Californian Kings

MAUREEN CHILD

Published in Great Britain 2014
by Mills & Boon, an imprint of Harlequin (UK) Limited,
Eton House, 18-24 Paradise Road, Richmond, Surrey, TW9 1SR

CALIFORNIAN KINGS © 2014 Harlequin Books S.A.

Conquering King's Heart, *Claiming King's Baby* and *Wedding at King's Convenience* were first published in Great Britain by Harlequin (UK) Limited.

Conquering King's Heart © 2009 Maureen Child
Claiming King's Baby © 2009 Maureen Child
Wedding at King's Convenience © 2009 Maureen Child

ISBN: 978-0-263-91200-5
eBook ISBN: 978-1-472-04495-2

05-0914

Harlequin (UK) Limited's policy is to use papers that are natural, renewable and recyclable products and made from wood grown in sustainable forests. The logging and manufacturing processes conform to the legal environmental regulations of the country of origin.

Printed and bound in Spain
by Blackprint CPI, Barcelona

Maureen Child is a California native who loves to travel. Every chance they get, she and her husband are taking off on another research trip. The author of more than sixty books, Maureen loves a happy ending and still swears that she has the best job in the world. She lives in Southern California with her husband, two children and a golden retriever with delusions of grandeur. Visit Maureen's website at www.maureenchild.com.

CONQUERING
KING'S HEART

BY
MAUREEN CHILD

To Patti Canterbury Hambleton.
For years of friendship and laughter.
For shared memories and too many adventures to count.
For always being a touchstone in my life.
I love you.

One

Jesse King loved women.

And they loved him right back.

Well, all except one.

Jesse walked into Bella's Beachwear and stopped just inside the store. His gaze wandered the well-kept if decrepit building and he shook his head at the stubbornness of women.

Hard to believe that Bella Cruz preferred this ramshackle building to what he was offering. He'd arrived in Morgan Beach, a tiny coastal town in southern California, nine months ago. He'd bought up several of the run-down, eclectic shops on Main Street, rehabbed some, razed others, then built the kind of stores and offices that would actually *attract* shoppers to the downtown district.

Everyone had been happy to sign on the dotted line. They'd accepted his buyout offers with barely disguised glee and most of them were now renting retail space from him. But not Bella Cruz. Oh, no. This woman had been working against him for months.

She'd spearheaded a sit-in campaign, getting a few of her friends to plant themselves in front of his bull-dozers for an afternoon. She'd held a protest march down Main Street that consisted of Bella herself, four women, two kids and a three-legged dog. And finally, she'd resorted to trying to pull off a candlelight vigil in memory of the "historic" buildings of Morgan Beach.

There had been five people standing outside his office holding candles the night the first big summer storm had blown in. Within minutes, they were all drenched, the candle flames drowned out. Bella was the only one left standing in the dark, glaring up at him as he looked at her through his office window.

"Why is she taking this all so personally?" he wondered. It wasn't as if he'd come to town to deliberately ruin her life.

He'd come here for the waves.

When professional surfers stopped riding competitively, they settled in a place where they could always find a good ride year-round. Most ended up in Hawaii, but, as a native Californian, Jesse had decided on Morgan Beach. His whole family still lived in the state and Morgan was close enough that he could keep in touch and far enough away from his three brothers that he wouldn't trip on them with every step. He liked his family. A lot. That didn't mean he wanted to live right on top of them.

So he was building himself a little kingdom here in this small town and the only thing keeping it from being absolutely perfect was Bella Cruz.

"The evil landlord stops by to gloat," a low, female voice said from somewhere nearby.

He turned around and spotted his nemesis, crouched behind the counter, rearranging a display of sunglasses, flip-flops and tote bags. Her dark brown eyes were fixed on him with the steely look of a woman about to spray a roach with Raid.

"You're not armed, are you?" he asked, walking toward her slowly. "Because you look as if you'd like to put me out of my misery."

"Out of *my* misery is more like it," she answered wryly. Then she stood up and Jesse took in her latest outfit.

Bella stood about five foot eight, which was good, because he liked his women tall enough that he didn't get a crick in his neck when he kissed them. Not that he was thinking about kissing Bella. It was just an observation.

She had wavy black hair that fell to the middle of her back, huge chocolate eyes and a lusciously full mouth he had yet to see curved into a smile. Pretty, he thought. Except for the clothes.

Every time he saw her she looked as if she were about to pose for the cover of *Amish Monthly*: loose-fitting cotton tops and full, floor-length skirts. Probably just as well, he told himself. He liked his women curvy and by the look of her, she had all the curves of a box. Seemed strange to him, though, that a woman who made her living designing and selling women's swim-wear looked as if she'd never worn one of her own garments.

"What do you want, Mr. King?"

He grinned deliberately. He knew the power of that smile. Enough women over the years had told him just what his dimples did to their knees. Bella's knees appeared to be rock solid. Oh, well. He wasn't interested in seducing her anyway. Or so he kept reminding himself.

"I wanted to tell you that we're going to start rehabbing this building next month."

"Rehabbing," she repeated and screwed up her face as if even the word itself were distasteful. "You mean knocking down the walls? Tearing up the hardwood floor? Getting rid of the leaded windows? That kind of rehabbing?"

He shook his head. "What is it exactly, that you have against well-insulated buildings and sound roofs?"

She crossed her arms under her breasts and Jesse was distracted for a moment. Apparently, she did have at least *one* good set of curves.

"My roof doesn't leak," she told him. "Robert Towner was an excellent landlord."

"Yes, so I've heard," he said with a sigh. "Repeatedly."

"You could take lessons from him."

"He didn't even bother to repaint the outside of your shop," Jesse pointed out.

"Why would he do that?" she demanded. "I painted it myself three years ago."

His mind boggled. "You actually *chose* to paint your business purple? On purpose?"

"It's lavender."

"Purple."

She inhaled sharply and gave him another glare that should have set his hair on fire. But Jesse was made of sterner stuff. He was a King. And Kings didn't cave for anybody.

"You won't be happy until every building on Main Street is beige with rust-colored trim, will you?" Shaking her head, she gave him a pitying look now, but it was wasted on Jesse. Kings didn't need anyone's pity. "We're all going to be Stepfords. Will we all march in lockstep, do you think? Dress alike?"

"Please God, no," he said, with a glance at her ensemble.

She colored briefly. "*My point is,* there's no individuality here anymore. Morgan Beach used to have personality."

"And wood rot."

"It was eclectic."

"Shabby."

"You're nothing but a corporate robot," she accused.

Jesse was stunned that anyone would describe him that way. He'd never set out to be a corporate anything. Hell, he'd gone out of his way to avoid the trap that all Kings eventually landed in. The business world. In fact, the King name had been a pain in his ass for most of his life.

His father, brothers, cousins—all Kings every-where—seemed to be locked into offices. Didn't matter to Jesse if those offices were luxurious penthouse suites. He'd never wanted anything to do with that world.

He'd watched his three older brothers slide into the family business concerns as if they'd been molded for the task. Even Justice, on his ranch, was a businessman first and foremost. But Jesse had broken away. Become a professional surfer and damn if he hadn't loved the life. While his brothers and cousins were wearing suits and running meetings, he was traveling the world, looking for the perfect ride. He did things his way. Lived his life the way he wanted to. He didn't answer to anyone.

Until his favorite surfboard maker went out of business a few years ago. Jesse had bought up the company be-cause he wanted access to the boards he favored. He'd done the same thing when he'd found the perfect wet suit. And the ideal swim trunks. Pretty soon, he'd actually done what he'd always insisted he wouldn't. Become a businessman. Not just a drone, either—the head of King Beach, a giant, diversified company that centered around life on the beach. Ironic that the thing he loved had even-tually turned him into what he'd never wanted to be.

"Look," he said quietly, shaking away thoughts that were too troubling to focus on. "We don't have to be enemies."

"Oh, yes, we do."

Damn, she was stubborn. For ten years, he'd been at the top of his sport. He'd won hundreds of competitions, been featured in magazine ads, partied with the most glamorous celebrities and last year had even been named California's Sexiest Bachelor. He had money, charm and all the women he could possibly want. So why was he torturing himself by standing here listening to Bella Cruz harp at him?

Because she intrigued him. Whether it was her obvious enmity for him, or her sheer hardheadedness, he wasn't sure. But there was something about Bella that got to him. Felt somehow…familiar.

Jesse pulled in a deep breath, leaned both hands on the counter and looked at her. "It's just some walls and windows, Ms. Cruz—or can I call you Bella?"

"No, you cannot, and it's not just walls and windows." She held out her arms as if physically trying to hug the ratty old building. "This place has a history. The whole town did. Until *you* showed up, that is."

She gave him a look that was heat and ice both at the same time. Impressive. She was practically vibrating with banked rage. He'd always found a way around a woman's temper. Until now.

For months, he'd been trying to worm his way into her good graces. It would have made life easier if she'd agreed to an easy working relationship. She had friends in Morgan Beach. She was successful—in her own, cottage-industry kind of way. And dammit, women *liked* Jesse King.

"The town's history is still here," Jesse told her, "along with buildings that won't collapse at the first sign of a stiff breeze."

"Yeah," she muttered, "you're a real humanitarian."

He laughed. "I'm just trying to run a business," he said and nearly winced at the words. When had he become his brothers? His father?

"No, you're trying to run *my* business."

"Trust me when I say I have zero interest in your company." Jesse glanced behind her to where one of her custom-designed swimsuits was tacked to the wall.

Jesse's company catered to men. He knew what a guy was looking for in a wet suit, bathing suit or whatever. He had no idea what women were looking for and wouldn't expand until he knew. Though his stockholders and managers were after him to expand to women's gear, Jesse was standing firm against them. He had no idea what to stock for women, yet; he'd rather focus on what he did best. Bella Cruz could *have* the female share of the market.

"Then why are you here?" she asked, and he heard the toe of her shoe tapping against the floor. "My rent's not due for another three weeks."

"So warm. So welcoming," he said, giving Bella another smile. It bounced off her like bullets off a tank. Woman was determined to hate him. Jesse shoved his hands into the pockets of his khaki slacks and walked off to study the racks.

"I'm very welcoming. To customers," she said.

"Yeah, the store's so packed I can hardly walk."

She huffed out a breath. "Summer's over. Sales slow down a little."

"Funny, everyone else says business is great."

"Worried about your rent?" she asked.

"Should I be?"

"No," Bella said quickly. "I have a small, but loyal clientele."

"Uh-huh."

"You're impossible," he thought he heard her mutter. Jesse smiled to himself. Good to know he was getting to her as thoroughly as she was getting to him.

Beyond the plate-glass window, Morgan Beach was going about its day. It was late morning and the surfers were packing it in for the day. He knew all too well that the best rides were just after dawn, before the water was crowded with kids and moms and wannabes with their little belly boards.

People were wandering the tidy sidewalks, sitting at sidewalk cafés and, in general, enjoying the day. While he was standing in a women's-wear shop talking to a female who practically hissed when she saw him. Jesse stifled a sigh of impatience.

He shifted his gaze to the interior of Bella's place. Pale, cream-colored walls were dotted with handmade swimsuits tacked up beside framed posters of some of the best beaches in the world. And Jesse should know. He'd surfed most of those beaches. For ten years, he'd hardly been out of the water. He'd snatched up trophies, endorsement deals, nice fat checks and plenty of attention from the surf bunnies who followed the circuit.

Sometimes he really missed that life. Like now, for instance.

"So, since I'm your landlord, why don't we play nice?"

"You're only my landlord because Robert Towner's kids sold you the building after he died. He promised me that they wouldn't, you know," she said, regret tingeing her voice. "He promised that I could stay here another five years."

"But that wasn't in his will," Jesse reminded her as he turned around to meet her hard gaze. "His kids decided to sell. Hardly my fault."

"Of course it was your fault—you offered them a small fortune for the building!"

He smiled. "Good business."

Bella smothered a sigh. What good would it do? Facts were facts and the fact was, Jesse King was now the owner of her building, despite Robert's promises.

Robert Towner had been a sweet old man, a surrogate grandfather to Bella. They'd had coffee every morning, dinner at least once a week. She'd seen him far more often than his own children had and she'd hoped to actually buy the building from him one day. Unfortunately, Robert had died in a car accident nearly a year ago. Despite his assurances, he hadn't made any provisions for Bella in his will.

A month or so after Robert's death, his children sold the building to Jesse King and Bella had been worried about her future ever since. Robert had always kept the rent low enough so she could afford this great location. But she knew that Jesse King wouldn't be doing the same.

He was making "improvements" right and left and

would soon be raising the rents to pay for them. Which meant that Bella would have to look for another shop to rent. She'd have to leave Main Street and relocate farther inland, losing at least a quarter of her business, since many of her customers were drop-ins off the beach.

Jesse King was going to ruin everything. Just as he had three years ago.

Not that he remembered. The bastard.

Bella really wanted to kick something. Preferably her new landlord. Which was so far out of her character, she blamed that notion on him, too. Jesse King was the kind of man who expected the world to roll over and beg whenever he crooked his finger. The trouble was, it usually did.

He looked over his shoulder at her and grinned. "I really irritate you on a personal level, don't I? I mean, this is more than me buying up Main Street, isn't it?"

Yes, it really was. Bella stiffened instinctively. The fact that he didn't even *know* why she loathed him was just infuriating. She couldn't tell him what he'd so obviously and embarrassingly forgotten.

"What do you want, Mr. King?"

He frowned a little. "Bella, we've known each other too long to stand on ceremony."

"We don't know each other at all," she corrected. He was going to call her Bella whether she wanted him to or not, it seemed.

"I know you love your shop," Jesse said, moving back to the counter. And her.

Why did he have to smell so good? And did his

eyes really have to be the deep, dark blue of the ocean? Did his smile *have* to cause dimples in his cheeks? And why had the sun bleached out lighter-colored streaks in his dark blond hair? Wasn't he gorgeous enough?

"You've got some nice stuff in here," he said, looking down into the glass display case at the sunglasses, flip-flops and tote bags. "Good eye for color, too. We're a lot alike, you and I. My company makes swimwear. So do you."

She laughed.

He scowled. "What's so funny?"

"Oh, nothing," she said, bracing her hands on the glass countertop. "It's just that my suits are handmade by local women from custom-woven organically sound fabrics and yours are stitched together by children hunched over dirty tables in sweatshops somewhere."

"I don't run sweatshops," he snapped.

"Are you so sure?"

"Yeah, I am. I'm not some Viking here to pillage and burn," he reminded her.

"Might as well be," she muttered. "You've changed the whole face of downtown in less than a year."

"And retail shopping is up 22 percent. I *should* be shot."

She simmered like a pot about to boil over. "There's more to life than profit."

"Yes, there's surfing. And there's great sex." He grinned again, clearly waiting to see if she'd be affected.

Bella would never let him know just how much that smile and his dimples did affect her. Or the casual mention of great sex. Women came too easily to Jesse King. She'd learned that lesson three years ago, when she'd been a card-carrying member of that adoring throng.

The World Surf competition had been in town and Morgan Beach partied for a week. Bella had been on the pier, watching the waves, when Jesse King had strolled up. He'd smiled then, too. And flirted. And teased. He'd kissed her in the moonlight, then taken her to the small bar at the end of the pier where they'd toasted each other with too many margaritas.

She could admit now that she'd been flattered by his attention. He was gorgeous. Famous. And, she'd thought back then, really a very nice guy underneath all the glamour.

That night, they'd wandered together along the sand, until the crowded pier and beach were far behind them. Then they stood at the ocean's edge and watched moonlight dance on the waves.

When Jesse kissed her, Bella was swept away by the magic of the moment and the heat and the delirious sensation of being *wanted*. They'd made love on the sand, with the sea wind rushing over them and the pulsing throb of the ocean whispering in the background.

Bella had seen stars.

Jesse had seen just one of the crowd.

She'd actually gone to see him the following day, in the harsh glare of sunlight. She'd wanted to talk to him about what had happened.

He'd said, "Good to see ya, babe," and walked right past her. He hadn't even remembered having sex with her. She was too stunned to even shout at him. She'd simply stared after him as he walked out of her life.

Bella looked at him now, and remembered every minute of their night together and the humiliation of the day after. But even that hadn't been enough to take away the luscious memory of lying in his arms in the moonlight.

She hated knowing that one night with Jesse had pretty much ruined her for other men. And she *really* hated knowing that he still didn't remember her. But then, why would he?

But not her.

At least, not again.

Everyone made mistakes, but only an idiot made the *same* mistake repeatedly.

Inhaling sharply, Bella told him, "Look, there's no point in arguing anymore. You've already won and I have a business to run. So if you're not here to tell me you're evicting me, I really have to get back to work."

"Evicting you? Why would I do that?"

"You own the building and I've done nothing but try to get rid of you for months."

"Yeah," he said, "but as you pointed out already, I've won that battle. What would be the point of evicting you?"

"Then why are you here?"

"To let you know about the coming rehab."

"Fine," Bella said. "Now I know. Thanks a bunch. Goodbye."

He grinned again and Bella's stomach pitched wildly.

"You know," Jesse said, "when a woman doesn't like me, I've just got to find out why."

"I've already told you why."

"There's more to it than that," he said, his gaze fixed on her. "Trust me when I say I will figure it out."

Two

Jesse couldn't figure out why he was still thinking about Bella. Why the scent of her still clung to him. Why one badly dressed woman with magic eyes was haunting him hours later. Clearly, he told himself, he'd been working too hard.

"According to research, women's beachwear outsells comparable styles for men two to one," Dave said.

Jesse's train of thought cut off as he leaned back in his desk chair. The fact that he actually *had* a desk chair hardly bothered him anymore.

"Dave," Jesse said, as patiently as he could, "I've told you already. I don't have any interest in catering to women—in the stores at least," he added with a smile.

"You're missing out on a gold mine, Mr. King," the

short, balding man said hurriedly. "And if you'll just give me one more moment of your time, I could show you what I mean."

Dave Michaels was the head buyer for King Beach and was constantly trying to push Jesse into expansion. But Jesse had a firm policy. He only sold products he knew and used personally. Products he believed in. Growing up as a King, he'd learned early on that success meant loving what you did. Knowing your business better than anyone else.

But he realized that Dave wouldn't give up until he'd had his chance to make a pitch.

"Fine, let's hear it." Jesse stood up, though, hating the feeling of being trapped behind a desk. Even though his desk was a sleek combination of chrome and glass, it always called up memories of his dad behind a mahogany desk the size of an aircraft carrier, waving at his sons, telling them to go and play, that he was too busy to join them.

Irritated at the memory, he turned his back on Dave to wander the perimeter of his office. Absently, he noticed the shelves filled with the trophies he'd won over the years. On the dark blue walls, there were framed photos of him in competitions, seascapes of some of his favorite beaches and assorted shots of his family. His lucky surfboard was propped up in one corner and the windows behind his desk offered a view of Main Street and the ocean beyond.

As if he needed that connection with the ocean he loved, Jesse moved to the windows and fixed his gaze on the water. Sunlight glinted off the surface of the sea and seemed to spotlight the lucky bastards waiting for the next ride atop their boards. That's where he should be, he thought wryly. How had he come to this, he wondered, not for the first time. How had he ended up exactly in his father's place?

His brothers were probably laughing their asses off just thinking about it.

"There's a store here in town with the kind of products we should be carrying," Dave was saying.

Jesse hardly heard the man. He was willing to do the job that he'd created for himself, but that didn't mean it would ever be his life's blood. Unlike the rest of his family, Jesse considered himself the anti-King, he thought with a half smile. He liked the money, liked the way he lived his life, liked the perks that being success-ful gave him. So he did the job, but it wasn't who he was. The job was simply that.

Work.

He did what he had to do so that he could do what he wanted to do. Enjoy life. Surf. Date gorgeous wom-en. He wasn't going to end up like his dad—a man who'd devoted everything to the King family dynasty and never really lived.

"If you'll only look at these photos, I'm sure you'll see that her products would be a perfect fit to King Beach's apparel line."

"*Her* products?"

"I know, I know," Dave countered quickly, holding up one hand to forestall Jesse's objections. "You don't want to add women's sportswear to the line, but if you'll just look…"

Jesse laughed shortly. "You just don't give up, do you Dave?"

"Not when I'm right."

"You should have been born a King," Jesse told him and reluctantly took the photos Dave was holding out to him. The sooner he finished work, the sooner he was out there in the sunlight.

"What am I looking at here?" Jesse asked, flipping through the stack of color photos. Bikinis. Sarongs. Beach cover-ups. All pretty, he supposed, but he didn't understand Dave's excitement. Nice enough swimsuits, Jesse thought, though he preferred his bikinis wrapped around gorgeous blondes.

"These suits," Dave said, "are growing in popularity. They're custom-designed, handcrafted with all 'green' fabrics, and the women who buy them swear there's nothing else like them."

Jesse suddenly had a bad feeling.

"There was a write-up in the Sunday magazine section of the newspaper last month and from the reports I'm getting, her sales are going through the roof."

Oh, yeah. That bad feeling kept getting…worse.

Jesse studied the photos more carefully. Some of them looked familiar. As in, he'd seen one of them just yesterday, tacked up to a wall in a crumbling shop on Main Street. "Bella's Beachwear?"

"Yes!" Dave grinned, pointed at one of the photos and said, "That one?" A cherry-red bikini. "My wife bought that one last week. Said it's the most flattering, comfortable suit she's ever owned and she wondered why *we* didn't offer something like it."

"It's nice that your wife's happy with her purchase," Jesse started.

"It's not just my wife, Mr. King," Dave interrupted, his eyes shining with enthusiasm. "Since we moved the business to Morgan Beach, all we've heard about is Bella's. She's got women coming in from all over the state to buy her suits."

Dave kept talking. "One of our guys in accounting did a projection. If we added her line to ours, the sky would literally be the limit on how well she'd do. That's not even saying how her line would influence King Beach sales."

Jesse shook his head. Though he was King enough to appreciate the thought of higher profit margins and headier success, he had his own plan for his business and when he branded women's wear, he would do it his way.

Dave told him flatly, "She's carved out a slice of the consumer pie that no one had really touched on before. We've checked into her and she's had other offers from major sportswear companies to buy her out, but she's turned them all down."

Intrigued in spite of himself, Jesse leaned back against the edge of his desk, folded his arms over his chest and said simply, "Explain."

Warming to his theme, Dave did. "Most swimsuits in this country and, hell, everywhere else, are designed and created for the so-called 'ideal' woman. A skinny one."

Jesse smiled. Skinny women in bikinis. What's not to smile about? Although he usually preferred a little more meat on his women.

As if he could read Jesse's mind, Dave said, "The majority of American women don't meet that standard. And thank God for it. Most women are curvy. They eat more than a lettuce leaf. And thanks to most designers, their needs are overlooked."

"You know, Dave, I like curves on a woman as much as the next guy," Jesse told him, "but not all women should wear a bikini. If Bella wants to sell to women who probably shouldn't be wearing suits anyway, let her do it. It's not for us."

Dave grimaced, then reached into his pocket for another photo. "I thought that would be your reaction," he said tightly. "So I came prepared. Look at this."

Jesse took the photo and his eyebrows lifted. "This is your wife."

"Yeah," Dave said, grinning now. "Normally Connie bans all cameras when we go swimming. Since she bought this suit, I couldn't get her to stop posing."

Jesse could understand why. Connie Michaels had given birth to three children over the last six years. She wasn't skinny, but she wasn't fat, either. And in the swimsuit she had purchased from Bella, she looked…great.

"She's really beautiful," Jesse mused.

Instantly, Dave plucked the photo from his hand. "Yeah, I think so. But my point is, if Bella's suits look this good on a normal-size woman, they'd look great on the skinny ones, too. I'm telling you, Mr. King, this is something you should think about."

"Fine. I'll think about it," Jesse told him, more to get Dave to drop the subject than anything else.

"Her sales are building steadily and I think she'd be a great asset to King Beach."

"Asset." Jesse murmured the word, remembering the look on Bella's face that morning during their "conversation." Oh, yeah. She'd already turned down offers from other companies. He could just see how pleased she'd be with *his* offer to buy out her business. Hell, she'd probably run him down with her car.

Not that it was going to be an issue because, "We don't sell women's wear yet."

Dave took a breath and said, "Word is Pipeline is looking to court Bella's Beachwear."

"Pipeline?" Jesse's major competitor, Nick Acona, ran Pipeline clothing and the fact that neither of them surfed anymore didn't get rid of the rivalry. If Nick was interested in Bella—that was almost enough to get Jesse involved.

"He says the way to increased sales is through women," Dave told him.

Jesse gave his assistant a hard look. He knew exactly what Dave was up to. And it was working. "I'll consider it."

"But—"

"Dave," he asked, "do you like your job?"

Dave grinned. He'd heard that threat before and didn't put much stock in it. "Yes, sir."

"Good. Let's keep it that way."

"Right." The man gathered up his notes, his research and the photos and headed for the door. "You did say you'd think about it, though."

"And I will." The truth was he knew he should expand into women's beachwear. He just hadn't found any he'd believed in enough to stock. Until now. The challenge would be in convincing Bella to come on board—before Pipeline got their hooks in her.

When Dave was gone, a spot of color caught his eye and Jesse bent down to pick up off the floor a photo Dave had left behind. A sea-green bikini with narrow straps on the halter top and silver rings at the hips, holding the bottom together.

Jesse caught himself trying to imagine Bella wearing that suit. He couldn't quite bring it off, though, and that was irritating, too. She wore those big, blousy tops and shapeless skirts, deliberately hiding her figure. Was it a studied plan to drive a man nuts?

Smiling to himself, Jesse tossed the photo onto his desk, turned around and looked down Main Street to Bella's place. He couldn't seem to get her out of his head. He kept remembering the battle-ready glint in her eye. Even if she dressed like a disaster refugee, there was something about her that…

Nope, forget it. He wasn't interested in Bella Cruz.

But there *was* a certain woman in Morgan Beach he was looking for. His mystery woman.

Narrowing his gaze on the sea, Jesse thought back to one night three years ago. He didn't remember much about that night or her… He'd won a huge competition that day and he'd been doing a lot of celebrating before he ran into her. Then there was more celebrating and finally, there was sex on the beach. Amazing, completely staggering, sex.

She'd been at the edges of his mind ever since. He couldn't recall her face, but he knew the sizzle of her touch. He couldn't remember the sound of her voice, but he knew the taste of her.

Oh, it was more than the waves that had brought him to Morgan Beach. His mystery woman was here. Somewhere. At least, he hoped so. She could have been in town for the competition, he supposed, but he liked to think that she lived here. That sooner or later, he'd run across her again.

And this time, when he got his hands on her, he wouldn't let her go.

His phone rang, thankfully silencing his thoughts. Automatically, he turned to snatch it up. "King."

"Jesse, it's Tom Harold. Just checking with you on the photo shoot scheduled for tomorrow."

"Right." More photos. But this was for a national campaign advertising King Beach and its end-of-summer sale. He might not have wanted to become a businessman, but now that he was, the King blood in his veins refused to let him be anything but a success.

"Yeah, we're set, Tom." He turned back to the window and stared out at the ocean. "The models will arrive first thing in the morning, and you can do the shoot on the beach. The mayor's cleared it for us to rope a section off."

"Perfect. I'll be there."

Jesse hung up, sat down at his desk and shoved thoughts of Bella out of his mind. There was plenty of paperwork—the one sure way to keep his thoughts too busy to wander.

"For Pete's sake, Bella," Kevin Walters told her over dinner that night, "stop antagonizing the man. Do you *want* him to end your lease?"

Kevin, with his dark red hair, tanned skin and blue eyes was Bella's best friend. They'd known each other for five years, ever since Bella had moved to Morgan Beach and rented her house from him. She could talk to him as she would any girlfriend and he was usually willing to give her the guy's point of view when she needed it. Tonight, however, she'd really rather he saw things from *her* perspective.

"No, I don't," she said quickly. She still had two months left on her lease and if Jesse King tossed her out, she'd have to sell suits out of her rental house; she didn't think Kevin would be thrilled with that solution. Which was just one more reason to be mad at Jesse King.

"You know, another couple of years in my location and I could have bought my house from you—"

He held up one hand. "I've offered to make you a deal."

"I don't need special deals, Kevin. You know I want to do this myself."

"Yeah, I know."

Reaching across the table to give his hand a pat,

Bella said, "I really do appreciate that you want to help me buy the place, Kevin. It's just that it wouldn't really be mine if I didn't do it all myself."

"Right. Like that shirt you're wearing?" He pointed to the heavily appliquéd, long-sleeved yellow muslin shirt that she wore with her best black skirt. "That's yours, right? So what? You did the weaving yourself? Stitched it all together and did the little flowers around the collar?"

"No…"

"So houses and shirts are different?"

"Well, yeah."

He shook his head and sighed. "Fine. Good. You want to buy the house and if you make King mad enough, he'll end your lease and then no house. So why continue to piss him off?"

Bella used her fork to poke at her vegetarian lasagna, then gave it up and dropped the fork to her plate with a clatter. Folding her arms atop the table, she looked at Kevin. "Because he doesn't even *remember* me. It's infuriating. Humiliating."

She'd confessed all one night during a monster movie marathon. And Kevin had immediately told her that she should have reminded Jesse of who she was when she'd run into him the following day. Of course he had. He was a guy.

Kevin shrugged and took a bite of his zucchini and potato casserole. "So tell him."

"*Tell* him?" Bella just stared at him. "You know, maybe I'd have been better off with a girl for a best friend. I wouldn't have to explain to another woman why *telling* Jesse that we'd slept together was a bad idea. She would know that instinctively."

Grinning, Kevin said, "Yes, but a girl best friend wouldn't come next door at ten at night to unclog your shower drain."

"Good point," Bella said. "But you've got a blind spot when it comes to Jesse."

"God, women always make everything harder than it has to be," Kevin muttered with a shake of his head. "This is why the battle of the sexes exists, you know. Because you guys are always on the battlefield ready for war and we're standing around on the sidelines saying, 'What's she mad about?'"

Bella laughed at the irritation in his gaze, which didn't appease him much.

"Let me guess," Kevin said with a tired sigh. "This is one of those If-he-doesn't-know-why-I'm-mad-I'm-sure-not-going-to-tell-him things, isn't it?"

"Yeah. And it's not a 'thing', it just is. He should know," Bella snapped and reached for her wineglass. "For Pete's sake, are there so many women in his wake that we're all just blurs to him?"

"Bella, honey," Kevin said, leaning back in the red leather booth, "you know I love you. But that is so female it has nothing to do with the world of man."

He was right and she knew it. Men and women came at the whole *sex* thing from completely different mind-sets. Even though she'd had too many margaritas that night, Bella had made a conscious decision to sleep with Jesse. And it hadn't been because he was rich or famous or gorgeous.

But because they'd really *talked* to each other. She'd felt a connection to him that she'd never felt before to anyone. That was the only reason she'd done what she did. Jesse, though, she realized by the next day, had only had sex with her because she was there. Willing. There'd been no meaning in it for him at all.

"If you wanted more from him than one night, you should have said something the next day," Kevin told her. "Made him remember. But no. Instead, you went all female on him and left him in the dark."

"I didn't put him in the dark," Bella reminded him.

For at least the tenth time, Bella went back over her conversation with Jesse King that morning three years ago. He'd looked right at her. Given her all his most practiced moves and never once remembered that they'd had sex! The man had had so many women, she'd been lost in the crowd from the moment she gave herself to him.

"Look, I know you don't like the guy, but he's here now and he's not going away," Kevin pointed out around another bite of his dinner. "He's moved the corporate offices here, he's opened his flagship store in town. Jesse King is here to stay, like it or not, and no protest is going to change that."

"I know," she grumbled.

"So if you're going to live in the same town with him, tell him what's bugging you. Otherwise, you're gonna drive yourself insane."

"You know," Bella told him, "I wasn't really looking for logic, here. I just wanted to enjoy my rant."

"Ah. Okay then, rant away. I'm listening."

"Sure, but you're not agreeing," she said, smiling.

"Nope, I'm not." Kevin shrugged. "I'm sorry you hate him and everything, but he seems like a nice enough guy to me."

"That's only because he bought that gold-and-emerald necklace from you." Kevin's store stocked work by local artists and jewelry designers, so he was always happy when he made a big sale.

He smiled and sighed. "Yeah, gotta say, a guy who spends a few thousand on a custom-made necklace without batting an eye? My kind of customer."

"Fine, fine. You're happy. The town's happy. Jesse's happy." She shoved her lasagna around on the plate. "I wrote a letter to the editor of the local paper."

"Uh-oh," Kevin muttered. "What kind of letter?"

She winced, regretting now what she'd done, but it was way too late to call it back. "Something about the corporations of America ruining small-town life."

He laughed. "Bella…"

"They probably won't even run it."

"Of course they will," he said. "Then you can expect another visit from Jesse King." Kevin paused, tipped his head to one side and looked at her. "Or is that what this is all about? You actually *want* him coming around, don't you?"

"No, I don't," she argued, wishing Kevin were just a little less observant. Could *she* help it if every time

Jesse King walked through her door she felt a zing of something amazing? It wasn't her fault that her hormones reacted when he was in the room. Heck, every female in America suffered from the same symptoms when it came to Jesse King.

And the very fact that he affected her so much was exactly *why* she was so bent on making him miserable. She probably should stop antagonizing him, as Kevin said, but she just couldn't bring herself to.

Bella had fought Jesse's takeover of Morgan Beach with everything she had. And still, she'd lost. He'd moved in, bought up property and immediately started ruining the only place she'd ever called home.

An only child, Bella had lost her parents at seven, gone into a series of nice, if impersonal foster homes and when she turned eighteen, she was out on her own. She didn't mind it so much, though the pangs for family never quite left her.

She'd put herself through college by making clothes for the girls who didn't have to worry about saving every cent. She'd sewn and knitted and crocheted her way to an education. Then she'd taken her first vacation ever, stumbled across Morgan Beach and never left.

She'd been here five years and she loved it. The tiny coastal town was everything she'd always dreamed of in a hometown. Small, friendly and close enough to big retail she could always indulge in a fun shopping trip when she felt the need. Even better, the close-knit feeling of the community fed that lack of family she'd always felt. People here cared about each other.

Now, with Jesse here, her beloved small town felt almost claustrophobic.

"Sell it to somebody else, Bella," Kevin said laughing. "Every time you say the guy's name, your eyes go all soft and shiny."

"They do not." Did they? Well, that was embarrassing as all get-out.

"Oh, yeah, they do, and I'll prove it. Look out the window."

She turned her head to glance out the window onto Main Street and was just in time to see Jesse King walking by. His dark blond, sun-streaked hair was too long. His blue jeans were faded and molded to his long legs and the white long-sleeved shirt he wore only accentuated his tan.

She sighed.

"Gotcha," Kevin said.

"You're so evil," Bella told him, but couldn't tear her gaze away from the man who was still occupying far too much of her thoughts.

Three

By the next morning, Bella had convinced herself that Kevin was right. She'd just have to suck it up and talk to Jesse. Tell him just what she thought of a man who could make love to a woman one night and forget her existence the following morning. She'd get everything off her chest and then she'd be fine.

She'd be over him.

Bella paused in front of her shop for a moment, and smiled to herself. Even Jesse King couldn't quash the thrill she experienced every time she walked into the world she'd built with her own talent.

But even as she enjoyed the sight of her place, once Jesse's "rehab" was finished, it would lose all its character. The creak in the front door would be "fixed." The pockmarked walls would be smoothed. The floor would be carpeted, all the gleaming floorboards covered up. Bella's Beachwear would survive, but it wouldn't be the same. The man had no more vision when it came to business than he had when it came to women.

It was all about the bottom line to men like Jesse.

A crowd was gathering across the street on the beach and she turned her head to look. As a few dozen people milled around, Bella caught glimpses of what was going on. She noticed the RVs parked on the sand, a bank of cameras, huge lights and electric fans. And in the middle of it all, Jesse King.

In spite of herself, she was curious. Bella hurried across Pacific Coast Highway and stepped up onto the sidewalk. She kept to the fringes of the interested crowd of onlookers and let her gaze slide over the goings-on.

Gorgeous male models, each of them wearing King Beachwear, were positioned around several surfboards, all planted nose down in the sand. Bella had to admit that the guys looked great, but her gaze kept straying to the female models they were using in the background. "Honestly, you'd think he could take a *little* interest in what the women were wearing."

"Why am I not surprised you've got a comment?"

She whipped her head around and looked up into Jesse's amused blue eyes. He'd managed to sneak up on her. Darn it.

"Let's hear it," he said, one corner of his mouth tipping up as he folded his arms across his chest. He glanced at the photo shoot, saw the photographer bustling around, arranging everything to his satisfaction. "What don't you like about all this?"

Bella bit down on her bottom lip. It wasn't any of her business, of course and she really shouldn't care at all, but then…her gaze went back to the very pretty, very thin women wearing generic swimsuits and she just couldn't stand it. "If you're going to all this trouble to shoot a big ad campaign, why not have *all* of the models look good?"

He frowned at her. "They do."

"Why do I bother?" she muttered, shaking her head. "Look at the blond girl in the back."

He did and smiled at the view.

Bella ignored that. "Her suit doesn't fit right. It's too tight across her hips—what there are of them—and too big at the bust."

"She looks fine to me," Jesse said with a shrug.

Bella pushed a strand of windblown hair out of her eyes, then pointed at a brunette talking to one of the male models. "What about her? That bikini is cut all wrong and the fabric is shiny, for heaven's sake. What did you do? Go down to the department store and snatch a bunch of suits off the clearance rack?"

Jesse frowned. "The girls look okay to me. Besides, this shoot isn't about *women's* suits. It's about King Beach. We're selling *guys'* clothes. The girls are just background."

"Do they have to be poorly fitted background?" she asked.

He sighed a little. "We've got a contract. We're giving the department store—"

"Hah!" she crowed, because she'd been so right about where they'd purchased the women's suits.

He scowled at her. "The store gets credit in the photo tagline."

"Fine," she said, wondering why she even cared about any of this. "Use one or two of them. But if you want this ad to look good, then *all* the models should be eye-catching."

One eyebrow lifted. "Meaning…"

She shouldn't have walked over here, she told herself. Shouldn't have gotten involved. What did it matter to her, after all, if his magazine ad didn't look as good as it could? Yet…

Bella's gaze slid back to the swimsuits the women were wearing and every one of her designer instincts stood up and growled. She simply couldn't stand it. Besides, Jesse King was so darn sure of himself. So arrogant, she really wanted to… "Meaning, women are the real shoppers of the world, Mr. King. If you had any sense, you'd know that. Those suits your models are wearing are so generic they should be marked *one size fits all* as long as they're size 0s. My suits are made to flatter a woman's figure. All women."

He grinned, looked her up and down, then stared into her eyes with a direct challenge. "Even you?"

Insulted, Bella lifted her chin and glared at him. She knew she was being manipulated, but at the moment, Bella didn't even care. He was so convinced that his way was the right way, she wanted to prove him completely wrong. One sure way to do that was to show him exactly what she meant.

"I'll be right back," she announced, then left him to walk over to the female models. She spoke to them briefly, got their sizes, then hurried across the street to her shop. It only took a few minutes for Bella to scurry back to the photo shoot, her arms filled with some of her designer suits.

"What do you think you're doing?" Jesse asked as she herded the women toward one of the RV trailers.

"You're about to find out," was all she said as she stepped into the trailer behind the models and firmly closed the door.

Minutes ticked past and Jesse frowned at the RV. He wasn't sure why he was letting Bella get away with this. He should have just headed her off at the pass, so to speak, and told her he didn't need her help to sell *his* sportswear. But damn if he'd been able to do that.

"Jesse, how much longer?"

He turned to look at Tom, the photographer, then shot a quick glance at his own wristwatch. "Give her another few minutes, Tom. As soon as she admits she was wrong to stick her nose in, we'll get back to the shoot."

"Fine by me," Tom told him, shifting a fast look at the cobalt-blue sky above. "But we've only got this section of the beach for the morning."

"You're right." Jesse's permit would end at noon, so there was no point in indulging Bella any further, even to get her to admit that she was wrong. He stalked over to the RV and knocked on the door. "Bella," he called out, "time's up. We need to finish the shoot."

The door to the RV opened and the models came out, smiling and primping. Jesse checked out each and every one of them as they walked past him. Even the skinniest of the models looked as if she had a figure now. The fabrics clung to their bodies and enhanced what few curves they had. It cost him to think it, but Bella had been right.

Tom, the photographer, let loose a low whistle and instantly started staging the women into far more prominent poses for the ad shoot. Jesse watched and shook his head, amazed, really, at the transformation. But where the hell was Bella?

Smiling to himself, he climbed the steps into the RV, stuck his head inside and shouted, "Lose your nerve? C'mon Bella, let's see you in one of those suits you're so proud of."

"Turn around." The sound of her voice came from right behind him and Jesse couldn't figure out how she'd gotten past him. But when he turned to look at her, he understood completely.

For months, he'd seen the woman around town, always buried under mountains of fabric. He'd naturally assumed that she had a body she was trying to hide.

He couldn't have been more wrong.

"Bella?" His gaze moved over her in a quick, thorough glance, then he looked again, giving her a more leisurely going over. The woman had enough curves to make any man sit up and beg.

"Wow," he said, walking a slow, tight circle around her, "you look…" *Familiar* was what he wanted to say, but he couldn't figure out why that would be, so he let it go in favor of, "amazing."

The bikini she wore was a deep red and clung to her body like a lover's hands. Her breasts were high and full, her waist was small, her hips rounded and just above her behind, at the small of her back, a tiny tattoo of the sun peeked at him. Her skin was smooth and the color of warm honey. Her long, dark brown hair hung down her back and swayed with her every movement. And her chocolate eyes were watching him with satisfaction.

"Thanks," she said, fisting her hands at her bare hips. "I believe I've made my point."

He grinned at her. "What point was that?"

"That the right bathing suit makes all the difference."

"Honey," he said, "with a body like that, you could wear one of *my* suits and look amazing."

She shook her head and he was fascinated with the way her hair danced and swayed. His body felt tight and need was a clamoring beast inside him. It was all he could do to keep his hands to himself, when what he *wanted* to do was pull her in close, kiss her until she couldn't talk and then find the closest flat surface, lay her down on it and bury himself inside her.

But judging from the fire flashing in her eyes at the moment, that little fantasy wasn't going to come true anytime soon.

"You're incredible," she said softly.

"What's that supposed to mean?"

"I only dressed your models—and myself—to prove

to you that I was right. That your way of doing things, mass-produced swimwear, isn't the *only* way. That *my* way is better."

"Not the way to make your fortune, though," he said, leaning one shoulder against the doorjamb as she gathered up her tentlike blouse and skirt.

"Who says I'm interested in that?" she demanded, whipping her hair out of her eyes long enough to glare at him.

"You're a businesswoman. Why wouldn't you want to succeed?"

"Success doesn't *have* to be your way."

"My way's not bad." It occurred to him that he was defending his business. The very business he had never intended to start. "Contracting out to manufacturers streamlines the business, allows you to reach more customers and—"

"—And cuts you off from the customers, too," she added. "You get so big you forget why you started your business in the first place. But that doesn't matter to a King, does it?" She walked close, poked him in the chest with her index finger and said, "Your whole family— you're like warlords or something. You swoop in, buy up what you want and never consider any way but yours."

"Hey, now," he argued, grabbing her finger and closing his fist around it. Warmth shot through him with the first contact of her skin against his, shattering his thoughts, obliterating whatever it was he'd been about to say.

He remembered feeling like this once before with the touch of a woman's skin. Remembered the slide of her skin against his, the heat of their joining, the taste of her mouth, the tight fit of his body locked inside hers. And just for a second, Jesse stared at her, refusing to believe that Bella Cruz might be his mystery woman.

"What are you doing?" she asked, trying to tug her hand free of his grasp. "Why are you looking at me like that?"

"No way," he murmured, more to himself than to her. It couldn't be. Not her. Not the woman who had been a thorn in his side from day one.

"What?" This time she succeeded in pulling free of him and then she took a hasty step or two backward just for good measure. "Look, um, I've got to get to my shop. I've spent too much time here already and—"

"Just a minute," he said, moving toward her, letting the RV door swing closed behind him. Inside, the trailer was filled with shadows, sunlight drifting through louvered shades on the windows. The scent of coffee and perfume hung in the air and from outside came the shouts and laughter of the crowd gathered to watch the photo shoot.

Jesse paid no attention to any of it. All he could see was her. Her chocolate eyes watched him warily even as he told himself that the only sure way to know if Bella was actually his mystery woman was to kiss her. To taste her. And damn if she was leaving this trailer until he'd done just that.

"Mr. King," she said, looking around as if for an exit

that wasn't barred by his tall, broad body, "*Jesse,* I really do need to get going now."

"Yeah," he said, moving closer still until her breath fanned against his chin as she looked up at him. "I know. But there's just one more thing we have to do first."

She licked her lips. "What's that?"

He smiled and dipped his head. "This," he whispered, then took her mouth with his.

She went stiff as a board for about a split second, then pliant, leaning into him, wrapping her arms around his neck. He pulled her in close, his hands at her waist, his fingertips nearly burning with the heat her skin engendered. Her lips parted under his and his tongue swept into her warmth and he knew.

That taste of her was something he would never forget. Something he'd been dreaming about for three years. He finally had her in his arms again. Finally could hold her, taste her, touch her and as realization flooded him, he broke the kiss abruptly, stared down into her glazed, dark brown eyes and said, "It's *you.*"

She staggered a little. "What?"

"You. On the beach. Three years ago."

She blinked up at him, rubbed her fingertips across her mouth and then drew in a long, shaky breath. "Congratulations," she said at last. "You finally remembered."

"You knew?" he demanded. "You remembered and didn't say anything to me?"

"Why would I?" she asked, gathering up the clothes

she'd dropped when he was kissing her. "You think I'm *proud* of that night?"

"You ought to be," he told her sharply. "We were great together."

"We were strangers. It was a huge mistake."

She tried to get past him, but Jesse grabbed her upper arm and stopped her dead. "I looked for you. The next day, I went back to the beach and looked all over."

"You thought I'd just be lying there on the sand, waiting for you?"

"That's not what I meant, damn it. But where the hell were you?"

Bella pushed her hand through her hair and glared at him. "You didn't look for me very hard. I went to see you the next morning and you blew right past me."

Frowning, Jesse tried to remember that, but truthfully, he'd been celebrating so much that most of that night and the following morning was a blur. All he'd really known was the touch of her. The taste of her. "When you saw me, did you tell me who you were?"

"Of course not!" This time, she did push past him, dragging her arm from his grasp.

"Well, how the hell would I know who you were otherwise?" he asked.

"Oh!" She looked at him the way she would a splotch of mud on her shirt. "What kind of man can't remember what the woman he's had sex with looks like?"

"One with a hangover," he told her. "As I recall, we both had a few margaritas that night."

"Yes, but I still knew who you were," she snapped, then

took a long, deep breath and said, "You said you went looking for me. Just how did you plan to identify me?"

"I don't know..." He scrubbed one hand across his jaw and over the back of his neck. "Dammit, Bella, you could have told me—if not the morning after, then any time since I came to town." He tilted his head to one side and studied her. "Is this why you've been so mad at me?"

"Please," she said with a sniff and a lift of her chin. "Could you think any more highly of yourself? This isn't personal, Jesse," she told him as she grabbed the doorknob and twisted it. "This is about you taking over my town. Don't you get it? I hate you and everything you stand for."

"You can't hate me," he told her, bracing one hand on the wall and leaning in toward her. "You don't know me well enough to hate me."

She laughed shortly, but her eyes didn't shine with humor. "I got to 'know' you well enough three years ago."

"Yeah," he said softly, "well, I think it's time we got to know each other all over again."

"Never. Going. To. Happen," she told him and opened the door.

"Never say never, Bella," he called after her and when she slammed the door, Jesse grinned. Three years he'd been thinking about that woman. And he wasn't going to rest until he got her back where he wanted her. In his bed.

Nothing a King liked better than a challenge.

"Get Dave Michaels in here," Jesse told his assistant as he stalked toward his office.

He closed the door, walked directly to the window

overlooking Main Street, Bella's shop and the ocean. He told himself he wanted to stare at the sea for a few minutes, gather his thoughts, let the never-ending roll and slap of the waves ease his mind as it always did.

But the truth was, he was watching Bella's shop.

"Dammit, why'd it have to be her?" he whispered, shoving both hands into the pockets of his slacks. His mystery woman had dogged his thoughts off and on for three years. After that one amazing night on the beach with her, he'd hung around town for a couple of weeks searching for her in every face he met. But she'd seemed to have disappeared. Hell, he'd actually come here to settle in Morgan Beach on the off chance that he might find her again.

"Karma really is a bitch," he muttered.

Sunlight spilled through the window and if the glass hadn't been tinted, Jesse would have been half-blinded by the brilliance of the light. The air conditioner clicked on and a soft hum of cool air pumped into the room. Even at the beach, September temperatures could spike into some serious heat.

There was a knock on his door, then Dave walked in asking, "You wanted to see me?"

Jesse turned and nodded. "Tell me everything you know about Bella Cruz."

Dave's face lit up. "Seriously? You're considering expanding?"

Was he? Yes, he was. He might not have started out wanting to be a businessman. But he'd become one anyway. And as a King, he wasn't going to do the job half-assed. That meant that it was time to stop treating King Beach like a hobby. He was going to make his company the biggest name in surf gear and swimwear in the world. To do that, he needed to get female customers.

Bella was his ticket there.

She might not know it yet, but it was only a matter of time before both Bella herself *and* her swimsuit line were taken over by Jesse King.

"Where do you want me to start?" Dave asked, walking into the office and dropping into one of the chairs opposite Jesse's desk.

"Personal," Jesse said flatly. "Family. Boyfriends. Husbands and/or exes. I want it all."

Dave frowned. "I thought this was about her business."

"It is," Jesse assured him, sitting down behind his desk. He leaned an elbow on the arm of his chair, watched the man opposite him and said, "To get the jump on Pipeline, I've got to move fast. That means having as much information as possible."

"It just seems sneaky."

"It's good business," Jesse told him. "Besides, to defeat your opponent, you have to know her first."

"Opponent?" Dave echoed, sounding a little uneasy. "She's not an opponent."

Jesse sighed, then grinned. "How long have you and Connie been married, Dave?"

"Thirteen years, why?"

"You've been out of the dating game so long, you've forgotten what it's really like." Jesse sat forward to lay his forearms on the desktop and continued, "Women and men are *always* opposing forces. That's the fun, after all. If we understood women, where would the challenge be?"

"Why does it have to be a challenge?"

Jesse chuckled. "Doesn't have to be," he said. "It just is. The trick is, knowing the woman you're interested in, figuring out how her mind works, if you can. Once you do that, everything comes more easily."

"If you say so," Dave said, but he didn't sound as if he believed him.

"Trust me on this. If I want to win Bella over, keep her from signing with Pipeline, then I've got to know her, don't I?"

"I guess you do," Dave said, then smiled. "I think Bella's stuff is going to be great for King Beach."

Jesse nodded. "It will. I'll see to it. But until I convince Bella of that, our plans are top secret. Nobody knows. Not even Connie."

Dave winced, then shrugged. "You got it, boss."

"Good." Jesse listened as Dave started talking, giving him all the information he had on Bella.

And while Dave talked, Jesse began to plan the way he would prove to Bella just how much *she* needed *him*.

Four

For the next couple of days, Jesse watched a steady stream of customers go in and out of Bella's shop. From the vantage point of his office window or from a seat in the sidewalk café on the beach, he had a perfect view of Bella's Beachwear and its all-too-intriguing owner. What had astounded Jesse was the *amount* of business she did. Bella had told him that her business was slowing down because the season was over. Well, if this was slow, he was impressed.

He still didn't like the idea of expanding. But he couldn't get the facts out of his head, either. Dave's research proved just how successful Bella had become in her niche market, and damn if he'd let Nick Acona grab up her business right from under his nose.

She was the perfect advertisement for her wares. A normal-size woman walked into her store frustrated by the offerings at chain stores, and left with a smile on her face. He'd been watching it for days.

"And there go two more," he said to no one as he set his hands on either side of his office's wide window and stared down at Main Street. A couple of women were just leaving Bella's, carrying huge, purple-and-white-striped shopping bags that looked stuffed to bursting. She had a good business, he admitted silently, but he could make it great.

If he bought her out, or better yet, simply absorbed her company into his, keeping her on as head designer, they could both make millions. Even though she'd probably fight him every inch of the way. He smiled to himself at the thought. Damn if he didn't like that about her. The way her brown eyes snapped with fury or irritation. The way she lifted her chin and gave him a glare that she fully expected would turn him to stone.

Most women he knew were so busy flirting with him, they'd never consider arguing with him. Bella was different. And now that he knew *she* was his mystery girl, she was even more appealing.

He wanted her. Badly. The woman he'd been thinking about for three years was here. Right in front of him. Ready to be taken again. He was more than ready to do the taking.

But *taking* wasn't right, either. He wanted to explore that fabulous body, feel the buzz of her skin beneath his and build new memories. Jesse smiled to himself. He wanted more than just one more night with her. He wasn't thinking about how *much* more, but that wasn't the point.

She was.

Hell, Jesse actually liked her. And dammit, he understood her. Watching Bella with her customers, he knew that her business was more than just work to her. He'd felt the same way back when he started. When he bought his first company, he'd actually gone in and learned how to shape and make the surfboards himself. He'd enjoyed being in on the ground floor, feeling a connection to the business that he never would have had simply as a suit. It had made it more than a company to him. It had made it a part of him.

And there was no doubt in his mind that was how Bella felt about her shop. He admired that about her, even as he knew that would be the sticking point to winning her over. She wouldn't want to let go of the reins of her shop.

She was going to be a hard sell. The difference was, he knew her secret. He knew that she was a woman of passion. A woman who'd rocked his world three years ago.

So what he had to do here was seduce her. Charm her. Flatter her. Get her into his bed and once he had her there, he'd be in a position to smooth her into his company.

When it was all over, she'd be rich and thanking him.

If there was one thing Jesse King knew, it was women.

"Jesse King's been with so many women, he can't tell us apart anymore. The entire female gender is like nothing more than a well-stocked candy store. He likes candy, so he just grazes his way through the aisles." Bella scowled and tapped her fingernails against one of the glass jewelry cases in Kevin's shop.

It had been three days since she'd seen Jesse. Three days and he hadn't made an effort to talk to her. Not a phone call. Not one of his annoying drop-ins at her store. Not even a brief sighting on the street. Not that she had been hoping for any of that, but she couldn't help feeling frustrated.

He'd seemed…excited to find out that she was the woman he'd been with three years ago on the beach. So much so that he'd been avoiding her ever since. Bella groaned internally. For heaven's sake, she was angry when he was around and even angrier when he wasn't. "Clearly, he's making me insane."

"Nothing wrong with a little insanity," Kevin told her.

"Easy enough to say when you're not the babbling idiot," Bella muttered and leaned over a glass display case to examine a new pair of earrings Kevin had stocked. "Is this turquoise?"

"God, you're plebian," he said with a laugh. "No, my little peasant, that's lapis lazuli. Antique. That stone— well, not that one in particular—was really popular back in the day with emperors and pharaohs."

"You know," Bella told him, tipping her head to one side and smiling up at him, "if I hadn't met your girl-friend, I'd swear you were gay."

"Straight men know good jewelry, too. Your surfer guy bought that great emerald piece from me, remember?"

Bella felt a twinge. Who had he bought it for? One of his celebrity dates? She had to be important to him. You didn't just buy emeralds for a casual fling. Of course, maybe Jesse did.

"Ah, yes, Mr. Thoughtful. Wonder which one of the slavering crowd gets the emeralds," Bella mused, stopping in front of a display case of sterling silver.

"Honey, you sound like a jealous wife."

Her head snapped up and she pinned him with a hard look. "I do not."

Kevin shrugged. "Yeah, you do."

Oh God, did she really? That was lowering. She wasn't jealous of Jesse's women. She was…heck, she didn't even know *what* she was anymore. Still… "I'm not jealous. I'm irritated."

"And hiding it nicely." Kevin bent over the glass case and looked into her eyes. "So he knows about three years ago."

"Yes, and had the nerve to tell me I should have told him who I was sooner."

"What an idiot," Kevin said chuckling. "Using logic."

"Oh, that's very funny," Bella said. "This has nothing to do with logic, anyway. He was completely insulting."

"Insulting?" Kevin shoved his hands into the pockets of his jeans and rocked back on his heels. "Jeez, Bella. Cut the guy a break."

Bella scowled. "He doesn't need a break from me. He makes his own breaks."

"He told you he remembered that night. Remembered *you*. How is that insulting?" Kevin demanded before adding, "And speak slowly, because I'm working with a Y chromosome here."

"It's insulting because he remembered the sex. He didn't remember *me*." Then there was the fact that he hadn't bothered to even talk to her once since his memory had been jogged. Oh, yes, being "remembered" by Jesse King was so-o-o flattering.

"Sure he did." Kevin gave a long-suffering sigh. "Women make this so much harder than it has to be. The guy remembered the sex *because* of you. So therefore he remembered you."

"Is it a genetic imperative that guys have to stick together?"

"Against women, hell, yes," Kevin admitted. "I love women, don't get me wrong, but you guys are enough to make a man old before his time."

"I don't know why," Bella said with a sniff. "We make perfect sense to each other."

"Exactly."

"Kevin, could you just be my best friend for a minute and not Jesse's brother-in-arms? Don't you get it? I could have been anyone as far as he knew," Bella argued.

"I *am* your best friend, and that's why I'm telling you the truth even though you don't want to hear it. You weren't just anyone to him. You're you. And he remembered. So cut him some slack."

"I can't believe you're still on his side," Bella said, eyes wide.

"The question is, why are you so against him?" Kevin leaned on the display case and grinned at her. "Seems to me you're awfully obsessed with Jesse."

"I'm not obsessed, I'm…focused," she finished lamely.

"Uh-huh."

Bella scowled at him. "We used to be together on this. Aren't you the one who helped me organize the protest march against corporate takeovers in Morgan Beach?"

He grinned. "You're the only one who's got a problem with him anymore."

"Fine. Lone wolf," she muttered. "That's me."

The bell over the door jangled and he gave her a quick grin. "Be back in a sec, Ms. Wolf, I've got a customer. Take a look at the new sterling earrings. Mrs. Latimer," he called out, hustling over to the tall, richly dressed woman entering the shop. "I've got some new jade you're going to love."

"Things are pretty darn sad when even your best friend isn't on your side," Bella muttered, strolling down the length of the counter again. Her gaze flicked past the gemstones, the twisted gold and the heavier sterling silver.

Kevin's shop sold jewelry made by local artisans. Here you could find everything from exquisite, high-priced jewels to skull rings and pentagrams. Eclectic, she thought. Like the town used to be. She ran her finger over the cool glass. "Jade. Emeralds. Diamonds."

"Which do you prefer?"

Bella felt her jaw drop. "What are you doing here?"

Jesse grinned at her, and carefully closed her mouth with the tip of one finger under her chin. "Came back to see if Kevin got in the matching earrings to a necklace I picked up here a couple of weeks ago."

"Ah, yes, the emeralds." Did she sound wistful? She didn't want to sound wistful.

"You have something against them?"

"Not a thing," Bella said, forcing a smile. "I just hope the woman you're buying them for appreciates the gesture. Hmm," she added, tipping her head to one side as she looked up at him, "I wonder. Do you remember *her* name?"

His eyes flashed and a muscle in his jaw ticked, but that was the only sign her barb had hit home.

"I do," he said. "But now I'm wondering why you care. Jealous?"

"Please." She glanced across the room at Kevin, who wasn't paying the slightest bit of attention to them, focused as he was on his customer. Great. No reprieves headed her way.

She wasn't jealous. She was pissy. Bella stared up into Jesse's beautiful eyes and told herself to remember that she was nothing to him. A blurry memory of one night that he hadn't even been able to recall the morning after.

Okay, that thought helped her weakened knees to strengthen a bit. He was charm personified. He knew just how to break down a woman's defenses. And Bella, despite knowing all that, was just as susceptible as the next woman. Dammit. But how was she supposed to react when she slept with him and was forgotten and some other nameless woman did the same thing and received emeralds?

"Who you buy jewelry for is none of my business," she said. "I just hope the poor woman knows what she's letting herself in for."

"Oh, I think she knows," he said, smiling now.

"Amazing to me how many women are sucked into your orbit," she said.

"As I recall, you liked my orbit just fine."

She scowled at him. "I thought you said you didn't recall much at all."

"Oh, the memories are hazy, but they're there." He leaned in toward her and lowered his voice even further until it was no more than a sexy rumble that rolled along her spine. "Lightly tanned skin in the moonlight. The buzz of something electrical when we touched. The sigh of your breath."

He paused and Bella shivered.

"Care to refresh my memory further?"

Indignation rose up hot and hideous inside her. He was the most appalling male on the face of the planet. Yes, sexy. Yes, gorgeous. But absolutely zero moral center.

"Oh, yeah," she hissed at him with a fierce shake of her head, "that's gonna happen. You're actually standing here, buying emeralds for one conquest, while trying to line up another. I feel so sorry for whoever this woman is, if I knew her name, I'd find her and warn her about you."

He leaned back against the glass case, looking completely at ease while Bella's insides were twisting themselves into hard, tight knots.

"Trust me when I say she doesn't need warning," Jesse told her.

"Why, I'll bet she's sitting at home thinking you're something special and has zero idea that you're trying to snuggle up to me and—"

"Snuggle?" he interrupted with a wink. "Nothing wrong with a good snuggle."

She stopped and gaped at him. "God, you really are a pig, aren't you?"

"I don't think pigs snuggle. Of course, to a pig, it might seem like snuggling…"

"You're making a joke out of this." Bella cut him off. "And it isn't funny."

He sighed. "Come on, Bella. It was a little funny. Now, why don't you and I go have lunch so we can talk about this?"

"Not a chance," Bella said, taking a step back just for good measure. Despite the fact that she knew Jesse King was bad news, her body continued to respond to him. And what did that say about her, she wondered. He was the only man who had affected her like this.

"There is absolutely *nothing* that would convince me to repeat a mistake I've spent three years trying to block out of my memory." All right, a little lie. But she couldn't very well admit to him what that night had meant to her. Besides, now that she was getting to know him a little better, she was beginning to rethink those blurry memories of pleasure.

His smile slipped a little and a quick flash of irritation sparked in his eyes. "If you'd really been trying to block that night out of your mind, you wouldn't be so mad right now about me buying jewelry for another woman."

She hissed in a breath and when she spoke again, her voice was low and sizzled with fury. "Are you serious? Is your ego really that big?"

"Bella, if you'd just shut up for a second…"

"Shut up?" Her eyes went wide and her head jerked back as if he'd slapped her. She shot another quick look at Kevin and his customer as if to reassure herself that they were absorbed in their own discussion. "Shut up? I can't believe you just said that to me."

"Bella, if you'll let me talk," he said, irritation beginning to color his voice.

"Oh, you've said plenty," she told him, riding the wave of anger that was cresting inside, threatening to choke her. "You're standing here trying to charm me, all the while you're buying expensive jewelry for some poor, misguided woman who probably thinks you love her."

"I do."

She actually gasped. Stung. Hurt. Furious. Amazing that all those emotions could crowd inside her at once, each clamoring for recognition. Pain jangled through her with sharp, jagged edges and she wondered why. Bella hadn't thought she'd really cared one way or another about Jesse King, but hearing him admit to her that he loved another woman was just…awful.

She shouldn't care. It shouldn't matter. Bella hadn't seen him in three years. She didn't want him in her life.

But oh God, knowing that it would never happen hit her on a level she hadn't really expected. And that made her even more furious with him.

"You bastard."

"Hey," he said, smiling now, "of course I love her. She's a great woman. Funny, smart…"

"Mazel tov," she snapped and tried to walk past him. "Don't bother sending me an invitation to the wedding."

"Wedding's over."

"What?" That stopped her dead in her tracks. Had she really been fantasizing about a married man all this time? "You're *married?*"

Jesse laughed and finally Kevin and his customer turned to look at them curiously. After a moment or two, they went back to business, though Kevin still managed to keep one eye on them while he worked and Bella tried to get herself under control.

This was even worse than she'd thought.

"You're married?" she repeated it, because she just couldn't believe this.

"No, I'm not. She is."

Better? She wondered, or worse? She voted worse. "Well, that makes you a real hero, doesn't it? Buying jewelry for a married woman."

"Her husband will understand."

"Oh, sure he will."

"You don't believe me," he said, smiling, "but my cousin Travis knows that I'm nuts about his wife, Julie."

"Yeah, I'll bet he does—" Bella broke off when his words finally registered. All her air left her in a rush as she noticed his wide smile and the pure enjoyment shining in his eyes. Still a little stunned, she whispered, *"What?"*

He reached out, took her hand in his and moved his thumb over her skin in a caress meant to be soothing, but was instead firing up her nerve endings. Why did it have to be Jesse King who could electrify her entire body with a single touch?

As if he knew exactly what she was thinking, his blue eyes danced with amusement and something more…intimate. "The necklace and earrings are for my cousin Travis's wife, Julie."

Bella blinked, shook her head as if she hadn't heard him correctly and repeated, just for clarification, "Your cousin's wife?"

"Yep," Jesse said, one corner of his mouth lifting into a half grin and Bella knew he was enjoying himself. "She just had a baby. Their second. A boy this time. Their little girl, Katie, is almost two and Colin was born a month ago."

"So you bought her emeralds," Bella said, feeling the last of her anger fade away to be replaced by a swell of something that felt a lot like tenderness. Which was a far more dangerous emotion to be entertaining about Jesse King.

"I did," he said. "She has green eyes, and Travis is always buying her emeralds, so when I saw that necklace here, I couldn't resist."

He bought an expensive necklace for his cousin's wife. Why did knowing that make Bella's heart soften toward him? Because he was close to his family. Clearly appreciated them. And she'd lived most of her life alone, so family was something of an elusive dream for her.

A small curl of envy wound through her for Julie King. Not only did she have a husband who loved her and two children, but she had cousins who cared enough to buy her something special to celebrate the birth of her child.

"So," he asked quietly, "am I still a pig?"

"Probably," Bella said on a sigh, "but not about this, obviously."

"You sound disappointed."

"No," Bella admitted, meeting his gaze squarely, "just confused."

"Well, now," Jesse said, still giving her that amazing smile of his, "I've gotta say, I consider that a step in the right direction."

"How's that?"

"Confusion means you're no longer so sure that I'm the devil incarnate and that means just maybe you're willing to take a chance."

Her heartbeat quickened and her stomach did a slow roll and spin. Darn it, her body was working against her. Bella knew, logically, that she should stay very far away from Jesse King. She'd already been burned once, so wouldn't it be the height of stupidity to stand in line to be burned again?

Yet…he was buying his cousin's wife emeralds. He was close enough to his family that he not only wanted to do something special for the new mom, but it felt right to him to do it. That said something about him, too, didn't it?

Life had been a lot easier when she had just hated him.

"What kind of chance?" she finally asked.

That smile of his brightened even further. "How about you give me the opportunity to take you around my offices. Show you I'm not the CEO of the evil empire that you think I am."

"Why do you care what I think?" she asked, instead of answering his question.

He studied her for a long minute before admitting, "I'm not sure, but I do."

"That's honest anyway."

"I'm just that kind of guy."

"Hmm. That's yet to be seen," Bella said softly, "but I'll take the tour of King Beach."

"That's good enough for now," he said. "How about in an hour?"

"Fine," she said, the fight gone out of her as her mind and heart and body all struggled to make sense of this latest insight into Jesse King.

"Okay. See you then." He walked out of Kevin's shop without a backward glance, leaving Bella feeling more confused than ever.

Five

Jesse waited for Bella on the sidewalk outside King Beach. For some weird reason, he felt almost like a teenager on a first date. Which was beyond stupid. Since not only wasn't this a date, but he'd already slept with Bella. So it wasn't as if this was the first time he would ever be alone with her.

Late-afternoon sunlight poured down on him from a brilliant blue sky. Traffic down Main Street was light, but the sidewalks were filled with people strolling in and out of the shops in the newly rehabbed business district. Everyone in Morgan Beach was happy with what he'd done there. Everyone but the one woman he was interested in.

Were the fates finally getting back at him? His entire

life, women had come easily to him. Now, there was Bella. A woman whose memory had haunted him for three years and now that he'd found her again she wanted nothing to do with him. Even worse, she had something going on with that Kevin guy. But what? he wondered. Was she in love with the other man?

Scowling at the thought, Jesse told himself it didn't matter. Whatever she felt for someone else could be dealt with. He wanted Bella and Jesse King didn't lose. Ever.

"Well, you look fierce."

He snapped out of his thoughts and looked down into chocolate-brown eyes. She'd slipped up on him unnoticed and he couldn't figure out how. Her scent alone should have alerted him. It was a blend of flowers and spice that somehow reminded him of summer nights. Well, *one* summer night in particular.

"Sorry," he said, smiling at her. "Just thinking."

"Couldn't have been happy thoughts."

"You might be surprised," he said and took her arm, turning her toward the front door of King Beach headquarters. When he took a step forward though, she didn't move. Turning to look down at her again, he asked, "What's the problem?"

She frowned, chewed at her bottom lip and finally admitted, "I feel as if I'm walking into enemy territory."

"Expecting an ambush?"

She whipped her long, thick, brown hair out of her way and stared up at him. "Honestly, I don't know what to expect."

"Well, then," Jesse said, enjoying her nervousness a bit, "let's get started and satisfy your curiosity."

He led her through the door and paused just inside the threshold. A receptionist's desk sat just opposite the door and the woman seated there was busily answering a phone that rang incessantly. Smiling at the woman, Jesse walked past her to the elevator bank, pushed the button and waited, still holding on to Bella as if he were worried that she'd bolt.

But she didn't. She stood there with an expression that made him think of martyrs about to be burned at the stake. He wished she would smile. Amazing how this one badly dressed woman could get to him so easily.

Over the last few days though, his mind had been filling in some blanks. Now that he knew who his mystery woman was, his memory of that night three years ago was becoming clearer. He could see her face now, as she'd looked in the moonlight. He could hear her voice, sighing. And he damn well remembered that she hadn't dressed like a Hungarian peasant back in the day. So he couldn't help wondering why she was dressing that way now.

Only one way to find out. "So, want to tell me why you wear those shapeless clothes?"

"Excuse me?" She turned her face up to his.

He waved one hand to encompass her loose, pale green shirt and flowing, floor-length yellow skirt. Maybe he shouldn't have said anything. After all, he was trying to charm and seduce her, not piss her off further.

But dammit, he'd seen the body she had hidden underneath all that fabric and he couldn't understand why she was so determined to disguise it. Especially, he thought, since she hadn't before. He distinctly remembered her wearing faded jeans and a low-necked, body-hugging T-shirt.

She flushed and Jesse was charmed. He couldn't remember the last time he'd seen a woman blush. But her one moment of embarrassment was gone an instant later. Her dark eyes flashed as she said, "Not that it's any of your business, but I like wearing natural fabrics."

He should have backed off, but couldn't help himself. "Natural, sure. But why…" He shook his head, clearly baffled.

The elevator chimed, the doors hissed open and Bella stepped inside. Turning around sharply, she lifted her chin, glared at him and said, "I stopped wearing form-fitting clothes three years ago when I discovered it attracted men who were interested in only one thing."

In the harsh, overhead glare of the fluorescent lights, she looked ferocious and proud. Like a female Viking. And Jesse felt a shot of admiration rip through him, along with a quick flash of shame. Because of *him,* she was dressing like a refugee from a rag factory? She was hiding that glorious body because he'd slept with her and disappeared from her life?

Vaguely disgusted with himself, he walked into the elevator beside her and punched the second-floor button. Strange, but until this moment, he'd never before considered what a woman thought of him after their time together was over. He'd always enjoyed himself, made sure his lady of the moment had a good time and then he'd moved on.

Uneasiness settled over him as he wondered how many other women he might have left wounded in his wake. He'd never thought of himself as a hurting women kind of guy. Hell, he *liked* women. But now…he had to wonder.

Still, he felt compelled to say something, so he said, "I don't think your strategy's working."

"Really?" she asked, her voice just carrying over the distantly annoying Muzak playing over the speakers. "I haven't been bothered by unwanted men in three years."

He found that hard to believe. "Then the men in this town are blind or extremely shortsighted and probably stupid to boot, so you're better off without them."

"Is that right?" She glanced up at him from beneath long, dark lashes.

"Damn straight," he told her, meeting her gaze squarely. Fine. He'd messed up. But that was in the past. And she might as well know that whatever she was wearing, she got to him on levels no one else ever had.

"The clothes are ugly, I grant you. But they don't disguise your eyes. Or your mouth." He lifted one hand and smoothed the pad of his thumb over her bottom lip. She pulled her head back quickly, and he smiled, shaking his head. "And even if you'd been dressed like this three years ago… I still would have noticed you."

She blinked at him, obviously surprised, and Jesse felt like a jerk. For the first time in his life, he was faced with a woman he'd used and walked away from. And for the first time in his life, he regretted what he'd done. A new experience for him. And not an entirely comfortable one.

The elevator opened, sparing them both from having to continue the conversation. A buzz of activity and conversation rolled toward them in a thick wave and Jesse smiled. He may not have started out as a business-man, but he certainly enjoyed the sights and sounds of his success. He knew all too well that it was because of him that this company was growing beyond all imagin-ings. And he had a real sense of pride in what he'd ac-complished in a few short years.

"Come on, Bella," he said, holding out one hand toward her and smiling. "Let me show you around the enemy camp."

She glanced from him to the room and back again before reluctantly slipping her hand into his and fol-lowing him out into the middle of organized chaos. Phones were ringing, printers were hissing as they shot sheet after sheet of paper onto trays and the low rumble of dozens of conversations almost sounded like the roar of the ocean.

He walked her through King Beach like a king over-seeing his estate. He made sure she saw all the latest technology and the swarms of people he had handling sales, marketing and publicity. Really getting into his spiel, Jesse pointed out the wall maps with the locations of the hundreds of King Beach stores and turned to bask in her admiration.

But Bella wasn't watching him or his presentation.

Instead, she was marching up and down the aisles, peeking into cubicles and rummaging in trash cans.

"What are you doing?" he asked, coming up behind her.

She straightened, spun around and faced him, holding an empty soda can aloft as if it were a gold nugget she'd scraped out of the earth. "Look at this! You don't even *recycle!*"

A muffled snort of laughter came from the guy whose cubicle had been invaded, but one steely look from Jesse ended his amusement fast. Everything he'd shown her. Everything he'd done to try to impress her hadn't meant a thing. No, she focused on empty soda cans. He admired her passion. She practically vibrated with it, and he wanted nothing more than to see it up close and personal again. Hell, there she stood, telling him off and his body was more than ready for her. Was it any wonder she fascinated him?

"Sure we recycle, Bella," he said, his voice patient. He shook his head and looked into her eyes, fired now with righteous indignation. "It's just not done up here. The janitorial staff handles it every night."

"Of course they do," she mumbled, dropping the can back into the trash, then glaring at him. "You hire someone to do the right thing for you rather than making the effort to do it yourself."

"What?"

"You heard me," she said, her voice low, but vehement. "You don't care what your company does as long as there's a healthy bottom line. You don't even ask your employees to recycle. How hard would it be to put *two* trash cans into every cubicle? Is it really so difficult to take personal responsibility for what your company produces?"

The resident of the cubicle hunched his shoulders, lowered his head and started typing, actively trying to ignore both of them. Jesse shook his head again, took Bella's arm and drew her out of the cubicle. He was not going to defend himself to her in front of his employees.

When they were far enough away from curious ears, he said, "In case you hadn't noticed, those cubicles are too small to cram much more into them."

"Easy excuse."

"What does it matter how the recycling gets done as long as it is done?"

"It's the principle of the thing," she muttered, folding her arms beneath her breasts and unintentionally, he was sure, outlining them nicely.

"The principle. So it's not recycling. It's having *me* recycle."

She frowned.

"I hire people to do that job."

"Hmph."

"Okay," Jesse said, leaning in closer to her, bending low so that he could look directly into her eyes. "Would it make you feel better if I fired the entire janitorial staff and did it all myself? Would that make the world a better place for you, Bella? Putting twenty people out of work? Does that help the environment?"

She was scowling now and her mouth was working

as if there were words locked behind her grimly closed lips fighting to get out. But after a few long seconds, her shoulders slumped, her mouth relaxed and she huffed out a breath. "All right, I suppose I can see your point."

Jesse grinned. She might be a hard case, but she could admit when she was wrong, which was more than he could say for a lot of people. She didn't look at all happy about seeing his point, but that didn't matter. She *had* seen it.

"I think I'm having a moment, here. I've just scored a point off Bella Cruz."

She snorted.

He held up a hand, grinned even more broadly and said, "Wait. Not finished relishing. I want to enjoy the glory of this small victory." Seconds ticked past, then with a deep breath said, "Okay, I'm done."

"Is everything a joke to you?" she asked, staring up at him.

"Who said I was joking?" Jesse teased. "Getting you to admit that I have a point about *anything* is well worth celebrating."

She rolled her eyes, but her lips twitched and Jesse felt as if he'd scored another victory.

"Now," he said, taking her hand in his, "how about finishing the tour?"

Her hand lay limply in his for a brief moment, then her fingers curled around his and this time, he kept his smile to himself. She walked beside him, spoke to a few of the people answering phones and Jesse watched as she charmed everyone. Apparently, his mystery woman had plenty of personality—she just wasn't using it on him.

Clearly, she didn't trust herself to relax around him. But that was fine with him. He didn't want her relaxed—he wanted her hot and bothered and poised on the edge of sexual heat. Then he wanted to take her over that edge.

Oh, yeah, he thought. He was going to have Bella again. He was going to wine her, dine her and seduce her until she begged him to take over her business and make her a millionaire. And once the business end of things was taken care of, he told himself, they'd go from there. Once she was a part of King Beach, it would be better for her. Better for him. Better for everyone.

He stood to one side as Bella chatted with a couple of the secretaries. They were both talking about her swimwear and how they wished they could find good suits like that everywhere. Say, for example, at King Beach. Jesse frowned a little to hear even his own employees saying that his company wasn't meeting the demands of all the consumers. But that only helped to convince him that the decision to absorb Bella's company into his own was the right one.

As if he'd heard Jesse's thoughts, Dave Michaels walked up, a stack of folders caught under one arm and an eager expression of welcome on his face. "Bella," he said, giving Jesse a nod of greeting, "we're delighted to have you here. Jesse told me he was going to give you a tour. Hope you don't mind if I call you Bella."

"Not at all," she said, stepping away from the two

women she'd been talking to as they went back to work. "This is all very…impressive."

She said *impressive,* but Jesse told himself she didn't sound impressed. She sounded just a little bit disgusted.

"Well, we're big and we're growing," Dave said, glee lacing his voice. "Which is just one of the reasons I'm glad you're here. As you know, King Beach doesn't really cater to women—"

Jesse's ears perked up and he shook his head wildly from behind Bella, hoping to head the man off. It wasn't time yet to hit her with the information that they were interested in buying out Bella's Beachwear. And when it *was* the right moment, Jesse intended to be the one to do the telling. Bella was a special case. She wasn't some ordinary CEO of a big company who would welcome a takeover if the money were right. He had to approach her cautiously or the whole thing would blow up in his face.

Dave caught the frantic motion and stopped himself midsentence. "But I have to tell you," he said, changing the subject smoothly, "my wife bought a bathing suit from you that she can't stop raving about."

"Isn't that nice?" Bella beamed at him as if the man had just presented her with a bouquet of roses. "I hope she comes back."

"Oh, she will. She's bringing her sisters to your shop next week," Dave assured her. "Connie's been bragging about your store so much, all three of them have insisted on visiting Bella's."

"Thank you, I'm always glad to hear about a satisfied customer."

"Yes, aren't we all," Jesse muttered, and jerked his head, silently telling Dave to take a hike.

Dave got the message. "Right. Well, I've got a few calls to make, so I'd better let you get on with your tour. Nice to see you here, Bella. Hope we see you again soon."

Bella watched him go, then turned to look at Jesse. "I like your friend."

"But not me," he added for her.

"Does it matter?" she asked and her voice was almost lost in the bustle of the office.

Yeah, it mattered. He wasn't sure why and he didn't like acknowledging the fact, even to himself. So he for damn sure wasn't going to let her know how he felt. That woman had enough power over him already.

"Let me show you my office," he said instead.

"Oh, Mr. King," a woman called out as she hurried up to meet them. "We've just heard back on the surfing exhibition plans. The city's approved everything and your guests have all agreed to take part."

"Good news, Sue," Jesse said, catching the gleam of curiosity in Bella's eyes. "Put a call in to Wiki, will you? Tell him I'll be getting in touch with him by tomorrow."

"Will do." The woman hurried off, the tap of her heels swallowed by the bustling noise of the busy office.

"Wiki?" Bella asked as Jesse took her arm and steered her toward his office at the back of the long, wide room.

"Danny Wikiloa," he said, opening the door for her. Once inside, he closed the door before adding, "He's a professional surfer. We competed against each other for years.

He's coming into town in two weeks for the exhibition. Doing it as a favor to me, actually, since he's retired, too."

"The exhibition," she murmured. "Everyone in town has been talking about it for days."

He stuffed both hands into his jeans pockets as he watched her wander the perimeter of his office. She noticed everything, pausing to look at the framed photos of different beaches. She hardly glanced at his surfing trophies, which stung a bit, but she seemed fascinated by the one wall where photos of his family were hanging.

"It's going to be fun," he said, walking over to join her. "Ten of the world's best surfers giving a one-day exhibition."

"You miss it, don't you? The competition, I mean."

He hadn't really admitted it to anyone else, but, "Yeah, I do. I like winning."

She nodded. "Not surprising. The whole King family is like that, aren't they?"

"Pretty much," he said and turned his back on the family photos so he could look instead at Bella. "We enjoy competing and we don't lose gracefully."

She tipped her head to one side, looked at him and said, "You can't always win."

"Don't see why not."

"You really don't, do you?"

"Nope," he told her and took the single step separating them. Standing alongside her, he looked up at the family photos and waved one hand at them. "Not a single one of those people is the type to settle for second place."

"Sometimes you don't have a choice," Bella said softly.

"There's always a choice, Bella." Jesse glanced at one familiar face and then another as he said, "The King family decided a long time ago that the only people who lose are the ones who expect to. We expect to win, so we do."

"Easy as that?"

He looked down at her and found her staring up at him. Those chocolate-brown eyes of hers looked deep and dark and filled with secrets. Secrets he wanted to know. To share. Lifting one hand, he cupped her cheek and said, "I never said it was easy. But winning shouldn't be. Takes all the fun out of it if everyone could do it."

"And fun's important to you, too," she said, stepping back, away from his touch, away from *him.*

"Should be important to everyone," he said, his palm still tingling from the touch of her skin against his. "What's life if you don't enjoy it? Hell, why do *any-thing* if you don't enjoy it?"

"And you enjoy what you do now?"

"Yeah," he said with a shrug. "I didn't think I would, you know. Never planned to be the suit-wearing guy, Mr. Businessman. But I'm good at it."

She looked toward the closed office door and the busy office beyond. "Yes, I guess you are."

"See, I'm enjoying this. We're agreeing on things."

"Don't get used to it," she told him wryly.

"Why not? We could make a great team, Bella."

She laughed a little. "We're so not a team, Jesse."

This was it, he thought. The moment. Time to slide an offer in here while she was still impressed by her tour. While she still liked him a little. It struck him then that he'd never had to work so hard to get a woman to like him. "We could be. Think about it. King Beach. Bella's Beachwear. A match made in heaven."

She stilled, slid an uneasy look at him and asked, "What kind of match?"

"Well, I wasn't going to bring this up so soon, but I don't like waiting, either. So I'll get right to it." He walked to his desk and leaned back against it. Through the wide window behind him, the sun splashed down on the view of Morgan Beach and the ocean stretching out to the horizon. "I want to buy Bella's Beachwear."

Six

"No." Bella blurted the word out instinctively.

"Jeez." He came up off the desk and took a step toward her. "At least let me finish my sentence."

"No need to, I'm not for sale." She should have known. Should have guessed that he was softening her up for something. She'd allowed herself to relax around him. All right, she'd actually been enjoying herself. The touch of his hand, that wicked smile of his, the way he seemed to focus so intently on her. All that had combined to weaken her defenses and now she was going to pay.

"I'm not trying to buy *you*, Bella. Just your business."

"That's what you don't get, Jesse. I *am* my business." Irritated, hurt and just a little angry at herself for walking into this mess, she continued, "You want to buy my swimwear, but to you it's just that. Bathing suits. Stick them on a rack, sell them to the masses."

Both his eyebrows rose. "There's something wrong with selling your product to people who want it?"

"No, but I'm not interested in the quick, easy sale." She took a deep breath, fisted her hands at her sides and tried once again to get through his hard head. "I'm interested in the *whole* woman. Helping ordinary women build their self-esteem. *You're* interested in making the young and skinny feel pretty. Well, guess what, they already do."

"Bella, I know you think I want to change what you do, but you couldn't be more wrong." He threw both hands up, then let them fall to his thighs. "I've been resisting selling women's stuff for years because how the hell do I know what women want to wear? Everything I stock I personally believe in. That's the reason I want *you* to be a part of King Beach. Because *you* believe in your stuff the way I believe in mine."

"It's not 'stuff.'"

He laughed and Bella simmered.

"I get it, I get it. Your line is not interchangeable with department store swimsuits."

"I'm not looking to be bought out or rolled over or absorbed by King Beach. You can't buy me up like you did this city, Jesse. I won't let you ruin the thing I love just for the sake of business."

"So you have something against becoming a millionaire?" he countered. "Because I promise you, join me and that's what you'll be."

For just one, brief, electrifying moment, she actually considered his offer and thought about what it would mean to her to be financially independent. She could buy her little house from Kevin. She could donate all the money she wanted to the different charities that had always tugged at her heart. She could…

Bella stopped, gasped and accused, "You're the devil."

He grinned. "Good. That means you're thinking about it."

"I did, for about thirty seconds."

"That's a start."

"No," Bella insisted. "It's not. I'm not set up for large-scale production. I'm a cottage industry and I like it that way. I know my weavers, my seamstresses. I personally choose fabrics, design styles. The women who work for me care as much about the product as I do. We're making a statement."

"Yes, but do you have to make it *poor?*" He grinned and said, "Think about this. You align with King Beach and you'll be creating more jobs. Better money for your weavers and seamstresses. We'll be able to use them, I know. Hell, they can probably teach the pros a thing or two."

"They *are* pros," she told him.

"I'm sure. But on a much smaller scale," he said. "Don't you see, Bella? Signing with me will get you and your company even more."

"I know you want my shop, but I'm not turning my business over to you."

"I don't just want your business, Bella," he said. "I want *you.*"

Oh God. A quick blast of something hot, delicious and practically mind-numbing shot through her. He wanted her. Jesse King wanted Bella Cruz. Did he mean that? And what exactly *did* he mean? Want? Want how? For how long? In what way? Oh God. Her stomach was a mess and in a split second, her mind took off on dozens of wild, crazy tangents that splintered again and again, teasing her with possibilities. Until he spoke again and shattered them all.

"I want you to run the business for us. You'll still be designing, you'll still have the final say in everything related to Bella's Beachwear—"

Just like that, the heat she'd been feeling drained away to be replaced by a chill snaking along her spine. Okay, fine. He didn't want *her*. He wanted her to work with him. For him. So much for dazzling daydreams, born to die within a few seconds of birth.

She had to stop setting herself up for disappointment. Jesse wasn't even on the same wavelength, and wishing it were different wasn't going to change a thing.

"This was your plan from the beginning, wasn't it?" she asked, and hoped she didn't sound as depressed as she felt at the moment. "All of your teasing and flirting was designed to get me off guard."

"That depends. Are you?"

She ignored that little quip. "All your talk about how King Beach doesn't cater to women was just that. Talk. You've been planning on trying to take me over from the very start."

"Considered it, yes. The day of the photo shoot

opened my eyes. But you've only got yourself to blame for that," he added, standing up straight and looking at her through eyes as blue as the sea. "You're the one who showed me what a difference your swimwear could make on a woman's body. You're the one who laid it all out for me. Is it my fault you started me thinking?"

She never should have done it, she thought now. Never should have put on one of her own suits. Never should have risen to his challenge just because she'd wanted to prove him wrong. She'd wanted to show off. And all that maneuver had done was dig her a deeper hole.

"It doesn't matter," she said, shaking her head as she watched him. "Nothing's changed. I haven't changed. I'm still not interested. Do you think you're the first company to try to buy me out? You're not. And you probably won't be the last. But I'm not selling, Jesse. This time, you lose."

"God, you're stubborn."

"I was just thinking the same thing about you," she countered and let the simmering fury inside bubble and boil. He was standing there smiling. As if he could change her opinion if he just smiled long enough. Did that technique work with most women? Of course it did. He probably never heard the word *no*.

Had to be a King thing.

"It's in your blood, isn't it?" she asked, voicing her thoughts. "You and every other member of the King family. You've always gotten what you wanted, so you expect nothing less. You've lived a charmed life," she told him. "Not many people do."

Instantly, he shifted position a bit, obviously uncomfortable with the turn of the conversation. "Okay, I grant you that. But if you think the King cousins were raised to be lazy or indulged or pampered, you've got us all wrong."

"Really." She glanced at the wall of family photos again and said, "None of these people look like they've had a rough life."

Jesse looked up, and pointed at one of them. "That's my brother, Justice."

Bella studied the photo. A gorgeous man with light brown hair, blue eyes narrowed, squinting at the sun. Justice King stood in an open field, arms folded across his chest, cowboy hat pulled low over his forehead. "Interesting name."

"My dad had just won a huge lawsuit the day he was born. Somehow he convinced mom that *Justice* was a perfectly reasonable name."

"Winning again."

"That's right," he said, smiling. "But let me tell you about Justice and the life of the pampered rich." Jesse eased down to sit on the arm of a brown leather chair. Looking up at her, he said, "Justice has a ranch about an hour from here. He's up at dawn every morning, checking his herds and his fences and the weather report. I swear he lives by the Weather Channel. As if the weather changes that much in southern California." Shaking his head, he laughed ruefully. "Our cousin Adam has a ranch too, farther north. He raises horses. Justice raises organically fed beef cattle. And grows acres of hay. He works twice as hard as any of his cowboys and wouldn't know how to be pampered if somebody paid him to try."

Bella frowned thoughtfully. "And that one?"

Jesse looked. "Ah, cousin Travis. He with the beautiful wife who loves emeralds." He pointed to a few other framed photos. "Those are his brothers, Jackson and Adam, with their wives, Casey and Gina. They've got kids, too. Two girls each. And I hear Gina's pregnant again." Getting into it now, he touched another photo of two smiling men. "This one is cousin Rico and his brother Nick at Rico's hotel in Mexico. For some reason their other brothers weren't around on that trip. And that's Nathan and Garret at some aunt's wedding. Their brothers Chance and Nash and Kieran are the three in that picture and—"

"How many of you are there?" she asked, amazement coloring her tone.

"Dozens and dozens. And probably more out there we haven't met!" Jesse laughed, obviously enjoying himself. "You can't kick a rock in California without turning up a King."

"It's…"

"Too much?" he offered, still smiling. "Way too many Kings running around?"

"It's wonderful," she finally said, and her voice was a little poignant. A minute or so ago, she'd been furious with him, trying to steamroll her into giving up the most important thing in the world to her, her business. Now that anger was pretty much gone, swamped by a tide of envy so thick she could barely breathe. She couldn't even imagine what it would be like to have so much family. As a kid, she'd hungered for parents. Or for a single brother or sister. Someone to whom she was linked. Jesse really *was* rich and she wondered if he even realized that the King family's real wealth wasn't in banks, but in each other.

Jesse's smile faded. "Are you okay?"

She nodded and pointed to another photo. She didn't want to talk about herself. "Who's that?"

"My eldest brother, Jefferson. He runs the King Studios. Makes movies and runs himself ragged because he doesn't trust anyone but himself to handle the details."

Jefferson King's photo made him look like a danger-ous man. He was wearing a white shirt, black slacks and giving the camera a hard glare, as if he resented being captured on film.

"How many brothers do you have?" Her voice was a whisper now and even she heard the yearning in it.

Softly now, he answered, "Three."

"Three brothers. And so many cousins…who is he?" she asked. "The marine?"

Jesse grinned even more broadly. "My brother Jericho. Now *there's* a pampered, lazy rich guy. A gunnery sergeant. Didn't want to be an officer. Said he'd rather serve with *real* marines. He's done two tours overseas," Jesse said and frowned when he added, "and he's about to be shipped out again."

Bella sighed, folded her arms beneath her breasts and looked at the man who still filled far too much of her thoughts. He wasn't what she'd expected. His whole *family* wasn't what she'd expected. Hardworking ranchers. Marines. And apparently they were all so close that it felt natural for Jesse to hang family photos in his office.

She envied him that connection. That solid base with so much family. Lives intertwined, bonds strengthened by years of love. What must it be like, she wondered, to have so much? To know that it was simply *there* whenever you needed it?

"Bella? You okay?"

"Yes," she said and looked at him. His blue eyes were narrowed on her and he was watching her as a soldier might keep a wary eye on a live grenade. "You just…surprised me, that's all."

"Why? Because I have a family?"

"No, because you love them so much."

"It surprises you to know that I love my family?" His features were as taut as his voice.

"You just never seemed…" She broke off, shook her head and said, "Never mind. It was nothing."

"Uh-huh," he said, moving in closer to her. "Well, if these pictures impressed you, you should know I have more."

She laughed shortly. "More?"

"Lots more pictures of everyone at home," he said, smiling again. "I ran out of wall space in here."

"This isn't fair," she said, looking from him to all the photos.

"What?"

"I thought I had you pegged," she admitted. "A

modern-day robber baron stomping his way through life, taking what he wanted and making no apologies."

"You weren't completely wrong," he said, "I do go after what I want and I don't let anybody stop me." He moved in even closer until all that separated them was an inch or two of space and Bella's own firm resolve.

Which was weakening, darn it.

She felt the heat of him sliding off his body, reaching for her, and it was so tempting to stand her ground, let him close that last inch or two of space so she could feel his tall, lean body pressed against her. Her memories of their one night together were still so vivid, it was all she could do to keep from flinging herself at him. But if she did that, then she'd be lost and she knew it. So she did the only thing she could. She stepped back—mentally and physically.

He sighed. "You don't have to be afraid of me, Bella."

"I'm not. Afraid I mean. Just…cautious."

"Cautious is okay," he allowed, giving her a small, wicked smile. "It just means that you take your time. But once you're sure of your footing, you'll move ahead."

She knew what he was talking about. There wasn't much subtext there. He wanted her. And oh God, she wanted him, too. But she'd wanted him three years ago, too. And what had that gotten her? One night of glory and three years of misery. Was she really ready to set herself up for that kind of pain again?

Jesse King wasn't the "forever" kind of guy. Bella wasn't the "temporary" kind of girl. So never the twain should meet.

"Why don't you go to dinner with me?"

"What?" Okay, that offer had come out of nowhere.

"Dinner," he repeated. "Usually considered the last meal of the day?"

His smile really was a weapon all its own. At least, for her, it was. "I don't know if that's a good idea."

"It's a great idea," he said, and closed the distance separating them again. "Look, you've been on a tour of the business. You've seen for yourself that the place isn't a sweatshop. Happy, well-paid employees, I must be a halfway decent boss, yes?"

"Yes…"

"And I'm not that hard to spend time with, am I?"

"No…"

"So we have a meal. We talk. We…"

"Jesse, I'm still not going to sell my business to you."

He cut her off, laid both hands on her shoulders and she felt the heat of his skin seeping through the fabric of her shirt and down, deep into her bones.

"I'm not talking about the business right now. I want you, Bella. I've wanted you for three years." His gaze moved over her like a warm caress. "Hell, I've *dreamed* of you for three years. You want me, too. I can feel it every time we're together."

"I don't always do what I want," she told him, and kept thinking, *Strong, Bella. Be tough. Be strong. Don't give in.* Unfortunately, her body wasn't listening.

"You should," he said with a quick grin. "But that's a talk for another time. Right now, I've got a deal for you."

Uh-oh. Making deals with a man who refused to

lose could never be considered a good idea. Warily, she asked, "What kind of deal?"

"A simple one. Perfect for both of us." He stroked his palms up and down her arms and the friction he caused was enough to kindle a sort of sweeping wildfire that began licking at her insides. "You think you know me, right?"

"All too well," she said.

He nodded. "Well, I think you're wrong and I'm willing to bet on it. If I manage to show you something about me that truly shocks you, we have sex. Again."

That one, three-letter word—*sex*—conjured up so many different emotions and needs, she could hardly draw a breath for the strangling effect on her lungs. "Now just a minute—"

"Come on, Bella. You've said yourself that you know exactly what kind of guy I am."

"Yes, but—" She waved a hand at the wall of family photos. "You've already surprised me there."

"Because I love my family," he said, as if he still couldn't believe that. "But I'm not talking about a surprise. I'm talking about *shock*. If I can really shock you, you have sex with me. Again."

"Stop saying *again*."

He grinned. "No reason to pretend you're insulted or anything," he pointed out a second later. "We've already had each other once. I'm just saying, it'd be nice to have each other *again*."

"You're doing that on purpose. Reminding me."

"Damn straight. Is it working?"

Yes, she almost shrieked. She was so out of her element here, Bella thought. Jesse King was a Major League Flirter. He could play this game in his sleep—probably did—where Bella was just lost. She didn't do the flirting thing. She was much more the honesty-is-the-best-policy type. Which probably explained the dearth of dates in her life.

Taking a deep breath, she met his gaze squarely, determined not to let him see just how rattled she actually was. But he'd know how crazy he was making her if she were too afraid to accept his deal, wouldn't he? She gave an inward sigh. "This deal. I know what happens if I lose. What do I get if I win?"

One eyebrow lifted and his mouth curved into a smile. "If I fail to shock you completely—and you've got to be honest—then I'll quit bugging you about buying your business."

Well. She hadn't expected that. This was too easy, Bella thought, watching him as he stood there staring at her with a smug smirk on his face. Clearly, he believed he would win this bet easily. But then, that was a part of who he was, wasn't it?

Hadn't he just told her that Kings never expect to lose?

And how satisfying would it be for her to knock him off his feet, so to speak? To beat him at the very deal *he'd* proposed? Oh, that would be sweet. The chance at doing just that was too tantalizing to turn down. Besides, he couldn't possibly shock her.

She knew exactly who Jesse King was.

"Okay," she said suddenly, before she could change

her mind, or listen to the outraged, rational screams rattling through her brain. "You're on. It's a deal."

"Friday night. Dinner and the bet."

She nodded. "Friday." Then she lifted her chin, held out her hand and waited.

"You want me to shake your hand?" he asked, glancing down briefly at her outstretched palm.

"Well, yes."

"Well," he countered, *"no."*

Then he caught her hand in his, pulled her in close and wrapped his arms around her. She was pressed so tightly to him, she felt every lean, muscular contour of his body— not to mention one specific part that left her no doubt as to just how he was feeling about her at the moment.

Bella looked up, met his gaze and held her breath as he lowered his head. The moment his lips met hers, everything stopped. Time screeched to a halt. The world probably stopped spinning on its axis. She knew for sure that she'd stopped breathing.

And more important, she didn't care.

Every cell in Bella's body leaped into life. Her blood rushed through her veins like a fiery flood. Her skin hummed. Her heart pounded frantically in her chest.

His mouth took hers in a hard, hot kiss that sizzled throughout her system like an out-of-control fireworks display. She felt alive and tingly and expectant. His tongue tangled with hers and heat dived through her, scalding everything she was, dragging her down, down into a kind of vortex where nothing was as it should be and everything shone with possibilities.

He gave her hunger and fed it.

He gave her passion and stoked it.

He gave her want and nurtured it.

Bella clung to him, pressing her body into his, relishing his hard, broad chest aligned with hers, loving the feel of that rigid proof of his desire for her pushing against her body. And while her brain shut down and her body sang, all Bella could think was, God help her if she really lost that bargain they'd just made.

Seven

For the next few days, Bella tried to put Jesse King and that kiss out of her mind. Which wasn't easy. Heck, the night she'd spent with him three years ago was still fresh in her mind. Having this latest example of his kissing prowess burned into her brain made it twice as hard to keep her mind from straying to him.

Still, if she kept busy, that helped. It was all the downtime, like sleeping, showering, washing dishes, taking a walk on the beach or even watching TV that was getting to her. The moment her brain had a free second, it leaped into thoughts of Jesse.

And her body wasn't far behind.

She'd almost been able to convince herself over the years that Jesse's kisses hadn't been *that* great. That the feel of his skin under her hands hadn't really felt like a slow burn. That his body wasn't actually that buff.

But a few short minutes alone in his office with him had shot down those little attempts at self-deception. Jesse was every bit as amazing as he had been three years ago. Her skin was still humming. And now that it was Friday, it was time to make good on the deal she'd made with him. Tonight, they'd have dinner. And if he managed to really shock her, they'd be having sex for dessert.

Oh, this was so not a good thing.

"Bella?" A voice called out from the dressing room and she walked toward the back of the store.

Desperately grateful for the distraction, Bella asked, "Do you need something?"

A blonde with big blue eyes poked her head up over the dressing-room door and grinned. "I need a smaller size in the silver swimsuit."

Bella laughed. "Didn't I tell you?"

The woman was a new customer and, like everyone else who came into her shop for the first time, she hadn't believed Bella when she'd advised that a well-made swimsuit would fit far differently than she was used to.

"I can't believe it," the blonde said, "but yeah, you were right."

"I'll be right back with a smaller size."

"Woo hoo, do I love hearing *that*," the woman said with a laugh.

Bella passed three other women looking through the racks of suits, sarongs and wraps as she headed for the hip-hugger bikini section. There she flipped through the suits hung on short plastic hangers until she found the silver mesh suit in a size 10. Smiling, she walked back to her customer, handed it over and went back to the front of the store.

September was generally a slower month than usual. She had plenty of walk-in business during the summer months, but by September, summer was ending and only the hard-core sun worshippers were out in abundance. Of course, she still had plenty of business from the female surfers in town.

When the door opened, she sent a smile of welcome, only to bite it back at the last minute. Jesse King strolled in, looking completely at home. He paused on the threshold, took a look around and smiled at her customers before focusing his attention on Bella.

God, she hated to admit what just seeing him could do to her. He was wearing his own sportswear, a red polo shirt with a collar and the KB logo in gold on the left breast, along with a pair of khaki slacks and brown suede boots. His dark blond hair was wind-ruffled and the sun-carved crinkles at the corners of his eyes deepened as he smiled.

"Morning, ladies," he said, as he headed across the store toward Bella.

"Oh my God! That's Jesse King," someone muttered and a soft giggle followed the declaration.

Naturally, he heard, and his grin widened.

Great, Bella thought. He was going to turn *her* customers into *his* groupies. She sensed more than saw the women in the store staring at him and she wanted to tell them all to turn off their hormones. But that would be like setting a filet mignon down in front of a hungry man and telling him not to eat it. An exercise in utter futility.

"Bella," he said, flattening his palms on the glass counter. Then he lowered his voice until it was just a rumble of sound. "Good to see you again. Miss me?"

"No." *Yes.* He'd stayed away from her for three days. No doubt he'd done it deliberately to drive her nuts. Well, it wasn't working! Oh, she told herself, of course it was working.

He smiled as if he'd heard that stray thought from her sex-starved hormones.

"I missed you," he said.

"Sure you did," Bella countered, congratulating herself silently on keeping her voice so steady. "Here to back out of our dinner date?" she asked with a little too much hope.

His grin broadened and, thankfully, Bella was close enough to the counter that she could hold on and keep her knees from buckling.

"Now why would I do that just when I'm set to get you where I want you so badly?" he asked.

Oh, boy. She really was in way over her head.

"No," he continued when she didn't speak. "I just came to tell you that I'll pick you up at seven, if that's okay."

"Oh, you don't have to," she said. "I can meet you wherever."

"On our first official date?" he countered. "I don't think so. I'll pick you up at your place."

"Fine," she said grudgingly, knowing this was one battle she wasn't going to win. "I'll write down my address."

"Oh, I know where you live."

"What? How?" Oh, she thought. The rental agreement.

"I made it a point to find out," he told her, then leaned across the counter, planted a quick, hard kiss on her open mouth and then winked at her. "So. See you at seven."

"Right. Seven."

"Excellent!" He slapped both hands against the glass counter then beat out a quick, drumlike tattoo of sound with his fingertips. "See you then."

Bella was pretty sure she heard one of her customers give a little sigh. Or, she thought sadly, it might have been her.

Then he turned, directed a brilliant smile at the customers still watching him, lifted a hand in farewell and said, "Ladies…"

The hushed whispers started almost the instant the door swung closed behind him. Bella didn't listen. Instead, she buried herself in work and tried not to think about the coming night.

Jesse left Bella's shop, walked down Main Street and turned left onto Pacific Coast Highway. A small café stood on the corner, with several tiny, round chrome tables clustered together on the sidewalk. There was a great view of the beach, the pier and the men hanging a wide sign reading *Surfing Exhibition—Come See the Champions*.

An exhibition had been his idea. Get a few of his friends together, have some fun in the ocean and rack up some great PR for his company all in one stroke. They'd bring plenty of tourists into town for the day, lots of money would be spent in the shops and he'd get another chance at the limelight. He hated to admit it, but he sort of missed the competition. The excitement of a meet. He didn't miss the press or the photographers, though the exhilaration of a win couldn't be beaten.

Smiling to himself, Jesse took a seat at one of the tables, drummed his fingertips on the shining silver tabletop and waited. When a young blond woman wearing shorts and a red shirt with *Christie's Café* emblazoned across her chest arrived, Jesse said, "Just a coffee, please."

"Sure, Mr. King," the girl said eagerly. "Hey, you're surfing in the exhibition, aren't you?"

"Yeah, I am," he told her, though his thoughts had moved on from the exhibition itself to the woman he thought might be there on the beach watching him.

"That's so great. Can't wait to see you in action!" She swung her long, blond ponytail behind her back and pushed out her breasts, just in case he hadn't noticed them.

Jesse nodded indifferently. He had. He just wasn't interested. Not so long ago, he'd have been smiling back at her, flirting, taking advantage of the gleam in her eyes. Now the only woman he was interested in had more of battle glint in her eyes than a gleam. And that, weirdly enough, was more of a draw for him than the eager blonde.

The waitress grinned hopefully, then disappeared into the café. Jesse was alone, except for the few stragglers taking up spots at the tables. He caught an interested glance cast his way a few times, but he ignored them. One downside to celebrity, he thought—you were never really alone.

"So," a deep voice said from behind him. "Thought we should talk."

Jesse turned his head and watched Bella's friend Kevin walk around him to take a seat in the chair opposite. Before he had a chance to speak, the waitress was back with Jesse's coffee.

"Hi, Kevin," she said. "The usual?"

"Yeah, Tiff. That'd be great." Kevin answered, though his gaze was locked on Jesse.

When she was gone again, Jesse measured the man opposite him. He had the look of a guard dog, which made Jesse wonder just what kind of friendship Kevin and Bella shared. Were they a couple? He didn't like the sound of that, but it was possible, because Jesse never had believed in men and women being merely "friends." But at the same time, he didn't think Bella was the kind of woman to be with one guy and kissing another. So just where did that leave Mr. Guard Dog? What was his interest here?

Jesse kept his irritation tightly wrapped. "What is it you want to talk about? Come to tell me you got those emerald earrings in?"

"No," Kevin said. "Next week. This is about Bella."

Of course it was. Just as well, though, Jesse told

himself. Best to have a little talk with this guy and get a few things straightened out. He wanted to know just where Kevin stood with Bella. Not that it would make a damn bit of difference to Jesse either way. He wanted Bella and he was going to have her. But it would be good to know just how many guys he was going to have to plow through to get to her.

"Fine. Let's talk," Jesse said congenially. "I'll start. Come to warn me off? Because I'll tell you straight up, it won't work."

Before Kevin could answer, the blonde was back, sliding a mug of coffee with cream in front of him. "Thanks," he muttered.

When neither of the men glanced at her again, the blonde pouted briefly and stomped off.

Finally, Kevin picked up his cup, took a sip and set it back down. "I figure Bella can tell you to take a hike if she wants to. That's not why I'm here."

One problem solved. "All right. Then why?"

"I want to know what's going on with you."

"And that's your business because…"

"Because I care about Bella."

Jesse didn't like how that sounded. He didn't like that Kevin felt he had the right to defend Bella. From *him*. His eyes narrowed, his gut clenched and his back teeth ground together. "You *care*. So, you're here to what? Be her white knight?"

"Does she need one?"

"If she does, it won't be you," Jesse told him.

"That's where you're wrong."

Had to give the guy points. He looked harmless, with his easy smile and casual pose. But there was steel inside him, too, which Jesse could admire even as he glared at him. "Have you slept with her?"

Kevin stared back. "No," he said, his voice low and tight.

"Good." Very good, Jesse thought. Even the idea of another man's hands on Bella was enough to set off an unfamiliar sort of rage inside him. He wasn't willing to question why that was. It was enough that the proprietary sensation was there. "Then if you're not her lover, or her husband or her father, what's this about?"

"I'm her friend. More than that," Kevin told him, cupping his coffee cup between his palms. "We're family."

Jesse studied the other man. "Is that right?"

"It is. She was pretty broken up three years ago when you split."

Jesse frowned, not liking the sound of that. He'd never spent a lot of time in self-examination. Usually the women he spent time with were after only what he was—an enjoyable evening. He knew now that Bella didn't fall into that category. Hell, maybe he'd known it back then, too, instinctively. He just hadn't wanted to acknowledge it.

"You're not going to do that to her again," Kevin told him.

"I don't usually take orders."

"Consider it a suggestion."

"Don't like them, either." Jesse braced his elbows on the table and watched Kevin carefully. There was no temper there, no outraged, jealous anger. Just concern. Maybe he was simply Bella's friend. And if so, then he couldn't really blame the guy for looking out for her. But that was Jesse's job now. If she needed protecting, he'd be doing it. What was between Jesse and Bella was nobody else's business. "I'm not asking your permission for anything."

Surprisingly, Kevin laughed. "Oh, hell, no. Man, Bella would kill me if she even knew I was talking to you."

Jesse smiled, but there wasn't much humor in the expression. "So why are you?"

He stood up, laid some money beneath his coffee cup and said, "Bella's not like the kind of woman you're used to. She's real. And she's breakable."

Jesse stood up, too, and slid a ten-dollar bill beneath his own cup in the same motion. "I'm not trying to break her."

"That's the problem," Kevin said with a shrug. "A guy like you can break a woman without even trying."

He left then and Jesse watched him go. *A guy like you.* What the hell did that mean? Was he so different from other men? He didn't think so. As for Bella—he wasn't looking to break her and damn if he would. Jesse wanted her. So Jesse would have her.

"Oh, for God's sake, stop checking the mirror," Bella muttered to herself even as she looked into the glass and smoothed her hands over her hair. She'd been ready for a half hour and had spent the extra time checking and rechecking her reflection.

"Very helpful," she said to the foolish woman looking back at her. Her hair was fine, loose and wavy,
hanging down around her shoulders. She wore a black,
floor-length skirt and a red blouse with short sleeves and
a scooped neckline. The tops of her breasts showed,
which made her a little uncomfortable. She stared at that
for a minute and thought seriously about changing her
shirt.

After all, it was mostly due to Jesse that she'd
stopped wearing tight or revealing clothes three years
ago. Was she crazy to stroll into the lion's lair looking
like a steak?

"Probably," she answered her own silent question, then
hissed out an impatient breath and stalked out of the small
bathroom, snapping the light off as she went. That's it. She
wasn't going to spend one more minute worrying about
what she was wearing or how she looked. Despite what
Jesse had said in the store that afternoon, this wasn't a *date*.
This was dinner. And a bet she had no intention of losing.

When the doorbell rang, she jumped, startled, then
grumbling under her breath, headed for the front door.
It didn't take long. Her house was small. An old beach
cottage, with one bedroom, a tiny bathroom, a ser-
viceable kitchen and a living room only big enough to
hold her worktable, a love-seat-size couch and one chair.
There were built-in bookcases, though, and room for a
TV and stereo. It was small, but it was hers and she
loved it, since it was the first real home she'd ever had.

She glanced around, making sure everything was
tidy before she opened the door. Jesse stood on her

small front porch lined with terra-cotta pots bursting with petunias, pansies and marigolds. The spicy scent of the flowers filled the sultry night air and rushed into her lungs as she inhaled sharply with her first sight of him.

He looked…edible.

His dark blond hair was a little long, hanging over the collar of his white, long-sleeved dress shirt. The collar was open, displaying just a bit of his tanned chest. He wore black slacks, black shoes and a smile that was designed to tempt angels out of heaven.

"You look nice," he said, his gaze resting just a little bit longer than necessary on her breasts. "Are you ready?"

Bella's stomach swirled with nerves that she tried to believe would fade away. But one look into Jesse's eyes assured her that the nervous feeling in her stomach was only going to get worse. All she had to do, she told herself, was to stay strong. *Sure,* she thought as his gaze locked on hers, *no problem.*

"Probably not," she admitted with a shrug, "but let's go anyway."

He laughed softly. "That's the spirit!"

Bella had to smile despite the butterflies still swarming in her stomach. Then she turned, picked up her purse and keys and stepped onto the porch beside him. He closed the door behind her, took her hand in his and said softly, "I've been waiting three years for tonight."

Jesse's house was, naturally, gorgeous. Bella knew it would be from the moment he steered his sports car up a winding driveway to a house that seemed to be perched on top of a hill. It was.

It was also the first shock of the evening.

"It's a 'green' house?" she asked, as they walked toward the front door.

"Right down to the bamboo floors and the recycled glass windows," he told her, grinning at the stunned bemusement on her face. "The builders use concrete. Good insulation, less steel needed for reinforcement and the foundations are easier to lay with less of an impact on the land and—" He broke off, staring at her. "What?"

Bella shook her head. She simply couldn't believe this. He was…more green than she was.

The house was designed to look like an old adobe Spanish-style home. It was surrounded by flowering bushes and dozens of trees. There were solar panels on the roof and wide windows overlooked the ocean, and even the front door looked…rustic.

"I don't believe this," she whispered.

He grinned even more widely. "Surprised? Maybe even…shocked?"

She snapped her head up and stared at him. He'd tricked her neatly because he had to know she never would have believed that he was so environmentally conscious. Why, he was the destroyer and pillager of historic districts. He was the man who was personally turning her beloved hometown into a cookie-cutter community.

And he had jute welcome mats.

Oh God.

She was really in trouble now.

"You set me up, didn't you?"

"You set yourself up, Bella," he said, laughing as he opened the door and ushered her inside. "You assumed you knew everything about me and you were willing to bet on it."

"But you let me," she countered, sweeping past him into the house. Just as she'd thought. It was even more perfect inside than out. Dammit.

"Hell, yes, I let you," he said, chuckling low in his throat so that it sounded like a rumbling freight train.

"You cheated. You knew I'd never expect something like this," she waved both hands out, encompassing the entire house. "I mean, I try to do things the 'green' way, but this is…"

"Why are you so surprised?"

"Are you kidding?" she demanded, glaring at him. "You're the guy who ripped out the heart of the business district and gave it all the personality of a damp rock."

He frowned at her. "That's business. And, just so you know, the materials used were all 'green.'"

"Why? Why do you care?"

"I'm a surfer, Bella. Of course I'm interested in the environment. I want clean oceans and air, I just don't broadcast what I do."

"No, you hide it."

"No, I don't. If you'd bothered to look a little deeper at me, you'd have found plenty of information. The 'Save the Waves' foundation? Mine. King Beach supports it."

She needed to sit down. Bella stared at him, amazed and…impressed. How was she supposed to reconcile her image of the corporate raider with this very unexpected side of Jesse King? Was it possible she'd been wrong about him? And if she were, what else had she been mistaken about?

Her gaze swept the interior. Bamboo floors, shining under coats of polish. Skylights cut into the ceiling allowed moonlight to drift into the foyer, giving the whole house a magical look. And it was working on Bella. She was beyond shocked. She was pleased. And almost proud. How ridiculous was that?

He tucked her hand through his elbow and led her down a long, wide hallway. "Come on. I asked the housekeeper to serve dinner on the patio."

On either side of them, the whitewashed walls were studded with family photos. Her heels tapped against the bamboo floor as she walked beside Jesse. She glanced at the photos as they passed, trying to take them all in. But there were just too many of them.

"Told you I had a lot more at home," he said. "I'll introduce you to all of them after dinner if you want."

Dinner. And, she thought, since he'd managed to absolutely shock her, *she* would be dessert. Unless she backed out. Ran away. Told him she'd changed her mind. He wouldn't be happy about it, but she had no doubt he'd let her leave. He might be arrogant and pushy, but he wasn't a bully.

"You're thinking too much," he said.

"You've given me a lot to think about."

"I knew you'd be shocked, but I still can't help wondering why," he said, leading her through a set of French doors onto a flagstone patio, Bella's breath caught in her throat.

A full moon was up and shining down on the ocean, laying a wide, silver ribbon of a path that looked as though all you had to do was follow it to find something wonderful. Stars winked out of a black sky and a sea wind slid over her skin like a caress. A small, round table was set with white linen, fine china and crystal. A bottle of wine stood open and "breathing" in the center of the table, and candle flames flickered wildly in the protective circle of hurricane-glass globes.

"Wow," she murmured.

"I agree."

She looked at him, but he wasn't looking at the view, or the setting. He was watching *her*. Was it part of his game? His routine for charming women? Or was this something else? Something just for her?

Oh, that thought was certainly a dangerous one.

"This is beautiful," she said, impressed in spite of her own misgivings about being there.

"It really is," he said, moving to the table, and pouring them each a glass of dark red wine. "I found this place the last time I was in Morgan. The setting was great, but I wanted a more organic kind of home. So I rehabbed it." He sent her a quick wink.

"Rehabbing seems to be a hobby of yours."

"Can't help myself. I'm a hands-on kind of guy."

Her stomach swirled and dipped again. Then she

recalled what he'd just said. "You bought this house three years ago?"

"Yeah." He walked toward her, holding out one of the glasses.

She accepted it, took a sip and said, "So you were always planning on moving here."

"Not always," he said. "Actually, it was meeting a certain woman on a pier one night that decided it for me."

He was just too smooth for her. He knew all the right words. Knew all the right moves. And she was floundering. If she had the slightest shred of sense, Bella knew she'd be running from him just as fast as her feet could take her. But she really didn't want to.

"Why do you do things like that?" she asked, her voice little more than a hush.

"Like what?" He sipped at his wine.

"Talk to me as if you're trying to seduce me."

"I am," he said. "I haven't exactly kept it a secret."

"But why play the game?" she asked, walking past him to set her wineglass on the table. With her back to him, Bella said softly, "You don't have to flatter me. Or flirt. Or any of the other things you do to get women. You already know I want you, too. So why bother pretending that you feel something for me that you don't?"

His features went still and, in the moonlight, his blue eyes glittered like silver. His jaw was tight, his hair rippled in the wind. "Who says I don't mean it?"

Eight

Bella turned to look at him and when her gaze locked with his, everything in her sizzled quietly. His eyes looked wild and flashed with heat and desire and something she couldn't quite identify. But whatever it was, there was an answering emotion roiling through her.

"What do you want from me, Jesse?"

He walked toward her, set his glass down beside hers and laid both hands on her shoulders. "Tonight, I just want you. And I don't want it to be because I won the stupid bet." He slid his hands up her shoulders, her neck, to cup her face between his palms. "I want you to come to my bed because you *want* to be there. Because we both *need* to be there."

Bella realized that he was giving her the chance to

back out. But she wouldn't. She'd known the minute
Jesse had come back to Morgan Beach that they were
headed down this road. That eventually, they would
wind up together again. If only for one more night. And
if it was going to be only one night, then she was determined to make the most of it.

She wasn't going to hide from what she was feeling
anymore. She wasn't going to pretend to hate him. She
wasn't going to lie to herself any longer. The simple
truth was that she'd fallen in love with him on that night
three years ago, when they'd talked about their pasts,
their futures, and shared an amazing blaze of passion
in the moonlight.

She hadn't wanted to love him. Hadn't expected to.
Had tried for three years to hide from the truth behind a
curtain of venom because she'd known it couldn't go
anywhere. Men like Jesse King didn't settle down. And
if they did, they didn't marry women like Bella. So it had
been easier to tell herself that she hated him, rather than
face the fact that she loved a man she would never have.

But she was done with that now. She did love him,
though she'd never tell him that. And she was going to
have another night with him—even if that was all she ever
got.

She reached up, wrapped her arms around his neck and
went up on her toes. "I want to be here, Jesse. With you."

"Thank God," he whispered as he bent his head to
take her mouth with his.

Bella's mind splintered as he parted her lips with his
tongue and swept inside, stealing what little breath she

had left and sharing his own. His tongue stroked hers, tangling them together in a prelude to a dance she'd spent three years hungering for. Her hands splayed against his broad back, holding him to her, as she gave him everything she had and took everything he offered.

His arms tightened around her body, pressing her to him, aligning her body along his with a need so fierce that it inflamed her own. Jesse lifted her easily, swung her up into his arms and Bella felt like a heroine in a romantic movie. Dazed, she lolled against him as he stalked across the patio, through the house and up a set of stairs. She paid no attention to where he was taking her and didn't care, as long as he started kissing her again really soon.

When he finally stopped and set her on her feet again, Bella took a quick look around. They were in his bedroom, obviously. A huge, bamboo four-poster bed took up most of the space. A skylight directly over the bed fanned moonlight onto a black-and-white quilt that looked handmade and what had to be a dozen pillows piled against the intricately carved headboard. Windows provided a view of the moon-kissed ocean and allowed the soft, cool sea wind to glide into the room.

"Like it?" he asked, reading her expression correctly.

"Oh, yes," she said, turning to look up at him.

"You'll like this, too," he told her, stepping past her to flip the quilt back, exposing clean white sheets. "Recycled cotton."

She sighed. "I think I just had an orgasm."

He laughed. "Not yet, baby. But soon. I promise."

Bella looked up at him. "And Kings always keep their promises?"

"Damn straight." He came to her then, hauling her up against him with a hard embrace that sent shivers of excitement scuttling down her spine.

She felt every hard inch of him and her body instantly went into eager mode. She forgot about everything else. Her business, her feud with him, everything. Bella didn't want to think. She wanted to feel.

And Jesse more than obliged.

His kiss turned hot and hungry and frantic. It was as if he couldn't taste her enough and she was right there with him. Her hands slid up and down his back, feeling the pull and flex of lean muscles honed by years of swimming in an ocean that he loved. His arms were like bands of steel, wrapped around her, holding her tightly to him. And when he cupped her bottom and pulled her in even closer, she felt the unmistakable hard length of him pushing into her.

Her body lit up inside and went hot and wet and ready for him. He seemed to sense what she was feeling because he took the hem of her shirt in his big hands and quickly peeled it up and over her head. In seconds, her skirt was gone, too, and she was standing in front of him in her white lace bra and panties.

His hands skimmed up and down her body, following her curves, cupping her breasts until she felt the heat of his touch through the fragile fabric. "Jesse…"

"Don't rush me," he said with a half smile. "I've been waiting a long time for this opportunity."

"No rush," she said and swayed a little unsteadily. "But I think my knees are melting."

That smile kicked up an extra notch. "Let's see what we can do about that."

He led her to the bed, and gave her a gentle push that sent her tumbling onto the mattress. The sheets were cool and smooth beneath her, and Jesse's hands were hard and hot as he continued to explore her. Bella's eyes slid shut on the sensations rippling through her body—there was too much sensory input. Too many feelings. Too many things rushing through her mind, vying for recognition. She was here, in Jesse's bed, with his big hands sliding over her skin, and she knew that no matter what else happened between them, nothing would take away the perfection of this night.

She opened her eyes when he stepped back from her and watched him as he quickly stripped out of his clothes. Through the skylight, a swath of moonlight fell across his naked body and Bella couldn't help thinking how beautiful he was. She smiled and he answered it.

"I remember," he said softly, "just how beautiful you are in moonlight."

"Funny," she answered, "I was just thinking the same thing about you."

One corner of his mouth lifted. "Men aren't beautiful, Bella."

"You are," she assured him and watched new hunger flash in his eyes.

"Enough talk," he told her and leaned over her on the

bed. In a few short seconds, he had her bra undone and off and was sliding her silky panties down her legs to fall to the floor. She twisted beneath him, trying to press herself even more tightly to him, to feel every inch of his hard, warm body along hers.

His hands seemed to be everywhere at once, she thought wildly as passion spiked and desire boiled. Her breasts, her belly, and lower still to the heart of her. Talented fingers and thumb stroked her center, making her writhe beneath him as need built into a firestorm that threatened to engulf her.

Again and again, he pushed her close to the edge of oblivion, only to ease back and keep her from reaching the peak of satisfaction that he held just out of reach. Her hips lifted into his hand as he lowered his head and took first one nipple and then the next into the heat of his mouth. His lips and tongue and teeth scraped and suckled at already too sensitized flesh and Bella was moaning now, from deep in her throat.

Her short, neat fingernails scraped at his back as she twisted beneath him. She slid her hands up, into his thick, golden hair and held him to her as his mouth continued to work at her breasts. "Jesse…"

"Soon," he promised, his words a whisper of a caress against her flesh.

It had to be soon, or she would die of the wanting. She felt her body coiling tighter and tighter and knew she couldn't take much more of his. "I need you. Inside. Jesse, please."

He lifted his head, stared down at her and she saw

the same passion she was feeling mirrored in his eyes. Her heart turned over in her chest and something wild and wonderful spilled through her bloodstream. There was more here than want. More than just need. There was a soul-deep connection between them. She felt it. Knew it. Recognized it.

Then he kissed her, plunging his tongue deeply into her mouth and thoughts scattered like dead leaves in a cold wind. His fingers continued to stroke and tease her, even as he moved to settle himself between her thighs.

She lifted her hips in silent invitation and when he eased back from their kiss, sitting on his haunches to look down at her, Bella felt like the most beautiful woman on the face of the planet. He looked at her with such a craving, she felt powerful and strong and enticing.

He parted her thighs farther, sliding his hands up and down the inside of her legs until she hissed in a breath and whispered brokenly, "Jesse, now."

"Yeah," he agreed, pushing his body into hers in one long, heated slide, *"now."*

She groaned as he filled her and her body stretched to accommodate him. He held perfectly still inside her for one long moment. Until she moved beneath him, showing him that she was ready for him. For all he could give her.

Jesse watched her eyes glaze and felt the thrumming of her heartbeat as he lowered his head to kiss her breasts, each in turn. His own heartbeat was galloping in his chest. He couldn't seem to catch his breath and he didn't care. This was what he'd been searching for these last three years. This woman. This moment. This link.

But as she sinuously moved beneath him, his mind blanked and his body took over. There would be time for thinking later. Much later. For now, he had everything he could want, right here in his arms.

He moved within her—sure, long strokes designed to draw the pleasure out, to stoke it so high they might both burn in the aftermath. Again and again, he laid claim to her and with every stroke. She met him, lifting her hips into him, sliding into a smooth rhythm he'd found with no one else. It was as if their bodies recognized what their minds had been fighting. That they belonged together. They *fit*.

He braced his hands on either side of her head, looked down into chocolate-brown eyes that sparkled and shone in the moonlight and gave himself up to what was happening. He felt her body stiffen, knew the moment when her climax claimed her and watched the magic in her eyes. Only then did he allow himself to follow after, his body shattering.

When the last of the tremors finally ceased, he collapsed atop her and felt her arms come around him, cradling him to her chest.

The night passed too quickly and Jesse couldn't seem to get enough of her. Again and again, they made love and each time was better than the one before. They came together, dozed briefly, then made love again. Finally, around 2:00 a.m., they threw on robes and raided the kitchen, at last getting around to eating the meal his housekeeper had left for them. It was cold, but they didn't care. They drank wine, ate their meal and then he had her as dessert on the kitchen table.

He couldn't keep his hands off her and even as he experienced it, Jesse knew how different this was for him. He'd never wanted a woman to stay the night with him before. And with Bella, he didn't want her to leave. As long as he kept her there, at his house, nothing would change.

Once the world intruded, everything would be different.

But he couldn't ignore the dawn. Jesse was used to waking up early. The habit came from all those years of pulling on a wet suit and heading to the beach to sit on a board and watch the rising sun blaze across the surface of the water. As far as he was concerned, the dawn was still the best part of the day.

Bella was sleeping when he slipped out of bed to start a pot of coffee. His housekeeper wouldn't arrive until noon, so breakfast would be up to him. He smiled as he thought about taking Bella some coffee and then convincing her to take a nice, hot shower with him.

Still smiling, he hit the button on the coffeepot, then walked through the quiet house to the front door. He stepped outside, picked up the paper off the porch, then went back into the house, unfolding the paper as he strolled at a leisurely pace back to the kitchen.

While he waited for the pot to brew, he leaned back against the counter and flipped through the thin, local paper, checking out the news and admiring the ad King

Beach was running. He finally hit the editorial page and paused to pour his first cup of the day. Taking a sip, he skimmed the letters to the editor and smiled as he read the complaints on everything from skateboarding kids to dogs being unwelcome on the beach.

"Gotta love a small town," he murmured, "there's always someone with something to say—"

Then he spotted one specific letter and scowled. He shot a glance at the floor above him, then deliberately took a breath, poured two more cups of coffee and tucking the paper under his arm, headed for the master bedroom. Bella was still snuggled under the quilt when he walked in and just for a second, he thought about ignoring the stupid newspaper in favor of joining her on the big bed.

Then he shook his head, and crossed the room. Sitting on the edge of the mattress, he set the coffee on the side table and reached down to smooth her hair back from her face. She was beautiful. And terribly sneaky.

"Bella," he said, "wake up."

"What? Why?" She pulled the pillow over her head and slipped deeper beneath the quilt.

Jesse plucked the pillow free, tossed it aside and said again, "Come on, wake up."

One brown eye opened and glared at him. "Jesse, it's still *dark*."

"It's dawn and the paper's here. The Morgan Beach weekly." He was watching her, waiting for her to respond.

"That's nice." She sniffed and blinked blearily at him. "I smell coffee."

"Have some," he said, offering her the cup as she scooted around and pushed a pillow behind her back. The sheet was drawn up, covering her breasts, and her hair was tousled. She looked beautiful. And so damn innocent.

Funny, in all his plans for her, he'd never once considered that she might still be working against him. Plotting. Planning. Turns out, he should have.

She took a sip, sighed, then blinked again, trying to focus on him. "Why are we awake?"

"I always wake up early."

"That's a hideous habit," she said sleepily, giving him a soft smile, "made slightly less hideous by the fact that you at least provide coffee."

"Uh-huh," he said, holding the newspaper up. "And reading material."

"What?" She stared at the paper he'd folded to a specific section. A second or two ticked past before her eyes went wide and she whispered, "Oh, no."

"Oh, yes," he said, both eyebrows rising high on his forehead. "Your letter to the editor was printed this morning."

"Jesse…"

"Wait, I want to read you my favorite part," he said, fixing his gaze on the short, to-the-point letter she'd written.

"Morgan Beach is selling its soul to a corporate raider who doesn't care what happens to us and our homes as long as his company makes a profit. We should all band together and let Jesse King

know that we won't be bought. We won't surrender who we are. Morgan Beach was here before Jesse King and it will be here long after he tires of playing at being a member of this community."

Bella's eyes closed and a groan slipped from her throat. She covered her eyes with one hand as if she couldn't bring herself to look at him. Her expression was one of pure misery and Jesse didn't mind admitting to himself that he was glad about that, at least.

"Very nice," he said, sarcasm icing his tone. "I especially like the 'corporate raider' part. Seems to be a theme with you. And the rest of it's pretty good, too. You should be a writer."

"I was angry."

"Was?" he repeated, picking up on that one word. "So you're not anymore?"

She hitched the sheet a little higher, then scooped one hand through her hair, swiping it back from her face. "I don't know."

"Great, you don't know," he said, standing up and walking to one of the windows. Jesse felt as if he'd been kicked in the gut. He had known all along that Bella had a problem with what he'd been doing since he hit town, but damn.

She'd just spent the night with him, all the time knowing that she'd taken another public shot at him.

Thoughts of the night before rushed through his mind. How could she have been so eager, so responsive, if this is how she still felt about him? Strange, but he felt used. And suddenly, he realized how all the women in his life must have been left feeling.

Hell of a time for an epiphany.

He stared blindly out at the ocean and tried to ignore the rustle of bedsheets that told him she was getting up. But even pissed, his insides twisted, knowing she was close by and naked. How twisted was that, he wondered, to want the one woman who hated his guts?

A moment later, she joined him at the window, his black-and-white quilt wrapped around her curvy body like a toga.

"I'd forgotten all about writing that letter," she said.

"If that's an apology, it sucks." He tossed the newspaper onto a chair and took a gulp of his coffee.

"It's not an apology," she said. "I meant it when I wrote it so I can't apologize for that."

He glanced at her. "Great." He paused, then asked, "Did you mean all that? Do you really think I don't care what happens to this place?"

"Jesse," she said with a shake of her head, "when I moved here, I loved it." She looked out the window at the ocean and the sunrise, just staining the horizon. "I'd never really had a home before. I...grew up in the foster system."

She said it so matter-of-factly, Jesse couldn't even offer sympathy. But he remembered how longingly she'd looked at the photos of his family, how she'd seemed so caught up in the fact that they were a huge, yet close group. And then he thought about what it must have been like to grow up alone. What it might have been like for him if he hadn't had his brothers and cousins. He couldn't help feeling a stab of sympathy for the little girl she'd once been, who'd had nowhere to call home.

And he wondered a bit that he could feel so much for her. He should have stayed pissed. Yet…looking at her, he just couldn't seem to hold on to the feeling.

"I loved the funky little buildings on Main Street," she was saying, "the slow pace of town life, the cottages on the beach. The sense of community. I saw it and knew that I belonged here, as if I'd never belonged anywhere before. I spent the first year here sliding into the town, making my place, fitting in." She turned her head and looked up at him. "You moved in and immediately started changing everything."

Frowning, Jesse thought he could understand now just why she'd been fighting him so hard for so long. "Nothing ever stays the same."

"I suppose not," she said wistfully and turned her head again to watch the sunrise splashing brilliant color across the ocean.

"So, change is bad, is that it?"

"Not bad, it's just *change,*" she argued. "I don't like it. I love this town. I loved what it was and I was angry at you for—"

"Buying up its soul?" he quoted, feeling the sting of the words again. He'd never meant to be a corporate raider. Hadn't wanted to be a corporate *anything.* And yet, somehow it had happened to him. He'd made his peace with it. Even come to enjoy what he'd made of his life. Until he found Bella. And now suddenly, he was left feeling that, somehow, the success he'd achieved was only failure, cleverly disguised.

She closed her eyes. "I'm sorry. I didn't mean to hurt you—well, no, I guess I did mean to. But that was before."

"Before you were back in my bed?" he asked, feeling a small stab of temper. "Guess it would be a little embarrassing to be attacking in public the same guy you're sleeping with in private."

"It's not that, Jesse," she said, clutching her toga to her chest tightly with one hand. "I think I might have been wrong about you and—"

"Might? *Might* have been wrong?" He laughed shortly. "Well, hell, Bella. That's damn nice of you."

With her free hand, Bella reached out, grabbed his upper arm and held on. Looking up into his eyes, she said, "I was wrong about you. I admit it. I wanted to hate you because it was easier that way. I wanted you to leave Morgan Beach because I didn't want to have to see you and not have you. I wanted…"

"What?" he asked, his voice low, his gaze fixed on her.

"You, Jesse," she said. "I wanted *you,* and couldn't admit it, even to myself."

He took a breath, inhaling the fresh, clean scent of her, then reached out and skimmed his fingers through her thick, soft hair. His gaze moved over her, settled on her mouth briefly and then lifted to meet her troubled eyes. "And now you're admitting it?"

She deliberately released her hold on the quilt and it swished to the floor at her feet. Moving into him, she slid her hands up over his chest and then hooked her arms behind his neck. "I'm admitting it. I'll even write a retraction to the paper, if you want."

He gave her a lazy smile, dismissing the irritation of seeing her letter in the paper in favor of enjoying having her in his arms. "I think I prefer a more private apology."

"Oh, I'm not apologizing," she corrected, going up on her toes to kiss him once, twice. "I'm just saying that I'm revising my opinion."

"Enough to consider making Bella's Beachwear a part of King Beach?" he asked.

She huffed out a breath. "Enough to think about considering it."

He laughed a little. "I can live with that."

Then he picked her up, carried her to the bed and lost himself once again in the wonder of her.

Nine

Everything was different, Bella thought.

Since that incredible night with Jesse a few days ago, they'd been together nearly every day. She was at King Beach or he was at her shop and they were talking business. He'd asked her advice on how to make his swimwear "greener" and had actually listened to her opinions. He was meeting her weavers and seamstresses and still trying to talk her into joining King Beach.

And for the first time, Bella was tempted. She still wasn't interested in success just for the sake of making money. But he'd dangled the hope of reaching women nationwide with her specialty suits and that was something she couldn't easily dismiss. With King Beach, she could find ways to make her cottage industry viable in a bigger setting and still maintain the kind of quality she insisted on.

But more than all that, being with Jesse was becoming the best part of her days. And nights. They were together every night now. At his house. At her house. On the beach, recapturing their very first time together. Her heart was full. She felt…amazing.

And she was terrified.

Bella was in love and just knew it wasn't going to end well. Despite how attentive he was now, Jesse King was simply not the forever kind of guy. Sooner or later, he'd get tired of what they had and he'd move on. And Bella knew the pain that was headed her way was something she might never recover from.

In self-defense, she should have started pulling away from him. Keeping a safe distance between her heart and Jesse. But she couldn't bring herself to give up what she could have now to protect herself in the future. Wasn't it better to enjoy what you had while you had it? There would always be time for pain later.

"You're thinking about him again."

She blinked, looked at Kevin and smiled. "How can you tell?"

"You're drooling."

Quickly, she lifted one hand to her mouth, then sneered at her best friend. "Oh, that's very funny."

He smiled at her over the lunch table. "You look happy, Bella. It's nice to see."

"I am happy," she said, but her voice carried a wary tone.

"But…"

"But," she said, stirring her iced tea, "it's not going to last, Kevin. One of these days, Jesse's going to move on and I'm not looking forward to it."

"How do you know?" He reached across the table and patted her hand. "Seems to me he's spending a lot of time with you. A guy doesn't do that if he's not interested."

"I know," she said, and pushed her plate aside. She wasn't really hungry anyway. "He's interested now. But how long can it last?"

"Jeez, Bella." Kevin shook his head at her. "Maybe you should give him a chance to screw up before you punish him."

"I'm not punishing him," she argued.

"Maybe not, but you're already rehearsing your goodbye speech."

"I'm just preparing myself," she countered, "and you'd think that my best friend would approve."

"Your best friend thinks you're nuts," Kevin told her, sitting back in his chair and crossing his arms over his chest. "Seriously, when you don't have him, you're miserable. When you *do* have him, you're crazy. Women are nuts."

"Thanks. Have you told Traci your theory?" His girl-friend, a model for one of the bigger agencies in California, was constantly traveling and had been gone from Morgan Beach for almost four weeks this time.

"Of course," he said. "She says I'm wrong. Just like you. But you're women. You can't see it."

"Uh-huh, and if we're crazy, why do you guys want to be with us?"

He grinned. "So where's Mr. Wonderful today anyway? You haven't had lunch with me in more than a week. Usually you're with him."

"He said he had to meet someone. Didn't say who." Bella frowned a little.

"So naturally, you're thinking it's some other woman."

Bella's eyes widened. "Well, I wasn't. Until now."

Kevin sighed. "Eat your alfalfa sprouts."

"She's making me insane," Jesse muttered.

"Not so hard to do if you ask me," Justice King told his younger brother and affixed his pliers to the end of the barbed wire before twisting it around a fence post.

"That's nice, thanks." Jesse shoved his hands into his jeans pockets and stared out over the rolling hills and fields of his brother's ranch. There was a cold wind blowing and afternoon sunshine spilled out of a sky studded with massive gray clouds. Idly, Jesse wondered if they might be in for an end-of-summer storm.

He'd made the two-hour trip to Justice's ranch in just under an hour and a half. He'd picked up a speeding ticket along the way, but it had still been worth it. He'd needed to get out of Morgan Beach. Needed a little distance from Bella. Needed to clear his head and driving fast was one sure way to do it.

He was seeing way too much of her, he told himself. Every day. Every night. She was becoming a part of him, threading herself so seamlessly into his life, he couldn't even imagine a way of getting her out again. When he was with her, he was touching her. When he wasn't with her, he was thinking about her.

What the *hell* was happening to his life?

"This is serious, Justice," he said, shooting a glare at his older brother. "She's slipping into my life and I'm letting it happen."

"Maybe that's a good thing," Justice told him, snipping off the end of the wire and tucking it into his jeans pocket. "Maybe you're tired of the babe-of-the-week routine. Ready for something different. Permanent."

His insides went cold and still. "Hold on, nobody said anything about permanent."

"Crap, you just went white." Justice laughed, walked back to his truck and set the pliers down in the locked down toolbox in the bed. "It's good to see."

"Yeah, because it worked out so well for you."

Instantly, Justice's grin faded. "What happened between me and Maggie has nothing to do with anything."

"Sure, we can talk about me, but not Maggie." Jesse kicked at the dirt, sent a spray of it toward the truck and glared at his brother.

"You came to me, Jesse. Remember?" Justice tugged the brim of his dust-colored cowboy hat down low over his eyes. "If you're having problems with a woman they're *your* problems, not mine."

"Fine. Forget it. Damn close-mouthed bastard." Justice never had told anyone what had gone wrong between him and his estranged wife, Maggie Ryan. The whole family had been nuts about Maggie, yet one day she and Justice had separated, neither of them offering an explanation.

That was a year ago, and still, his brother was completely mute on the subject.

After a minute or two, Jesse blurted, "Look, you're the only one of us to ever get married. Who the hell else should I ask?"

"Try Travis. Or Jackson. Or hell, even Adam," Justice told him, ticking off the names of three King cousins who'd all been happily married for a couple of years now.

"They're not around—you are."

"Lucky me."

"How the hell is a man supposed to deal with having only one woman in his life?" Jesse asked. "I've never done that before. Never had a long-standing girlfriend. Never wanted one. I like the no-strings-attached approach to dating, you know?"

"So, have no strings," Justice told him.

"But Bella's not that kind of woman," Jesse muttered, shoving one hand through his hair. "She's got strings all over the damn place and I keep getting tangled up in them."

"You don't want them?" Justice said quietly, as he closed the gate on the back of the truck. "Cut them and move on. End of story."

Jesse looked at his brother and sighed. Justice was right, he knew it. And yet, "That's the problem. For the first time in my life, I don't know if I want to move on."

* * *

The surfing exhibition had drawn a great crowd. People from up and down the state had gathered in Morgan Beach to watch the show and so far, it had been worth it.

Some of the best surfers in the world were riding the waves, making it look effortless as they skimmed the surface of the water, riding in a tunnel of water, then shooting out into the open, their boards kicking up fantail wakes behind them. The sun slipped in and out of banks of heavy clouds, its golden light glancing off the surface of the water in nearly blinding flashes. The scent of hot dogs and beer wafted over the noisy crowd and seagulls shrieked in accompaniment. The exhibition was proving to be a great end-of-summer celebration and the crowds would no doubt spill over into the Main Street shops later. But for now, Bella had her shop closed so she could watch the show. And Jesse.

She had a great seat in the bleachers set up in the sand for the day. At the end of a row, she looked down to her left at the path the surfers took in and out of the water. And she wasn't alone, either. Jesse's cousin, Jackson, his wife, Casey, and their daughters, Mia and Molly, were in town. They'd actually come to southern California to take the girls to Disneyland, but hadn't been able to resist watching Jesse surf in the competition.

"He's really good, isn't he?" Casey whispered, her gaze locked on the ocean where Jesse was maneuvering his long board in and out of a six-foot wave.

Cheers erupted from the stands and Bella grinned,

caught up in the excitement of watching Jesse do what he did best. He had so much grace and style, he eclipsed every other surfer out there easily. And everyone in the stands seemed to recognize that, too.

"He really is good," Bella answered, never taking her eyes off the man who'd become such a huge part of her life. She couldn't even believe how charmed her life was lately. Every spare moment was spent with Jesse and she grew more in love with him every day. The only worry was that she didn't know how he felt.

Did he share her feelings? Or was this all just a fun fling that he'd move on from eventually? And if it was, how would she ever get through it?

She closed her eyes, sighed and told herself not to worry about that now. Just to enjoy this moment for what it was. She was building so many memories, her heart was full of them.

"Of course he is," Jackson said, "he's a King, isn't he? Molly, honey, don't eat the paper."

"Paper?" Casey demanded, tearing her gaze from the ocean to look at her younger daughter. "What paper?"

"Nothing, don't worry about it," Jackson told her. "Let's just consider it fiber."

Bella laughed, Casey sighed and reached across her husband to lift her two-year-old daughter onto her lap. "Honestly, Jackson."

"I didn't tell her to eat the paper the cookie came in, did I, Mia?" He tickled his older daughter and as the girl laughed, Bella sighed.

Jesse's cousin and his family had arrived in town the night before and since then, they'd all had a wonderful time together. Jesse was like a different person when he was with the two little girls. They clearly adored him and he was crazy about them. Watching him with Jackson's daughters, Bella hadn't been able to stop the tiny bubble of something dangerously maternal rising inside her. And she wondered what it would be like to be Jesse's wife. To have his children. To feel that sort of warmth surrounding her for the rest of her life.

But the truth was, as much as she loved him, as much as she wanted him, Bella wasn't sure he felt the same way. Yes, he was a wonderful lover. But did it go any further than that? Was she in love and he in lust? She wished she knew.

"Where's Uncle Jesse?" Mia demanded, standing on her father's lap and staring out at the sea.

"There he is," Bella said and pointed to the surfer sitting atop his board, waiting for his next ride. "See? When the next wave comes, he'll stand up and ride it all the way in to the beach."

"Can I?" Mia asked.

"Sure," Jackson told her. "When you're thirty."

Casey caught Bella's eye and winked. "He's a little overprotective."

"I think it's nice," Bella said.

"Me, too, actually," Casey admitted. "He and his brothers guard their kids like trained pit bulls. It's really amazing to watch. And when the kids are all together, it's hysterical, seeing all the King boys riding herd on them."

"It's not funny," Jackson told her, "it's stressful."

"I think it sounds wonderful." Bella smiled, but Casey looked at her with sympathy.

Leaning in closely, she whispered, "Falling for a King isn't easy, Bella. They'll make you nuts if you let them. But I promise, it's completely worth it."

She nodded, but couldn't help thinking that it would be worth it if the King you loved, loved you back. Otherwise, it was just torture.

"There he goes!" Mia shouted, jumping up and down on her daddy's lap and pointing excitedly at Jesse.

Bella stilled her thoughts and focused on his last ride of the day. It was perfect. Jesse lay across his board and paddled fiercely until the crest of the rising wave caught up to him. Then he stood, shook back his hair and walked up and down the length of the board with an easy grace that was beautiful to watch. His arms were relaxed at his sides and even from a distance, Bella could see his grin while he used his body to direct the board in and out of the wave. The roar of the ocean was lost in the roar of the crowd's appreciation. His ride ended as his board skimmed the lacy froth of the dying wave. He jumped off as he neared the shore, then picked up the board, tucked it under his arm and trotted up the beach.

Bella watched as literally hundreds of bikini-clad women raced toward him, all of them eagerly attempting to capture his attention. He ran past them all as if he didn't even see them. Bella's breath caught as he headed right toward her. Her heart pounded hard in her chest as he dropped his board to the sand, looked up at her and asked, "How'd I do?"

"Great!" Jackson shouted then grunted when his wife's elbow met his midsection. "Hey, what was that for?"

"He wasn't talking to you," Casey muttered.

Jesse grinned wider. "She's right. I wasn't. Bella. How'd I do?"

"You were wonderful," she said, aware now that people all around them were watching, listening.

"That's what I like to hear. Now I need my prize."

Bella laughed. "No trophies today, remember?"

"Who's talking about a trophy?" Jesse asked, and reaching up, plucked her from the bleachers and dragged her down to him. "This is the only reward I'm interested in."

Then he kissed her. Long and hard and deep, sweeping her backward into a romantic dip that had the audience surrounding them cheering in approval.

Vaguely, Bella was aware of the crowd's applause and even of the sound of cameras clicking as pictures were snapped. But she didn't care. How could she when Jesse's arms were around her and his mouth was fused to hers? Electricity hummed through her body and sent sparks shooting through her bloodstream.

He'd sought her out. Come to her. Kissed her in front of the whole world and for the first time in her life, Bella felt like a princess. Like she mattered. Her heart turned over in her chest and she felt even more deeply in love, though she wouldn't have thought that possible.

Finally, after what felt like a lifetime, he broke the kiss, lifted his head to stare into her eyes and Bella thought she saw…love shining back at her.

Then he grinned, the moment was gone and she couldn't be sure it had even happened. Instantly, the crowd surrounded them, congratulating Jesse on his win and he draped one arm around her shoulders, holding her close to his side.

Did he love her?

She didn't know. But the sun was shining and he was holding her tight and just for the moment, that was enough.

Later that night at Bella's house, they sat out on the top step of the back porch, sipping wine and watching the clouds sail past the moon. From Mrs. Clayton's house next door, came the sounds of a game show playing on TV and from down the street came the howl of a dog. On the other side of Bella's place, Kevin's house was dark.

The spicy scent of chrysanthemums planted along the back fence filled the air, and Jesse took a deep breath, drawing it deep, knowing that he would always associate that scent with this night. With this woman.

He draped one arm around her and smiled when she leaned into him, laying her head on his shoulder. "It was a good day."

"It was," she agreed, taking a sip of wine. "You were amazing out on the water."

"Not bad for a corporate raider, huh?" he asked, his tone light and teasing.

She huffed out a breath. "Not going to let me forget that anytime soon, are you?"

"No, I figure that's good for at least six months' worth of teasing."

"Six months?"

"At least," he said, looking down into those chocolate eyes of hers.

"So you think we'll still be together," she said, "like this, I mean, in six months?"

He frowned and felt her tense up alongside him. "Well, yeah. Why wouldn't we be?"

She tipped her head back and stared up at the moon as clouds drifted across its face. "I just didn't know how you felt. What you expected."

"I don't *expect* anything, Bella," he said, turning on the step to face her more fully. "We're good together, aren't we?"

"Yes."

"The sex is great."

"Yes," she said, smiling.

"Well, then." That was settled. It was like he'd told Justice, he didn't want to move on. He liked being with Bella. He liked who he *was* with Bella. But he felt hesitation in her and he knew that she was thinking again. Trying to lay out a plan. Or see into the future. "Why should we try to put a time stamp on this? Or define it somehow? Look, nobody knows what's going to happen to them a day from now, let alone six months from now. But here, tonight, I can't imagine being anywhere else."

It was the closest he'd ever come to telling a woman that he didn't want to lose her.

She looked at him for a long moment, then smiled and laid one hand on his forearm. "Me, either."

Jesse smiled. Problem averted. For now, anyway.

She changed the subject abruptly though and he had to wonder if she did it on purpose, trying to keep him off balance. If so, she was damn good at it.

"I liked your cousin and his family."

His smile broadened. "Yeah. Always good to see them and the kids."

"I envy you that," she whispered.

"What?" He kissed the top of her head, silently encouraging her to continue.

"Your family. You're all so connected. And you were so good with those little girls…"

He dismissed that easily. "They're great kids. Not hard to have fun with them."

"Yes," she said, tipping her head back to look up at him, "but a lot of men wouldn't bother to get down on the floor and give 'pony rides' for an hour."

He laughed, but she only looked at him, so his laughter faded away quickly. "What is it?"

"I've been doing a lot of thinking lately."

"Okay…" Her expression was serious. Damn near solemn, and Jesse braced himself for whatever might be coming.

"And I've come to the conclusion that you aren't quite the man I thought you were in the beginning."

He smiled at her. "Good to know."

She straightened up and looked him square in the eye. "There's more. Jesse, you know I never wanted to expand my business."

"Yeah," he said wryly, relaxing just a bit. "I think you've made that pretty clear."

"Well, I've changed my mind."

"What?" That surprised him and he wondered idly if he'd ever be able to read Bella. He watched her, trying to determine her emotions, but her eyes were clear and direct and whatever she was feeling, she kept hidden too well for him to decipher.

Finally, she smiled, lifted her hand and cupped his cheek in her palm. He felt the warmth of her slide deep inside him.

"I've decided to join King Beach," she said. "You've convinced me that I can trust you, Jesse. And I think, together, we can do some amazing things."

He caught her hand in his and squeezed it. Strange, but over the last couple of weeks, he'd forgotten about trying to merge her company into King Beach. He'd been too focused on getting her into bed. And then keeping her there once he had her. Her making this announcement out of the blue really threw him.

He was utterly touched. For weeks, he'd been trying to make her see reason. To join King Beach. Now that she had, he felt a little…uneasy. But why? He'd bought up companies before. Hell, he'd gotten his start that way. But for Bella to join him was a real statement on her part. She was trusting him not to ruin what she loved. "You won't be sorry, Bella."

"I know," she said, leaning into him for a kiss. "I believe in you, Jesse."

The wind kicked up, carrying the scent of the sea, and a trickle of worry sprang up out of nowhere inside him. Promptly, Jesse shut it down. This was what he'd wanted. And hell, he'd done even better than he'd thought. Not only did he have her business, but he had *Bella*.

What could possibly go wrong?

Three days after the exhibition, life was back to normal in Morgan Beach. Except for one thing.

Jesse was nervous.

This was not normal. Not for him anyway.

He was worried about his relationship with Bella now that they would be going into business together. What if she found out that he'd planned to seduce her into handing over the reins? She'd be hurt, pissed. He hadn't expected to care, but he did.

And he couldn't bear the thought of losing her.

But he didn't like hiding the truth from her, either. He'd learned long ago that hidden secrets had a way of showing up when you least expected them to bite you in the ass.

So what did that say? What the hell was he feeling and why now of all times? Bella had sneaked up on him and he'd never seen it coming. She'd gotten beneath his finely tuned radar and had carved out a spot for herself in his heart. Hell, he hadn't even known he could feel everything he was feeling for her. Hadn't guessed he was capable of it.

For years, he'd steered clear of anything that looked like it might lead to something permanent. Carefully, deliberately, he'd only dated women who were interested in having a good time. The future-in-their-eyes type he left strictly alone.

So how the hell had this happened to him?

Which wasn't really important now anyway. The real question was, what was he going to do about it?

For three days now, he'd kept his distance from Bella, trying to work out in his own mind just what he was feeling and what he wanted to do about it. This was a whole new ball game for him. He'd never before even contemplated a future with a woman. He'd never before *wanted* to. Now, he couldn't imagine the rest of his life without Bella beside him.

God knew, he hadn't meant to get so involved. He'd wanted Bella mostly to prove something to Nick Acona. Now it had gone way beyond that. And damn if he knew how to handle it.

He stood up from his desk, turned around and stared out the bank of windows at Main Street and the ocean beyond. Black clouds hovered on the horizon, pushing toward shore and he knew that by evening, there'd be a storm blowing in. Which suited how he was feeling just fine. His insides were raging, in a tumult. He'd never thought of himself as the marrying kind of guy. But Bella was definitely the marriage kind of woman. Which left them exactly where?

His parents' marriage hadn't gone well, what with his father always buried in work. And Justice's marriage had split apart, though no one knew why. So how the hell was he supposed to make it work?

"Mr. King?"

"Yeah?" He glanced over his shoulder, irritated at the interruption as he watched Dave Michaels step into the office. "What is it, Dave?"

Dave blinked at Jesse's tone, but said, "I've got the paperwork drawn up for Bella to look over and sign."

"Right. Fine. Just…leave it on my desk, will you?" He turned back to stare outside again, his thoughts racing in circles. He'd convinced Bella to take a chance. To sign with King Beach. To trust him not to screw up the business she loved.

And he couldn't help feeling guilty about it all. He'd won. This was what he'd set out to do. To seduce her and persuade her to join his company. Everything had gone according to his original plan. He'd submarined her. Coaxed her into sharing the most important thing in her life.

The only trouble was, while he was seducing her, *he* was the one who'd been falling.

He'd stumbled into a snare that only tightened when he tried to escape. But then, he told himself, maybe that was because he didn't really want to get free.

He groaned and shoved one hand through his hair. His life had been a lot less complicated before he'd come to Morgan Beach.

There were two customers in her store, a new order just arriving from the seamstresses and a tidy profit sitting in the bank, thanks to the sales made on the day of the surfing exhibition.

So why wasn't Bella happier?

She frowned as she fitted the new swimwear onto hangers and sorted them by size and style. She knew the answer to that question. Because she hadn't seen Jesse since she'd agreed to join King Beach.

Oh, she'd talked to him on the phone several times. He was busy. Had meetings. Decisions had to be made. Papers drawn up. He said all the right things, and when she was talking to him it all made perfect sense. It was later, when she was alone, that the niggling doubts crept into her mind to torture her.

She missed Jesse, too. Missed his smile. His laugh. The feel of his arms sliding around her. The whisper of his breath against her neck.

But if he was feeling the same things, why was he staying away from her?

Bella shook her head, tried to dismiss her thoughts and smiled at a woman browsing through the racks. She went back to her work, all the time her mind whirling with possibilities, each worse than the one before.

He'd gotten what he wanted, now he didn't need to see her anymore. She shook her head, not liking the sound of that at all.

Romancing her had simply been part of the plan, to wear down her defenses and get hold of her company. That one she liked even less. He couldn't have been pretending, could he? Was anyone that good an actor?

He was feeling guilty for stealing her company under false pretenses, so he couldn't bring himself to face her. Hmph. She didn't think so. Jesse King didn't do guilt.

"So what's going on?" she muttered, her stomach twisting itself into knots.

And why was she standing around wringing her hands about it? For heaven's sake, all she had to do was go to him and tell him she wanted to know what was going on. They were partners now, weren't they? In business *and* in life. If she had questions, then she'd take them straight to Jesse. This might have nothing to do with her, after all. It might be a family problem. Something she could help him with.

Nodding to herself, Bella decided that as soon as these customers left the shop, she'd go to the King Beach office and make Jesse talk to her.

The front door opened, the bell above it jangling, and Bella looked up. A man in a three-piece suit approached the counter. "Bella Cruz?"

"Yes," she said, giving him her best, I'm-the-owner-welcome-to-my-store-smile. "How can I help you?"

He nodded, tucked one hand into the inside pocket of his suit jacket and withdrew an envelope. "I was instructed to deliver this." He handed it over. "Have a nice day."

Then he turned and left. Before the bell had stopped jangling again, Bella had the envelope open and was pulling the folded, single sheet of paper from inside. She read it. Then read it again.

Her insides iced over and a cold, hard knot of pain

settled in the pit of her stomach. The letters on the paper blurred as tears swam in her eyes. Determinedly though, she blinked them back. She wasn't going to cry. She was going to scream. Fury erupted, clawing at her throat, nearly choking her.

This couldn't be right, she thought, her gaze locked on a few, select words. Had to be a mistake. But then, a quiet, logical voice in her mind whispered, it explains a lot, doesn't it? Why Jesse'd been avoiding her, for example. And as her thoughts raced, the sense of betrayal blossomed inside her until she thought she would explode.

She'd wondered what was going on.

Now she knew.

But she couldn't do a thing about it until her customers were gone. With that thought in mind, she plastered on a helpful smile, tucked the paper into the pocket of her skirt and went to work. The sooner she helped these women find what they'd come for, the sooner she could face Jesse King.

If he thought she'd simply disappear, he was sadly mistaken.

He was about to find out exactly what Bella thought of him.

Ten

A knock on his office door had Jesse frowning an hour later. Before he could shout, *come in,* the door opened and Dave Michaels stuck his head inside. He looked worried. Never a good sign.

"Boss, there's a problem."

"What? What problem?"

"Oh," Bella said, pushing past Dave to stomp into the office, "there's more than just a problem."

Dave's expression went from concerned to panicked. Jesse hardly noticed though, because his attention was focused on the absolutely infuriated woman standing in front of his desk. Bella's eyes were flashing like danger signals and her mouth was flattened into a grim slash. She was practically vibrating with rage.

"Thanks, Dave," Jesse said, waving one hand to dismiss the man. "I'll take it from here."

Obviously grateful for the reprieve, Dave backed out and closed the door behind him.

Jesse stood up from his chair, walked around the desk and headed for Bella. Worry raced through him, but he squelched it. He'd fix whatever was wrong.

She backed up, shook her head at him and held out one hand to stave him off. "Don't you even come near me, you bastard."

Surprised, he stared at her. "Now just a minute…"

"It was all a game, wasn't it?" she said, her voice cold, tight, pitched low enough that he had to strain to hear her. She wasn't shouting or shrieking. Trust Bella to be different from every other woman he'd ever known. The few times he'd faced down a furious woman, they'd railed and screamed at him, and one had even tossed a vase at him.

Not Bella, though.

And the icy cold had him more worried than heat would have.

"What are you talking about?" He took a step toward her, but she shoved her hand out again as if trying to use telekinesis or something to hold him back.

"This," she snapped, reaching into a pocket of her skirt, "I'm talking about *this*." She dragged out a sheet of paper, crumpled it in one fist and then threw it at him.

Jesse snatched it out of the air, scanned it quickly and felt his heart sink. "What the hell?"

"Don't recognize your own handiwork?" she sneered. "Allow me to explain. That is an eviction notice. Giving me three weeks to vacate the property. The property *you* own."

"Bella, you have to know this is a mistake."

"No, I don't. It's all there in black and white," she snapped. Her face was pale and the two bright spots of color on her cheeks stood out in sharp relief. "It's all perfectly clear, Mr. King."

"I'm not evicting you."

"Really?" She tipped her head to one side and glared at him. "Because that paper makes it all pretty official. My lease is up in three weeks and you want me out. All very cut-and-dried."

"I didn't order this—" Jesse broke off, let his head fall back and closed his eyes as he silently cursed his business manager to hell and back.

When he'd first bought Bella's building from the late owner's family, he'd told his business manager to leave her alone until the end of her lease. Well, her lease was up in just a few weeks and apparently, his manager had kept track. Jesse hadn't even *thought* about her damn lease in weeks. Turns out, he should have been paying closer attention.

"Okay, let me explain."

"There is nothing you can say to me that will explain this."

Getting angrier himself by the second, Jesse defended himself. "I told you, this is a mistake. Yes, I admit that eviction plans were drawn up a few months ago, but I told my business manager not to do anything until your lease was almost up—"

"Congratulations, he follows orders exceedingly well."

"I never really planned to evict you, Bella. I wanted a chance to convince you to come on board with my company. And I just…forgot to inform my manager."

"You *forgot?*" Her eyes were wide and horrified. "You *forgot* to tell someone *not* to evict me?"

"Yeah, I grant you, that sounds bad. But in my defense I've been pretty busy the last few weeks. With *you.*"

"So it's my fault." She shook her head in amazement.

"Okay, calm down, Bella. We can talk about this, straighten it all out." He walked toward her again, but stopped when she snarled at him.

"If you touch me now, I swear to God, I'll get violent."

Judging by the look in her eyes, he believed her. A wise man knew when to back off. So Jesse stopped stock-still and met her gaze squarely. "I've said it a million times now. This is a mistake, Bella. You can't believe I'd want you thrown out of your store."

"Why wouldn't I?"

"Dammit Bella, I…*care* about you."

"Don't choke on the words," she told him.

This was not going well. He should have known. Should have kept a closer watch on his business manager, but he'd had so many balls in the air lately, it hadn't been easy keeping an eye on everything. Which she would never accept as an explanation, and he didn't blame her.

He reached up, grabbed his hair with both hands and gave it a yank out of pure frustration. "This doesn't make sense. Think about it. Hell, you just agreed to join my company, why would I do this to you now?"

She laughed shortly, but there was no humor in it and her eyes only gleamed darker. "That, I grant you was a mistake. You messed up there, didn't you? You should have had me sign the papers before you sent your little man with his eviction notice. Bad move there, Mr. Corporate Raider."

"Are we back to that now? I thought we were past that. I thought we understood each other."

"I thought a lot of things, too," she told him. "I thought you were more than you seemed. That there was a heart in there somewhere. But it looks like we both made mistakes."

"Bella—" She was still coldly furious and that worried him. If she were yelling or shouting or calling him names, Jesse thought, he'd have more of a chance of reaching her. As it was, the ice in her eyes made it plain that she wasn't going to listen to a thing he said.

But he was certainly going to try.

Hell, he cared about her. A lot. Maybe more than cared. Maybe it was love. Maybe he'd fallen in love and hadn't even realized it until it was too late.

Jesse staggered. God. He really was an idiot. Was he really going to lose her just when he realized how much he needed her? No way. No way was he going to let her walk away from him now. He had to tell her. Say the words he'd never said to anyone before. Then she'd believe him. She had to.

"Bella, I love you."

She blinked and then choked out a laugh. "Getting desperate are we? Pulling out the big guns?"

Not the response he'd hoped for. Or the one he'd been counting on. "Dammit, I mean it. You're the only woman I've ever said that to."

"And I'm supposed to believe that, right?"

"Yes!" How could she not believe him? How could she not see that she was killing him?

"Well, I don't," she said, her voice even lower now. "Why should I? I agreed to join King Beach and you disappeared. I haven't seen you in days. Because you'd gotten what you wanted."

"That wasn't it," he said, wishing to hell he knew a way to get out of this mess. That he knew what words to say to convince her. "I was thinking. About us. Our…future."

She gave that short, sad laugh again and it tore at something deep inside him. "We don't have a future, Jesse. We never did. All we ever had was a night on the beach three years ago. Because all the rest of it," she added, her voice dropping now to a husky whisper, "wasn't real. These last few weeks. The time we've been together, it was all an act."

"No." He lifted his chin, met her stormy eyes and willed her to believe.

She didn't.

"All the romance," she said. "The seduction. The lovemaking, the laughter. All of it. You never wanted me. You wanted my business. It was all a game."

He felt the sharp slap of shame and hated the feeling.

He'd dreaded this moment, had hoped to avoid it. Would give anything to be able to tell her she was wrong. But he wouldn't win her now by lying.

"That's how it started, yeah," he admitted, and watched the resulting pain flash in her eyes. He felt like the bastard she'd called him. "I heard Nick Acona was after your business, and—"

"So you deliberately came after me to best your friend?"

"That was part of it…" he hedged.

"All of it," she corrected.

"But that's not how it is now."

"Sure," she said with a short nod. Her mouth twisted and pain shimmered in the depths of her eyes. "I believe you. It wasn't a game. And I believe you love me. Why not?"

"Bella, dammit." He took one step toward her and stopped. If he got too close, he'd reach for her and it would kill him if she wouldn't let him touch her. His heart ached, his throat was tight and dry and Jesse felt as if he were fighting for his life. And losing.

He shoved one hand through his hair again and wished for the right words. Finally though, he simply had to start. "I admit I started seeing you in the beginning because I wanted your business. I wanted to beat Nick out. But I wanted you again, too. You haunted me for three years!"

Her mouth worked, but she didn't say anything, she just stood there, watching him, and Jesse felt like a bug under a microscope.

"Everything changed. So damn fast." He laughed a little, shook his head and scrubbed one hand across the back of his neck. "Hell, Bella, I stopped thinking about just your business weeks ago. And I forgot about the blasted eviction notice because I was spending so much time with you, nothing else mattered."

Her expression stayed blank. The hurt remained in her eyes. "I don't believe you."

"I know." He took the eviction notice and ripped it in half. Then ripped those halves again. Tossing them to the floor, he said quietly, "Forget about this, Bella. Stay in the damn shop. Stay rent-free! And forget about King Beach taking over Bella's Beachwear. I don't want your business. I just want you. I don't want to lose you."

"You already have." Bella looked at him and felt her heart break. Nothing he said now could change the fact that he had deliberately set out to seduce her business out from under her. How could she ever trust that he was telling her the truth?

Pain was so sharp and thick inside her that she could hardly draw a breath. He'd said *I love you*. And just hours ago, she would have given anything to hear those words from him. Now it was too late. Now he used those words too easily in an attempt to gloss over what he'd done.

She'd lost everything.

In one fell swoop, it was all gone. Dreams. Hopes. A future with the man she loved. It was all dust, blowing out to sea.

"Besides, I was never really yours to lose," she whispered, realizing the stark truth.

"I don't accept that," he told her and in his blue eyes, she read a determination to fight.

Well, it was too late for that.

"You have to accept it, Jesse," she said, shaking her head and backing away from him. Her fury was gone. The righteous indignation that had spurred her to come here to witness the destruction of everything she cared about had faded away. All that was left now was the pain.

Stepping back from him was the hardest thing she'd ever had to do, but if she didn't pull away now, she'd never be able to live with herself. "It's over. All of it."

"Bella, if you'll just listen—"

"No." She headed for the door, never taking her eyes off him. "I'll move out of the shop. I'll be gone before the end of the month."

"I don't give a damn about that shop. You don't *have* to move out," he snapped.

"Yes, I do." Her hand closed around the doorknob. She glanced back at him over her shoulder and knew she'd keep this picture of him in her mind always. Backlit by the sun glancing off the ocean behind him, his hair was golden, his eyes in shadow and his jaw tight and hard.

Everything in her wanted to run to him, throw her arms around him and pretend for one more day that what they'd shared was real. That what she felt was reciprocated. That, for once, she had someone who loved her.

But if it wasn't real, then none of it mattered.

Sighing, she told him, "You won't be getting my

business. Because *I* am my business and you'll never have me. You don't deserve me, Jesse."

His features tightened and his body flinched as if she'd struck him a physical blow.

"Bella," he said softly, "give us a chance. Give me a chance."

"No more chances. I should have known this was how it would end," she said sadly. "You've never made a commitment to anything in your life. I get that now. And I know that's why you would never commit to me."

"You're wrong," he argued. "I've made plenty of commitments and if you'd just listen—"

She interrupted him. "Jesse, you drifted into owning your company. You hired someone else to build your 'green' house. All you had to do was show up and live in it. You pay someone to recycle your trash. You pay people to run the Save the Waves foundation. Don't you get it? You hire people to make commitments for you, so you never have to bother." She shook her head. "That's not how I want to live my life."

"Bella, don't go." Three words that sounded as though they'd been forced from his throat.

It was too little, too late.

"If it helps, I won't be signing with Nick Acona, either."

"Bella…"

"Goodbye, Jesse." She opened the door, left the office and closed it behind her with a quiet snick of sound.

Two days later, Jesse was still stunned.

No one had ever told him off the way Bella had.

No one had ever been so right about him.

He'd wanted to argue with her, to refute everything she'd said to him, but she'd pegged him perfectly.

He *had* gone through life looking for the easiest route. He'd stumbled into a business that suited him, and only when it was placed right in front of him had he made the effort to grow it successfully. He *did* take a backseat in the running of his ocean foundation. He'd found good people to run it, then salved his conscience by writing hefty checks.

And damn it, she was right about something else, too. He *could* put two trashcans into every cubicle at the office. The janitorial staff would probably thank him profusely for making that job a little easier.

It was a hell of a thing when you got a wake-up call from the woman you loved and she was telling you that you didn't deserve her.

Even worse, he thought, when she was right.

Bella had made him take a good, hard look at himself and Jesse hadn't liked what he'd seen. He'd wanted to go to her house that night. To face her down, admit that everything she'd said to him was right on the money. To even, as hard as it was to swallow, beg her to hear him out. But he'd known that she would still be way too furious to listen to anything he had to say. And who could blame her?

So he'd given it a couple of days. Time enough for that icy temper of hers to thaw a little. Time enough for him to come up with at least a half-baked plan he hoped would work to convince her to come back to him.

A cold sea wind was blasting in off the ocean when

he left King Beach to walk the short block to Bella's shop. Dark clouds studded the sky and seabirds were headed inland. A sure sign that the storm that had been building for days was finally coming in for a landing. Good, he thought. A storm would clear the air and maybe, he told himself, that's just what he and Bella needed, too.

Taking a deep breath of the cold air, he headed for Bella's, walked up to the front door and—it was locked. Scowling, he thought for a second that she'd gone to lunch or something. But it was three in the afternoon, so that wouldn't wash. Cupping one hand over his eyes, he leaned in close to the window and peered inside.

The shop was empty.

Everything was gone. The swimsuit racks stood naked, the cash register was gone from the counter. The walls had been stripped of the swimsuits and posters Bella had had hanging there. Panic rose up in his chest. Not really believing what he was seeing, Jesse moved to another window, one that afforded a peek into the back of the shop, but he didn't feel any better once he checked that one out, too.

Her supplies of fabric were gone. Her worktable was bare and the boxes of new inventory were missing. The entire shop was vacant and as he stood there, locked out on the sidewalk, Jesse felt as empty as the building in front of him.

But damn if he was going to stay that way.

He went back to King Beach, got his car and drove to her house. The tidy flowerbeds, the small patch of lawn, the bright red front door all called to him, made him remember days and nights with her. Memories he didn't want to give up. Promises of a future he didn't want to lose.

He stalked up the front walk, pounded on that red door and waited for a response that didn't come. Looking into the windows, he sighed in relief when he noted that her things were still here, at least. She hadn't skipped town on him. Not that that would have stopped him. It just would have taken him longer to find her.

"Bella!" he called, pounding on the door again. "Bella, open up and talk to me, dammit!"

He waited what seemed like several lifetimes, but she never came to the door. He glanced next door at her friend Kevin's house, but the place was dark and there were no cars in the driveway, so she wasn't hiding out with him. Where the hell was she? Sitting in the living room, listening to him make an ass of himself?

Desperation clawing at his insides, Jesse shouted, "Fine! I'll just sit here on your porch until you come out!"

He spent the next few hours doing just that. He waved at the neighbors, ordered a pizza when he got hungry and he was still sitting there late that night when the brewing storm finally blew into Morgan Beach.

Eleven

The following afternoon, Jesse went to Kevin's shop, determined to get the man to tell him where Bella was. If anyone knew, her best friend would. He pushed the door open and stopped dead.

There was Kevin, with a tall, leggy blonde wrapped around him like shrink-wrap on a DVD. Their kiss was steamy enough to fog up the windows and only ended reluctantly when they heard Jesse's entrance.

The blonde glanced at him, then tucked her face into Kevin's chest on a laugh. "Oops."

Kevin only grinned. "It's okay, Trace. Jesse, this is my girlfriend, Traci Bennett. Traci, Jesse King."

She looked at him and Jesse realized that he recognized her. Her face was in dozens of magazine ads. She was tall, beautiful and dressed in quiet elegance, and all he could think was that he wished he were looking at a short, badly dressed, curvy brunette.

"You're the ex-surfer who's been rebuilding around here," Traci said. "Good job, by the way. Love what you've done to the place."

"Thanks." She liked it. Bella hated it.

"It's nice to meet you," she said. "Um, sorry about your walking in on the kiss, but I've been gone four weeks, and I really missed Kevin."

"No problem," Jesse said, stuffing his hands into the pockets of his slacks. If he could have had his way, he'd be with Bella right now, doing the same damn thing. "I just need to talk to him for a few minutes, if you don't mind."

"Not at all." She reached up, rubbed lipstick off Kevin's smiling mouth with her thumb, then turned and picked up her purse off the counter. "I'll let you guys talk. I'll see you later at my place, honey?"

Kevin's eyes gleamed. "Oh, yeah."

She was gone a moment later, leaving a trail of expensive perfume behind her. Jesse looked at Kevin. "So, you really do have a girlfriend."

"I really do. But is that what you came to talk to me about?" he asked, folding his arms over his chest and giving Jesse the kind of hard stare reserved for bad dogs and crazed children.

Apparently, Bella'd already talked over the situation with her friend and it was no surprise whose side Kevin was on. Fine. He could take whatever the guy had to say.

Hell, he deserved it. But Jesse wasn't leaving here without knowing how to find Bella.

"No, it's not *your* girlfriend I'm worried about," he admitted.

"What I thought." Kevin nodded toward the front door. "Flip the closed sign then come to the back."

Jesse did as Kevin asked, locked the front door, then followed Kevin into what looked like a miniwarehouse. The walls were crowded with shelves filled with boxes and gift wrap and ribbon and more jewelry than one person could use in several lifetimes.

There was also a small sink, a refrigerator, a tiny table and two chairs. Kevin pointed at the table, said, "Take a seat," and turned for the fridge. "Beer?"

"Sure."

Once they were both seated and Kevin had had a sip of his beer, he asked, "So, why are you looking for Bella?"

"Why?" Jesse just stared at him. "Because I have to talk to her."

"Seems to me you guys said everything that needed saying."

"She told you."

"She did." Kevin took another pull at his beer, then set the bottle down on the table, leaned back in his chair and glared at Jesse. "She cried."

"Dammit." He hadn't thought it possible to feel worse than he had been feeling, but he'd been wrong. He hated knowing that she'd cried. Hated even more knowing that he'd caused her tears. "She moved out of her shop."

"You evicted her."

Jesse groaned. "No, I didn't. I tore up the notice. Told her she could stay." Why was nobody listening to him?

"And you think she'd stay after that?"

"No, not Bella," Jesse whispered. "She's got too much pride for that. And she's too hardheaded."

Kevin laughed. "That sounds like pot and kettle talk."

"What the hell does she want from me?" Jesse demanded, unamused and feeling just a little desperate. The longer he went without talking to her, the worse his chances of fixing this were.

"Seems like she doesn't want anything from you," Kevin said thoughtfully.

Jesse cupped the cold beer bottle between his palms and felt the iciness creep inside him. But there was nothing different about that for him. He'd felt cold to the bone for days now. Without Bella…

"She left her shop," he said softly. "She's not at her house and when I call her cell, I get dumped into voice mail instantly."

Kevin sighed and picked up his beer for another sip. "She doesn't want to talk to you, man. She wants you to leave her alone."

"No, she doesn't," Jesse insisted, his gaze spearing into Kevin's. "She loves me."

"She did."

Jesse snorted. "What? She's stopped? Just like that? Turned it off and moved on?"

Kevin shook his head. "Why'd you come to me if you don't want to hear what I'm telling you?"

"I didn't come here looking for advice," he muttered. "I came here looking for Bella."

"She's not here."

"Yeah," Jesse told him with a hard look. "I can see that. So where is she?"

"Now why would I tell you that?" Kevin wondered aloud. "You already broke her heart."

Jesse winced. It hadn't been easy coming to Bella's friend. But whether he wanted to admit it or not, he needed help. He had to find her. Talk to her. Convince her to come back to him. Convince her to take a chance. And if anyone would know where she was, it was Kevin.

Jesse could just admit to the man that he loved Bella. But that was private. Between the two of them. He'd tell her. Again and again until she believed him. But damn if he'd tell her best friend. "I have to talk to her."

"And tell her what?"

"Everything."

"Didn't go so well for you the last time," Kevin said.

"No," Jesse admitted. "She didn't exactly give me a chance, though. She came into the office, reamed me out, then disappeared."

Kevin smiled, took a sip of his beer and said, "So what are you going to do about it?"

"Apparently," Jesse told him, "I'm going to sit in the back room of her friend's shop and be tortured."

"Besides that, I mean."

"I'm going to find her." Jesse glared at him again. "Even if you don't tell me where she is, I'll find her.

Then I'll tie her to a chair if I have to, to make sure she listens to me. Then I'm going to tell her that she loves me and that we're damn well getting married."

"I'd almost like to see that," Kevin mused.

"Enjoying this, are you?"

"Not as much I thought I would." Kevin leaned forward, bracing his arms on the table. "I told you before, that Bella's family to me. You hurt her badly, twice, but I'm willing to give you another chance because I know she's nuts about you."

Hope leaped up in Jesse's chest.

"But," Kevin added, his eyes steely, his features grim, "I'm warning you now. You hurt her again and I'll find a way to hurt you back."

"Understood." It was a measure of just how far gone he was that Jesse was willing to accept that threat from Kevin without batting an eye. Ordinarily, nobody told Jesse King what to do or how to do it. But as Bella's only "family," Jesse figured Kevin was within his rights.

The other man studied him for a long moment or two, then nodded and said, "All right. She's been staying at my place, but she went back home this morning."

"Thanks." Jesse jumped to his feet and headed for the front door.

An hour later, Bella was curled up on her couch feeling sorry for herself when a knock at the door sounded. Her head snapped up. She knew without even looking out the window that it was Jesse. She seemed to be able to sense his presence. Even when she didn't want to.

But she couldn't hide from him forever. She'd had a couple of days to cry and wallow in her misery. Now it was time to reclaim her life. This was her house. Her hometown. And she wasn't going to give it up because she'd made the mistake of loving a man who was incapable of loving her back.

She ran her fingers under her eyes, wiping away any stray teardrops, then checked her reflection in the closest mirror. Her hair was a mess, she wasn't wearing makeup and she looked like exactly what she was. A woman who'd spent too much time lately crying.

He knocked again, louder this time and Bella steeled herself as she opened the door. Her heart squeezed in her chest. He looked so good and she'd missed him so much.

"Bella," he whispered, a relieved smile creasing his features. "Thank God. I've been looking for you for days."

"What do you want, Jesse?" she asked, hugging the edge of the door close, positioning herself across the entryway so he couldn't slip into the house.

He inhaled sharply, blew the breath out in a rush and nodded. "Right. Okay. There's a lot I want to talk to you about, but let's start with this." He held out a sheaf of papers.

She sighed, took them and glanced at the bold, black letters across the top. *Deed.* "What?"

"It's the deed to your building, Bella," he said quickly, giving her that half smile she loved so much. "I want you to have it. Do whatever you want with it. Expand your business or close it. It's yours. No strings."

She looked down at the paper in her hand, then lifted her gaze to his beautiful blue eyes. Shaking her head, she said, "Don't you get it, Jesse? I don't want this. I don't want anything from you." She threw the deed over his head and watched it flutter in the wind until it landed on her lawn. "Now, please. Just go away."

She closed the door on him and tried not to remember the stunned surprise flickering in his gaze. Then she leaned back against the door and let the tears fall again. She'd thought she was finished crying, but apparently, there were more tears locked inside.

He didn't understand. This wasn't about her shop. Her business. Or King Beach. This was about *them.* This was about how she loved him and how wrong she'd been.

"Bella," he said, his voice coming through the door clearly, "don't do this."

She held her breath, closed her eyes and waited him out. Finally, she heard his footsteps as he left the porch and took the steps. When she didn't hear anything else, she slowly sank to the floor, hugged her knees to her chest and sat there silently until she heard him turn and walk away. She'd done the right thing, Bella knew. She had to be strong. She couldn't let herself be hurt again. She just didn't think she would survive another broken heart.

Turning him away was the only thing she could do. Right now, he was reacting to having lost her. He'd already told her that Kings didn't lose, so naturally, he wouldn't give up easily. But eventually, if she stayed strong enough, he'd give up and go away.

Bright and early the next morning though, he was back, pounding on her front door. "Bella! Bella, open up! Talk to me, dammit."

She staggered from bed in the semidarkness of the night just as dawn broke. She hadn't planned to answer the door if he came back. Wouldn't have actually, if he hadn't kept shouting her name so loudly. If she didn't open her door, Mrs. Clayton next door would be calling the police in a few minutes.

Clutching her pale pink robe to her chest, she threw the door open. Cold wind scuttled past her and sent a chill zipping through her body. The sky behind him was a pale violet and studded with dark clouds. The sun hadn't risen yet, but it was close.

Jesse looked as if he hadn't slept. His hair was wild, as if he'd been driving his fingers through it all night. His white shirt was wrinkled, there was a day's growth of whiskers on his jaw and his eyes were shadowed. He held a latte from the diner in each hand. "I brought you coffee."

She sighed, reached out and took one. Fine. He knew her weakness. But that didn't mean anything. Nor did the fact that she'd accepted the coffee.

"Jesse, you have to stop."

"No, I don't," he told her, stepping in close. "I won't stop. Not until you hear me out."

Bella sighed again, heavier this time. He looked as bad as she felt. Why drag this on for either of them? Wouldn't it be easier to just let him say what he felt that he had to say? Then maybe he'd go away. "Okay, talk."

He blinked at her. "Can't I come in?"

"No."

He huffed out a breath, muttered something she didn't quite catch and let his head fall back. "Fine. You don't want me in your house, I'll just say it right here." His gaze met hers. "Bella, I *love* you."

Her breath caught. How amazing that pain could just keep growing. "Jesse…don't…"

"I do." He reached out and when she would have shut the door, he slapped one hand against it, preventing her from closing herself off from him again. "Look, I know I screwed up. I know you're hurt. And pissed. And you've got every right to be. But dammit, Bella, I've never felt this way before. Maybe that's why I'm messing it up so badly. It's all new to me. *You're* new to me. But that doesn't make it less true. I love you, Bella. I really do."

Her throat was closing on her and her vision was blurring. She really didn't want to cry in front of him, but if she didn't get the door closed fast that was exactly what was going to happen and her humiliation would be complete.

His words echoed over and over again in her mind and she wanted to hold on to them. But how could she? She would have given anything to believe him. To hear those words and hold them close. Instead, she said, "How can I believe you, Jesse? You lied to me right from the beginning."

Sorrow glimmered in his eyes and his mouth tightened into a hard, flat line. "I know and I'm sorry. Sorrier than you realize. As I said, I made mistakes. But loving you isn't one of them, Bella. You have to believe me. You have to know that what I feel is real. I want to marry you." He laughed shortly. "There's a sentence I never thought I'd hear myself say."

She shivered and fought to keep her tears from falling. "Stop. Please."

"No," he told her sincerely, his blue eyes fixed on hers, "I'll never stop. You're the soul of me, Bella. You're the piece of me that was always missing. Hell, I didn't even know I was incomplete until I found you." He slid his hand over the door to rest atop hers. "And I can't lose you now. I won't go back to being alone."

Just that one touch of his skin against hers sent heat she hadn't known in days skimming through her system. Still, Bella couldn't believe. Couldn't risk it.

"You were my mystery woman, Bella," he said. "But I see now the only mystery is how I ever managed to live without you in my life. Give me a chance to make it all up to you, Bella. Give *us* that chance."

She stared into his eyes, longing to believe, but just too shattered to try. "I really wish I could believe you, Jesse. But I just can't."

Then she closed the door and let the tears fall.

Late that night, Jesse muttered a curse as the heavens opened up on him. He'd never had to work so hard for anything in his life. Always, things had come easily to him. Always, he'd walked through life, taking what he wanted, leaving the rest behind. Until now.

Now, everything rested on his being able to convince one woman—*the* woman—that she was the most important thing in his world. That she *was* his world.

And he wasn't going to lose.

She was stubborn?

He was more stubborn.

If she thought he was going to give up and go away, then she had a big surprise in store for her. He stepped out of his car and was instantly drenched.

Naturally, it was pouring rain. Wouldn't want this to be easy at all. He stared at Bella's house, glanced at the neighbors on either side. Kevin was probably with Traci and Mrs. Clayton's house was dark. No one would see him. Then he shifted his gaze to Bella's bedroom window. She was in there. Snuggled under her blankets. Alone.

But not for long.

He swiped his wet hair out of his eyes and headed directly across the lawn toward her bedroom. He was through going to the front door, asking her to let him in. Enough already. She was going to listen to him. She was going to *believe* him. And he damn well wasn't going to leave until she did.

He smiled as he lifted her window, glad that it was still unlocked. The last time they'd stayed at her house, he'd noticed that the lock was faulty and had been going to replace it for her. Now he was grateful that he hadn't.

The wood window frame, still soaked from the previous storm, screeched a little as it slid up and Jesse winced. He paused, looked over his shoulder and noticed a light come on in at Mrs. Clayton's. Of course it couldn't have been Kevin who'd heard him. Had to be the neighbor he hadn't met. If she looked out and saw him climbing through a window, she'd be calling the cops any second now.

No time to waste.

He climbed in, hit his shin on the windowsill and muffled the curse that flew from his mouth. On the bed, Bella stirred beneath her blankets and turned so that the dim light of the rainy night fell across her features. Jesse's chest tightened. He loved her more than he'd ever thought it was possible to love anyone.

The room was small and filled with shadows. But he didn't need to see to know where his destination was.

Walking quietly toward the bed, he shrugged out of his jacket and tossed it onto the floor with a sodden splat. Shaking his head, he sat down beside her, laid one hand on her hip and whispered, "Bella. Bella, wake up."

She turned toward him with a slow, languid movement, opened her eyes sleepily and stared up at him. A second passed before she blinked and said, *"Jesse?"*

"Were you expecting someone else?" he asked wryly.

"No, and I wasn't expecting you, either." She scooted back from him, but Jesse wasn't going to lose his momentum now.

He reached out, grabbed her and pulled her to him.

"You're soaking wet!"

"It's raining outside."

"How did you get in here?" She was squirming,

trying to get free of him, but Jesse only tightened his hold on her.

"Climbed through your window." He looked down into her eyes. "You really need to get that latch fixed."

"Apparently."

"Look, Bella, Mrs. Clayton saw me climbing in, I think, so I've gotta talk fast, because she's probably calling the cops to report a break-and-entry."

"Oh, for heaven's sake!"

"You see what I'm willing to do for you?" He asked the question with a wide grin. He was soaking wet, cold down to the bone and yet he hadn't felt so warm in days. Just having her here, beside him, made everything all right. Still smiling, he said, "I'm probably going to get arrested, so now you have to listen to me."

"Jesse, you're crazy."

"Probably."

She swung her hair back from her face and looked up at him, eyes shining. "Why are you doing all this? Why do you keep trying?"

"Because you're worth it," he told her, his voice deep and low. "You're worth anything."

"Jesse, I want to believe you, I really do."

"Because you love me," he said, tracing the pads of his thumbs across her cheekbones. "Why won't you admit it?"

Her eyes closed and a single tear slid from beneath her eyelid. He kissed it away.

"I can't. If I do, you'll break my heart again," she

said, her voice almost lost in the steady patter of the rain falling outside.

Jesse's own heart ached at the misery in her voice and at the knowledge that he'd caused her so much pain. But he could fix that. He would make it his personal mission to see to it that she never cried again.

"No more tears, Bella. You're killing me."

"I can't seem to stop," she admitted, lifting her gaze to look at him again.

"God, I love you so much." He cupped her face in his palms and let his gaze move over her features hungrily. Like a man starved and finally given a feast, he couldn't seem to get his fill of her. "I swear I'll never make you cry again."

She actually laughed at that. "Oh, Jesse, you can't make that kind of promise."

The tightness in his chest eased a little. She wasn't trying to escape from him anymore. She wasn't trying to push him away. That was a start, anyway.

"I will promise it, though." He met her gaze and held it. "Believe me, Bella. I will spend the rest of my life trying to make you smile. Making sure you never doubt again how much I love you."

She chewed at her bottom lip and drew one shaky breath.

Reaching into his slacks pocket, he pulled out the box he'd been carrying all day. He'd gone shopping at Kevin's place that morning right after he left Bella. He flipped the red velvet lid back, displaying the ring that had made him think of Bella the moment he saw it.

"Jesse…"

He reached for her left hand and though she was trembling slightly, she didn't pull away. Slowly, he slid the ring onto her finger and held it in place while they both stared down at it, shining in the darkness.

"It's a yellow diamond," he said, "and when I saw it at Kevin's I thought of you. Those yellow shirts you wear. The way you love the sun. The brightness I feel in the world when I'm with you."

She lifted her free hand and covered her mouth while her eyes drenched and spilled over.

"Now see, I've already broken my promise and made you cry again," he whispered, leaning in to kiss her forehead with a gentle reverence.

"Doesn't count," she whispered. "Tears of happiness don't count."

He smiled and relief washed over him. He was forgiven.

"I love you, Bella. I want to marry you. Have babies with you. Build a life together."

She pulled in another shuddering breath, lifted her gaze to his and said, "I want that, too, Jesse. I love you so much."

"Finally," he said, a wide grin on his face. "You're going to have to say that a lot, you know. Don't think I'll ever get tired of hearing it."

"I can do that," she said.

Taking both of her hands in his, he said, "I'm making a commitment, Bella. To you. To us. I even put recycling cans in the cubicles at the office."

She laughed then, a delightful sound that rippled out around him and settled over Jesse like a blessing.

"Oh, Jesse, you really are crazy, aren't you?"

"Crazy about you? Oh, yeah, baby. Count on it."

Outside, flashing red-and-yellow lights lit up the darkness and Jesse grimaced. "That'll be the police. Honey, would you mind coming out and explaining to the nice officers that this is just the beginning of our very interesting lives?"

Epilogue

Three months later, Bella burst from her office into Jesse's, a wide grin on her face as she waved a sheet of paper in the air as if she were waving the winner's flag at a car race.

"It's here! And it's wonderful! *You're* wonderful!" She flung herself at him and Jesse jumped up from his chair to catch her, arms coming around her in a tight embrace.

His wife.

He didn't think he'd ever get tired of the sound of those two words. *His wife*. He and Bella had been married for a month now and the difference in his life was staggering. He felt more alive than he ever had and it was all because of her.

"What's here and just how wonderful am I?" he asked, bending his head to nibble at her neck.

Since Bella's office was right next to his now, there was a connecting door the two of them alone used. That way they could be together whenever they wanted and without the rest of the office giving them knowing winks and smiles.

Not that he minded.

Bella hummed low in her throat as his lips and tongue moved over her neck. He loved the way she was dressing these days. Jeans that clung to her amazing legs, shirts that were actually her size and usually with nicely scooped out necklines, giving him much easier access.

"That's not fair," she whispered. "You know I can't think straight when you do that."

"Good," he murmured. "No thinking required."

And with the new rules of the office—no one entered without knocking and receiving a response—they were free to do whatever they liked. Jesse smiled to himself. There were several things he could think of to occupy them both for at least an hour or two.

"Jesse…" she squirmed in his grasp. "I didn't come in here for this. I just wanted to show you. To thank you…"

"Ooh, good. I love being thanked by my wife."

She laughed and tossed the paper she'd been holding onto his desk so that she could wrap both arms around his neck. She kissed him then, long and deep, and then pulled back to look up at him. "You say that a lot, you know? *My wife.*"

He grinned at her. "Get used to it. My wife. *Mine.*"

"Just the way I like it," she whispered, and kissed him again, giving him everything he could ever have wanted. Making every dream come true. Making his life just as it should be.

And when she stepped away from him, backing toward the office sofa with a secretive smile, he followed willingly. But first, he glanced at the paper she'd brought into the office and he smiled.

It was the new national ad for King Beach.

Good to know she approved.

The glossy paper carried their pictures, shots of their beachwear and the slogan *Bella and the King. Together at Last.*

It was perfect.

* * * * *

CLAIMING
KING'S BABY

BY
MAUREEN CHILD

To the Estrada Family:
Steve, Rose, Alicia, Lettie, Patti and Amanda.
Good friends. Great neighbours.
We love you guys.

One

Justice King opened the front door and faced his past.

She stood there staring at him out of pale blue eyes he'd tried desperately to forget. Her long, light red hair whipped around her head in a cold, fierce wind, and her delectable mouth curved into a cynical half smile.

"Hello, Justice," said a voice that haunted his dreams. "Been a while."

Eight months and twenty-five days, he thought but didn't say. His gaze moved over her in a quick but thorough inspection. She was tall, with the same stubborn tilt to her chin that he remembered and the same pale sprinkle of freckles across her nose. Her full breasts rose and fell quickly with each of her rapid breaths, and that more than anything else told him she was nervous.

Well, then, she shouldn't have come.

His gaze locked back on hers. "What're you doing here, Maggie?"

"Aren't you going to invite me in?"

"Nope," he said flatly. One thing he didn't need was to have her close enough to touch again.

"Is that any way to talk to your wife?" she asked and walked past him into the ranch house.

His wife.

Automatically, his left thumb moved to play with the gold wedding band he'd stopped wearing the day he had allowed her to walk away. Memories crashed into his mind, and he closed his eyes against the onslaught.

But nothing could stop the images crowding his brain. Maggie, naked, stretched out on his bed, welcoming him. Maggie, shouting at him through her tears. Maggie, leaving without a backward glance. And last, Justice saw himself, closing the door behind her and just as firmly shuttering away his heart.

Nothing had changed.

They were still the same people they'd been when they married and when they split.

So he pulled himself together, and closed the front door behind them. Then he turned to face her.

Watery winter sunlight poured from the skylight onto the gleaming wood floors and glanced off the mirror hanging on the closest wall. A pedestal table held an empty cobalt vase—there'd been no flowers in this hall since Maggie left—and the silence in the house slammed down on top of them both.

Seconds ticked past, marked only by the tapping of Maggie's shoe against the floor. Justice waited her out, knowing that she wouldn't be able to be quiet for long. She never had been comfortable with silence. Maggie was the most talkative woman he'd ever known. Damned if he hadn't missed that.

Three feet of empty space separated them and still, Justice felt the pull of her. His body was heavy and aching and everything in him clawed at him to reach out for her. To ease the pain of doing without her for far too long.

Yet he called on his own reserves of strength to keep from taking what he'd missed so badly.

"Where's Mrs. Carey?" Maggie asked suddenly, her voice shattering the quiet.

"She's on vacation." Justice cursed inwardly, wishing to hell his housekeeper had picked some other time to take a cruise to Jamaica.

"Good for her," Maggie said, then tipped her head to one side. "Glad to see me?"

Glad wasn't the word he'd use. *Stunned* would be about right. When Maggie had left, she'd sworn that he would never see her again. And he hadn't, not counting the nights she appeared in his dreams just to torment him.

"What are you doing here, Maggie?"

"Well, now, that's the question, isn't it?"

She turned away and walked slowly down the hall, bypassing the more formal living room before stepping into the great room. Justice followed, watching as she looked around the room as if reacquainting herself with the place.

She looked from the floor-to-ceiling bookshelves on two walls to the river stone hearth, tall and wide enough for a man to stand in it upright. The log walls, with the white chinking between them that looked like horizontal striping. The plush chairs and sofas she'd bought for the room, gathered together into conversation areas, and the wide bank of windows that displayed an unimpeded view of the ranch's expansive front yard. Ancient trees spread shade across most of the lawn, flowers in the neatly tended beds dipped and swayed with the ocean wind and from a distance came the muffled roar of the ranch tractor moving across the feed grain fields.

"You haven't changed anything," she whispered.

"Haven't had time," he lied.

"Of course." Maggie spun around to face him and her eyes were flashing.

Justice felt a surge of desire shoot through him with the force of a lightning strike. Her temper had always had that effect on him. They'd been like oil and water, sliding against each other but never really blending into a cohesive whole. And maybe that was part of the attraction, he mused.

Maggie wasn't the kind of woman to change for a man. She was who she was, take her or leave her. He'd always wanted to take her. And God help him, if she came too close to him right now, he'd take her again.

"Look," she said, those blue eyes of hers still snapping with sparks of irritation, "I didn't come here to fight."

"Why are you here?"

"To bring you this."

She reached into her oversize, black leather bag and pulled out a legal-size manila envelope. Her fingers traced the silver clasp briefly as if she were hesitating about handing it over. Then a second later, she did.

Justice took it, glanced at it and asked, "What is it?"

"The divorce papers." She folded her arms across her chest. "You didn't sign the copy the lawyers sent you, so I thought I'd bring a set in person. Harder to ignore me if I'm standing right in front of you, don't you think?"

Justice tossed the envelope onto the nearest chair, stuffed his hands into the back pockets of his jeans and stared her down. "I wasn't ignoring you."

"Ah," she said with a sharp nod, "so you were just what? Playing games? Trying to make me furious?"

He couldn't help the half smile that curved his mouth. "If I was, looks like I managed it."

"Damn right you did." She walked toward him and stopped just out of arm's reach. As if she knew if she came any closer, the heat between them would erupt into an inferno neither of them would survive.

He'd always said she was smart.

"Justice, you told me months ago that our marriage was over. So sign the damn papers already."

"What's your hurry?" The question popped out before he could call it back. Gritting his teeth, he just went with it and asked the question he really wanted the answer to. "Got some other guy lined up?"

She jerked her head back as if he'd slapped her.

"This is *not* about getting another man into my life," she told him. "This is about getting a man *out* of my life. You, Justice. We're not together. We're not going to be together. You made that plain enough."

"You leaving wasn't my idea," he countered.

"No, it was just your fault," she snapped.

"You're the one who packed, Maggie."

"You gave me no choice." Her voice broke and Justice hissed in a breath in response.

Shaking her head, she held up one hand as if for peace and whispered, "Let's just finish this, okay?"

"You think a signed paper will finish it?" He moved in, dragging his hands from his pockets so that he could grab her shoulders before she could skitter away. God, the feel of her under his hands again fed the cold, empty places inside him. Damn, he'd missed her.

"You finished it yourself, remember?"

"You're the one who walked out," Justice reminded her again.

"And you're the one who let me," she snapped, her gaze locked on his as she stiffened in his grasp.

"What was I supposed to do?" he demanded. "Tie you to a chair?"

She laughed without humor. "No, you wouldn't do that, would you, Justice? You wouldn't try to make me stay. You wouldn't come after me."

Her words jabbed at him but he didn't say anything. Hell, no, he hadn't chased after her. He'd had his pride, hadn't he? What was he supposed to do, beg her to stay? She'd made it clear that as far as she was concerned, their marriage was over. So he should have done what exactly?

She flipped her hair back out of her face and gave him a glare that should have set him on fire. "So here we are again on the carousel of pain. I blame you. You blame me. I yell, you get all stoic and stone-faced and nothing changes."

He scowled at her. "I don't get stone-faced."

"Oh, please, Justice. You're doing it right now." She

choked out a laugh and tried to squirm free of his grip. It didn't work. She tipped her head back, and her angry eyes focused on his and the mouth he wanted to taste more than anything flattened into a grim slash. "Our fights were always one-sided. I shout and you close up."

"Shouting's supposed to be a good thing?"

"At least I would have known you cared enough to fight!"

His fingers on her shoulders tightened, and he met that furious glare with one of his own. "You knew damn well I cared. You still left."

"Because you had to have it all your way. A marriage is *two* people. Not just one really pushy person." She sucked in a breath, fought his grip for another second or two, then sighed. "Let me go, Justice."

"I already did," he told her. "You're the one who came back."

"I didn't come back for this." She pushed at his chest.

"Bullshit, Maggie." His voice dropped to a whisper, a rough scrape of sound as the words clawed their way out of his throat. "You could have sent your lawyer. Hell, you could have mailed the papers again. But you didn't. You came here. To *me*."

"To look you in the eye and demand that you sign them."

"Really?" He dipped his head, inhaled the soft, flowery scent of her and held it inside as long as he could. "Is that really why you're here, Maggie? The papers?"

"Yes," she said, closing her eyes, sliding her hands up his chest. "I want it over, Justice. If we're done, I need all of this to be finally over."

The feel of her touching Justice sparked the banked fires within and set them free to engulf his body. It had always been like this between them. Chemistry, pure and simple. Combustion. Whenever they touched, their bodies lit up like the neon streets of Vegas.

That, at least, hadn't changed.

"We'll never be done, Maggie." His gaze moved over her. He loved the flush in her cheeks and the way her mouth was parted on the sigh that slipped from between her lips. "What's between us will never be over."

"I used to believe that." Her eyes opened; she stared up at him and shook her head. "But it has to be over, Justice. If I stay, we'll only hurt each other again."

Undoubtedly. He couldn't give her the one thing she wanted, so he had to let her go. For her sake. Still, she was here, now. In his arms. And the past several months had been so long without her.

He'd tried to bury her memory with other women, but he hadn't been able to. Hadn't been able to want any woman as he wanted her. Only her.

His body was hard and tight and aching so badly it was all he could do not to groan with the pain of needing her. The past didn't matter anymore. The future was a hazy blur. But the present buzzed and burned with an intensity that shook him to his bones.

"If we're really done, then all we have is now, Maggie," he said, bending to touch the tip of his tongue to her parted lips. She hissed in a breath of air, and he knew she felt exactly as he did. "And if you leave now, you'll kill me."

She swayed into him even as she shook her head. Her

hands slid up over his shoulder, and she drove her fingers up, into his always-too-long dark brown hair. The touch of her was molten. The scent of her was dizzying. The taste of her was all he needed.

"God, I've missed you," she admitted, her mouth moving against his. "You bastard, you've still got my heart."

"You ripped mine out when you left, Maggie," he confessed. His gaze locked with hers, and in those pale blue depths he read passion and need and all the emotions that were charging through him. "But you're back now and damned if I'll let you leave again. Not now. Not yet."

His mouth came down hard on hers, and it was as if he was alive again. For months, he'd been a walking dead man. A hollowed-out excuse for a human being. Breathing. Eating. Working. But so empty there was nothing for him but routine. He'd lost himself in the ranch workings. Buried himself in the minutiae of business so that he had no time to think. No time to wonder what she was doing. Where she was.

Months of being without her fired the desire nearly choking him, and Justice gave himself up to it. He skimmed his hands up and down her spine, sliding them over the curve of her bottom, cupping her, pressing her into him until she could feel the hard proof of his need.

She groaned into his mouth and strained against him. Justice tore his mouth from hers and lowered his head to taste the long, elegant line of her throat. Her scent invaded him. Her heat swamped him. And he could think only of taking what he'd wanted for so long.

He nibbled at her soft, smooth skin, feeling her shivers of pleasure as she cocked her head to one side, allowing him greater access. She'd always liked it when he kissed her neck. When his teeth scraped her skin, when his tongue drew taut, damp circles just beneath her ear.

He slid one hand around, to the front of her. He cupped her center with the palm of his hand. Even through the fabric of her tailored slacks, he felt her heat, her need, pulsing at him.

"Justice…"

"Damn it, Maggie," he whispered, lifting his head to look down at her. "If you tell me to stop, I'll…"

She smiled. "You'll what?"

He sighed and let his forehead drop to hers. "I'll stop."

Maggie shifted her hold on him, moving to cup his face between her palms. She hadn't come here for this, though if she were to be completely honest, she'd have had to admit that she'd hoped he would hold her again. Love her again. She'd missed him so much that the pain of losing him was a constant ache in her heart. Now, having his hands and mouth on her again was like a surprise blessing from the suddenly benevolent fates.

When she'd first left him, she'd prayed that he'd follow her, take her home and make everything right. When he hadn't, it had broken her heart. But she'd tried to go on. To rebuild her life. She found a new job. Found an apartment. Made friends.

And still there was something missing.

A part of her she'd left here, at the ranch.

With him.

Looking up into the dark blue eyes that had captivated her from the first, she said, "Don't stop, Justice. Please don't stop."

He kissed her, hard and long and deep. His tongue pushed into her mouth, claiming her in a frenzy of passion so strong she felt the tide of it swamp her, threaten to drown her in an overload of sensation.

From the top of her head to the tips of her toes, Maggie felt a rush of heat that was incredible. As if she were literally on fire, she felt her skin burn, her blood boil and her heart thunder in her chest. While his mouth took hers, his clever fingers unzipped her slacks so that he could slide one hand down the front of her, beneath the fragile elastic of her panties to the swollen, hot flesh awaiting him.

She shivered as he stroked her intimately. She parted her legs for him, letting her slacks slide down to pool on the floor. She didn't care where they were. Didn't care about anything but feeling his hands on her again. Maggie nearly wept as he pushed first one finger and then two deep inside her.

Sucking in a gulp of air, she let her head fall back as she rode his hand, rocking her hips, seeking the release only he could give her. The passion she'd only ever found with him. She heard his own breath coming hard and fast as he continued to stroke her body inside and out. His thumb worked that so sensitive bud of flesh at the heart of her, and Maggie felt her brain sizzle as tension coiled inside her, tighter, tighter.

"Come for me, Maggie," he whispered. "Let me watch you shatter."

She couldn't have denied him even if she'd wanted

to. It had been too long. She'd missed him too much.
Maggie held on to his shoulders, fingers curling into the
soft fabric of the long-sleeved shirt he wore, digging into
his hard muscles.

Her mind spun, splintering with thoughts, images,
while her body burned and spiraled even closer to its
reward. She'd never felt anything like this with any man
before him. And after Justice…she'd had no interest in
other men. He was the one. She'd known it the moment
she'd met him three years before. One look across a
crowded dance floor at a charity event and she'd known.
Instantly. It was as if everything in the world had held
utterly still for one breathless moment.

Just like now.

There was nothing in the world but him and his
hands. His touch. His scent. "Justice—I need…"

"I know, baby. I know just what you need. Take it. Take
me." He touched her deeper, pushing his fingers inside
her, stroking her until her breath strangled in her throat.

Until she could only groan and hold on to him. Until
her body trembled and the incredible tension within
shattered under an onslaught of pleasure so deep, so
overwhelming, all she could do was shout his name as
wave after wave of completion rolled over her, through
her, leaving her dazed and breathless.

And when the tremors finally died away, Maggie
stared up into Justice's lake-blue eyes and watched him
smile. She was standing in the living room, with her
pants down, trembling with the force of her reaction to
him. She should have been…embarrassed. After all,
anyone could have walked into the ranch house.

Instead, all Maggie felt was passion stirring inside again. His hands were talented, heaven knew. But she wanted more. She wanted the slide of Justice's body into hers.

Licking her lips, she blew out a breath and said, "That was…"

"…just the beginning," he finished for her.

TWO

Sounded good to Maggie.

Yet… She glanced around the empty room before looking back at him. "Mrs. Carey's not here, but—"

"Nobody's here," he said quickly. "No one's coming. No one is going to interrupt us."

Maggie sighed in relief. She didn't want any interruptions. Justice was right about one thing—their past was gone. The future was gray and hazy. All she had was today. This minute. This one small slice of time, and she was going to relish every second of it.

Her fingers speared through his thick, soft hair, her nails dragging along his scalp. He always kept it too long, she thought idly, loving the way the dark brown mass lay across his collar. He had a day's worth of dark stubble on his jaws, and he looked so damned sexy he made her quiver.

Her breasts ached for his touch and as if he'd heard that stray thought, he pulled back from her slightly, just far enough so that his fingers could work the buttons on her pale pink silk blouse. Quickly, they fell free and then he was sliding the fabric off her shoulders to drop to the floor. She stepped out of her slacks, kicked off her half boots and slipped her lacy panties off.

Then he undid her bra, tossing it aside, and her breasts were free, his hands cupping her. His thumbs moved over her peaked nipples until she whimpered with the pleasure and the desire pumping fresh and new through her system. As if that climax hadn't even happened, her body was hot and trembling again.

Need crashed down on her, and at her core she ached and burned for him.

"You're beautiful," he whispered, drawing his mouth from hers, glancing down at her breasts, cupped in his palms. "So damn beautiful."

"I want you, Justice. Now. Please, now."

One corner of his mouth tipped into a wicked smile. His eyes flashed and in an instant he'd swept her up into his arms, stalked across the room and dropped her onto one of the wide sofas. She stared up at him as he tugged his shirt up and over his head. And her mouth watered. His skin, so tanned, so strong, so sculpted. God, she remembered all the nights she'd lain in his arms, held against that broad, warm chest. And she trembled at the rise of passion inside her.

She scooted back on the sofa until her head was

resting on a pillow. Maggie held her arms out toward him. "What're you waiting for, cowboy?"

His eyes gleamed, his jaw went tight and hard. He finished undressing in a split second but still Maggie thought he was taking too long. She didn't want to wait. She was hot and wet and so ready for him that she thought she'd explode and die if he didn't take her soon.

He came to her and Maggie's gaze dipped to his erection, long and thick and hard. Her breath caught on a gasp of anticipation as Justice leaned down, tore the back cushions off the sofa and tossed them to the floor to make more room for them on the overstuffed couch. The dark green chenille fabric was soft and cool against her skin, but Maggie hardly noticed that slight chill. There was far too much heat simmering inside her, and when Justice covered her body with his, she could have sworn she felt actual flames sweeping over them.

"I've missed you, babe," he told her, bracing himself on his hands, lowering his mouth to hers, tasting, nibbling.

"Oh, Justice, I've missed you, too." She lifted her hips for him, parting her thighs, welcoming him home. He pushed his body into hers with one hard stroke. She groaned, loving the long, deep slide of his flesh claiming hers. He filled her and she lifted her legs higher, hooking them around his waist, opening herself so that she could take him even deeper.

And still it wasn't enough. Wasn't nearly enough. She groaned, twisting and writhing beneath him as he moved in and out of her depths in plunging strokes that fanned the flames engulfing her.

It had been too long, she thought wildly. She didn't

want soft and romantic. She wanted hard and fast and frantic. She wanted to know that he felt the same crushing need she did. She wanted to feel the strength of his passion.

"Harder, Justice," she whispered. "Take me harder."

He looked down at her and his eyes flashed. "I'm holding back, Maggie. It's been too long. I don't want to hurt you."

She cupped his face in her palms, fought to steady her breath and finally shook her head and smiled. "The only thing that hurts is when you hold back. Justice, I *need* you. All of you."

His jaw clenched tight, he swept one arm around her back, holding her to him even as he pushed off the couch. With their bodies locked together, her legs wrapped around his waist, he eased her onto the oriental carpet covering the hardwood floors. With her flat on her back, he levered himself over her, hands at either side of her head. Grinning down at her, he muttered, "Told you when you bought 'em those damn couches were too soft."

She grinned right back at him. "For sitting, they're perfect. For this…yeah. Too soft."

She lifted her hips then, taking him deeper inside. When he withdrew a moment later, she nearly groaned, but then he was back, driving himself into her, pistoning his hips against hers and she felt all of him. Took all of him. His need joined hers.

He lifted her legs, hooking them over his shoulders, tipping her hips higher so that he could delve even deeper, and Maggie groaned in appreciation. She slapped her hands onto the carpet and hung on as he moved faster and faster, driving them both to a shuddering climax that hovered just out of reach.

"Yes, Justice," she said, her voice nothing more than a strained hush of sound. "Just like that."

Again and again, his body claimed hers, pushing into her soft, hot folds, taking everything she offered and giving all that she could have wanted. She looked up into his eyes, saw the flash of something delicious wink in their depths and knew in that one blindingly clear instant that she would never be whole without him.

Without him.

That one random thought hovered at the edges of her mind and filled her eyes with tears even as her body began to sing and hum with the building tensions that rippled through her senses.

He touched her at their joining. Rubbing his thumb over that one spot that held so many incredible sensations. And as he touched her, Maggie hurtled eagerly toward the enormous climax waiting for her. As her body exploded with the force of completion, she screamed his name, and still she heard the quiet voice in the back of her mind whispering, *Is this our last time together?*

Then Justice gave himself over to his own release, her name an agonized groan sliding from his throat. When he collapsed atop her, Maggie held him close as the last of the tremors rippled through their joined bodies and eased them into oblivion.

And if her heart broke just a little, she wouldn't let him know it.

* * *

The rest of the weekend passed in a blurry haze of passion. But for a few necessary trips to the kitchen, Justice and Maggie never left the master bedroom.

After that first time in the living room, Justice made a call to his ranch manager, Phil, and told him to handle the ranch problems himself for the next few days. It hadn't exactly been a promise of forever, but Maggie had been happy for it.

All the same, she was crazy and she knew it. Setting herself up for another fall. As long as Justice King was the man she loved, she wasn't going to find any peace. Because they couldn't be together without causing each other pain and being apart was killing her.

How was that fair?

She sighed a little, her gaze still fixed on him. The only light in the room came from the river stone hearth, where a dying fire sputtered and flickered. Outside, a winter storm battered at the log mansion, tiny fists of rain tapping at the glass. And within Maggie, a different sort of storm raged.

What was she supposed to do? She'd tried living without him and had spent the most miserable nine months of her life. She'd tried to lose herself in her work, but it was an empty way to live. The sad truth was she wanted Justice. And without him, she'd never be really happy.

He was the most amazing lover she'd ever known. Every touch burned, every breath caressed, every whispered word was a promise of seduction that kept her hovering on the brink of a new climax no matter how many times he pushed her over the edge. Her skin hummed long after he stopped touching her. She closed her eyes and felt him inside her. Felt their hearts pounding in rhythm and couldn't help wondering, as she always had, how two people could be so close and so far apart at the same time.

Now she watched him get out of bed and walk naked across the bedroom. His body was long and lean and tanned from all the years of working in the sun. His dark brown hair hung past his shoulders. She'd always found that hair of his to be sexy as hell and what made it even sexier was that he was oblivious to just how good he looked. How dangerous. Her heartbeat quickened as her gaze moved over his back, and down over his butt. He moved with a stealthy grace that was completely innate. Everything about him was, she had to admit, fabulous. He was enough to make any woman toss her panties in the air and shout hallelujah. And she was no different.

He went into a crouch in front of the hearth. The fire was dying and he set a fresh log on the fading flames. Instantly the fire blazed into life, licking at the new wood, hissing and snapping.

Maggie watched Justice. His legs were muscled and toned from hours spent in a saddle. His back and shoulders were broad and sculpted from the hard work he never spared himself. As a King, he could have hired men to do the hard work around the ranch. But she knew it had always been a matter of pride to him that *he* be out there with those who worked for him.

Justice King was a man out of time, she thought, sweeping one arm across the empty space in the bed where he'd been lying only moments ago. He would have been completely at home in medieval times. He would have been a Highlander, she mused, her imagination dressing him in a war-torn plaid and placing a claymore in his fist.

As if he knew she was watching him, Justice turned his face to her, and the flickering light of the fire threw dancing shadows across his features. He looked hard and strong and suddenly so unapproachable that Maggie's heart gave a lurch.

She was setting herself up for pain and she knew it. He was her husband, but the bonds holding them together were frayed and tattered. In bed they were combustible and so damn good it made her heart hurt. It was when they were *out* of bed that things got complicated. They wanted different things. They each held so tightly to their own bottom line that compromise was unthinkable.

But it was Sunday night. The end of the weekend. She'd have to return to her world soon, and knowing that this time with him was nearly over was already bringing agonizing pain.

The storm blowing in off the coast howled outside the window. Rain hammered at the glass, wind whistled under the eaves and, Justice noticed, Maggie had started thinking.

Never had been a good thing, Justice told himself as he watched his wife study him. Whenever Maggie got that look on her face—an expression that said she had something to say he wasn't going to like—Justice knew trouble was coming.

But then, he'd been halfway prepared for that since this "lost" weekend had begun. Nothing had changed.

He and Maggie, despite the obvious chemistry they shared, were still miles apart in the things that mattered, and great sex wasn't going to alter that any.

Her red-gold hair spilled across her pillow like hot silk. She held the dark blue sheet to her breasts even as she slid one creamy white leg free of the covers. She made a picture that engraved itself in Justice's mind, and he knew that no matter how long he lived, he would always see her as she was right at this moment.

He also knew that this last image of her would torment him forever.

"Justice," she said, "we have to talk."

"Why?" He stood up, crossed to the chair where he'd tossed his jeans and tugged them on. A man needed his pants on when he had a conversation with Maggie King.

"Don't."

He glanced at her. "Don't what?"

"Don't shut me out. Not this time. Not now."

"I'm not doing anything, Maggie."

"That's my point." She sat up, the mattress beneath her shifting a little with her movements.

Justice turned his head to look at her, and everything in him roared at him to stalk to her side, grab her and hold her so damn tight she wouldn't have the breath to start another argument neither of them could win.

Her hair tumbled around her shoulders, and she lifted one hand to impatiently push the mass behind her shoulders. "You're not going to ask me to stay, are you?"

He shouldn't have to, Justice told himself. She was his damn wife. Why should he have to ask her to be with him? She was the one who'd left.

He didn't say any of that, though, just shook his head and buttoned the fly of his jeans. He didn't speak again until his bare feet were braced wide apart. A man could lose his balance all too easily when talking to Maggie. "What good would it do to ask you to stay? Eventually, you'd leave again."

"I wouldn't have to if you'd bend a little."

"I won't bend on this," he assured her, though it cost him as he noted the flash of pain in her eyes that was there and then gone in a blink.

"Why not?" She pushed out of the bed, dropping the sheet and facing him, naked and proud.

His body hardened instantly, despite just how many times they'd made love over the past few hours. Seemed his dick was always ready when it came to Maggie.

"We are who we are," he told her, folding his arms across his chest. "You want kids. I don't. End of story."

Her mouth worked and he knew she was struggling not to shout and rail at him. But then, Maggie's hot Irish temper was one of the things that had first drawn him to her. She blazed like a sun during an argument— standing her ground no matter who stood against her. He admired that trait even though it made him a little crazy sometimes.

"Damn it, Justice!" She stalked to the chair where she'd left her clothes and grabbed her bra and panties. Slipping them on, she shook her head and kept talking. "You're willing to give up what we have because you don't want a child?"

Irritation raced through him; he couldn't stop it. But he wasn't going to get into this argument again.

"I told you how I felt before we got married, Maggie," he reminded her, in a calm, patient tone he knew would drive her to distraction.

As expected, she whipped her hair back out of her eyes, glared at him fiercely, then picked up her pale pink blouse and put it on. While her fingers did up the buttons, she snapped, "Yes, but I just thought you didn't want kids that instant. I never thought you meant *ever.*"

"Your mistake," he said softly.

"But one you didn't bother to clear up," she countered.

"Maggie," he said tightly, "do we really have to do this again?"

"Why the hell not?" she demanded. Then pointing to the bed, she snapped, "We just spent an incredible weekend together, Justice. And you're telling me you feel *nothing?*"

He'd be a liar if he tried. But admitting what he was feeling still wouldn't change a thing. "I didn't say that."

"You didn't have to," she told him. "The very fact that you're willing to let me walk…*again*…tells me every-thing I need to know."

His back teeth ground together until he wouldn't have been surprised to find them nothing more than gritty powder in his mouth. She thought she knew him, thought she knew what he was doing and why, but she didn't have a clue. And never would, he reminded himself.

"Hell, Justice, you wouldn't back down even if you did change your mind, would you? Oh, no. Not Justice King. His pride motivates his every action—"

He inhaled deeply and folded his arms across his bare chest. "Maggie…"

She held up one hand to cut off whatever else he might say, and though he felt a kick to his own temper, he shut up and let her have her say.

"You know what? I'm sick to death of your pride, Justice. The great Justice King. Master of his Universe." She slapped both hands to her hips and lifted her chin. "You're so busy arranging the world to your specifications that there is absolutely no compromise in you."

"Why the hell should there be?" Justice took a half step toward her and stopped. Only because he knew if he got close enough to inhale her scent, he'd be lost again. He'd toss her back into the bed, bury himself inside her—and what would that solve? Not a thing. Sooner or later, they'd end up right here. Back at the fight that had finally finished their marriage.

"Because there were *two* of us in our marriage, Justice. Not just you."

"Right," he said with a brief, hard nod. He didn't like arguments. Didn't think they solved anything. If two people were far enough apart on an issue, then shouting at each other over it wasn't going to help any. But there was only just so much he was willing to take. "You want compromise? We each give a little? So how would you manage that here, Maggie? Have *half* a child?"

"Not funny at all, Justice." Maggie huffed out a breath. "You knew what family meant to me. What it still means to me."

"And you knew how I felt, too." Keeping his gaze steady and cool on hers, he said, "There's no compromise here, Maggie, and you know it. I can't give you what you want, and you can't be happy without it."

As if all the air had left her body, she slumped, the flash of temper gone only to be replaced by a well of defeat that glimmered in her eyes. And that tore at him. He hated seeing Maggie's spirit shattered. Hated even more that he was the one who'd caused it. But that couldn't be helped. Not now. Not ever.

"Fine," she said softly. "That's it, then. We end it. Again."

She picked up her slacks and put them on. Shaking her head, she zipped them up, tucked the tail of her shirt into the waistband and then stepped into her boots. Lifting her arms, she gathered up the tangle of her hair and deftly wound it into a knot at the back of her head, capturing that wild mass and hiding it away.

When she was finished, she stared at him for a long moment, and even from across the room Justice would have spared her this rehashing of the argument that had finally torn them apart. But this weekend had proven to him as nothing else ever would, that the best thing he could do for her was to step back. Let her hate him if she had to. Better for her to move the hell on with her life.

Even if the thought of her moving on to another man was enough to carve his heart right out of his chest.

Maggie picked up her purse, slung it over her shoulder and stared at him. "So, I guess the only thing left to say is thanks for the weekend."

"Maggie…"

Shaking her head again, she started walking toward the door. When she came close to him, she stopped and looked up at him. "Sign the damn divorce papers, Justice."

She took another step and he stopped her with one hand on her arm. "It's pouring down rain out there. Why don't you stay put for a while and wait out the storm before you go."

Maggie pulled her arm free of his grasp and started walking again. "I can't stay here. Not another minute. Besides, we're not a couple, Justice. You don't have the right to worry about me anymore."

A few seconds later, he heard the front door slam. Justice walked to the windows and looked down on the yard. The wind tore her hair free of its tidy knot and sent long strands of red flying about her face. She was drenched by the rain almost instantly. She climbed into the car and fired up the engine. Justice saw the headlights come on, saw the rain slash in front of those twin beams and stood there in silence as she steered the car down the drive and off the ranch.

Chest tight, he watched until her taillights disappeared into the darkness. Then he punched his fist against the window and relished the pain.

Three

Justice threw his cane across the room and listened to it hit the far wall with a satisfying clatter. He hated needing the damn thing. Hated the fact that he was less than he used to be. Hated knowing that he needed help, and he sure as hell hated having his brother here to tell him so.

He glared at Jefferson, his eldest brother, then pushed up and out of the chair he was sitting in. Justice gathered up his pride and dignity and used every ounce of his will to make sure he hobbled only a little as he lurched from the chair to the window overlooking the front yard. Sunlight splashed through the glass into the room, bathing everything in a brilliant wash of light.

Justice narrowed his eyes at his brother, and when he was no more than a foot away from him, he stopped and said, "I told you I can walk. I don't need another damn therapist."

Jefferson shook his head and stuffed both hands into the pockets of what was probably a five-thousand-dollar suit. "You are the most stubborn jackass I've ever known. And being a member of this family, that's saying something."

"Very amusing," Justice told him and oh-so-casually shot out one hand to brace himself against the log wall. His knuckles were white with the effort to support himself and take the pressure off his bad leg. But he'd be damned if he'd show that weakness to Jefferson. "Now, get out."

"That's the attitude that ended up bringing me here."

"How's that?"

"You've chased off three physical therapists in the past month, Justice."

"I didn't bring 'em here," he pointed out.

Jefferson scowled at him, then sighed. "Dude, you broke your leg in three places. You've had surgery. The bones are healed but the muscles are weak. You need a physical therapist and you damn well know it."

"Don't call me 'dude,' and I'm getting along fine."

"Yeah, I can see that." Jefferson shot a quick glance to Justice's white-knuckled grip on the wall.

"Don't you have some inane movie to make somewhere?" Justice countered. As head of King Studios, Jefferson was the man in charge of the film division of the King empire. The man loved Hollywood. Loved traveling around the world, making deals, looking for talent, scouting locations himself. He was as footloose as Justice was rooted to this ranch.

"First I'm taking care of my idiot brother."

Justice leaned a little harder against the log wall. If Jefferson didn't leave soon, Justice was going to fall on his ass. Whether he wanted to admit it aloud or not, his healing leg was still too weak to be much good. And that irritated the hell out of him.

A stupid accident had caused all of this. His horse had stumbled into a gopher hole one fine morning a few months back. Justice had been thrown clear, but then the horse rolled across his leg, shattering it but good. The horse had recovered nicely. Justice, though, was having a tougher time. After surgery, he now carried enough metal in his bones to make getting through airport security a nightmare, and his muscles were now so flabby and weak it was all he could do to force himself to move.

"It's your own damn fault you're in this fix anyway," Jefferson said, as if reading Justice's mind. "If you'd been riding in a ranch jeep instead of sitting on top of your horse, this wouldn't have happened."

"Spoken like a man who's forgotten what it was like to ride herd."

"Damn right," Jefferson told him. "I put a lot of effort into forgetting about predawn rides to round up cattle. Or having to go and find a cow so dumb it got lost on its own home ranch."

This is why Jeff was the Hollywood mogul and Justice was the man on the ranch. His brothers had all bolted from the home ranch as soon as they were old enough, each of them chasing his own dream. But Justice's dreams were all here on this ranch. Here is where he felt most alive. Here, where the clear air and the open land could let a man breathe. He didn't mind the hard work. Hell, he relished it. And his brother knew why he'd been astride a horse.

"You grew up here, Jeff," he said. "You know damn well a horse is better for getting down into the canyons. And they don't have engines that scare the cattle and cause stress that will shut down milk production for the calves, not to mention running the jeeps on the grasslands only tears them up and—"

"Save it," Jeff interrupted, holding up both hands to stave off a lecture. "I heard it all from Dad, thanks."

"Fine, then. No more ranch talk. Just answer this." Justice reached down and idly rubbed at his aching leg. "Who asked you to butt into my life and start hiring physical therapists I don't even want?"

"Actually," Jefferson answered with a grin, "Jesse and Jericho asked me to. Mrs. Carey kept us posted on the situation with the therapists, and we all want you back on your feet."

He snorted. "Yeah? Why're you the only one here, then?"

Jefferson shrugged. "You know Jesse won't leave Bella alone right now. You'd think she was the only woman in the world to ever get pregnant."

Justice nodded, distracted from the argument at the moment by thoughts of their youngest brother. "True. You know he even sent me a book? *How to Be a Great Uncle.*"

"He sent the same one to me and Jericho. Weird how he did this turnaround from wandering surfer to home-and-hearth expectant father."

Justice swallowed hard. He was glad for his brother, but he didn't want to think about Jesse's imminent fatherhood. Changing the subject, he asked, "So where's Jericho?"

"On leave," Jefferson told him. "If you'd open your e-mails once in a while, you'd know that. He's shipping out again soon, and he had some leave coming to him so he took it. He's soaking up some sun at cousin Rico's hotel in Mexico."

Jericho was a career marine. He loved the life and he was good at his job, but Justice hated that his brother was about to head back into harm's way. Why hadn't he been opening his e-mails? Truth? Because he'd been in a piss-poor mood since the accident. He should have known, though, that his brothers wouldn't just leave him alone in his misery.

"That's why you're here, then," Justice said. "You got the short straw."

"Pretty much."

"I should have been an only child," Justice muttered.

"Maybe in your next life," Jefferson told him, then pulled one hand free of his slacks pocket to check the time on his gold watch.

"If I'm keeping you," Justice answered with a bared teeth grin, "feel free to get the hell out."

"I've got time," his brother assured him. "I'm not leaving until the new therapist arrives and I can make sure you don't scare her off."

Wounded pride took a bite out of Justice and he practically snarled at his brother. "Why don't you all just leave me the hell alone? I didn't ask for your help and I don't want it. Just like I don't want these damn therapists moving in here like some kind of invasion." He winced as his leg pained him, then finished by saying, "I'm not even gonna let this one in, Jeff. So you might as well head her off."

"Oh," Jefferson told him with a satisfied smile, "I think you'll let this one stay."

"You're wrong."

The doorbell rang just then and Justice heard his housekeeper's footsteps as she hustled along the hall toward the door. Something way too close to panic for Justice's own comfort rose up inside him. He shot Jefferson a quick look and said, "Just get rid of her, all right? I don't want help. I'll get back on my feet my own way."

"You've been doing it your own way for long enough, Justice," Jefferson told him. "You can hardly stand without sweat popping out on your forehead."

From a distance, Justice heard Mrs. Carey's voice, welcoming whoever had just arrived. He made another try at convincing his brother to take his latest attempt at help and leave.

"I want to do this on my own."

"That's how you do everything, you stubborn bastard. But everybody needs help sometimes, Justice," his brother said. "Even you."

"Damn it, Jefferson—"

The sound of two women's voices rippled through the house like music, rising and falling and finally dropping into hushed whispers. That couldn't be a good sign. Already his housekeeper was siding with the new therapist. Wasn't anyone loyal anymore? Justice scraped his free hand through his hair, then scrubbed his palm across his face.

He hated feeling out of control. And ever since his accident, that sensation had only been mounting. He'd had to trust in daily reports from his ranch manager rather than going out to ride his own land. He'd had to count on his housekeeper to take care of the tasks that needed doing around here. He wanted his damn life back, and he wasn't going to get it by depending on some stranger to come in and work on his leg.

He'd regain control only if he managed to come back from his injuries on his own. If that didn't make sense to anyone but him, well, he didn't care. This was *his* life, his ranch and, by God, he was going to do things the way he always had.

His way.

He heard someone coming and shot a sidelong glance at the open doorway, preparing himself to fire whoever it was the minute she walked in. His brothers could just butt the hell out of his life.

Footsteps sounded quick and light on the wood floor, and something inside Justice tightened. He had a weird feeling. There was no explanation for it, but for some reason his gut twisted into knots. Glancing at his brother, he muttered, "Just who the hell did you hire?"

Then a too-familiar voice announced from the doorway, "Me, Justice. He hired me."

Maggie.

His gaze shot to her, taking her in all at once as a man dying of thirst would near drown himself with his first taste of water. She was wearing blue jeans, black boots and a long-sleeved, green T-shirt. She looked curvier than he remembered, more lush somehow. Her hair was a tumble of wild curls around her shoulders and framing her face with fiery, silken strands. Her blue eyes were fixed on him and her mouth was curved into a half smile.

"Surprise," she said softly.

That about covered it, he thought. Surprise. Shock. Stunned stupid.

He was going to kill Jefferson first chance he got.

But for now he had to manage to stay on his feet long enough to convince Maggie that he didn't need her help. Damn it, she was the absolute last person in the world he wanted feeling sorry for him. Lifting his chin, he narrowed his gaze on her and said, "There's been a mistake, Maggie. I don't need you here, so you can go."

She flinched—actually flinched—and Justice felt like the bastard Jefferson had called him just a moment or two ago. But it was best for her to leave right away. He didn't want her here.

"Justice," his brother said in a long-suffering sigh.

"It's okay, Jeff," Maggie said, walking into the room, head held high, pale blue eyes glinting with the light of battle. "I'm more than used to your brother's crabby attitude."

"I'm not crabby."

"No," she said with a tight smile, "you're the very soul of congenial hospitality. I just feel all warm and fuzzy inside." Then she took a hard look at him. "Why are you standing?"

"What?"

Beside him, Jeff muffled a laugh and tried to disguise it with a cough. It didn't work.

"You heard me," Maggie said, rushing across the

room. When Justice didn't move, she grumbled something unintelligible, then dragged a chair over to him. She pushed him down onto it, and it was all Justice could do to hide the relief that getting off his feet gave him. "Honestly, Justice, don't you have any sense at all? You can't put all your weight on your bad leg or you'll be flat on your back again. Why aren't you using a cane at least?"

"Don't have one," he muttered.

"He threw it across the room," Jeff provided.

"Of course he did," Maggie said. She spotted the cane, then walked to retrieve it. When she came back to his side, she thrust it at him and ordered, "If you're going to stand, you're going to use the cane."

"I don't take orders from you, Maggie," he said.

"You do now."

"In case you didn't notice the lack of welcome, I'm firing you."

"You can't fire me," she told him, leaning down to stare him dead in the eye. "Jefferson hired me. He's paying me to get you back on your feet."

"He had no right to." Justice sent his brother a hard glare, but Jefferson was rocking back and forth on his heels, clearly enjoying himself.

Maggie straightened up, fisted her hands at her hips and stared down at him with the stern look of a general about to order troops into battle. "He did hire me, though, Justice. Oh, and by the way, I've heard about the other three therapists who've come and gone from here—"

Justice looked past her to glare at his brother but looked back to Maggie again when she continued.

"—and you're not going to scare me off by throwing your cane. Or by being rude and nasty. So no need to try."

"I don't want you here."

"Yes," she said and a flicker of something sharp and sad shot through her eyes. "You've made that plain a number of times. But you can just suck it up. Because I'm here. And I'm staying. Until you can stand up without brackets of pain lining the sides of your mouth or gritting your teeth to keep from moaning. So you know what? Your best plan of action is to do exactly what I tell you to do."

"Why's that?"

"Because, Justice," she said, bracing her hands on the arms of his chair and leaning in until their faces were just a breath apart, "if you listen to me, you'll heal. And the sooner that happens, the sooner you'll get rid of me."

"Can't argue with her there," Jeff pointed out.

Justice didn't even glance at his brother. His gaze was locked with Maggie's. Her scent wafted to him like the scent of wildflowers on a summer wind. Her eyes shone with a silent challenge. Now that he was over the initial shock of seeing her walk into his life again, he could only hope to God she walked back out really soon.

Just being this close to her was torture. His body was pressing against the thick denim fabric of his jeans. Good thing she'd pushed him into a chair so damn fast or she and his brother would have been all too aware of the kind of effect she had on him.

Maggie stared into Justice's eyes and felt her heart hammer in her chest. Seeing him again was like balm to an open wound. But seeing him hurt tore at her. So she was both relieved and miserable to be here.

Yet how could she have turned down Jefferson's request that she come to the ranch and help out? Justice was still her husband. Though he probably didn't realize that. No doubt he'd never even noticed that though he had signed the divorce papers and mailed them to her, she had never filed them with the courts. Naturally, even if he had noticed, Justice would have been too stubborn to call her and find out what was going on.

And as for Maggie? Well, she had had her own reasons for keeping quiet.

Strange. The last time she'd left this ranch, she'd been determined to sever the bond between her and Justice once and for all. But that plan had died soon enough when things had changed. Her life had taken a turn she hadn't expected. Hadn't planned for. A rush of something sweet and fulfilling swept through her and Maggie almost smiled. Nothing Justice did or said could make her regret what her life was now.

In fact, that was one of the reasons she'd come to help him, she told herself. Of course she would have come anyway, because she couldn't bear the thought of Justice being in pain and needing help he didn't have. But there was more. Maggie had leaped at Jefferson's request to come to the ranch, because she'd wanted the chance to show her husband what he was missing. To maybe open his stubborn eyes to the possibilities stretched out in front of him.

Now, though, as she stood right in front of him and actually *watched* a shutter come down over his eyes, effectively blocking her out, she wondered if coming here had been the right thing to do after all.

Still, she *was* here. And since she was, she would at least get Justice back on his feet.

"So, what's it going to be, Justice?" she asked. "Going to play the tough, stoic cowboy? Or are you going to cooperate with me?"

"I didn't ask you to come," he told her, ignoring his brother standing just a foot or so away.

"Of course you didn't," Maggie retorted. "Everyone knows the great Justice King doesn't need anyone or anything. You're getting along fine, right?" She straightened up and took a step back. "So why don't you just get up out of that chair and walk me to the door."

His features tightened and his eyes flashed dangerously, and just for a second or two Maggie was half afraid he'd try to do just that and end up falling on his face. But the moment passed and he only glared at her. "Fine. You can stay."

"Wow." She placed one hand on her chest as if she were sighing in gratitude. "Thank you."

Justice glowered at her.

Jefferson cleared his throat and drew both of their gazes to him. "Well, then, looks like my work here is done. Justice, try not to be too big of an ass. Maggie," he said, moving to plant a quick kiss on her forehead, "best of luck."

Then he left and they were alone.

"Jefferson shouldn't have called you," Justice said quietly.

"Who else would he call?" Maggie looked at his white-knuckled grip on the cane he held in his right fist. He was angry, she knew. But more than that, he was frustrated. Her husband wasn't the kind of man to accept limitations in himself. Having to use a cane to support a weakened leg would gnaw at him. No wonder he was as charming as a mountain lion with its foot caught in a trap.

He blew out a breath. "I could get Mrs. Carey to throw you out."

Maggie laughed shortly. "She wouldn't do it. She likes me. Besides, you need me."

"I don't need your help or your pity. I can do this on my own."

A flare of indignation burst into life inside her. "That is so typical, Justice. You go through your life self-sufficient and expecting everyone else to do the same. Do it yourself or don't do it. That's your style."

"Nothing wrong with that," he argued. "A man's got to stand on his own."

"Why?" She threw both hands high and let them fall. "Why does it always have to be your way? Why can't you see that everyone needs someone else at *some* point?"

"I don't," he told her.

"Oh, no, not you. Not Justice King. You never ask for help. Never admit to needing anyone or anything. Heck, you've never even said the word *please*."

"Why the hell should I?" he demanded.

"You're a hard man," Maggie said.

"Best you remember that."

"Fine. I'll remember." She stepped up close to him, helped him up from the chair despite his resistance and when he was standing, looked him dead in the eye and said, "As long as *you* remember that if you want to get your life back, you're going to have to take orders from me for a change."

Late that night Justice lay alone in the bed he used to share with his wife. He was exhausted, in pain and furious. He didn't want Maggie looking at him and seeing a patient. Yet, all afternoon she'd been with him, taking notes on his progress, telling him what he'd been doing wrong and then massaging his leg muscles with an impersonal competence that tore at him.

Every time she'd touched him, his body had reacted. He hadn't been able to hide his erection, but she'd ignored it—which infuriated him. It was as if he meant nothing to her. As if this were just a job.

Which it probably was.

Hell, what did he expect? They were divorced.

Grabbing the phone off the nightstand, he stabbed in a number from memory and waited impatiently while it rang. When his brother answered, Justice snapped, "Get her out of my house."

"No."

"Damn it, Jefferson," Justice raged quietly with a quick look at the closed door of his bedroom. For all he knew Maggie or Mrs. Carey was out wandering the hall, and he didn't want to be overheard. Which was the only thing that kept his voice low. "I don't want her here. I made my peace with her leaving, and having her here again only makes everything harder."

"Too bad," Jefferson shot back. "Justice, you need help whether you want to admit it or not. Maggie's a great therapist and you know it. She can get you back on your feet if you'll just swallow your damn pride and do what she tells you."

Justice hung up on his brother, but that didn't make him feel any better. *Swallow his pride?* Hell, his pride was all he had. It had gotten him through some tough times—watching Maggie walk out of his life, for instance—and damned if he was going to let it go now, when he needed it the most.

He scooted off the edge of the bed, too filled with frustration to try to sleep anyway. He could watch the flat-screen television he'd had installed a year ago, but he was too keyed up to sit still for a movie and too pissed off already to watch the news.

Disgusted by the need for it, Justice reached for his cane and pried himself off the mattress, using the thickly carved oak stick for balance. His injured leg ached like a bad tooth, and that only served to feed the irritation already clawing at his insides. Shaking his head, he hobbled toward the window but stopped dead when he heard…something.

Frowning, he turned toward the doorway and the hall beyond. He waited for that noise to come again, and when it did, his scowl deepened. What the hell?

He made his way to the door, flung it open and stood on the threshold, glancing up and down the hallway. The wall sconces were lit, throwing golden light over the narrow, dark red-and-green carpet, which lay like a path down the polished oak floors. The hallway was empty, and yet…

There it was again.

Sounded like a cat mewling. Justice moved toward

the sound with slow, uncertain steps. Just one more reason to hate his damn cane and his own leg for betraying him. A few months ago he'd have stalked down this hallway with long strides. Now he was reduced to an ungainly stagger.

He followed the sound to the last door at the end of the hallway. The room Maggie was to stay in while she was on the ranch. At least he'd been able to order *that* much. He'd wanted her as far from his bedroom as possible to avoid the inevitable temptation.

Outside her door he cocked his head and listened. The house made its usual groaning noises as night settled in and the temperature dropped. Seconds ticked past and then he heard it again. That soft, wailing sound that he couldn't quite place. Was she crying? Missing him? Regretting coming to the ranch?

He should knock, he told himself. But if he did and she told him to go away, he'd have to. So instead, Justice turned the knob, threw open the door and felt the world fall out from beneath his feet.

Maggie.

Holding a baby.

She looked up at him and smiled. "Hello, Justice. I'd like you to meet Jonas. My son."

Four

"What? Who? How? What?" Justice jolted back a step, hit the doorjamb and simply stared at the woman and baby on the wide, king-size bed.

Maggie's gaze locked on his as she answered his questions in order. "My son. Jonas. The usual way. And again, my son."

Pain like Justice had never known before shot through him with a swiftness that stole his breath and nearly knocked him off his feet.

Maggie had a son.

Which meant she had a lover.

She was with someone else.

Everything in him went cold and hard. Amazing, really, how big the pain was. He'd told himself he was over her. Assured himself that their marriage was done and that it was for the best. For both of them. Yet now, when he was slapped with the proof that what they'd shared was over, the sharp stab of regret was hard enough to steal his breath. The thought of Maggie lying in another man's arms almost killed him. But then, what had he expected? That they'd get a divorce and she'd join a convent? Not his Maggie. She had too much fire.

Clearly, it hadn't taken her too long to move on. Her son looked to be several months old, which meant that she'd rolled out of his bed into someone else's real damn fast. Which made him wonder whether she'd been involved with someone else already when they'd had that last weekend together. That thought chewed on Justice, too. All the time they'd been rolling around in his bed, she'd had another guy waiting for her? What the hell was up with that?

He wanted to shout. To rage. But he didn't. He locked up everything inside him and refused to let her see that he was affected at all. Damned if he'd give her the satisfaction of knowing that she still had the power to cut him.

He had his pride, after all.

"Not going to say anything else?" she asked, swinging her legs off the bed and lifting the baby to sit at her hip.

He wiped one hand across his whiskered jaw and fought for indifference. "What do you want me to say? Congratulations? Fine. I said it." His gaze stayed locked on hers. He wouldn't look at the chubby-cheeked infant making insensible noises and gurgles.

"Don't you want to know who his father is?" she asked, moving closer with small, deliberate steps.

Why the hell was she doing this? Did she really enjoy

rubbing the fact of her new relationship in his face? He hoped she was enjoying the show because, yeah, he did want to know. Then he wanted to find the guy and beat the crap out of him. But that wasn't going to happen. "None of my business, is it?"

"Actually, yes," she said, turning her head to plant a kiss on the baby's brow before looking back at Justice. "It sort of is. Especially since *you're* his father."

Another jolt went through Justice, and he wondered idly how many lightning strikes a man could survive in one night. Whatever game she was trying to run wouldn't work. She didn't have any way of knowing it, of course, but there was no possible way he was that baby's father.

So why the hell would she lie? Was the real father not interested in his kid? Is that why Maggie sought to convince Justice that he was the father instead? Or was it about money? Maybe she was trying to get some child support out of this. That would be stupid, though. All it would take was a paternity test and they'd all know the truth.

Maggie wasn't a fool. Which brought him right back to the question at hand.

What was she up to?

And why?

He stared at her, reading a challenge in her eyes. He still couldn't bring himself to look at the child. It was there, though, in his peripheral vision. A babbling, chortling statement on Justice's failure as a husband and Maggie's desire for family, provided by some other guy.

Pain grabbed at him again, making the constant ache

in his leg seem like nothing more substantial than a stubbed toe.

"Nice try," he said, fixing his gaze on her with a cold distance he hoped was easily read.

"What's that mean?"

"It means, Maggie, I'm *not* his father, so don't bother trying to pawn him off on me."

"Pawn him—" She stopped speaking, gulped in air and tightened her hold on the baby, who was slapping tiny fists against her shoulder. "That's not what I'm trying to do."

"Really?" Justice swallowed past the knot in his throat and managed to give her a tight smile that was more of a baring of his teeth than anything else. "Then why is he here?"

"Because I am, you dolt!" Maggie took another step closer to him, and Justice forced himself to hold his ground. With the weakness in his leg, if he tried to step back, he might just go down on his ass, and wouldn't that be a fine end to an already spectacular day?

"I'm his mother," Maggie told him. "He goes where I go. And I thought maybe his daddy would like a look at him."

One more twist of the knife into his gut. He hadn't been able to give her the one thing she'd really wanted from him. Now seeing her with the child she used to dream of was torture. Especially since she was looking into his eyes and lying.

"I'm not buying it, Maggie, so just drop it, all right? I'm not that kid's father. I'm not anybody's father. So why the song and dance?"

"How can you know you're not?" she argued, clearly willing to stick to whatever game plan she'd had in mind when she got here. "Look at Jonas. Look at him! He has your eyes, Justice. He has your hair. Heck, he's even as stubborn as you are."

As if to prove her point, the baby gave up slapping at her shoulder for attention, reached out and grabbed hold of Maggie's gold, dangling earring. He gave it a tug, squealing in a high-pitched tone that made Justice wince. Gently, Maggie pried that tiny fist off her earring and gave her son a bright smile.

"Don't pull, sweetie," she murmured, and her son cooed at her in delight.

That softness in her voice, the love shining in her eyes, got to him as nothing else could have. Justice swallowed hard and finally forced himself to look at the child. Bright red cheeks, sparkling dark blue eyes and a thatch of black hair. He wore a diaper and a black T-shirt that read Cowboy in Training and was waving and kicking his chubby arms and legs.

Something inside him shifted. If he and Maggie had been able to have children, this is just what he would have expected their child to look like. Maybe that's why she thought her ploy would work on him. The kid looked enough like Justice that she probably thought she could convince him he was the father and then talk him out of a paternity test.

Sure. Why would she think he'd insist on that anyway? They had been married. The timing for the child was about right. She'd have no reason to think that he wouldn't believe her claims. But that meant that whoever had fathered the boy had turned his back on them. Which, weirdly, pissed him off on Maggie's behalf. What the hell kind of man would do that to her? Or to the baby? Who wouldn't claim his own child?

He watched the boy bouncing up and down on Maggie's hip, laughing and drooling, and told himself that if there were even the slightest chance the boy was actually his, Justice would do everything in his power to take care of him. But he knew the truth, even if Maggie didn't.

"He's a good-looking boy."

Maggie melted. "Thank you."

"But he's not mine."

She wanted to argue. He could see it in her face. Hell, he knew her well enough to know that there was nothing Maggie liked more than a good argument. But this one she'd lose before she even started.

He couldn't be Jonas's father. Ten years before, Justice had been in a vicious car accident. His injuries were severe enough to keep him in a hospital for weeks. And during his stay and the interminable testing that was done, a doctor had told him that the accident had left him unlikely to ever father children.

The doctor had used all sorts of complicated medical terms to describe his condition, but the upshot was that Jonas couldn't be his. Maggie had no way of knowing that, of course, since Justice had never told anyone about the doctor's prognosis. Not even his brothers.

Before he and Maggie got married, when she started talking about having a family, he'd told her that he didn't want kids. Better to let her believe he chose to remain childless rather than have her think he was less than a man.

His spine stiffened as that thought scuttled through his brain. He hadn't told her the truth then and he wouldn't now. Damned if he'd see a flash of pity in her eyes for him. Bad enough that she was here to see him struggle to do something as simple as *walk*.

"So who were you with, Maggie?" he asked, his voice a low and dark hum. "Why didn't he want his kid?"

"I was with *you,* you big jerk," she said tightly. "I didn't tell you about the baby before because I assumed from everything you'd said that you wouldn't want to know."

"What's changed, then?" he asked.

"I'm here, Justice. I came here to help you. And I decided that no matter what, you had the right to know about Jonas."

If it were possible, Maggie would have said that Justice's features went even harder. But what was harder than stone? His eyes were flat and dark. His jaw was clenched. He was doing what he always had done. Shutting down. Shutting her out. But why?

Yes, she knew he'd said he didn't want children, but she'd been so sure that the moment he saw his son, he'd feel differently. That Jonas would melt away his father's reservations about having a family.

She'd even, in her wildest fantasies, imagined Justice admitting he was wrong for the first time in his life. In her little dream world, Justice had taken one look at his son, then begged Maggie's forgiveness and asked her to stay, to let them be a family. She should have known better. "Idiot."

"I'm not an idiot," he told her.

"I wasn't talking to you," she countered. He was so close to her and yet so very far away.

The house was quiet, tucked in for the night. Outside the windows was the moonlit darkness, the ever-present sea wind blowing, rattling the windowpanes and sending tree branches scratching against the roof.

Justice stood not a foot from her, close enough that she felt the heat of his body reaching out for her. Close enough that she wanted to lean into him and touch him as she'd wanted to during the therapeutic massage she'd given him earlier.

Instantly, warmth spiraled through her as she remembered his response to her hands moving on the weakened muscles in his leg. His erection hadn't been weak, though, and hadn't been easy to ignore, especially since being near him only made her want the big dummy more than ever.

"Look," Justice muttered, breaking the spell holding Maggie in place, "I'm willing to do the therapy routine. I don't like it, but I need to get back on my feet. If you can help with that, great. But if you staying here is gonna work, you're going to have to drop all of this crap about me being your baby's father. I don't want to hear it again."

"So you want me to lie," she said.

"I want you to stop lying."

"Fine. No lies. You are Jonas's father."

He gritted his teeth and muttered, "Damn it, Maggie!"

"Don't you swear in front of my son." She glanced at Jonas and though he was only six months old, she could see that he was confused and worried about what was happening. His big eyes looked watery, and his lower lip trembled as if he were getting ready to let a wail loose.

Justice barked out a harsh laugh. "You think he understood that?"

She glanced at the baby's big blue eyes, so much like his father's, and stroked a fingertip along his jaw soothingly. "I think he understands tone," she said quietly. "And I don't want you using that tone in front of him."

He blew out a breath, scowled ferociously for a second, then said, "Fine. I won't cuss in front of the kid. But you quit playing games."

"I'm not playing."

"You're doing something, Maggie, and I can tell you now, it's not going to work."

She stared up at him and shook her head. "I knew you were stubborn, Justice, but I never imagined you could be *this* thick-headed."

"And I never figured you for a cheat." He turned and started to painstakingly make his way out of the room into the hall.

Just for a second she watched him walk away and her heart ached at the difficulty he had. Seeing a man as strong and independent as Justice leaning on a cane tore at her. His injuries weren't permanent, but she knew what it was costing his pride to haltingly move away from her.

But though she felt for him, she wasn't about to let him get away with what he'd just said.

"*Cheat? A cheat?*" Maggie inhaled sharply, cast another guilty glance at her son and gave him a smile she didn't feel. She wouldn't upset her baby for the sake of a man who was so blind he couldn't see the truth when it was staring him in the face. "I am not a cheat or a liar, Justice King."

He didn't look back at her. He just kept moving awkwardly down the hall, his cane tapping against the floor runner. If his plan was to escape her, he'd have to be able to move a lot faster than that, Maggie told herself. Quickly, she walked down the hall, stepped out in front of him and forced him to stop.

"Get out of the way," he murmured, staring past her, down the hall at his open bedroom door.

"You can think whatever you like of me, but you will, by God, not ignore me," she told him, and the fact that he kept avoiding meeting her eyes only further infuriated her. This had so not gone the way she'd hoped and expected.

When Jefferson called her, asking her to come help Justice, she'd taken it as a sign. That this was the way they would come together again. That the time was finally right for Justice to meet the son he didn't know about. Apparently, she had been wrong.

"Are you too cowardly to even look at me?" she demanded, knowing that the charge of coward would get his attention.

Instantly, he turned his dark blue gaze on her and she saw carefully banked anger simmering up from their depths. Well, good. At least he was feeling *something*.

"Don't push me, Maggie. For both our sakes. If you want me to watch my tone around your son, then don't you push me."

He was furious—she could see that. But beyond the anger there was hurt. And that tore at her. He didn't have to be hurt, darn it. She was offering him their son, not the plague.

"Justice," she said softly, smoothing one hand up and down her baby's back, "you know me better than anyone. You know I wouldn't lie to you about this. You are my son's father."

He snorted.

Insulted and stung by his obvious distrust, she stepped back from him. How could he believe that she was lying? How could he have ever claimed to love her and *not* know that she was incapable of trying to trick him in this way? What the hell kind of a husband was he, anyway?

"I'm trying to be understanding," she said, but her temper simmered just beneath the words. "I know this is probably all a surprise."

"You could say that."

"But I'm not going to say it to you again. I won't argue. I won't force you to admit your responsibilities—"

"I always face my responsibilities, Maggie. You should know that."

"And you should know I'm not a liar."

He blew out a breath, cocked his head to one side and stared into her eyes. "So what? We call it a draw? A standoff? An armed truce?"

"Call it whatever you want, Justice," Maggie said, before he could say something else that would hurt her. "All I'm going to say is that if you don't believe me about Jonas, then it's your loss, Justice. We created a beautiful, healthy son together. And I love him enough for both of us."

"Maggie…"

She placed one hand on the back of her son's head, holding him to her tenderly. "And in case you were wondering why I waited until now to tell you about Jonas... It's because I was worried about how you'd react." She laughed shortly, sharply. "Imagine that. Wonder why?"

He muttered something under his breath, and judging by the expression on his face, she was just as happy she'd missed it.

"The sad truth is, Justice, I never wanted my son to know that his own father hadn't wanted him."

His eyes went colder, harder than before, and Maggie shivered a little under his direct gaze. A second passed, then two, and neither of them spoke. The hall light was soft and golden, throwing delicate shadows around the wide, empty passage. They were alone in the world, the three of them, with an invisible and apparently impenetrable wall separating Maggie and her son from the man who should have welcomed them with open arms.

At last, Justice turned his gaze to the boy who was watching him curiously. Maggie watched her husband's features soften briefly before freezing up into that hardened, take-no-prisoners expression she knew so well. After several long moments he lifted his gaze to hers, and when he spoke, his voice was so soft she had to hold her breath to hear him.

"You're wrong, Maggie. If I *was* his father, I would want him."

Then he brushed past her, the tip of his cane making a muffled thumping sound as he made his way to his room. He didn't look back.

And that nearly broke Maggie's heart.

Five

"Run the calves and their mamas to the seaward pasture," Justice told Phil, his ranch manager, three days later. "You can leave the young bulls in the canyons for now. Keep them away from the heifers as much as you can."

"I know, boss." Phil turned the brim of his hat between his hands as he stood opposite the massive desk in Justice's study.

Phil was in his early fifties, with a tall, lanky body that belied his strength. He was a no-BS kind of guy who knew his job and loved the ranch almost as much as his boss. Phil's face was tanned as hard and craggy as leather from years spent in the sun. His forehead, though, was a good two shades lighter than the rest of him, since his hat was usually on and pulled down low.

He shifted uneasily from foot to foot, as if eager to get outside and back on his horse.

"We've got most of the herd settled into their pastures now," he said. "There was a fence break in the north field, but two of the boys are out there now fixing it."

"Okay." Justice tapped a pen against the top of his desk and tried to focus the useless energy burning inside him. Sitting behind a desk was making him itchy. If things were as they should be, he'd be out on his own horse right now. Making sure things were getting done to his specifications. Justice wasn't a man to sit inside and order his people around. He preferred having his hand in everything that went on at King Ranch.

Phil Hawkins was a good manager, but he wasn't the boss.

Yet even as he thought it, Justice knew he was lying to himself. His itchy feeling had nothing to do with not trusting his crew. It was all about how he hated being trapped in the damn house. Now more than ever.

The past few days, he'd felt as if he was being stalked. Maggie was following him around, insisting on therapy sessions or swims in the heated pool or nagging at him to use the damn cane he'd come to hate. Hell, he'd had to sneak away just to get a few minutes alone in his office to go over ranch business with Phil.

Everywhere he went, it seemed, there was Maggie. Back in the day, they'd have been falling into each other's arms every other minute. But nothing was as it had once been. These days, she looked at him as if he were just another patient to her. Someone to feel bad for. To fix up. To take care of.

Well, he didn't need taking care of. Or if he did, he'd never admit it. He didn't want her being *paid* to be here. Didn't want to be her latest mission. Her cause. Didn't want her touching him with indifference.

That angry thought flashed through his mind at the same time a twinge of pain sliced at his leg. Damn thing was near useless. And three days of Maggie's torture hadn't brought him any closer to healing and getting on with his life. Instead, she seemed to be settling in. Making herself comfortable in the log house that used to be her home.

She was sliding into the rhythm of ranch life as if she'd never left it. She was up with the dawn every day and blast if it didn't seem she was deliberately close enough to him every morning so that Justice heard her talking to her son. Heard the baby's nonsensical prattle and cooing noises. Could listen in on what he wasn't a part of.

She was everywhere. Her or the baby. Or both. He heard her laughing with Mrs. Carey, smelled her perfume in every room of the house and caught her playing with her son on several occasions. She and the baby had completely taken over his house.

There were toys scattered everywhere, a walker with bells, whistles and electronic voices singing out an alphabet song. There was a squawking chicken, a squeaky dog and a teddy bear with a weird, tinny voice that sang songs about sharing and caring. Hell, coming down the stairs this morning, he'd almost killed himself when his cane had come down on a ball with a clown's face stamped on it. There were cloth books, cardboard books and diapers stashed everywhere just in case the kid needed a change. That boy had to go through a hundred of them a day. And what was with all the books? It was not as if the baby could read.

"Uh, boss?"

"What?" Justice shook his head, rubbed at his aching leg and shifted his gaze back to Phil. That woman was now sneaking into his thoughts so that he couldn't even *talk* about ranch business. "Sorry," he said. "My mind wandered. What?"

Phil's lips twitched as if he knew where his boss's mind had slipped off to. But he was smart enough not to say anything. "The new grasses in the east field are coming in fine, just like you said they would. Looks like a winner to me."

"That's good news," Justice said absentmindedly. They'd replanted one of the pastures with a hardier stock of field grass, and if it held up to its hype, then the herd would have something to look forward to in a few months.

Running an organic cattle ranch was more work, but Justice was convinced it was worth it in the long run. The cowboys he had working for him spent most of their time switching the cattle around to different pastures, keeping the grass fresh and the animals on the move. His cows didn't stand in dirty stalls to be force-fed grains. King cattle roamed open fields as they'd been meant to.

Cattle weren't born to eat corn, for God's sake. They were grazers. And keeping his herds moving across natural field grasses made the meat more tender and sweet and brought higher prices from the consumer. He had almost sixty thousand acres of prime grassland here on the coast and another forty thousand running alongside his cousin Adam's ranch in central California.

Justice had made the change over to natural grazing and organic ranching nearly ten years ago, as soon as he took over the day-to-day running of King Ranch. His father hadn't put much stock in it, but Justice had been determined to run the outfit his way. And in that time, he'd been able to expand and even open his own online beef operation.

He only wished his father had lived to see what he'd made of the place. But his parents had died in the same accident that had claimed Justice's chances of ever making his own family. So he had to content himself with knowing that he'd made a success of the family spread and that his father would have been proud.

"Oh, and we got another offer on Caleb," Phil was saying, and Justice focused on the man.

"What was it?"

"Thirty-five thousand."

"No," Justice told him. "Caleb's too valuable a stud to let him go for that. If the would-be buyer wants to pay for calves out of Caleb, we'll do that. But we're not selling our top breeding bull."

Phil grinned. "That's what I told him."

Some of Justice's competitors were more convinced it was his breeding stock that made his cattle so much better than others, and they were continually trying to buy bulls. They were either too stupid or too lazy to realize that fresh calves weren't going to change anything. To get the results Justice had, they were going to have to redo their operations completely.

The door to the study swung open after a perfunctory knock, and both men turned to look. Maggie stood in the open doorway. Faded jeans clung to her legs and the King Cattle T-shirt she wore in bright blue made her eyes shine like sapphires. She gave Phil a big smile. "You guys finished?"

"Yes, ma'am," Phil said.

"No," Justice said.

His ranch manager winced a little as he realized that he'd blown things for his boss.

Maggie looked at her husband. "Which is it? Yes or no?"

Frowning, Justice scowled at his foreman, silently calling him *traitor*. Phil just shrugged, though, as if to say it was too late now.

"We're finished for the time being," Justice reluctantly admitted.

"Good. Time for your exercises," Maggie told him, walking into the room and heading for his desk.

"Then I'll just go—" Phil waved his hat in the direction of the door "—back to work." He nodded at her. "Maggie, good to see you."

"You, too," she said, giving the other man the kind of brilliant smile that Justice hadn't seen directed at him in far too long.

"He hasn't changed at all," Maggie mused.

"You haven't been gone that long."

"Funny," she said, "feels like a lifetime to me."

"I guess it would." Justice didn't want her in here.

This was his office. His retreat. The one room in the whole place that hadn't been colored by her scent. By her presence. But it was too late now.

As she wandered the room, running her fingertips across the leather spines of the books in the shelves, he told himself that from now on, he'd see her here. He'd feel her here. He'd be able to close his eyes and imagine her with him, the sound of her voice, the sway of her hips, the way the sunlight through the window made her hair shine like a fire at midnight.

Squirming uncomfortably in his chair now, Justice said, "You know, if you don't mind, I've got some paperwork to catch up on. Things pile up if you don't stay on top of them. Think I'll skip the exercises this morning."

She gave him the sort of smile she would have given a little boy trying to get away with cutting school. "I don't think so. But if you want, we can change things up a little. Instead of a half hour on the treadmill, we could walk around the ranch yard."

Sounded like a plan to him. He hated that damn treadmill with a raging passion. What the hell good was it, when a man had the whole world to walk in? Who would choose to walk on a conveyor belt? And if she didn't have him on that treadmill, she had him doing lunges and squats, with his back up against the wall. He felt like a lab rat, moving from one maze to the next. Always inside. Always moving and getting exactly nowhere.

The thought of getting outside was a blessing. Outside. Into the air, where her perfume would get lost in the wind rather than clinging to every breath he took. "Fine."

He pushed up from his black leather chair, and as he

stepped around the edge of the desk, Maggie approached and held out his cane. He took it, his fingers brushing against hers just enough to kindle a brand-new fire in his gut. He pulled back, tightened his grip on the head of the blasted cane and started for the door.

"You're walking easier," she noted.

Irritation spiked inside him. He remembered a time when she had watched his ass for a different reason. "Yeah," he admitted. "It still hurts like a bitch, but maybe it's a little better."

"Wow. Quite the compliment to my skills."

He stopped and turned to look at her. "Maybe I'm doing well enough to just cut the therapy short."

"Ooh, good effort," she said and walked past him toward the front door.

Now it was his turn to watch her ass, and he for damn sure wasn't doing it to check out her ability to walk. Then something struck him: the fact that she didn't have her son on her hip. "Uh, don't you have to watch…"

"Jonas?" she provided.

"Yeah."

"Mrs. Carey has him. She loves watching him," Maggie said, striding down the hall to the front door. Her boots, which clacked against the wood floor, sounded like a quickening heartbeat. "Says he reminds her so much of you it's almost eerie."

Justice scowled at her back. She managed to get one or two of those pointed digs in every day. Trying to make him see something that wasn't there. A connection between her son and him.

He should just tell her, he thought, snatching his

battered gray felt hat off the hook by the door. Tell her that he was sterile and be done with it. Then she could stop playing whatever game she was playing and he wouldn't have to put up with any of this anymore.

But if he did that, she'd know. Know everything. Why he'd let her go. Why he'd lied. Why he felt less than a man because he hadn't been able to give her the one thing she'd wanted. And, damn it, once he told her the truth, she'd feel sorry for him—and he couldn't stand that. Better for him if she thought him a bastard.

Maggie listened to the uncertain steps of her husband coming up behind her and stopped on the porch to wait for him. She took that moment to admire the sweep of land stretching out in front of her. She'd missed this place almost as much as she'd missed Justice. The wide yard was neatly tended, the flower beds were spilling over with bright, colorful blossoms and from somewhere close by, the lowing of a cow sounded almost like a song.

Just for a second or two, all of Maggie's thoughts and worries drifted away, just drained out of her system as if they'd never been there. She took a deep breath of the sweet air and smiled at two herd dogs, a mutt and a Lab, chasing each other across the front yard. Then she sensed Justice coming up behind her, and in an instant tension coiled deep in the pit of her stomach.

She would always sense him. Always be aware of him on a deep, cellular level. He touched something inside her that no one else ever had. And when they were apart, she felt his absence keenly. But feeling connected to a man who clearly didn't share the sentiment was just a recipe for disaster.

"It's really beautiful," she whispered.

"It is."

His deep voice rumbled along her spine and tingled through her system. Why did it have to be *him* who did this to her? she wondered and glanced over her shoulder at him. He wasn't looking at the ranch; he was watching her, and her knees went a little wobbly. Maggie had to lock them just to keep upright. The man's eyes should be illegal. His smile was even more lethal—thank heaven she didn't see it often.

"You used to love it here," he said quietly, letting his gaze slide from her to where the dogs chased each other in dizzying circles.

"I did," she admitted and took a deep breath.

From the moment she had first seen this ranch, it had felt like home to her. As if it had only been waiting for her to arrive, the ranch had welcomed her. Maggie had always been amazed that she could stand on her porch and feel as though she were in the middle of the country, when in reality the city was just a short freeway ride away.

Here on the King Ranch it was as if time had not exactly stood still but at least had taken a break, slowed down. She'd always thought this would be a perfect place for her children to grow up. She'd imagined watching four or five King kids racing through the yard laughing, running to her and Justice for hugs and kisses and growing up learning to care for the ranch as much as their father did.

But those dreams had died the night she'd left Justice so many months ago.

Now she was nothing more than a barely tolerated visitor, and Jonas would never know what it was like to grow up among his father's memories.

Or to grow up with his father's love.

Justice was deliberately closing himself off from not only her but also the child they'd made together. That was something she couldn't forgive. Or understand. Justice had always been a hard man, but he was also a man devoted to family. To his brothers and the King heritage. So how could he turn his back on his own son?

In the past three days, Justice had done everything in his power to avoid so much as being in the same room with Jonas. Her heart twisted painfully in her chest, but she wouldn't *force* him to care, even if she could. Because then his love wouldn't mean a thing. To her or her son. So she would be professional and keep her emotions tightly leashed if it killed her.

"Loving this place didn't keep you here," he pointed out unnecessarily.

"No, it didn't," she said. "It couldn't."

He shook his head and frowned, squinting out from beneath the brim of his hat. "It could have. You chose to leave."

"I'm not going over that same old argument again, Justice."

"Me neither," he said with a shrug. "I'm just reminding you."

Maggie inhaled slowly, deeply. She told herself to bank her temper, to not let him get to her. It wasn't easy, especially since Justice had always known exactly which of her buttons to push to get a reaction. But as satisfying as it would be to shout and rage and give in to her frustration by telling him just what she was thinking, it wouldn't do a darn bit of good.

"We should walk." She spoke up fast, before her temper could override her more rational side. Then she turned to offer him her arm so she could assist him getting down the short flight of steps leading from the porch to the yard.

Instantly, he scowled at her and stepped around her, the tip of his cane slamming down onto the porch. "I'm not completely helpless, Maggie. I can get around without holding on to your arm. You're half my size."

"And trained to help ambulatory patients get around. I'm stronger than I look, Justice. You should remember that."

He shot her one hard, stony glare. "I'm not one of your patients, damn it."

"Well, yeah," she countered, feeling the first threads of her patience begin to unravel, "technically, you are."

"I don't want to be—don't you get that?"

She felt the cold of his stare slice right into her, but Maggie had practice in facing down his crab-ass attitude. "Yes, Justice. I get it. Despite the great trouble you've taken in trying to hide how you feel about me being here, I get it."

His mouth flattened into a grim line, and she glared right back at him.

"You still won't leave, though, will you?"

"No. I won't. Not until you're on the mend."

"I am mending."

"Not fast enough and you know it. So suck it up and let's get the job done, all right?"

"Stubbornest damn woman I've ever known," he muttered darkly and, using his cane to take most of his weight, took the steps to the drive. The minute his feet hit the drive, both ranch dogs stopped their playing, leaped up, ears perked, then with yips of delight, charged at him.

"Oh, for heaven's sake." Maggie jumped out in front of him to keep the too-exuberant dogs from crashing into Justice and bowling him right over, but it wasn't necessary.

"Angel. Spike." Justice's voice was like thunder, and when he snapped his fingers, both dogs instantly obeyed. As one, they skidded to a stop and dropped to the ground, their chins on their front paws as they looked up at him.

Maggie laughed in spite of herself. Going down on one knee, she petted each of the dogs in turn, then looked up at the man watching her. "I'd forgotten just how good you were at that. The dogs always did listen to you."

One corner of his mouth quirked briefly. "Too bad I could never get you to do the same."

Straightening up, Maggie met his gaze. "I never was the kind of woman to jump at the snap of your fingers, Justice. Not for you, not for anyone."

"Wouldn't have had you jump," he told her.

"Really. And what command would you have had me follow if you could?"

He shifted his gaze from hers, looked toward the barn and the pastures beyond and said softly, "Stay."

Six

A ping of regret echoed inside Maggie at his statement, sending out ripples of reaction like the energy released when a tuning fork was struck. Her entire body seemed to ache as she watched him walk away, keeping his gaze averted.

"You would have told me to stay?" she repeated, hearing the break in her own voice and hating it. "How can you say that to me now?"

He didn't answer her, just kept walking slowly, carefully. The only sign of his own emotions being engaged was how tightly he held on to his cane. Maggie's back teeth ground together. The man was just infuriating. She could tell that he was regretting what he had said, but that was just too bad for him.

The first time she'd walked away from him and their

marriage, it had nearly ripped her heart out of her chest. He hadn't said a word to her. He'd watched her go, and she'd felt then that he hadn't really cared. She'd told herself through her tears that clearly their marriage hadn't been everything she'd thought it was. That the dream of family she was giving up on had been based in her own fantasies, not reality.

She'd thought that Justice couldn't possibly have loved her as much as she loved him. Not if he could let her go without a word.

Then months later, they shared that last weekend together—and created Jonas—and still, he'd let her go. He'd stayed crouched behind his walls and locked away whatever he was thinking or feeling. He'd simply shot down her dreams again and dismissed her.

And even then she hadn't been able to file the signed divorce papers when he'd returned them to her. Instead, she'd tucked them away, gone through her pregnancy, delivered their son and waited. Hoping that Justice would come to her.

Naturally, he hadn't.

"How could you do it?" she whispered and thought she saw his shoulders flinch. "How could you let me leave when you wanted me to stay? Why, Justice? You didn't say a *word* to me when I left. Either time."

He stopped dead and even the cool wind sliding in off the ocean seemed to still. The dogs went quiet and it felt as if the world had taken a breath and held it.

"What was there to say?" His jaw tightened and he bit off each word as if it tasted bitter.

"You could have asked me to stay."

"No," he said, heading once more for the barn. "I couldn't."

Maggie sighed and walked after him, measuring her steps to match his more halting ones. Of course he couldn't ask her to stay, she thought.

"Oh, no, not you. Not Justice King," she grumbled and kicked at the dirt. "Don't want anyone to know you're actually capable of feeling something."

He stopped again and this time he turned his head to look at her. "I feel plenty, Maggie," he said. "You should know that better than anyone."

"How can I know that, Justice?" She threw her hands high, then let them fall to her sides again. "You won't tell me what you're thinking. You never did. We laughed, we made love but you never let me *inside,* Justice. Not once."

Something in his dark blue eyes flashed. "You got in. You just didn't stay long enough to notice."

Had she? She couldn't be sure. In the beginning of their marriage, it was all heat and fire. They hadn't been able to keep their hands off each other. They took long rides, they spent lazy rainy days in bed and Maggie would have told anyone who had asked that she and Justice were truly happy.

But, God knew, it hadn't taken much to shake the foundations of what they'd shared, so how real could any of it have been?

Her shoulders slumped as she watched him continue on to the barn. He held himself straighter, taller, as if knowing she'd be watching and not wanting to look anything but his usual, strong self. How typical was that, Maggie thought.

Justice King never admitted weakness. He'd always been a man unable to ask for anything—not even for help if he needed it—because he would never acknowledge needing assistance in the first place. He was always so self-reliant that it was nearly a religion to him. She'd known that from the beginning of their relationship, and still she wished things had been different.

But if wishes were horses, as the old saying went…

Maggie was shaken and not too proud to admit it, at least to herself. Pushing her turbulent thoughts to a back corner of her mind to be examined later, she took a deep breath, forced some lightheartedness into her voice and quickly changed the subject.

"So," she asked, glancing back at the two dogs trotting behind them, "why are Angel and Spike here instead of out with the herd?"

There was a pause before he answered, as if he were grateful for the reprieve.

"We're training two new dogs to help out," he said. "Phil thought it best to give these two a couple days off while the new pups are put through their paces."

She'd been a rancher's wife long enough to know the value of herd dogs. When the dogs worked the cattle, they could get into tight places a cowboy and his horse couldn't. The right dog could get a herd moving and keep it moving while never scaring the cattle into a stampede, which could cause injury both to cowboys and to herd. These dogs were well trained and were spoiled rotten by the cowboys, as she remembered. She'd teased Justice once that apparently sheepherders had been right about using dogs in their work and that finally ranchers had caught on.

She smiled, remembering how Justice had reacted—chasing her through the house and up the stairs, laughing, until he'd caught up to her in their bedroom. Then he'd spent the next several hours convincing her to take it back. No cattleman alive had ever taken advice from a sheepherder, he'd told her, least of all him.

Spike and Angel darted past Justice and Maggie, heading through the open doors of a barn that was two stories tall and built to match the main house's log construction. The shadows were deep, and the only sound coming from the barn was that deep, insistent lowing Maggie had heard earlier.

"Hey, you two, come away from there!" A sudden shout came from inside the barn, and almost instantly both dogs scuttled back outside and took off in a fast lope across the dirt. If they'd been children, Maggie was sure they would have been laughing.

"What's that about?" she asked, watching the dogs race each other to the water tank kept as a sort of swimming pool for herd dogs.

"Mike's got a cow and her calf in there. Probably didn't want the dogs getting too close," Justice told her, walking through the barn to the last stall on the right. There he leaned one arm on the top of the wood partition, clearly to take some weight off his leg, and watched as an older man expertly ran his hands up and down a nearly three-month-old calf's foreleg.

"How's he doing?"

"Better," Mike said, without looking up. "Swelling's down, so he and his mama can go back out to pasture tomorrow." Then he did lift his gaze and smiled when he spotted Maggie. "Well, now, you're a sight for sore eyes. Good to see you back home, Maggie."

"Thanks, Mike." She'd gotten more of a welcome from the cowboys and hired hands than she had from her own husband, she thought wryly. "So what happened to this little guy?"

Maggie wandered into the stall, keeping one wary eye on the calf's mother, then sank to one knee beside the smaller animal. He was, like most of Justice's herd, Black Angus. His black hide was the color of the shadows filling the barn, and his big brown eyes watched her with interest.

"Not sure, really," Mike said. "One of the boys saw the little guy limping out on the range, so he brought them in. But whatever was wrong, looks like it's all right now."

The calf wasn't small anymore. He was about six months old and wearing the King Ranch brand on his flank. He was well on his way to being the size of his father, which would put him, full grown, at about eleven hundred pounds. But the way he cuddled up to his mother, looking for food and comfort, made him seem like little more than an overlarge puppy.

The mingled aromas of hay and leather and cow mingled together in the vast barn and somehow made a soothing sort of scent. Maggie never would have believed she was capable of thinking that, since before meeting and marrying Justice, she had been a devout city girl. She'd once thought that there was nothing lovelier than a crowded shopping mall with a good-size latte stand. She had never liked the outdoors as a kid and had considered staying in a motel as close to camping as she ever wanted to get.

And yet being on the King Ranch had been so easy. Was it just because she'd loved Justice so much? Or was it because her heart had finally figured out where she belonged?

But then, she asked herself sadly, what did it matter now?

"See you later, Mike," she said, then tugged at Justice's arm. "Let's get you moving again. Gotta get your exercise in whether you want to or not."

"I never noticed that slave-driver mentality of yours before," Justice muttered as they left the barn and wandered around the side of the main house.

"You just didn't pay attention," she told him. "It was always there."

He was moving less easily, she noticed, and instinctively she slowed her pace. He fell into her rhythm and his steps evened out again. She knew how much he hated this. Knew that he detested having to depend on others to do things for him. And she knew he was in pain, though heaven knew he'd be roasted over live coals and still not admit to that. So she started talking, filling the silence so he would have to concentrate on something other than how hard it was to walk.

"Phil said you planted new grasses?" That was a brilliant stroke, Maggie thought. Get the man talking about the ranch and the prairie grass pastures and he'd get so involved, he wouldn't notice anything else. Not even pain.

"On the high pasture," he told her, easing around the corner of the log house to walk toward a rose garden that had originally been planted by his mother. "With the herd rotation, we'll keep the cattle off that grass until winter, and if it holds and we get some rain this fall, we'll have plenty of rich feed for the herd."

"Sounds good," she murmured, knowing her input wasn't needed.

"It was a risk, taking the cattle off that section early in the rotation, but we wanted to try out the new grasses and it had to have time to settle in and grow before winter, so…" He shrugged, looked down at her and unexpectedly smiled. "You're taking my mind off my leg, aren't you?"

"Well," she said, enjoying the full measure of a Justice King smile for as long as she could, "yeah. I am. Is it working?"

"It is," he said with a nod. "But I'm going to stop talking about it before you fall asleep while walking."

"It was interesting," she argued.

"Sure. That's why your eyes are glazed over."

Maggie sighed. "Okay, so the pastures aren't exactly thrilling conversational tidbits. But if you're talking about the ranch, you're not thinking about your leg."

He stopped, reached down and rubbed his thigh as if just the mention of it had fired up the aching muscles. He tipped his head back and looked up at the sky, a broad expanse of blue, dotted with thick white clouds. "I'm tired of thinking about my leg. Tired of the cane. Tired of being in the house when I should be on the ranch."

"Justice—"

"It's all right, Maggie," he said with a shake of his head. "I'm just impatient, that's all."

She nodded, understanding. She'd seen this before, usually in men, but some women had the same reaction. They felt as though their worlds would fall apart and crash if they weren't on top of everything at all times. Only they were capable of running their business, their homes, their children. It was a hard thing to accept help, especially since it meant also accepting that you could be replaced. However briefly.

"The garden looks good," she said abruptly.

He turned his head to look. "It does. Mom's roses are just starting to bloom."

Maggie led the way down the wide dirt path, lined on either side by pale, cream-colored bricks. The perfume of the roses was thicker the farther they went into the garden, and she inhaled deeply, dragging that scent into her lungs.

The rose garden spread out just behind the ranch house. A huge flagstone patio off the kitchen and great room led directly here, and Maggie had often had her morning coffee at the kitchen table, staring out at the garden Justice said his mother had loved.

The garden was laid out in circles, each round containing a different color and kind of rose. Justice's mother had turned this section of the ranch into a spring and summer wonder. Soon, Maggie knew, the garden would be bursting with color and scent.

She heard him behind her and turned to look at him. Behind him, the house sat, windows glistening in the sun. To her right was a stone bench, and she heard the splash of the water from the fountain that sat directly in the middle of the garden.

Justice was looking at her through narrowed eyes and, not for the first time, Maggie wondered what he was thinking about. What he saw when he looked at her. Did he have the same regrets she did? When he looked at the roses his mother had planted, did he see Maggie there, too? Was she imprinted on this house, his memories? Or had she become someone he didn't *want* to think about at all?

Well, that was depressing, she told herself and shook off the feeling deliberately. Instead, she cocked her head to one side, looked up at him and asked, "Do you remember that summer storm?"

After a second or two, he smiled and nodded. "Hard to forget that one." He glanced around at the neatly laid out flower beds, then kicked at one of the bricks at his feet. "It's the reason we laid these bricks, remember?"

A soft wind blew in and lifted her hair off her neck and Maggie grinned. "How could I forget? It rained so hard the roses were coming up out of the ground." She looked around and saw the place as it had been that long-ago night. "The ground couldn't hold any more water. And the roots of the bushes were pulling up just from the weight of the bushes themselves." She and Justice had raced outside, determined to save his mother's garden. "We were running around here for two hours, in the rain and the mud, propping up the rose bushes, trying to keep them all from being washed away."

"We did it, too," he mused, looking around now, as if reassuring himself that they'd been successful.

"Yeah, we did." She took a breath and asked, "Remember how we celebrated?"

His gaze fixed on hers, and she felt the heat of that stare slide right down into her bones. "You mean how we made love out here, covered in mud, laughing like loons?"

"Yes," she said, "that's what I mean." She took an instinctive step toward him. The past mingled with the present, memory tangling with fresh need. Her mouth went dry, her insides melted and something low and deep within her pulsed with desire. Passion. She remembered the feel of his hands on her. The taste of his mouth on hers. The heavy weight of him pressing her down, into cold, sodden earth. And she remembered she hadn't felt the cold. Hadn't noticed the rain. All she'd been aware of was Justice.

Some things didn't change.

The sun was blazing out of a spring sky. They were on opposite sides of a very large fence that snaked between them. Their marriage was supposedly over, and all that was keeping her here on the ranch was the fact that he needed her to help him be whole again.

And yet, none of that mattered.

She took another step toward him. He moved closer, too, his gaze locked on hers, heat sizzling in those dark blue depths until Maggie almost needed to fan herself. What he wanted was there on his face. As she was sure it was on hers. She needed him. Always had. Probably always would.

Standing here surrounded by memories was just stoking those needs, magnifying them with the images from the past. She didn't care. Maggie lifted one hand, cupped his cheek in her palm and felt the scratch of beard stubble against her skin. It felt good. Right. He closed his eyes at her touch, blew out a breath and moved even closer to her.

"Maggie…"

A baby's cry broke them apart.

Jolting, Maggie turned toward the sound and saw Mrs. Carey hurrying across the patio and down the steps, carrying a very fussy Jonas on her hip. The older woman had cropped gray hair and was wearing jeans and a long-sleeved T-shirt. Her tennis shoes didn't make a sound as she scurried toward them, an apologetic expression on her face.

Maggie walked to meet the woman, holding out her arms for her son. Jonas practically flung himself at his mother and wrapped his arms around her neck.

"I'm so sorry for interrupting," Mrs. Carey said, glancing from Maggie to Justice with a shrug. "But Jonas looked out the window, saw his mama and there was just no holding him back."

"It's okay, Mrs. Carey," Maggie told her, running one hand up and down her son's back in a soothing gesture that was already quieting the baby's cries and sniffles. The look on the housekeeper's face told Maggie she *really* regretted interrupting whatever had been going on. But maybe it was for the best, she thought. Maybe things would have gotten even more complicated if she and Justice had allowed themselves to be swept away by memories.

It only took another moment for Jonas to lift his head from Maggie's shoulder and give her a watery smile. "There now, no reason to cry, is there, little man?"

Jonas huffed out a tiny breath, grabbed hold of one

of Maggie's earrings, then turned his victorious smile on Justice and Mrs. Carey. As if he were saying, *See? I have my mommy. Just like I wanted.*

Justice moved off a little and sat down hard on the stone bench. "I'm done exercising, Maggie. Why don't you take your son into the house?"

Mrs. Carey, standing behind her boss, made a face at him that almost set Maggie laughing. But the truth was she was just too torn to smile about the situation. There her stubborn husband sat, with his son within arm's reach, and Justice had withdrawn from them. Sealed himself off behind that damn wall of his. Well, Maggie thought, maybe it was past time she tore some of that wall down. Whether he liked it or not.

Giving into the urge, Maggie jostled Jonas on her hip a bit, then asked, "Jonas, you want to go see your daddy?"

Justice's head snapped up and his eyes were wide and horrified briefly before they narrowed into dangerous slits. "I'm not his daddy."

"You are the most hardheaded, stubborn, foolish man I have ever known," Mrs. Carey muttered darkly. "Not enough sense to see the truth even when it's staring right at you with your own eyes."

"You might want to remember who you work for," Justice told her without looking at her, keeping his eyes fixed on Maggie and the boy.

"I believe I just described who I work for," Mrs. Carey told him. "Now I'm going back to the kitchen. Put a roast in for dinner."

When she was gone, Maggie stared at Justice for another minute, while the baby laughed and babbled to himself. But her mind was made up. She was going to force Justice to acknowledge their son. No more of this letting him avoid the baby, scuttling out of rooms just as she entered. No more walking a wide berth around the situation. It was time for him to be shaken up a bit. And there was no better way to do it than this.

"Here you go, sweetie. Go see your daddy." Maggie swung Jonas down and before Justice could get off the bench, she plopped the baby into his lap.

Both baby and man wore the same startled expression, and they looked so much alike that Maggie actually laughed.

Justice didn't hear her. He was holding his breath and watching the baby on his lap as if it were a live grenade. He expected the tiny boy to start shrieking in protest at being handed over to a stranger. But instead, Jonas looked up at him and a slow, cautious smile curved his tiny mouth.

He had two teeth, on the bottom, Justice noted, and a stream of drool sliding out of his mouth. His hair was black, his eyes a dark blue and his arms and legs were chubby pistons, moving at an incredible rate. Justice kept one hand on the boy's back and felt the rapid beat of the baby's heart beneath his hand.

For days he'd steered clear of the child, told himself the baby was none of his concern. He hadn't wanted to be touched by the child. Hadn't wanted to look at Jonas and know that Maggie had found what she needed with some other man. Staying away had been much easier.

Yet now, as he considered that, he realized that for the first time in his life, he'd behaved like a coward.

He'd run from the child and what he meant to save his own ass. To protect himself.

What did that say about him?

Jonas laughed and Justice turned his attention to Maggie, who was watching them both with tears in her eyes. His heart turned over in his chest, and just for an instant he let himself believe it was real. That he and Maggie were together again. That Jonas was his son.

Then the sound of a car engine out front shattered the quiet. A moment later that engine was shut off and the solid slam of a car door followed. Before he could wonder who had arrived, Mrs. Carey shouted from inside, "Jesse and Bella are here!"

Justice stared up at Maggie, the moment over. "Take the baby."

Seven

"I can't tell you how glad I'll be to finally have this baby," Bella said with a groan as she eased back into one of the comfy chairs in the great room. Her long, dark hair lay across her shoulder in a thick braid and silver hoops winked from her ears. A wry smile curved her mouth as she ran one hand over her belly. "It's not all about wanting to sleep on my stomach again, though. I'm just so anxious to meet whoever's in there."

"You didn't find out the baby's sex?" Mrs. Carey asked.

"No," Bella said. "We decided to be surprised."

Maggie grinned. She'd felt the same way. She hadn't wanted to know the sex of her baby before she saw him for the first time. And she remembered all too clearly what the last couple of weeks of pregnancy were like. No wonder Bella was fidgety. There was the discomfort, of course. But more than that, there was a sense of breathless expectation that clung to every moment.

"And," Bella was saying, "I don't think Jesse can take much more of this. The man's on a constant red alert. Every time I breathe too deeply, he bolts for the phone, ready to call 911. He's so nervous that he's awake every couple of hours during the night, waking me up to make sure I'm all right."

"That's just as it should be," Mrs. Carey said, from her seat on the couch, where she held Jonas in the crook of her arm and fed him his afternoon bottle. "A man should be wrapped up in the birth of his child." She sniffed. "Some men, at least, know what to do."

It was really nice having the King family housekeeper on her side, Maggie mused, but at the same time, she felt she owed Justice some sort of defense.

"To be fair," Maggie said, "Justice didn't know I was pregnant."

"Would have if he hadn't been too stubborn to go after you in the first place," she countered with a sharp nod that said, that's all there is to it. "If he had, then you would have been here, at home while you were carrying this little sweetheart. And I wouldn't have had to wait so long to meet him."

It would have been nice, Maggie thought, to have been here, surrounded by love and concern during her pregnancy. Instead, she'd lived alone, in her apartment a half hour away in Long Beach. Thank God she'd had her own family for support.

"I can't believe you went through your whole pregnancy on your own," Bella said softly, her hands still moving restlessly over the mound of her belly. "I don't know what I would have done without Jesse."

"It wasn't easy," Maggie admitted, pouring Bella another glass of lemonade before slumping back into her own chair. She shot a quick look at her baby, happily ensconced in Mrs. Carey's arms, and remembered those months of loneliness. She'd missed Justice so much then and had nearly called him dozens of times. But her own pride had discounted that notion every time it presented itself. "I had my family," she said, reminding herself that she'd never really been completely alone. Besides, she didn't want these women feeling sorry for her. She hadn't had Justice with her, but she hadn't been miserable the whole time, either.

"That's good," Bella said softly, as if she understood exactly what Maggie was trying to do.

"My parents live in Arizona, but they were on the phone all the time and were really supportive. Both of my sisters were fabulous." Maggie grinned suddenly with a memory. "My sister Mary Theresa was even in the delivery room with me. Matrice was great, really. Don't know what I would have done without her there."

"I'm glad you weren't alone," Mrs. Carey said quietly, "but a woman should have her man at her side when her children are born."

In a perfect world, Maggie thought but didn't say. Instead, she sighed and said, "I wanted to tell him. I really did. But at the same time, Justice had already told me that he didn't want children."

Mrs. Carey snorted. "Darn fool. Don't know why he'd say that raised in this family, one of four kids. Why wouldn't he want children? Especially," she added, bending to kiss Jonas's forehead, "this little darling."

Maggie gave her a smile, delighted that Jonas had an honorary grandmother to dote on him. "I didn't understand why, either, but he'd made himself clear. So I couldn't very well show up here pregnant knowing how he felt about it. And besides…"

"You wanted him to want you for *you*, not for the baby," Bella said for her.

"Exactly," Maggie said on another sigh. She may have just met Bella King, but she had a feeling the two of them could be very close friends. But that wasn't likely to happen either, since the minute Justice recovered, she'd be leaving again—and this time she knew it would be for good. There'd be no coming back here, not if Justice could turn his back on his son.

With a heavy heart, Maggie glanced around the room and idly noted the splash of sunshine lying across polished floors and gleaming tables. The scent of freshly cut flowers hung in the air, and the only sounds were those made by her hungry son as he devoted himself to his snack.

"I understand that completely," Bella told her. "If I'd been in your situation, I would have done the same thing. You know, Jesse told me how happy you and his brother were together. And I can tell you he was really surprised when you two split up."

Mrs. Carey huffed out a disgusted breath.

"He wasn't the only one." Maggie felt a quick sting of tears behind her eyes, and she blinked fiercely to keep them at bay. The time for tears was long past. "I would never have believed that Justice and I wouldn't be together forever. But he's just so darn…"

"Stubborn. Bullheaded," Mrs. Carey supplied.

"That about covers it," Maggie said with a laugh, relieved to feel her emotions settle again.

"So is Jesse," Bella said, then went on to describe life with a husband who rarely let her walk across the room without an escort. She started in by telling them how her office at King Beach had been outfitted with a resting chaise and that Jesse made sure she took a nap every afternoon.

While Maggie listened, she tried to hide the pain she felt. The envy, wrapping itself around her heart, for what Bella shared with her husband. Jesse had already come into the room twice in the past hour, ordering his wife to put her feet up, getting her a pillow for her aching back.

It was easy to imagine that Bella's whole pregnancy had been like that. With her eager, loving husband dancing attendance on her. And Maggie couldn't help but remember what her own pregnancy had been like. Sure, she'd had her parents and her sisters, but she hadn't had Justice. She hadn't had the luxury of lying in bed beside the father of her child while they spun daydreams about their baby's future. She hadn't been able to share the excitement of a new ultrasound photo. Hadn't been able to hold Justice's hand to her belly so that he could feel Jonas moving around inside her.

They'd both missed so much. Maybe she should have come to Justice immediately on finding out she was pregnant. Maybe she should have given him the chance then to acknowledge their child, to let them both into his life. But she'd been so sure she wouldn't be welcome. And frankly, his actions over the past few days supported her decision.

But then she remembered the look in Justice's eyes just an hour or so ago when she'd dropped Jonas into his lap. There had been an unexpected tenderness on his face, underlying the surprise and wariness. Maybe, she thought wistfully, if she'd just stood her ground long ago, things might have been different. Now, though, she'd never know for sure.

"You all right, honey?"

Mrs. Carey's concerned voice brought Maggie out of her thoughts to focus on what was happening. She shot a look at Bella in time to see a quick flash of pain dart over her features. "Bella?"

"I'm okay," she said, taking a deep breath. "It's just that my back's been bothering me all day. Probably just spasms from carrying around all this extra weight."

"A backache?" Maggie asked.

"All day?" Mrs. Carey added.

Bella grimaced, then said, "I probably just need another cookie."

"Um," Maggie started, "just when exactly are you due, Bella?"

"Oh, not for two weeks yet." She groaned a little as she pushed herself forward to reach for the plate on the table in front of her.

Maggie and Mrs. Carey exchanged a long, knowing look.

* * *

"You're crazy, you know that, right?" Jesse took a long pull of his beer and stretched his legs out in front of him, crossing them at the ankle.

Justice shot a look at his younger brother in time to see him shaking his head in disgust. The sun was hot, the breeze was cool and the patio was empty except for him and Jesse.

Maggie, Bella and Mrs. Carey were all in the house cooing over Jonas and talking about Bella's due-any-minute baby. He scowled to himself and took a drink of his own beer. Justice and Maggie had already legally separated by the time Bella and Jesse got together, but you wouldn't have known it from the way Maggie and Bella had instantly bonded. They were like two old friends already, and their chatter had eventually chased Jesse and Justice out to the patio for some quiet.

At least, that had been the plan.

"Crazy? Me?" Justice laughed shortly. "I'm not the one hauling my extremely pregnant wife around when she should be at home."

"Bella gets antsy sitting around the house. Besides, we're only forty minutes from the hospital—and you're changing the subject."

"Damn straight. Take the hint."

Jesse grinned, completely unfazed by Justice's snarl. "Why should I?"

"Because it's none of your business."

"When's that ever stopped a King?"

True, Justice thought. Never had a King been born who knew enough to keep his nose out of his brother's business.

"Look," Jesse said, "Jeff called, told me he'd hired Maggie, so I thought I'd bring Bella over to meet her sister-in-law. Nobody told me you had a son."

"I don't."

Laughing shortly, Jesse said, "You're so busy being a tight ass you don't even see it, do you?"

"I'm not talking about this with you, Jesse."

"Fine. Then I'll talk. You listen."

A cloud scudded across the sun, tossing the patio into shadow and dropping the temperature suddenly. Justice frowned at his brother, but Jesse paid no attention. He sat up, braced his forearms on his thighs and held his beer bottle between his palms. "I thought your leg was hurt, not your eyes."

"What's that supposed to mean?"

"It means, you dumb jerk, that Jonas looks just like you and you'd have to be blind not to see it."

"Black hair and blue eyes doesn't make him mine."

"It's more than that and you know it. The shape of his face. His nose. His hands. Damn it, Justice, he's a carbon copy of you."

"He can't be."

"Why the hell not?" Jesse's voice dropped and his gaze narrowed. "Why can't he be your son?"

Irritated beyond measure, pushed beyond endurance, Justice awkwardly got out of his chair and grabbed for his hated cane. Then he walked a few uneasy steps away from Jesse, stared out at the rose garden and told his brother what he'd never told another living soul before.

"Because I can't have kids."

"Says who?"

Justice choked out a laugh. Figured Jesse wouldn't react with any kind of tact. Just accept what his brother said and let it go. "A doctor. Right after the accident that killed Mom and Dad and laid me up for weeks."

"You never said anything."

He laughed again, a sound that was harsh and miserable even to his own ears. "Would you have?"

"No," Jesse said, standing up to walk to his side. "I guess not. But, Justice, doctors make mistakes."

He took a drink of his beer, letting the frothy cold liquid coat his insides and put out the fires of humiliation and regret burning within. "Not about that."

"God, you're an idiot."

"I'm getting awful tired of people calling me names," Justice muttered.

"You deserve it. How do you know that doctor wasn't wrong?" Jesse stepped out in front of him, forcing Justice to meet his gaze. "Did you ever get a second opinion?"

"You think I *liked* getting that news? Why would I go to someone else to hear the same damn thing again?"

Shaking his head wildly as if he couldn't believe what he'd just heard, Jesse blinked at his brother and said, "I don't know, to make sure the guy was right? Justice, you get a second opinion from vets on your cattle! Why wouldn't you do that for yourself?"

Justice wiped one hand across his face, then took another long swallow of his beer. He didn't like defending himself and liked even less the vague notion that his younger brother might be right. What if that doctor *had* been wrong? What if it had all been a mistake?

His heartbeat thundered in his chest and his mouth

went dry. If that were true, then he'd let Maggie walk out of his life for no reason at all. And worse, he had a son he'd only just met.

"No, he wasn't wrong," Justice muttered, refusing to accept the possibility. "He couldn't have been."

"Why?" Jesse demanded. "Because if he was wrong, that means you've wasted time with Maggie, neglected your son and are the Grand Poobah of Idiots?"

Grinding his back teeth together, Justice barely managed to mutter, "Pretty much."

"Well, here's something else for you to think about, your majesty. Even if he was right at the time, things change. But you never bothered to find out, did you? Damn, Justice. You really are—"

"—an idiot. Yeah, I know. Thanks for not saying it again."

"Give me time," Jesse told him with a half grin. "I'll get around to it."

"I'm sure. Y'know, I just told Jeff that I should have been born an only child."

"Like you could have made it through life without us!" Jesse laughed and clapped Justice on the shoulder. "Now, you know what you've got to do, right?"

"I have a feeling you're about to tell me."

"As you like to say, damn straight. Get a paternity test, Justice. It's easy. It's fast. And it'll tell you flat out if the doctor was wrong or not."

Paternity test. It would be easier, he thought, than finding another doctor and going through testing again himself. And he'd have his answer. One way or the other. A thread of worry snaked its way through his system, reminding him that if the results came back as negative, then he'd have to acknowledge that Maggie had lied to him. And that she had another man in her life. He ignored that worry completely.

"Maybe you're right," he murmured.

Jesse laughed. "Hell, it was worth the drive to the ranch just to hear you say that."

"Funny. That's really funny."

"This isn't." Jesse's smile faded and his voice dropped a notch. "Get this straightened out, Justice. Because if you don't, you're going to lose Maggie, your son, everything. Then you'll be a miserable bastard for the rest of your life and speaking as one of the people who'd have to put up with it, we'd rather not see that."

"You made your point." Justice had had more advice from people in the past couple of weeks than he'd had in the past five years. And he was damn tired of it.

"Glad to hear it. Now, how about another beer?"

"What the hell—"

"*Justice!*"

Maggie's shout had him spinning around and nearly toppling over but for Jesse's hand on his arm steadying him. She stood in the open doorway leading to the kitchen, and the wind swept her fiery hair into a dancing tangle around her head. "What is it?"

"It's Bella," Maggie called back, her gaze sliding from Justice to Jesse, who was already sprinting for the house. "It's time."

"How much longer?"

Maggie looked up at Justice and smiled. They'd been at the hospital for nearly five hours already and it felt like days. Funny, but when she herself had been in labor, it had seemed that time was rushing by, breathlessly. Now that she was expected to do nothing but sit and wait, time was at a crawl.

"No way to tell," she told him, tossing aside a six-month-old magazine she hadn't been reading anyway. "First-time babies can take anywhere from a few hours to a couple of days to make their appearance."

Justice looked horrified and Maggie stifled a laugh. He'd been a nervous wreck since they first bundled Jesse and Bella into the ranch SUV and hit the freeway. Neither of them had trusted Jesse to drive. He'd been practically vibrating with nerves when he called Bella's doctor to tell her they were headed to the hospital. Leaving Jonas with Mrs. Carey, Maggie had ridden shotgun while Justice drove and Jesse hovered over Bella on the backseat.

As soon as they had arrived at the sprawling medical center in Irvine, Jesse and Bella had been taken off to Maternity. Justice and Maggie, meanwhile, had been directed to the waiting room, which boasted the most uncomfortable chairs in the world. Short backs, narrow seats and hardwood arms made getting comfy a nearly impossible feat.

But, she supposed, comfort wasn't a real issue, since mostly the people waiting for news from the delivery room were too nervous to sit anyway. Still, she kept giving it a shot. "Justice, sit down and give your leg a rest, why don't you?"

"My leg's fine," he said, but his tight-lipped expression told the real truth. She knew he was in pain, but the man would never admit it.

"Okay, then sit down because you're making me nervous," she said.

He looked at her for a long minute, then took a seat beside her. A television was tuned to a twenty-four-hour comedy channel, the canned laughter and muttered conversations becoming a sort of white noise in the background. The walls were a pale hospital green and the carpet was multicolored, probably in an attempt to keep it from showing wear over the years. The scent of burned coffee hung in the air, a nasty layer over the medicinal stench of antiseptic.

"I hate waiting," Justice muttered, throwing a glance at the door opening onto the hallway that led to Labor and Delivery.

"No kidding? You hide it well." Maggie patted his arm absentmindedly.

Two other people, an older couple, were waiting in that room with them, having arrived just a half hour ago. The woman leaned forward and excitedly confided, "My daughter's about to make me a grandmother. It's a boy. His name will be Charlie, after my husband."

"Congratulations," Maggie said. "We're waiting to become an aunt and uncle."

"Isn't it wonderful?" The woman was practically glowing as she reached out blindly and took her husband's hand. "So thrilling to be a part of a miracle. Even in a small way."

Beside her, Justice shifted in his chair, but Maggie ignored him. "You're right, it is."

"The waiting is difficult, though," the woman admitted. "I'd do much better if I only knew what was happening…."

Whatever the woman might have said next was lost forever when a nurse in surgical scrubs poked her head in the door, smiling and asked, "Mr. and Mrs. Baker?"

"Yes!" The expectant grandmother leaped up out of her chair and would have rushed blindly at the nurse if her husband hadn't dropped both hands onto her shoulders. "That's us. How is Alison? Our daughter?"

"She's doing great and said to tell you that Charlie is calling for you."

"Ohmygoodness!" The woman turned her face into her husband's chest and, after a quick hug, looked back at the nurse. "We can see them now?"

"Of course. Follow me."

"What about us?" Justice demanded.

The nurse turned a questioning look on him. "I'm sorry?"

"It's nothing," Maggie told her, taking Justice's hand and giving it a squeeze. "Never mind."

"Good luck to you, dear," the new grandma said as they hustled out of the room after the nurse.

"What do you mean it's nothing?" Justice asked when they were gone. "We were here long before them!"

Maggie laughed at her husband's impatience. "Not exactly how it works, Justice."

"Well, it damn well should." He pushed up and out of his chair again, marched to the door and looked out. Then he turned back to her and said, "I feel like the walls are closing in on me in here. I don't think I can stay in this little room another minute."

"I'm kind of with you on that," Maggie said. "Let's take a walk."

For the next several hours, Justice and Maggie prowled the hallways of the hospital, checking in occasionally with the maternity ward. They wandered down to the nursery to look at the new babies and once again ran into the Bakers, who proudly pointed out little Charlie. They checked in with the nurses' station to get updates on Bella, and Maggie called the ranch to be assured by Mrs. Carey that Jonas had had his supper and his bath and was now sleeping soundly. She was told not to worry and to be sure to call the minute the baby was born.

"How did you do it?" Justice asked quietly when they were once more in the dreaded waiting room.

"Hmm? Do what?"

"This," he said, waving a hand as if to encompass the hospital, the maternity ward and all they contained. "How did you do it alone?"

"I wasn't alone," she told him. "Matrice was with me."

"Your sister." He blew out a breath. "You should have told me. I would have been here."

Outside, night crouched at the windows. The lights in the waiting room were dim, and thankfully, they had shut off the television, since they were the only two people in the room. Now she almost wished for that background noise so that the silence between them wouldn't seem so overwhelming.

Looking into Justice's eyes now, she would have liked to believe he was right. That had she called him from the hospital, he would have rushed right over to be at her side. But she knew better. In her heart of hearts, she just knew.

"No, you wouldn't have, Justice," she said with a sigh. "You wouldn't have believed me then any more than you do now."

He pushed one hand through his long black hair, scrubbed the other across the back of his neck and admitted, "Maybe you're right. Maybe I wouldn't have believed you. But I would have come to you anyway, Maggie. I would have been with you through this."

Something inside her eased just a little. To know that—to believe that he would have come whether or not he thought he was her baby's father was a gift. Yet even as she admitted that, there was another voice inside her demanding to be heard.

"Do you really think I would have wanted you here if you thought I was lying to you?" Before he could answer, she added, "And do you really believe that I would have called you to watch me give birth to another man's child?"

He watched her as long silent moments ticked past. Finally, though, he said, "No. You wouldn't have. To both questions." He rubbed absentmindedly at his thigh. "You really threw me hard, Maggie. Showing up at the ranch the way you did. With a boy you claim to be mine."

God, she was tired of defending herself. Sighing, she said, "He is yours. I'm not just claiming it."

He studied Maggie, his gaze moving over her features until she shifted uneasily under his steady regard. Eventually, he spoke. "I have something to tell you."

"What?" Maggie held her breath as hope jumped up inside her and waved its arms and legs excitedly. Was he finally going to admit that he knew Jonas was his? That she wasn't lying? Was he going to ask her to stay with him? Be a family?

"Mr. and Mrs. King?"

Maggie groaned at the interruption and turned her head to look at the nurse stationed in the doorway. Hours ago, she would have welcomed the woman. Now? What terrible timing. But the nurse was smiling and Maggie was already standing up to join Justice when she said, "Yes, that's us. Are Bella and the baby all right?"

"Everyone's fine," the nurse assured them. "Even the happy father is coming around."

"Coming around?" Justice repeated. "What—"

"He got a little light-headed in the delivery room," the nurse hedged.

"You mean he *fainted?*" Justice asked her, grinning like a big brother who would now have something on his sibling for the rest of his life.

"Justice…" Maggie said.

"You've been invited in to meet the newest member of your family," the nurse told them. "If you'll follow me."

"What was it?" Maggie asked. "Girl or boy?"

"I'll let the new mom tell you that," she said, leading them through a set of double doors and down a brightly lit hallway.

Two immensely pregnant women were wandering the halls, shuffling with slow steps as they hung on to IV poles for support. Their husbands were right on their heels, murmuring encouragement. In one room a woman moaned, and from yet another a new baby's indignant wail rose up like a discordant symphony.

Maggie felt Justice's hand on the small of her back and relished that small intimacy. Here at least, they were together. A team. Two people who had survived hours of expectation and were now about to be rewarded.

In Bella's room the new mom lay back, exhausted and gorgeous against her pillows, a tightly wrapped bundle cradled in her arms. Jesse stood beside her, still looking a little pale and glassy-eyed but happier than they'd ever seen him.

Maggie hurried forward, held on to the bedrail, stared down into a red, wrinkly face and declared it, "Beautiful. Just beautiful, Bella. So…boy or girl?"

"Boy," Jesse said proudly. "And we're keeping the J-name thing going, too. Uncle Justice, Aunt Maggie, I want you to meet Joshua."

Justice moved in closer, leaning over Maggie to get a good look at the newest King. She felt his breath on her cheek as he reached over, pulled the tightly wrapped white blanket down a bit so he could get a better view of the baby. She felt his indrawn breath as he studied his brother's son and heard the soft sigh escape him as he looked at Bella.

"He's a beauty, Bella. Good thing he looks like you."

"Hey!" Jesse grinned.

"Don't you think you'd better sit down?" Justice asked, a teasing note in his voice. "I hear the delivery was a little rough on you."

Jesse scowled and cast a disgusted glance at the open door even as Bella laughed delightedly. "Big-mouth nurse," he muttered before turning a look back on Justice. He jerked his head to one side, silently telling his brother he wanted to talk in private.

When they were far enough from the two women in the room, Jesse said, "I'm a father now, too, Justice. And I'm telling you, Jonas is your son. Don't lose this. Don't blow everything for your pride."

Justice, though, turned to look at Bella and Maggie, illuminated by the overhead light, both women looking down on that tiny boy with delirious smiles. "Now's not the time, Jesse."

"There's no better time, Justice," his brother told him. "Don't waste another minute."

Jesse moved back to his wife then, and Maggie soon joined Justice to go back to the ranch, leaving the new family to settle in together. As they stepped out of the hospital into the cold, clear night, Justice stopped, took a deep breath and thought about what Jesse had said to him, both here and at the ranch. What if he was right about all of it? What if Justice had been clinging to bad information for ten years?

"Wasn't he beautiful," Maggie asked, hunching deeper into the sweater she'd brought along with her. "So tiny. So perfect. So…" She stopped talking then, looked up at Justice and asked, "What is it? Is something wrong?"

He met her gaze and knew what he had to do. For all their sakes, it was time for the truth to come out.

"I want a paternity test run on Jonas."

Eight

A few days later, Justice was still feeling the effects of Maggie's fury. After an hour of lunges, wall squats and some fast walking on a treadmill, Maggie still wasn't finished with him.

She'd set up a massage table in the pool house behind the main house and had him stretched out atop it like a prisoner on a rack. Sunlight drifted in through heavily tinted windows that allowed the people inside to enjoy the view but kept anyone outside from peering in. The bubbling of the hot tub at one end of the pool sounded overly loud in the strained quiet, and quiet purr of the air conditioner sounded like a continuous sigh.

Justice paid no attention to his surroundings, though. Instead, he kept a wary eye on Maggie. Her hands were sure, her professional demeanor was firmly in place but her eyes were flashing with suppressed rage. He winced as she took hold of his foot and, lifting it, pushed his leg toward his chest. Muscles he'd been working hard stretched and pulled, and he ground his teeth together to keep any moans from sliding out of his throat.

He curled his hands around the edges of the table and held on while she forced him to push against her hands. Resistance training, she called it. Torture was more like it, Justice thought.

"You're enjoying this," he muttered.

"No, I'm not."

"Bullshit. You're pissed off and you're getting a charge out of making me pay."

"Justice," she said on a rush of breath, "I'm a professional physical therapist. I would never, under any circumstances, harm a patient under my care. Now push against me."

He did and still managed to say, "You're not trying to hurt me—I get that. But if it's a by-product, it won't bother you much, I'm thinking."

"I'm doing what's best for your rehabilitation," she said, "and resisting torturing you, despite how tempting the idea might be."

He pushed into her grip, focusing his strength, and he had to admit that since she'd been manhandling him, his leg was stronger and getting better every day. It still ached, but it was manageable and he rarely needed the cane anymore.

"I didn't ask for the test specifically to piss you off," he muttered, unwilling to leave it alone. Wanting her to see his side.

She inhaled sharply, set his leg down on the table and fisted her hands at her hips. "What do you want me to say, Justice? That I'm fine with you arranging for our son to be poked with a needle because you don't trust me? Not gonna happen."

She'd argued with him, of course, that night at the hospital. Her temper had flared and shone like a beacon as she faced him down and told him just what she thought of a man who would put an infant through an unnecessary test. But Justice hadn't been swayed.

The day he'd found out he couldn't father children, the news had almost killed him. Not only had he lost his parents—his past—in that accident, he'd lost his future as well. He was no different than any other man. He'd dreamed of family, of passing on King Ranch to another generation who would love and care for it as he had. And to have those dreams shattered in an instant had been devastating.

Yet now that Jesse had planted all of those thoughts in his mind, he had to wonder: had the doctor been wrong? He had to know the truth. Had to know if Jonas was his. If he really did have a son. And nothing Maggie said had changed his mind.

They'd arranged for the paternity test the next morning, taking the baby to one of the King laboratories. Sometimes, he told himself, it paid to be a member of a huge, successful family. The Kings had their fingers in just about every pie worth having in California. No matter what one of them might need, there was generally a cousin who could provide it.

They'd put a rush on the paternity test, and even with

that it would be another few days before they had the
results. Justice had never been good at waiting, and this
time it was even harder. There was so much riding on
the outcome of this test. Not just his pride, he told
himself, but the direction of his very future.

She poured some liquid into her hands, scrubbed
her palms together, then began what she called "deep
tissue mobilization." In other words, a hard massage,
he thought and sighed as her fingers and palms worked
magic on his leg. His surgical scar was white and
fresh-looking despite being completely healed. Her
hands on his leg felt like a blessing. Her touch was
sure, firm and, just as she said, professional. He
wanted more. He wanted her hands on other parts of
him, too. But he wasn't going to get that, not when she
was this furious.

"How does this feel?" she asked, working from the sole
of his foot, up his calf to his thigh and back down again.

If she glanced at the erection pushing at the fly of his
shorts, she'd know just how it felt, he thought and
grimly tried to bring his body under control. "Good," he
said bluntly. "It's all good."

"You're improving, Justice. I'm glad to see it."

"Are you?"

"Of course I am. That's why I'm here, remember?
And the sooner you're back on your own feet, the sooner
I can take Jonas and leave."

He reached out, grabbed one of her hands and held
on. "You're not going anywhere until those test results
come back in, Maggie."

She pulled her hand free of his grip. "I'm not going

anywhere until my job is done," she corrected. "When it is, you won't be able to stop me from leaving."

He ran one hand over his face. "Damn it, Maggie, don't you see why I had to do this?"

"No. I don't see." She grabbed up a towel, dried her hands and continued, "You had my word, Justice. You could have believed me."

"I don't just want your word. I want proof." He pushed up onto his elbows and stared at Maggie.

Her hair was in a thick ponytail at the back of her neck. She wasn't wearing makeup, but then, she didn't really need any. Her eyes were hot and filled with fury, and her delectable mouth kept working as if she were biting back hundreds of words she wanted to fling at him.

The day was warm and she wore jeans shorts and a sleeveless T-shirt for their exercise session. Her skin was smooth and pale, and Justice wanted nothing more than to grab her, pull her down on top of him and bury himself inside her. With that mental image firmly planted in his mind, he could almost *feel* her damp heat surrounding him. Feel her body moving on his. See her as she leaned over him, brushing his chest with her bare breasts.

Damn it.

He swung his legs off the table in a hurry, hoping she hadn't seen his erection, hard and all too eager for her. Around Maggie, he seemed to be little better than a teenager. Always hard. Always ready.

"Come on," she said, stepping around the table to wrap one arm around his waist. "You need to sit in the hot tub awhile. Ease your muscles."

He thought about refusing her offer to help him walk

to the far end of the pool. Then he told himself he'd be a fool for not taking the opportunity to touch her. Her scent rose up to greet him, and the soft fall of her hair against his skin felt like silk. He draped one arm across her shoulders and, with her aid, walked barefoot across the cool, sky-blue tiles lining the edge of the pool.

"Here you go," she said as they reached the partitioned-off area of the pool. There was a bench along the half circle of the hot tub, and Justice lowered himself onto it, hissing a little as the warm, bubbling water caressed his body.

"I turned the heat down a bit," Maggie was saying. "I don't want you parboiled, just warm and relaxed."

He doubted he'd ever be fully relaxed when she was around, but he didn't bother telling her that. Instead, he just looked up at her, standing on the tiles, watching him with her "professional mien" in place. Where was *his* Maggie? The one with fire in her eye. The one who turned him inside out with a single touch.

"Why don't you join me?" he asked. She started to refuse but he kept talking. "You look like you need to relax as much as I do, Maggie."

She bit her lip, blew out a breath and said, "I'm too mad at you, Justice. There wouldn't be any relaxing. For either of us."

"Fine, then," he said, slapping the frothing water with the flat of his hand. "Sit down and yell at me. You always did feel better after a good rant."

Her lips twitched and he knew he'd won.

"I don't have a bathing suit."

"I won't tell if you don't," he coaxed, mouth dry,

wanting—no, *needing* to see her strip down to nothing to join him in the warm, bubbling water.

She took a deep breath and blew it out again. "Okay. But just for a few minutes. Then I should go in and take care of Jonas."

"He's fine with Mrs. Carey."

"I know that," she countered, stepping out of her jean shorts to reveal pale pink silk panties, "but he's *my* son and my responsibility."

Justice just nodded. He didn't trust himself to speak anyway. She lifted the hem of her shirt and tugged it up and over her head, giving him his first look at a wisp of a pale pink bra that exactly matched her panties. Maggie always had loved good lingerie. And he'd always considered himself a lucky bastard.

When she stepped into the water, though, he stopped her. "Aren't you going to take those off?"

She glanced down at herself, then at him. Laughing, she told him, "I don't think so. It's not safe to be naked around you, Justice."

Since his erection was now pushing against the button fly of his own shorts, demanding to be set free, he had to silently agree with her.

She eased down onto the bench opposite him and with a sigh, tipped her head back onto the rim of the pool. "God, you were right. This feels amazing."

Her lean, toned legs half floated in the water, directly in front of one of the jets, and Justice's mouth watered as he watched her. He reached down and readjusted himself, hoping to ease his discomfort. It didn't help. But he knew what would. Deftly, he undid the buttons on his shorts and pushed them off, shoving them to the floor of the pool. Instantly, his aching groin was eased, free of the constricting shorts. But he needed more.

He needed *Maggie.*

He moved closer to her while her eyes were closed. His gaze locked on her breasts, bobbing just above the water's edge, her dark, rosy nipples perfectly defined by the wet silk. She might have thought she was protecting herself by staying semiclothed, but all she'd managed to do was tempt even more thoroughly. Wet silk clung to her skin, displaying far more than it hid.

When he was close enough, he reached out to slide one hand up her calf. Instantly, her eyes flew open and she floundered a bit, until she was again seated on the bench, gaze fixed on him. "What're you doing?"

Justice moved closer still. "Helping us both relax."

"I don't think so," she said, shaking her head and scooting farther from him.

"Don't be so skittish, Maggie," he soothed. "It's not like we're strangers."

She held up one finger, holding him at bay. "No, we're not strangers, Justice. That's why we shouldn't do this. It'll only confuse things even more than they already are."

"Impossible," he countered, coming closer. The warm water felt great on his skin, the slide of his hand along her wet leg, once he took hold of her again, felt even better.

"Okay, maybe you have a point," she said, nodding. "But I'm still mad at you."

He grinned briefly. "Some of our best sex happened when you were mad at me."

"Okay," she admitted with a quick nod, "that's true, too. But that doesn't mean I want you now."

"Liar." He took hold of her foot and pulled her toward him, sliding his hands up her legs as she floated to him in the frothing water.

She hissed in a breath. "You're cheating."

"Damn straight."

"Justice, this won't solve anything."

"Maybe it doesn't have to," he told her, his hands now gripping her bottom. "Maybe it just has to happen."

She looked at him and squirmed in his grip, as if she were trying to get comfortable. "Maybe," she acknowledged. "But maybe we shouldn't let it."

"Too late," he whispered and moved off the bench so that he could turn her in his grasp, holding her floating body in front of the pulsing jets of water streaming into the tub.

"Cheating again!" she accused on a sigh as her legs parted and the thrum of the warm, pulsing water caressed her center.

While the hot tub worked its magic, Justice worked some of his own. Supporting her head with one arm, he used his free hand to undo the front clasp of her bra, freeing her breasts, her hard nipples. He dipped his head and took first one, then the other, into his mouth, rolling his tongue across their sensitive tips, feeling Maggie shudder beneath him as tumultuous sensations gathered within her.

He couldn't seem to taste her enough. How had he lived these long months without her in his arms? He suckled her, and she whimpered, both from his attentions and the steady beat of the water on her tender flesh. He knew what she was feeling because he felt it, too.

The hunger. The need. The raw urgency racing through his bloodstream. He had to have her. Reaching down, he tore her panties down and off her legs and then held her thighs apart so that the warm water could caress her even more intimately.

She grabbed at his shoulders and groaned from deep in her throat as she lifted her hips into the water jet, aching, needing. He watched her face as her eyes swam with desire and her breath caught in her throat. Then she turned her gaze on him and whispered, "I want you inside me, Justice."

That was all he needed to hear. He pulled her toward him, locked his mouth onto hers and eased them both down onto the bench. She straddled him, her knees at either side of his hips, and then lowered herself down onto him, inch by slow, incredible inch. She took him inside, into the heat. Into the heart of her, and Justice couldn't look away from her amazing eyes while he filled her, pushing himself deeply into her body.

Their gazes fixed on each other, they moved as one, racing toward the inevitable finish that they both so desperately needed. Justice felt whole. Felt complete. Felt as if nothing else in the world mattered but this moment. This woman. She was all. She was everything. And when her lips parted and she cried out his name as her body trembled and shook with the force of her release, he knew he'd never seen anything more lovely.

Only moments later, he gave himself up to the

wildness calling him and willingly followed her into a dazzling world that only lovers knew.

"It didn't change anything," Maggie muttered while she dressed Jonas in his pajamas that night. Her son smiled and laughed, a rolling, full-throated sound that never failed to tear at her heart.

She had him lying on her bed, since the two of them were still sharing a room. Thank heaven it was at the opposite end of the hall from the master bedroom. After what had happened between them that afternoon, she didn't think it would be a wise idea to be too close to him.

"You think it's funny, do you?" she asked her son, smiling at him as she bent to plant a kiss on his belly. "You think Mommy is making a fool of herself? You're right, she probably is. And you know what? She's still not sorry."

The baby pulled at her hair, and Maggie gently untangled his fingers. She put first one chubby foot then the next into his footed blue sleeper, then swiftly did up the zipper, snapping the jammies closed at the neck. Jonas kicked and squirmed on Maggie's bed until she scooped him up and cuddled him close.

Nothing in the world smelled better than a baby fresh from his bath. His skin was soft and warm and the heavy, solid weight of her son in her arms eased the ache in her heart substantially.

She didn't regret making love with Justice that afternoon, but at the same time she could admit that it had probably been a mistake. Nothing was settled between them. She was still furious with him for insisting on a paternity test when any fool could look at Jonas and know without a doubt he was Justice's son. And she was frustrated by the fact that no matter how hard she tried to get past the barriers Justice had erected around his own heart, they still stood tall and strong against her.

"But you know what really gets to me, sweetie?" she crooned, keeping her voice light and soothing as she bounced her son on her knee. "Your daddy wants a paternity test yet he's still avoiding you. Why's that, hmm? Do you know? Can you tell Mommy?"

Jonas laughed and cooed and waved his arms as if he were trying to fly, and Maggie smiled at the tiny boy who had so filled her heart. She couldn't imagine her life without Jonas now. He was a part of her. Yet, the man who was his father was still a stranger to him.

"Well, little man," she said, making her decision in an instant, "it's time we changed all that, don't you think? It's time your daddy discovered just what he's been missing. I want him to know you. To know what we could all have had together."

Jonas burbled something that Maggie took to be agreement. Pushing off the bed, she carried the baby out of the room, along the hall and down the stairs, following the sound of the evening news on a television.

She spotted Justice the moment she walked into the great room. He was sprawled in one of the comfortable chairs positioned around the room, his gaze fixed on a flat-screen TV on the opposite wall. While a news anchor rambled on about the top stories of the day, Maggie crossed the room with determined steps.

When she got close, he looked up, directly into her eyes. She felt a quick thrilling rush through her system as heat pooled in the pit of her stomach and then slipped lower. Oh, he was dangerous, she told herself, with his dark eyes, long black hair and stern features. Then his gaze shifted to the baby and a wariness shone in his eyes briefly. Which told Maggie she was doing exactly the right thing. So she took a breath, steadied herself and forced a smile.

"I brought your son to say good-night."

He sat up straighter, narrowed his gaze on her and said, "Not necessary."

"Oh, it is, Justice," she told him, and in a sure, swift movement set the baby onto Justice's lap. The two of them blinked at each other, and Maggie would have been hard-pressed to say which of them looked more surprised by her actions.

"Maggie, the test isn't in yet, so—"

"He's your son, Justice. The test will prove that, even to you, very soon. So you might as well start getting to know him."

"I don't think—"

"You should know him, Justice," she said, not letting him finish. "And there's no time like now. So, you two be good and I'll go get his bottle."

Justice's eyes widened in horror. "You're leaving me alone with him?"

Maggie laughed. "Welcome to fatherhood."

She left the room after that but stayed in the hall, peeking into the room so she could watch the two men in her life interact. Justice looked as though he were holding a ticking time bomb and Jonas looked uncertain about the whole situation.

When the baby's lower lip began to tremble, Maggie almost went back inside. Then she heard Justice say, "Now don't cry, Jonas. Everything's going to be all right."

And in the hall, Maggie had to wonder if he'd just lied to his son for the first time.

As the days passed, Justice felt the strength in his leg continue to grow. But as his body healed, his heart was being torn open. Being with Maggie and yet separate from her was harder than he would ever have thought possible. Those few stolen moments in the hot tub hadn't been repeated, and now that time with her seemed almost like a dream. A dream that continued to haunt him no matter where he was or what he was doing.

He stood at the paddock in the bright sunshine and leaned his forearms atop the uppermost rail in the fence. With his hat pulled low over his eyes, Justice stared out at the horses being saddle-trained and told himself that he'd do well to simply concentrate on work.

Now that he was getting around better, he'd begun to take up more of the reins of the operation again, and it was good to feel more himself. Though he wasn't up yet for taking his own horse out onto the range, he would be soon. Until then, he spent as little time as possible inside the house—though he was seeing more of the baby these days. It seemed as though both Maggie and Mrs. Carey were bound and determined to see him connect with the child.

And to be honest, Justice was enjoying himself. That little boy had a way of tugging at a man's heart. Father or not, he was being drawn deeper into the web of feeling, caring. Only that morning, Jonas had curled his little fist around Justice's finger and that tiny, fierce grip had taken hold of him more deeply than he would have thought possible.

The exercise-and-massage sessions Maggie had devised were getting less tiring as he healed, and he both hated that fact and was relieved by it. One-on-one time with Maggie was dangerous because he wanted her now more than ever. He hated missing those moments, but he also needed the space to do some serious thinking. Once the paternity test results came in, he would know if Maggie had been lying to him all this time. He would know if the baby boy he was becoming more fond of every day was his son.

And he would know what he had to do.

If Maggie was lying, then he'd have to let her go again. No matter how much he still loved her, no matter how much he'd come to care for the boy, he wouldn't be used. By anyone. But even as he thought it, a voice in his head shouted at him that it wasn't in Maggie's nature to lie. She was as forthright and honest a person as he'd ever known.

Which meant that as far as she knew, she was telling the absolute truth. Jonas was his son. If the tests proved it out, then Justice was going to be a part of the boy's life, whether or not Maggie was happy about that.

However the chips fell, he and Maggie had some tough choices headed their way. So why clutter everything up further with sex?

"Hey, boss!"

Justice turned toward the voice and spotted Mike leading one of the young horses around the perimeter of the ring. "What?"

Mike pointed toward the house. "Looks like your boy there is a born ranch hand!"

Justice swiveled his head to look and saw Maggie and Jonas on the flagstone patio. She was kneeling beside Jonas, who sat astride a rocking horse that had been in the King family for decades. Mrs. Carey must have hauled it down from the attic, Justice mused, a smile on his face as he watched Jonas hold on to the reins and rock unsteadily, his mother's arm wrapped firmly around him.

Even from a distance, he heard the baby's delighted laugh and Maggie's soft chuckle, and the mingled sounds went straight to his heart. If she was lying, how the hell was Justice going to stand losing her and the baby?

Nine

Maggie was putting her laundry away when she noticed the corner of a brown envelope peeking out from beneath a stack of T-shirts.

The signed divorce papers.

She set the laundry down, reached into the drawer for the large manila envelope and carefully opened the metal tabs. Pulling the papers free, she let her gaze drift over the legalese that would have, if she'd only filed the damn things with the court, ended her marriage.

But then, that was the problem. Despite going to the trouble of getting the papers, of having Justice sign them, Maggie never really had wanted the marriage to be over. So now, she simply kept the signed documents with her. As a sort of talisman, she supposed. As long as she had them, she was still connected to

Justice. Jonas still had a father. And she had a chance at getting back what she and Justice had lost. Was she just fooling herself, though? Torturing herself with thoughts of reconciliation?

Sex between them was still off-the-charts great. But was that it? Was that all they shared now?

Sadly, she slid the papers back into the envelope, then dropped the package back into her drawer. Turning from the dresser, she walked to the open window overlooking the front of the house and stared out at the storm blowing in off the ocean.

The white sheers at the window billowed in the wind gusting in under the sash like ghosts fighting to be free of earth. Tree limbs clattered and seagulls wheeled and danced in the sky, taking refuge inland from the approaching storm. She closed the window against the cold wind and told herself firmly that when she got back to her own apartment, she had to file those divorce papers. But even as she thought it, she knew she wouldn't do it.

"You're crazy, Maggie," she whispered.

"I always liked that about you."

She spun around quickly, hand splayed across her chest as if to keep her heart in place. "Nothing like a jolt of adrenaline to get the morning off to a great start."

"Didn't mean to startle you," Justice said as he walked into her room with slow, but even steps. "Thought you would have heard me coming down the hall."

She watched him as he moved without hesitating, or limping. He was nearly back to normal and hadn't used his cane in a couple of days. Soon, he wouldn't need her at all. Well, wasn't that a cheery thought?

"No, without the tapping of the cane giving you away, you're pretty stealthy."

He nodded, reached down to rub his thigh and said, "It's good to be rid of it."

"I'm sure it is." She moved back to the dresser and tucked her laundry into the proper drawers, then straightened, gave him a bright smile and said, "Well, I really should go down and get Jonas. Mrs. Carey's had him most of the morning."

"It can wait another minute." He moved to stand between her and the door and Maggie knew the only way she'd get past him was to brush up against him. And she didn't think that was a good idea. Not since her body remembered their time in the hot tub all too well and was just itching for more.

So instead she stopped, hitched one hip higher than the other and folded her arms over her chest. "Okay. What do you need, Justice?"

His gaze locked on hers, he said, "I think it's time you and I had a talk about what's going to happen when the test results come in."

"What do you mean?" Wariness crept into her voice, but she really couldn't help it.

"I mean, in a few days we'll know the truth. And if it turns out that Jonas really is my son…"

She bristled. God, she hated that he didn't trust her and instead needed substantiating proof from a laboratory.

"—then I'm going to want him raised here," Justice was saying and Maggie listened up. "On the ranch."

A sinking sensation opened up in the pit of her

stomach and her heart dropped into it. She shook her head. "No way."

"What?"

"You can't just take my son."

"If he's my son, too," Justice argued, "I can take my share of him."

She laughed shortly, a harsh scrape against her throat. "What do you plan to do? Cut him in half?"

He scowled and walked past her to sit on the edge of the bed. Rubbing his leg, he said, "Nothing so dramatic. If Jonas is mine, I want him raised here. I want him growing up where I did. This ranch is his heritage, and he should get to know it and love it like I do."

"All of a sudden you're worried about his *heritage?*" Maggie stalked across the floor toward him and stopped just before she got within strangling range. Because the way she was feeling at the moment, she really didn't trust herself. "Up until last week you wouldn't even admit to the possibility of his being your son. Now he has a heritage and you want to take him from me? I don't think so."

"Don't fight me on this, Maggie," Justice said, wincing a little as if his leg was paining him. "You'll lose."

For the first time since she'd arrived at the ranch, she wasn't concerned with Justice's pain. With the discomfort of his injury. In fact, she hoped his leg ached like a bitch. Why should she be the only one in pain here? All she knew was that he was going to take her baby from her. Well, it would have to be over her dead body.

She took a deep breath, held on to her heartache like a shield and said, "Oh, no, I won't lose. He's mine,

Justice. He's nearly six months old and up until little more than a week ago, you'd never seen him!"

"Because you didn't bother to tell me of his existence."

"You didn't believe me when I *did* tell you."

"Not the point." He waved that argument aside with a flick of his hand.

"It's exactly the point, Justice, and you know it."

Outside, clouds rolled in, the wind kicked up into a fierce dance and rain suddenly pounded on the windowpanes with a vicious rhythm.

Feeling as ragged and frenetic as the storm, Maggie stepped back from him and said firmly, "Jonas is going to be raised in the city. By me. My apartment is lovely. There's a park close by and good schools and—"

"A park?" Justice pushed off the bed and grimaced a little but kept coming, walking toward Maggie until she backed up just to keep a distance between them. "You want to give him a park when I've got thousands of acres here? The city's no place for a boy to grow up. He couldn't even have a *dog* in your apartment."

"Of course he can," she argued, temper spiking, desperation growing. "Pets are allowed in my building. We'll get a little dog as soon as he's old enough. A poodle, maybe."

He barked out a sharp laugh. "A *poodle?* What the hell kind of dog is that for a growing boy?"

"What do you want him to have, a pit bull?"

"The herd dogs. They're well-trained—he'll love 'em. We've got a new litter due in a few weeks, too. He'll have a puppy to grow up with and he'll love that, too."

He probably would, but that wasn't the point either,

Maggie thought, surrendering to the fires inside her, letting her temper boil until she wouldn't have been surprised to feel steam coming out of her own ears.

"That's not your decision to make."

"Damn straight it is. If Jonas is my son, I won't be separated from him."

"You never even *wanted* children, remember?" She was shouting now and didn't give a damn who heard her. The rain hammered the windows, the wind rattled the glass and Maggie felt as if she were in the center of the storm. This was a fight she was determined to win. She wouldn't give ground.

"Of course I did!" Justice's shout was even louder than hers. "I lied to you because I thought I couldn't have kids."

Dumbfounded, Maggie just stared at him for a second or two. A heartbeat passed, then another, as her brain clicked through information and presented her with a really infuriating picture. Eventually that temper kicked back in and all hell was cut loose.

"You lied to me?" she demanded. "Deliberately let me believe you just didn't want kids when you knew you couldn't have them at all? Why would you do that?"

She rushed him and pushed at his chest with both hands, so furious she could hardly breathe, let alone shout, yet somehow she managed. "You let me walk away from you rather than tell me the truth? What were you thinking?"

"I didn't want you to know," he said, capturing both of her wrists and holding them tightly. His gaze pierced into hers, and Maggie saw shame and anger and regret all tangled up together in his eyes. "I didn't want anyone to know. You think I wanted to tell you I was less than a man?"

Maggie just blinked at him. She couldn't believe this. Couldn't get her mind around it at all. "Are you a Neanderthal? Being able to father a child is not a measure of your manhood, you big dolt!"

"To me it is."

She saw the truth of that statement on his face, and it didn't calm her down any. Yanking her hands free of his grip, she wheeled around and started pacing the circumference of the room in fast, furious steps.

"All this time, we've been apart because you thought you were sterile?" She sent him a quick look and saw her words hit home.

His mouth tightened, his jaw clenched and every muscle in his body looked to be rigid, unforgiving. He didn't accept weakness, and of course that's how he would have seen himself. She knew that about him if nothing else. So, yes, she could understand that he would have thought it better to get a divorce than to confess to his wife that he was less than he thought he should be.

That's what she got for marrying a man whose pride was his major motivator. How typical of Justice. Then she stopped dead, studied her husband and hit him with what she'd just realized.

"It's your damn pride, isn't it?" she murmured, never taking her eyes off him. "That's what's at the bottom of all this. Why you didn't fight for me. Why you let me go. For the sake of your damn pride."

"Nothing wrong with pride, Maggie," he told her in

a voice that just barely carried over the sound of the storm raging outside.

"Unless you hold that pride more precious than anything else. Because that's what you did, Justice. Rather than admit to me you couldn't have children, you let our marriage end." The slap of that truth hurt her deeply. He'd chosen his own image of himself over their marriage. Over their love. "*That* was easier for you than losing your pride."

"You're the one who walked."

"So you keep reminding me," she said, moving back toward him now with slow, sure steps. "But you could have kept me, Justice. You could have stopped me with two words. *Please stay.* That's all you had to say and you know it. Hell, you admitted to me just the other day that you would have liked to say it. But you couldn't do it."

She shook her head as she stared up into dark blue eyes that suddenly looked as cold and deep as a storm-tossed ocean. "I loved you enough that I would have stayed with you if I thought you wanted me to. Instead you pulled away and closed yourself off and I had nothing. No children. No husband. So why the hell would I stay?"

He flinched and looked uncomfortable, but that was fleeting. In a heartbeat, he was back to being his stone-faced, in-control self.

"This is useless, Maggie." He pushed one hand through his hair, cast a quick look at the window and the storm beyond, then shifted his gaze back to her. "What's past is past. We can't change it. But know this. If Jonas is my son, I'm not going to give him up. If that boy is a King, he's going to be raised by Kings."

He left her then, walking quietly away without a backward glance, and when he was gone, Maggie felt cold right down to the bone. That icy pit in the bottom of her stomach was still there and now tangled with knots of nerves.

Everything Justice had just said had also been motivated by his pride, his pride in his child, and while she might ordinarily cheer for that, right now all it meant to her was that Justice would be a fierce opponent.

As that thought flew through her mind, Maggie realized that with his money and his family's power behind him, he might very well roll right over her and win custody if it ever went to court. Then what would she do?

She couldn't lose her son.

Everything in her went cold and still. Fear rocketed through her system, successfully dousing the fires of her temper.

This was so much more dangerous than she'd ever thought.

"I'll run away. I swear I will," Maggie said into the phone a half hour later. "I'll take Jonas and disappear."

"Calm down, sweetie," Matrice urged her. "Now just tell me what happened without the hysterics, okay?"

Sitting on her bed, watching her son stare out the window at the play of the storm outside, Maggie went over her whole fight with Justice. She told her elder sister everything, sparing neither of them, and by the time she was finished talking, she had to admit she felt better already, just for the spewing factor.

"I can't believe he'd be that dumb," Matrice said. "If

he'd just told you the truth before, none of this would have happened."

"I already covered that, believe me," Maggie told her and smiled when Jonas kicked his little legs as if he were desperately trying to get up and run.

"I know, but, oh, hold on—" She half covered the mouthpiece so that her voice was muffled as she said, "Danny, don't pour oatmeal on the cat, honey. That's a bad choice. Sorry," she told Maggie when she was back. "We're getting a late start on breakfast and Danny apparently wants to share."

Maggie smiled, thinking of her almost two-year-old nephew. The little boy attacked each day as if determined to get as much out of it as he could. Maggie could hardly wait to watch Jonas at that age. She looked down at her son, trying to grab hold of his own toes, and smiled. There was so much to look forward to. So much she could lose if Justice meant what he said and actually tried to take her son.

Fear galloped along her spine and Maggie took a deep breath, trying to rein it in.

"Mags? You there?" Matrice's voice brought Maggie back to earth and grounded her in the present.

Her older sister was matter-of-fact and down-to-earth, and she had enough common sense to talk Maggie off the proverbial ledge when she had to. Today, that talent was essential.

"I'm here, Matrice. Worried and a little nauseous, but I'm here."

"You don't have to worry."

"Easy for you to say."

Matrice laughed. "Honey, I'd be worried, too, if I actually believed that Justice would take you to court over your son."

"What makes you think he won't?"

"Because I'm brilliant and insightful. That's why you called me, remember?"

True. But still, Matrice hadn't seen Justice's face. His stern, determined expression.

"It's not going to go to court, I promise you, so relax a little, okay?"

"You don't know that," Maggie assured her, reaching out to smooth her hand across her son's inky black hair and skim her fingertips along his cheek. Instantly, Jonas made a grab for her finger and held on, as if he'd caught a prize. He couldn't possibly realize that he also had a grip on his mother's heart. "Justice is single-minded if nothing else, remember? And now that he's focused on Jonas and being a part of his life, there's nothing that will stop him. He'll do whatever he has to, to ensure he wins."

"But he can't win if he alienates you, and he knows it."

"Maybe. But he's so focused on Jonas."

Matrice chuckled. "That's not a bad thing, honey. You *wanted* him in Jonas's life, remember? That was one of the reasons you took the job when Jeff offered it. You wanted Justice to get to know his son. To want to be in his life."

"Yeah…" Okay, yes, that had been the plan. "But I didn't mean for him to take my son from me."

"He's not going to."

"You can't be sure of that."

"Yes, I can."

"How?" Maggie asked, really wanting to be convinced.

Her sister sighed into the phone. "Justice loves you, Mags. He always has. He wouldn't hurt you like that, and if you think about it, you'll see that's true."

"Yes, but…"

"And please, he's going to take the baby from you? Can you see him raising a baby on his own? It would be pitiful. Why, my own Tom hardly knows which end of the diaper goes under Danny's behind!"

"True," Maggie said, smiling now as her nerves began to unwind a little. She remembered the still-awkward way Justice held his son and knew that he'd be lost if he had to take care of the baby on his own. Then something occurred to her. "But he has Mrs. Carey and she's crazy about Jonas!"

"She's crazy about you, too," Matrice insisted. "No way would that woman help Justice take your son from you."

"Maybe not," she said with a sigh, lifting her gaze from the grinning baby to the stormy skies beyond the window. "But, Matrice, I can't help thinking this is going to get uglier before it gets any better."

"My money's on you, kid," her sister said.

A few hours later Justice studied the ranch report spread out on his desk, but he couldn't keep his mind from wandering. He'd put a call into King Labs and was unable to get an answer from them yet. What the hell was taking so long? Why couldn't they just finish the damn test and end the waiting?

He leaned back in his chair then, willing to admit at

least to himself that his mind wasn't on the ranch. Instead, it was tangled up with thoughts of Maggie and the boy who might be his son. And if he wasn't? he asked himself. What then? Then, he thought, Maggie would leave, taking Jonas with her, and life at the ranch would once again be quiet as the grave.

Was he really willing to go back to living like that?

Justice scrubbed both hands over his face. No, he wasn't. He hated the idea of once more being alone in this house but for Mrs. Carey. He didn't like the idea of not seeing toys everywhere. Of not hearing the baby cry or Maggie's laughter ringing through the halls.

But did he have a choice? Had there been too many lies to patch up a marriage that had once been so shining and right? Great sex wasn't enough. Not when there had been so many harsh words between a couple. Not when distrust roared up at every corner. And, as he'd told himself before, great sex only complicated things. Remembering the look on her face when he'd finally confessed the truth to her, Justice had to acknowledge that maybe what they'd once shared was too shattered to put back together. And if their marriage was really over, what was left?

A small boy who would need both of them.

He accepted that if Jonas wasn't his, then Maggie was lying to him. But hadn't he lied to her, too? Hadn't he done just what she'd accused him of doing—chosen his pride over their marriage? Was her lie so much more terrible than his? Would it be so bad to accept another man's child as his own?

People adopted every day. Why couldn't he?

Warming to his thoughts, Justice stood up and walked to the wide windows overlooking the ranch yard. The storm was still raging, matching the way he was feeling exactly. He laid one hand on the cold glass and felt the tiny slaps of the rain as the drops bounced against his palm.

All he had to do was accept Jonas and he would have an heir. He'd have a boy he could raise and teach. Did it really matter who had created him as long as Justice raised him?

A small voice in his mind whispered *yes, it matters*. And his pride stirred and did battle with his desires. He couldn't ask her to be his wife again. That was done. Maggie and he might be finished, but they could have something different, he thought now. Something less than a marriage, less than lovers and more than friendship. It could work.

He could have Maggie *and* a son if he was willing to bend.

The question was, could he?

When the study door opened behind him, Justice didn't even have to turn around to know she was there. Watching him. He felt the power of her gaze and waited for her to approach. Her steps were muffled against the thick rugs spread across the wood floor, but he heard her anyway. That sure, confident step was purely Maggie.

She stopped directly behind him, and he could have sworn he felt the heat of her body reaching out for his.

"I won't lose my son, Justice," she said, and though her voice was quiet, there was a ring of steel in her tone.

He admired that. Hell, he'd always admired Maggie.

Justice turned around to face her, and his gaze swept her up and down, noting the faded jeans, the cream-colored sweater and the wild tangle of her fiery hair. Her blue eyes were calm and fixed on him, but her chin was lifted into fighting mode and he knew she was ready to draw a line in the sand.

So he cut her off before she could.

"You don't have to," he said and saw the brief flash of confusion on her face. "I've been thinking about this since this morning, and an idea just came to me."

She tipped her head to one side to watch him warily. "What kind of idea?"

He leaned back against the window jamb, folded his arms across his chest and said, "I want you to move back to the ranch. You and Jonas."

"You mean once the test results are in."

"No," he said. "I mean now."

She shook her head as if she didn't quite understand what he was saying. And hell, who could blame her.

"But you don't even believe that Jonas is yours yet."

"Doesn't matter," he said and actually felt the ring of truth in that statement resonate in his soul. He'd made up his mind. Jonas would be his. Biologically or legally. "I can adopt him legally. Either way, he'll still be my son."

"I see," she said, though he was guessing she really didn't, since her features were carefully blank. "So, you want me to move back in as your wife?"

Step carefully, King, he told himself.

"No," he said quietly, "we're divorced and that's probably best. Maggie, we were always too combustible for our own good. I know our marriage is over. But there's no reason you can't move in here anyway. We can raise Jonas together and have a platonic relationship."

Her jaw dropped.

He smiled. It wasn't easy to surprise Maggie King.

"Platonic?" She repeated the word as if she couldn't quite believe he'd actually said it. "Whatever we have together, Justice, it's never been platonic."

"Doesn't mean it can't be," he countered. God knew, he wouldn't enjoy it much, but if that's what it took to have her and the baby in his world, then that's what he'd do. "We could have a good life, Maggie. We'd be close…friends."

"We'll never be just friends, Justice," she told him. "Don't you get that? There's too much between us. Too much passion to be stoppered up in a jar and set on a shelf somewhere to make things easier for you."

"You're taking this all the wrong way, Maggie. That's not what I'm trying to do."

"Isn't it?" She pushed both hands through her hair and growled briefly under her breath as if she were trying to get hold of her temper. "You've decided Jonas will be your son whether he is or not. You've decided that I can be your friend and live here at the ranch. But you're not saying anything about trying for something more, because Justice King doesn't make mistakes."

"What the hell are you talking about?"

"Don't you think I know what you're doing?" She laughed then, hard and fast. "God, I know you even better than you know yourself. You won't ask me to live with you as your wife again because that would mean you made a mistake when you let me leave you. And you don't make mistakes, do you, Justice?"

He just stared at her. How was a man supposed to unravel the wild logic women came up with? "How the hell did you twist this around like that?"

"Because I know you." She laughed shortly and shook her head while she waved one finger at him. "You don't want platonic, Justice, any more than I do. You just figure that's the easiest way to get me to agree. Then, once I'm living here at the ranch, you can change things. You've probably got it all planned out in your mind. I can just see it," she continued, wiggling her fingers in wide circles that got smaller and smaller. "You'll work it around to the arrangement that will suit you best. And what suits you, Justice, is me in your bed. You want *me*. You want our bodies tangled together. You want hot breath and soul-stealing kisses."

He took a long, slow breath and then swallowed hard. Figured Maggie would make this more difficult than it had to be. Figured she would see right through his "platonic" offer, too. The woman always had been way too smart. "Of course I want you—that's obvious enough—but it doesn't mean we can't live as friends."

"Oh, of course it does. It would be impossible. You and I, Justice, were never meant for platonic." Then she went up on her toes, wrapped her arms around his neck and pulled him in for a long, deep kiss that held as much fury as passion.

Justice would have sworn he felt heat swamp him from the top of his head to the bottoms of his feet. She was fire and light and heat and seduction. His arms snaked around her middle, held on tight and pressed her to him, aligning her body to his. He was tight and hard for her in an instant and knew she was making her point all too well.

Then the kiss was over and she was looking up into his eyes. "Deny that, if you can. We're not friends. We're lovers." Her arms dropped from around his neck. "Or we were. Now, I'm not sure what we are anymore. The only thing I'm sure of is, I won't lose my son."

She turned her back on him and stomped out of the room without once looking back. But why should she? She'd made her point.

His arms felt empty without her in them. His body was on fire and slowly cooling now that Maggie was gone. Damn it, he hated the cold. He wanted the heat. He wanted *her*. And he always would. She was right. They couldn't live together as friends. So what did that leave them?

They had a past.

They might have a future.

All it would cost him was his pride.

Ten

"You're as stubborn as he is, I swear." Mrs. Carey gave her soup pot a stir, then fisted her hands at her hips. "That poor baby is going to have a head like a rock thanks to his parents."

Maggie sat at the kitchen table, drinking tea she didn't want and staring through the window at Justice as he carried Jonas around the ranch yard. Spring sunshine fell out of a perfect sky. Angel and Spike were racing in circles, making Jonas laugh with delight, and the wide grin on Justice's face stole her breath away.

Yet here she sat in the kitchen. It was a bright, cheery room, with dozens of cabinets, miles of countertop and the comforting scent of homemade soup bubbling on the stove. But Maggie didn't feel comforted. More like... disconnected.

At the end of a very long week, she felt as though she were walking a tightwire fifty feet off the ground with no net beneath her. Days crawled past and she and Justice might as well have been living in separate homes. She hadn't touched him in days, though she'd dreamed about him every night. Thought about him every waking moment.

And still there didn't seem to be an answer.

"What am I supposed to do?" Maggie asked with a shake of her head. "He wants us to be *friends*."

Mrs. Carey snorted. "Anyone can see you two weren't destined for friendship."

Smiling wryly, Maggie said, "I agree, but what if that's all that's left to us?"

Mrs. Carey walked to the table, sat down opposite her and folded her hands neatly on top of a brick-red placemat. Staring Maggie in the eyes, she asked bluntly, "If all that's left is friendship, why does the air sizzle when the two of you are together?"

Maggie laughed. "Excuse me?"

"Do I look like I'm a hundred and fifty years old?" Mrs. Carey snorted again and clucked her tongue. "Because I'm not. And anyone with half an eye could have seen the way you two were around each other the past couple of weeks. I nearly caught fire myself, just watching the two of you look at each other."

No point in denying the truth, Maggie thought. So she didn't try. "Not lately, though."

"No," Mrs. Carey allowed. "What I've got to wonder is why? What changed?"

"What hasn't?" Reaching for a cookie from the plate

in the center of the table, Maggie took a bite, chewed, then swallowed. "He wants Jonas, but he hasn't said he wants *me*."

"Pfft." The older woman waved away that statement with one dismissive hand. "You know he does."

"What I know and what I need to hear are two different things," Maggie said, letting her gaze slide once again to the two most important men in her life. She looked out the window just in time to see Justice plant a kiss on Jonas's forehead.

Her heart melted. She'd wished for this for so long, that Justice would know and love his son, and now it was happening. The only problem was that she should have been more specific in her wishes. She should have hoped that the *three* of them would find one another.

"Maggie, you more than anybody know that Justice doesn't always say what he's feeling," Mrs. Carey said softly, drawing her gaze away from the window. "You love him. I can see it in you."

"Yeah, I love him," she admitted. "But that doesn't change anything."

The other woman laughed. "Oh, honey. It changes everything. With love, anything's possible. You just can't give up."

"I'm not the one giving up," she retorted, defending herself. "Justice is the one who won't budge."

"Hmm…"

"What's that mean?"

"Nothing at all," Mrs. Carey said with a sigh. "Just seems to me that people as stubborn as you and Justice have an obligation to the world to stick together. Spare two other people from having to put up with either of you."

She had to laugh. One thing about Justice's house-keeper, you never had to wonder what she was thinking.

"Now, why don't you go outside and join your men?"

She wanted to. She really did. But things were so strained between Justice and her at the moment that she wasn't at all sure she'd be welcomed. Besides, now that Justice was almost back to full strength, she'd be leaving soon and taking Jonas with her, no matter what the baby's father thought about it. So why not let the two of them have some time together while they could?

But, oh, the thought of leaving the ranch again, leaving *Justice* again, was killing her. And the fear that he might make good on his promise and try to take her son was chilling. Pain was gathering on the near horizon, and she knew that when it finally caught up to her, it was going to be soul crushing.

"No," Maggie said, standing up slowly. It was time she started getting used to the fact that she wasn't going to be with Justice. Brace for the coming pain as best she could. "I think I'll go upstairs, take a long bath and start getting ready for tonight."

Mrs. Carey nodded. "It's good that you're going with him."

Maybe it was, Maggie thought, but maybe it would turn out to be an exercise in torture for both of them. She'd agreed days ago to attend the Feed the Hungry charity dance with Justice.

Feed the Hungry was a local foundation the King Ranch donated hundreds of thousands of dollars every year to in order to stock local food banks. Maggie had even helped plan the event when she and Justice were still together. So attending with him had seemed like a good idea when he'd first broached the subject.

But now…she wasn't so sure. Looking down at the woman still seated at the table, she asked, "Are you certain you don't mind babysitting while we go? Because if you do, I can stay home and—"

"It's a joy to watch that baby, and you well know it," Mrs. Carey told her with a smile. "So if you're thinking of chickening out at the last minute, you can't use me as an excuse."

Maggie's lips twitched. "Some friend you are."

"Honey, I am your friend. And as your friend, I'm telling you to go upstairs. Take a bath. Do your hair and makeup and wear that gorgeous dress you bought yesterday." She stood up, came around the table and gave Maggie a brief, hard hug. "Then you go out with your husband. Dance. Talk. And maybe remember just what it is you two have together before it's too late."

Justice hated getting dressed up.

He felt uncomfortable in the tailored tux and wished to hell he was wearing jeans and his boots. He even had a headache from gathering up his hair and tying it into a neat ponytail at the back of his neck. He didn't get why it mattered what he wore to this damn thing. Why couldn't he just write a check and be done with it?

Scowling, he glanced around the hallway and noted that the cobalt blue vase held a huge bouquet of roses, their scent spilling through the entryway. Now that

Maggie was back on the ranch, the vases were filled again; he knew that when she was gone, it would be just one more thing he would miss. She'd made her mark on this place as well as on him. And nothing would be the same after she left.

His leg was better now, so he knew that she'd be planning to go soon. He couldn't let that happen. Not this time. He had to find a way to make her stay. Not just because of Jonas but also because without Maggie, Justice didn't feel complete.

He shot his cuffs, checked his watch and frowned. Maggie always had kept him waiting. Back in the day, he'd stood at the bottom of these steps, hollering up for her to get a move on, and she'd always insisted that she would be worth the wait.

"Damned if that isn't still true," he murmured when he spotted her at the top of the stairs.

Her long, red-gold hair fell loosely around her shoulders, the way he liked it best. Long, dangling gold earrings glittered and shone in the light tossed from a wall sconce. She wore a strapless, floor-length dark green dress that clung to her curves until practically nothing was left to the imagination. The bodice was low-cut, exposing the tops of her breasts, and the skirt fell in graceful folds around her legs. She carried a black cashmere wrap folded neatly across her arm.

She stood there, smiling at him, and his breath caught in his lungs. Her cheeks were pink and her blue eyes sparkled as she enjoyed his reaction to her. If she only knew just how strong his response was. Suddenly, his tux felt even more uncomfortable than it had before as his body tightened and pushed at the elegant fabric.

"Well?" she asked, making a slow turn at the top of the stairs.

Justice hissed in a breath. The back was cut so low she was practically naked. The line of her spine drew his gaze, and he followed it down to the curve of her behind, just barely hidden by the green silk. His hands itched to touch her. It took everything he had to keep from vaulting up the stairs—bad leg or not—crushing her to him and carrying her off to the closest bed.

She'd been right, he told himself. They weren't friends. They'd never *be* friends. He wanted her desperately and doubted that feeling would ever fade.

But she was waiting for him to say something, watching him now with steady eyes. He didn't disappoint her.

"You're beautiful," he whispered, his voice straining to be heard past the knot in his throat. "Every man in the room is going to want you."

She came down the stairs slowly, one hand on the banister, each step measured and careful. He got peeks of her sandaled feet as she moved and noticed a gold toe ring he'd never paid attention to before. Sexy as hell, he thought, and grimly fought a losing battle to get his own body back under control.

"I'm not interested in every man," she said when she was just a step or two above him.

"Good thing," he told her. "I'd hate to have to bring a club to fight them off with."

She gave him a dazzling smile that sent his heartbeat into overdrive.

"I think that's the nicest thing you've ever said to me, Justice."

Then he'd been a damn fool, he thought. He should have always told her how beautiful she was. How important to him she was. But he hadn't found the words and so he'd lost her. Maybe, though, there was time enough for him to take another shot at it.

He reached out, took one of her hands in his and helped her down the last two steps. When she was standing right in front of him, he inhaled, drawing her scent into his body as if taking all of her in. He lifted one hand, smoothed her hair back from her cheek, touched her cool, soft skin and felt only fire.

"Maggie, I—"

"Well, now, don't you both look wonderful," Mrs. Carey said as she walked into the hall, Jonas on her hip.

Justice didn't know if he was relieved or irritated by the interruption.

The baby kicked his legs, waved his arms and, with drool streaming down his chin, reached for his mother. Maggie moved to take him, but Mrs. Carey stepped back. "Oh, no, you don't," she said, laughing. "He'll have you covered in drool in no time—you don't want to ruin that dress."

Maggie sighed and Justice watched her eyes warm as she looked at her son. He felt it, too, he realized, looking at the baby safe in the housekeeper's arms. A wild, huge love for a tiny child he wasn't even sure was his yet. But the more time he spent with the baby, the more he saw of him, the more he cared for him. He and Maggie were linked through this child, he knew. But would it be enough to start over? To rebuild what they'd lost?

"She's right," he said, keeping a tight grip on Maggie's hand. "We're late anyway."

Maggie lifted one eyebrow at him. "Was that a dig?"

He gave her a half smile. "Just a fact. You always did make us late for everything."

"I like to make an entrance."

"You do a hell of a job, I'll give you that," he said and was rewarded by a quick grin. Her smile sucker punched him, and he had to steady himself again before looking at Mrs. Carey. When he did, he found the older woman giving him a knowing look. She saw too much for Justice's comfort. Always had.

"Goodnight, little man," Maggie whispered as she leaned in to Jonas and kissed his cheek. Then she cupped her hand around the back of his head and just held on to him for a long moment. Pulling back, then she said, "Does he feel a little warm to you?"

"Warm?" Justice repeated, reaching out to place his palm on the baby's forehead, a sudden, sharp stab of worry slicing through him. "You think he has a fever?"

"Maybe we should check before we go," Maggie said. "It won't take long and—"

"He'll be fine—don't you worry." Mrs. Carey shook her head at both of them. "I know how to take care of a baby and if I need you, I'll call your cell."

"You've got the number, right?" Maggie asked, digging in her small cocktail purse to drag out her cell phone and make sure it was on.

"Of course I do, you've given it to me three times just today."

"My number's programmed on your phone, too, right?" Justice asked, patting his pants pocket to assure himself he had his phone, as well.

"I have your number, too. And the police," Mrs. Carey said, herding them toward the front door. "And the hospital and probably the National Guard. Go. Dance. Have fun."

Frowning a little at the bum's rush they were receiving, Justice took hold of Maggie's elbow and steered her onto the porch. "We're going, but we're only a few miles away and—"

"I know where Stevenson Hall is, Justice. Haven't I lived here most of my life?" Mrs. Carey shooed them off with one hand. "Go on, have some fun, for heaven's sake. The baby's fine and he's going to stay fine."

"If you're sure…" Maggie didn't sound at all pleased about leaving now and her gaze was fixed on the smiling baby.

"Go."

Justice took Maggie's wrap from her, draped it over her bare shoulders, then took her arm and threaded it through his. Giving his housekeeper one more look, he said, "She's right. Jonas will be fine, and if we have to, we can be back home in ten minutes."

"All right, then," Maggie said unenthusiastically. She looked at Mrs. Carey. "You promise to call me if he needs me?"

"Absolutely," she said. "Drive safe."

Then she closed the door and Maggie and Justice were standing on the dimly lit porch all alone. Her scent

drifted to him and the heat of her body called to him—
and Justice could only think he'd never been less interested in going anywhere. It wasn't worry over the baby
making him want to stay home. It was the idea of having
this elegantly dressed, absolutely beautiful Maggie King
all to himself.

But he had an obligation to the charity the King Ranch
funded, so he would go. "We don't have to stay long,"
he said, leading her down the porch and across the drive
to where one of the ranch hands had parked the SUV.

"I know." Maggie threw one last glance at the house
behind her, then turned to look at Justice. "Jonas is
probably fine, and besides, I want a dance with a handsome man in a tux tonight."

His mouth quirked slightly. "Anyone I know?"

She laughed as he'd meant her to, then said, "Maybe
Mrs. Carey is right. Maybe we should try to relax and
enjoy the night."

"Maybe," he said, sliding one hand down her arm.
"But for God's sake don't tell her that."

Maggie laughed again as she swung herself inside the
car after he opened the door for her, and Justice told
himself to enjoy what he had while he had it. He knew
all too well just how quickly things could change.

The charity ball was a huge success.

The banquet hall at the local art center was packed
with the county's movers and shakers. A band was
playing dance music on the stage, and formally dressed
waiters moved through the crowd carrying trays of ap-
petizers. Helium-filled balloons in an array of colors

filled the ceiling and occasionally fell limply to the floor below. Women dressed in jewel-toned gowns swirled in the arms of tuxedo-clad men, and Maggie was left to visit with friends instead of dancing with her husband as she wanted to.

She spotted Justice across the room, standing in a knot of people. Even from a distance, her breath caught in her chest just watching him. He was magnificent in a tuxedo. She knew he hated formal wear, but even in a tux, his raw strength and sensuality bled through until most women would have had to fan themselves after a peek at him.

Maggie frowned when she saw him rub idly at his thigh. She probably should have put her foot down about attending this dance, but he was so damn proud. So reluctant to be treated as if he needed help. And the truth was, he was well on the way to being one hundred percent again, so a small ache or pain wasn't going to stop him anyway.

The men clustered around Justice were no doubt asking his advice on any number of things, she thought, while absentmindedly keeping track of the conversations around her. But that was how it had always been. People turned instinctively to Justice. He was a man who somehow gave off the air of being in complete control, and to most people that was simply irresistible.

She was no different. She looked at Justice and knew she wanted him with every breath in her body. He was the one. The only one for her. Sighing, she turned her head and smiled at the still-speaking woman beside her.

So when Justice came up behind her a moment or

two later, she was so startled she jumped as he laid one hand on her back. Heat spilled through her as his fingers caressed her spine with a delicate touch. She closed her eyes, sighed a little and took a breath, hoping to regain her balance. Then, looking up at him, she asked, "Having a good time?"

He dipped his head to hers and murmured, "Hell, no, but it might get better if you dance with me."

Maggie smiled, then asked, "You sure you're up to it? Your leg, I mean."

"The leg's fine. A little achy." He held out a hand. "So? A dance with the guy who brought you?"

"Oh, honey, if he was asking me to dance, I wouldn't hesitate." A few chuckles resulted from that statement by a woman old enough to be Justice's grandmother.

"Mrs. Barton," Maggie said with a teasing laugh, "you'd better be careful. I've got my eye on you."

As Justice led her through the crowd to the mobbed dance floor, Maggie felt a swell of pride inside her. There were any number of women in this room who would give anything to be on Justice's arm. And for tonight, at least, that woman was her.

She went into his arms as if it was the only place on earth she belonged. When he held her so tightly to him she could feel the strength of his body pressing into hers, Maggie nearly sighed with pleasure. Then he turned her lazily in time to the swell of the music, and she smiled, enjoying the moment. All around them, couples swayed in time and snatches of conversations lifted and fell in the air.

When Justice's step faltered, Maggie frowned. "Are you okay?"

He gritted his teeth. "I'm fine."

"We don't have to dance, Justice."

He hissed out a breath. "I said I'm fine, Maggie. The leg aches a little. That's all."

"I'm just concerned."

"You don't have to be, damn it," he ground out, then clamped his lips tightly together for a second before saying, "I don't need you to worry about me, all right? Can we just dance?"

But the magic of the moment was ruined for Maggie. *I don't need you.* His words repeated over and over again in her mind. "That's the problem, Justice," she blurted while still following his lead around the floor.

"What?" He was frowning again now, and damned if that expression didn't make him look more sexy. More dangerous.

"You don't need me."

"I said I don't need you to worry about me—there's a difference."

"No," she insisted, staring up at him as they made another turn. "There isn't. I need *you*. I always have."

"That's good, because—"

"No," she interrupted him, uncaring about the people surrounding them on the floor. They probably couldn't overhear the conversation over the music, but even if they could, that wouldn't have stopped her. "It isn't good, Justice. It's the reason I can't be with you."

"You *are* with me."

His hand tightened around hers and his eyes

narrowed into slits. Maggie shook her head at his fierce expression. "Not for much longer. Yes, I need you, but I can't be with you, because I want to be needed, too."

"What the hell does that mean?" he demanded, holding her closer, as if half afraid she was going to bolt. "Of course I need you."

She laughed shortly, but there was no humor in it, only misery. "No, you don't. You wouldn't even let me help you a second ago when your leg hurt."

"That's different, Maggie. I don't need a therapist."

"No," she said, her temper building, frothing, despite the fact that she was in the middle of a crowd that was slowly beginning to take notice. "You don't want to need anyone. You won't admit that you can't do every-thing yourself. It's your pride, Justice. It always comes down to your pride."

Justice's voice was low and tight. There were too many damn people around them. Too many who might be listening in. "My pride helped me build the ranch into one of the biggest in the country. My pride got me through when you walked out."

"Your pride is the *reason* I walked out, remember?"

"You're not walking this time," he told her, his grip on her hand and around her waist making that point clear. "This time we *have* to be together."

"Why?"

"Because I got a text from Sean at the lab. The results of the test are in. I'm Jonas's father."

Both of her eyebrows arched high on her forehead as she tried to pull free from his grasp. "If you're waiting for me to be surprised, don't bother."

"I know. I should have listened. I should have believed."

"Yes, you should have."

He felt as if a two-thousand-pound rock had been lifted off his shoulders. He felt change in the air, and it damn near made him laugh with the possibilities of it all. "Don't you get it, Maggie? This changes everything. I'm his father. That means the doctor was wrong. I *can* give you children."

"I already knew that, Justice," she said, glancing to the side as another couple moved in close.

"Which is why we're getting married," he said, the decision made and delivered like an order.

"Excuse me?" She stopped dancing, dragging him to a sudden halt.

"I said we're getting married."

Maggie frowned at someone who jostled her, then turned to him and announced, "I can't marry you. I'm already married."

"You're married?" Justice stared at her as if she were speaking Greek. "What do you mean you're *married*? We've been sleeping together!"

Several heads turned toward them now, and Justice scowled at the most obvious eavesdroppers, shaming them into looking away.

Maggie flushed right up to the roots of her hair, but it was fury, not embarrassment, staining her cheeks. "I'm married to *you,* Justice!"

She spun around on her heel and pushed her way through the crowd. Justice was left staring after her, stunned by her declaration and furious that he hadn't known about this before. He started after her, his steps long and sure. When he caught up with her, he grabbed her arm, turned her to face him and, ignoring the crowd, said, "I signed those divorce papers, Maggie! How the hell are we married?"

"I never filed them, you big jerk." And once again, she pulled free and made her way to the exit. Justice was right behind her, ignoring the wild rustle of conversations and laughter filling the hall behind him.

No doubt people would be talking about this night for a damn long time, he told himself while he took off after Maggie. Mostly, he suspected they'd be calling him a fool, and he'd have to agree.

He and Maggie were still married and he hadn't even known it. When he reached the front door, he raced outside and spotted Maggie walking with furious steps down the sidewalk in the direction of home. Racing for the parking lot, Justice found his car, started it up and chased down his errant wife.

Driving alongside her while she was muttering to herself and bristling with unleashed fury, he rolled down the passenger window and ordered, "Get in the car, Maggie."

"I don't *need* you, Justice." She made sure of the emphasis on the word *need,* and flipped her hair back behind her shoulders. "I'll walk."

"You can't walk it."

"Watch me."

"It's ten miles to the ranch."

She slowed a little, shot him a furious glare and said, "If I get in that car, don't you *dare* speak to me."

"We have to talk about this, Maggie."

"No, we don't. We've said plenty. In front of the whole town, no less. So if you can't promise me silence, I'll walk."

"You're freezing."

"I'm too mad to be cold."

"Damn it, Maggie!" He slammed on the brakes, threw the car into Park and jumped out, racing down the sidewalk to catch up to her. His leg ached like a son of a bitch, but he ignored the pulsing pain in his quest to catch the most infuriating woman he'd ever known. When he grabbed hold of her, he wasn't even surprised to feel her turn into a hundred and twenty pounds of fighting fury.

"Let me go, you big bully!" She wrenched free from his grasp, and when his hand clutched at her forearm again, she swung one leg back to kick him in the shins. He dodged that move and still didn't release her. "Don't touch me. You humiliated me in front of the whole town—"

His eyes went wide. "I humiliated *you?*"

"You told the whole damn room we've been sleeping together."

"And you told 'em we're *married.* Who cares?"

"I do, in case you haven't noticed."

"So, now whose pride is the problem?" That one question delivered in a quiet, reasonable tone did what all of his arguments hadn't. They shut her up but fast, despite how resentful she looked about it.

"Fine. I'll take the ride. But I'm not talking to you, Justice. Not tonight. Not *ever.*"

He smiled to himself as he led her back to the car. One thing in this world he was sure of. Maggie Ryan King wouldn't be able to keep a vow of silence if her own life depended on it.

Eleven

By the time they reached the ranch, Maggie's temper had died into a slow burn. She could still see the shocked, delighted expressions on the faces of the people surrounding them at the ball. She just knew that by tomorrow the story was going to be all over the county.

And there wasn't a damn thing she could do about it. God, she felt like an idiot. She'd been harboring too many dreams about Justice, and seeing them shattered in an instant—in front of an audience—was just humiliating.

She had the door open and was jumping to the ground almost before the car had rolled to a stop.

"Damn it, Maggie! Wait a minute."

She ignored him and marched toward the house. She'd had enough. All she wanted now was to go inside, hug her baby and go to bed. Then when she woke up, she'd pack and get the heck out of Justice's house before he'd even had his morning coffee.

"Maggie, wait for me."

She glanced over her shoulder and hesitated when she saw him limp slightly. But a moment later, she reminded herself that he didn't want her help. He didn't need a therapist. He didn't need her.

Fumbling in her clutch purse for the front door key, she blew out a breath as Justice came up behind her, then reached past her to unlock the door and open it up.

"Thank you."

"You're welcome."

She hurried to the stairs, but his hand on her arm stopped her. "Maggie, at least talk to me."

Turning her gaze up to his, she stared into those dark blue eyes and felt a sigh slide from her throat. "What's left to say?"

"I'm so glad you're home. I was just getting ready to call you!"

They both turned to look up at the head of the stairs, where Mrs. Carey stood, holding a fretful Jonas. Instantly, Maggie gathered the hem of her dress, hiked it above her knees and raced up the stairs. Justice was just a step or two behind her.

Scooping her son into her arms, Maggie cuddled him close and inhaled sharply. "He's burning up!"

Justice came close, laid his hand on the back of Jonas's neck and shot a look at Mrs. Carey. "How long?"

She wrung her hands together. "He's been uneasy all night, but just in the past half hour or so, his fever's climbed. I tried calling the doctor but couldn't get him, so I was going to call you."

"It'll be fine, Mrs. Carey. Don't worry." He plucked Jonas from Maggie's arms and held him close to his chest. With his free hand, he took Maggie's and curled his fingers around hers. She immediately felt better, linked to his warmth and strength. When she looked up at him, she saw the calm, stoic expression she was used to.

Tonight, that was a comfort. She was so scared for Jonas that having Justice beside her, taking charge and looking confident, filled her with the same kind of certainty.

"We'll take him to the E.R.," Justice was saying, already starting down the stairs, taking Maggie with him.

"Don't you want to at least change clothes first?" Mrs. Carey called after them.

"Nope."

The emergency room in any city was a miserable place, Justice thought as he paced back and forth across the pale green linoleum. The smells, the sounds, the suffering, it all piled up on a person the minute he or she walked in the doors. They shouldn't have to be there. Kids shouldn't be allowed to get sick. There should be some sort of cosmic law against making a child who didn't even understand what was happening to him feel so bad. If he had his way, he thought, glancing over his shoulder to where Maggie sat on a gurney cradling Jonas in her lap, he'd see to it that his son was never in a place like this one again.

Everything in Justice tightened as he realized that

what he was feeling was sheer terror with a thick layer of helplessness. And that was new. Justice had never in his life faced a situation that he couldn't fix—except for the time when Maggie had left him. Yet even then, he reminded himself, he could have stopped her if he'd let go of his own pride long enough to admit what was really important.

She'd been right, he realized. At the dance, when she'd accused him of letting their marriage dissolve because of his pride. But damn it, was a man supposed to lay down everything he was for the sake of the woman he loved?

Love.

That one word resonated inside him and seemed to echo over and over again. He loved her completely, desperately, and a life without her seemed like the worst kind of prison sentence.

His gaze fixed on Maggie now, he saw tears glimmering in her eyes. Saw her hand tremble as she stroked their son's back. Then she lifted her gaze to his, and he read absolute trust in those pale blue depths. She was looking to him to fix this. To make it right. She was turning to him despite the hard words and the hurt feelings that lay between them. Justice felt a stir of something elemental inside, and as he held her gaze, he swore to himself that he wouldn't let her down. And when this crisis with Jonas was past, he would do whatever he had to do to keep Maggie in his life.

As soon as they got Jonas taken care of and settled down in his own bed back at the ranch, he was going to tell her that he loved her. Tell her what she meant to him and how empty his life was without her—and his pride be damned.

"Justice, he feels so hot." She cradled the baby's head to her chest and rocked as Jonas sniffled and cried softly, rubbing tiny fists against his eyes.

His heart turned over as he watched the baby and reacted to Maggie's fears.

"I know," he said, "but don't worry, all right? Everything's gonna be fine, and I'm gonna get someone in here to see him even if I have to buy the damn hospital."

Someone out in the waiting room was crying, a moan came from behind a green curtain and nurses carrying clipboards hurried up and down a crowded hallway, their shoes squeaking on the floor. They'd been there an hour already, and but for a nurse checking Jonas's temperature when they first arrived, no one had come to check on the baby.

Maggie forced a smile. "I don't think buying the place is going to be necessary."

"It is if it's the only way I can get somebody's attention." He shot a glare over his shoulder at the hallway and the hospital beyond. "Damn it, he's a baby. He shouldn't have to wait as long as an adult."

Maggie sighed and smiled a little in spite of her obvious fear. "I'm glad you're here with me."

He stopped and stared at her. "You are?"

"God, yes," she said on a choked laugh. "I'd be a gibbering idiot right now if you weren't here with me, pacing in circles like a crazy person and threatening to buy hospitals."

He walked toward her and went into a crouch in front

of her so that he could look at her and his son. He dragged the backs of his fingers across Jonas's too-warm cheek and felt a well of love fill his heart. The baby turned his head, looked at Justice and sighed. A tiny movement. A small breath. And dark blue eyes looking into his with innocence and confusion.

And in that instant, that one, timeless moment, Justice finally completed the fall into an overpowering love for his son. It had been coming on him for days, and maybe it was all instinctual. Like a cow in the spring that can pick out her own calf from the herd.

Nature, drawing families together, bonding them with an indefinable something that in humans was explained as love. A love so rich, so pure, so overwhelming, it nearly brought him to his knees. There was absolutely nothing on this earth that Justice wouldn't do for that boy. Nowhere he wouldn't go. Nothing he wouldn't dare.

"It'll be all right, son," he whispered, his voice breaking as his eyes misted over. "Your daddy's going to see to it."

Maggie reached for his hand and held on. Linked together, a silent moment of complete understanding passed between them, and Justice couldn't help wondering how many other parents had been in this room. How many others had waited interminably for help.

"This is ridiculous," he said. "There should be more doctors. More nurses. People shouldn't have to wait. I swear, I'm going to talk to the city council. Hell, I'll donate an extra wing to this place and pay to see it's better staffed."

"Justice…"

"What the hell is taking so long?" he muttered, squeezing Maggie's hand to relieve his own impatience. "I don't get it. What do you have to do to get seen around here, bleed from an eyeball?"

"Well, wouldn't that be festive?" A woman's voice came from right behind him.

Justice whirled around to face a doctor, in her late fifties, maybe, with short, gray hair, soft brown eyes and an understanding smile on her face.

"I didn't see you."

"Clearly, and as to your earlier question, I'm sorry about the wait, but I'm here now. Let's take a look at your son, shall we?"

As the doctor walked past him toward the baby, she took the stethoscope off from around her neck and fitted the ear pieces into her ears. "Lay him down on the gurney, please," she said softly.

Maggie did but kept one hand on Jonas's belly, as if to reassure both of them. Justice stepped up behind her and laid one hand on her shoulder, linking the three of them together, into a unit.

"Let's just listen to your heart, little guy," the doctor crooned, giving Jonas a smile. She moved her stethoscope around the baby's narrow chest and made a note on a chart. Justice tried to read it but couldn't get a good look.

Then she checked his temperature and looked in his eyes. Finally, when the baby's patience evaporated and he let loose a wail, the doctor looked up and smiled.

"What is it? What's wrong with him?" Maggie reached to her shoulder to lay her hand over Justice's.

"Let me guess," the doctor said, hooking her stethoscope around her neck again before scooping Jonas up in capable hands and swaying to soothe his tears. "This is your first baby."

"Yes, but what does that have to do with anything?" Justice asked.

Jonas's tears had subsided, and he was suddenly fascinated by the doctor's stethoscope.

"Babies sometimes spike fevers," the doctor was saying. "Not sure why, really. Could be a new tooth. Could be he didn't feel well. Could be growing pains." Still smiling, she handed Jonas to his mother and looked from Maggie to Justice.

"The point is, he's fine. You have a perfectly healthy son." She checked her chart. "According to this, his temperature has already dropped. You can take him home, give him a tepid bath, it'll make him feel better. Then just keep an eye on him, and if you're worried about anything at all, you can either call me—" she wrote down a phone number on the back of her card "—or bring him back in."

Justice took the business card she handed him. He glanced at her name and nodded. "Thanks, Dr. Rosen. We appreciate it."

She grinned at him. "It's my pleasure. But if you meant what you were saying earlier, the hospital could use the extra wing and I've got lots of ideas."

Justice stared down at her and found himself smiling. There was so much relief coursing through his veins at the moment that he would have built the woman her own clinic if she'd asked him to. And he had the distinct feeling she knew it. As it was, he tucked her card into his breast pocket and said, "Give me a few days, and we'll talk about those ideas."

Her eyebrows shot straight up in surprise, but she recovered quickly. "You've got a deal, Mr. King."

When she left, Maggie leaned in close to Justice and he slid his arms around her and their son, holding them tightly to him. He rested his chin on top of Maggie's head and took a long minute to simply enjoy this feeling.

He had his family in his arms, and there was simply no way he would lose them now.

The ride back to the ranch was quiet and Maggie was grateful.

There were too many thoughts whirling through her mind for her to be able to hold any kind of rational conversation. Behind her in his car seat, Jonas slept fretfully. Soft whimpers and sighs drifted to her, and she turned in her seat to look at him, needing to reassure herself that he was safe. And healthy.

When she faced the front again, she took a moment to study Justice's profile in the muted light from the dashboard. His eyes were fixed on the road ahead of them. His mouth was firm and tight, his jaw clenched as if he, too, were having trouble relaxing from the scare they'd had. In the shadows he looked fierce and proud and untouchable.

But the memory of his arms coming around her, holding her and the baby, was so strong and fresh in her mind that she knew he was right now hiding his emotions from her. Which was probably just as well, she thought. Now that they were back on solid ground, now that they knew Jonas was fine, everything would return to the way it was. The way it had to be.

God, she could still hear him at the dance. *We'll get married.* Did he actually think that she would stay with him just because Jonas was his son? Or because he knew now that he could give her more children? Didn't he see that a marriage for the sake of the children was a mistake for everyone involved?

She blew out a breath as Justice steered the car down the long drive to the ranch house. Before he'd even turned off the engine, the front door flew open and a wide slice of lamplight cut into the darkness. Mrs. Carey stood on the threshold, wearing a floor-length terry cloth robe, fisted in one hand at her neck.

"Thank goodness, you're back. He's really all right?" she called out. "I've been so worried."

Maggie stepped out of the car. "He's fine, Mrs. Carey."

"Go on to bed," Justice added as he came around the front of the car. "We'll talk in the morning."

The older woman nodded and turned for the stairs, leaving the front door open with the lamplight shining like a path in the darkness.

Maggie went to the backseat, opened the door and deftly undid the straps holding Jonas in his car seat. He stirred a little, but as soon as his head was nestled onto his mother's shoulder, he went back to sleep. Having her child cuddled in close gave Maggie the strength she was going to need when she spoke to Justice. So she held on to Jonas as if he were a talisman as they headed for the house.

Once inside, Justice closed the door and silence descended on them. It had been one of the longest nights of Maggie's life—and it wasn't over yet. She couldn't wait until morning to say what had to be said. She didn't know if she'd find the will to have this conversation in the morning; by then, she might have talked herself out of it, and she couldn't allow that to happen no matter how her heart was breaking.

"Quite a night," Justice said, splintering the quiet with his deep, rumbling voice.

"Yes, it was." She turned her gaze up to his and stared into those dark blue eyes for a long moment. God, how she would miss him. *Say it now, Maggie,* she told herself firmly. *Do it and get it over with.* "Justice…"

He watched her, waiting, and she could see by his rigid stance that he wasn't expecting good news.

"I'm going to be leaving tomorrow," she said, the words bursting from her in a determined rush.

"What?" He took a step toward her, but Maggie backed up, stroking one hand up and down Jonas's spine. "Why?"

"You know why," she said sadly, feeling the sudden sting of tears. She blinked them back, desperate to at least complete this last part of their marriage with a little dignity. "Your leg's nearly healed. You don't need me, Justice, and it's time I actually moved on with my life."

"Move on?" He shook his head, ground his teeth together and said, "Now you want to move on? Now when we know I'm Jonas's father? Now that we can have the big family you always wanted?"

"It's not about that," she said with a sigh.

"I signed those divorce papers a hell of a long time ago, Maggie, but you never filed them. Why?"

She shook her head now. "You know why."

"Because you love me."

"Yes, all right?" She raised her voice and immediately regretted it when Jonas stirred against her. Hushing him, Maggie lowered her voice again and said, "I did. Still do. But when I go home, I'm finally going to file those divorce papers, Justice."

"Why now?" He stared at her, his features shadowed by the overhead light.

"Because I'm not going to stay married to you for the sake of our son," she told him, willing him to understand. "It wouldn't be right for any of us. Don't you see, Justice? I love you, but I need to be loved in return. I want to be needed. I want a man to share Jonas's life with me. I want a man who'll stand beside me—"

"Like I did tonight, you mean?"

"Yes," she said quickly, breathlessly. "Like you did tonight. But, Justice, that's not who you are normally. You don't let people in. You don't let yourself *need* anyone." She blew out a breath, bit down on her trembling lower lip and said, "You'd rather be right than be in love. Your pride is more important to you than anything or anyone. And I can't live like that. I won't."

She turned for the stairs, her heart heavy, her soul empty. She picked up the hem of her dress, took one step and was stopped by a single word from Justice.

"Please."

Stunned to her core, Maggie slowly turned to look at him. He stood alone in the entryway, a solitary man in the shadows though he stood beneath an overhead light. There was hunger in his eyes and a taut, uncomfortable expression on his face.

She'd almost convinced herself she had imagined him speaking when he said again, louder this time, "Please stay."

Maggie swayed in place, shocked by his words, astonished that he would swallow his pride and so damn hopeful she nearly couldn't breathe. "Justice? I don't think I've ever heard you say that before."

"You haven't." Justice went to her then, desperate to make her hear him. Make her understand everything he'd learned in the past few hours. It had been coming on for days, he knew, but the time spent in that emergency room, sharing their fears, standing beside her, wanting to take on the world to help his son, had coalesced everything into a very clear vision.

Without Maggie, he had nothing.

She'd knocked the floor out from under his feet by telling him she was going to leave him again. And if he allowed it this time, he knew it would be permanent. If he clung to his pride and refused to bend, he would lose everything that had ever mattered to him.

So he threw his pride out the proverbial window and risked everything by going to her. Two long steps brought him to her side. He reached for her but stopped himself. First, he would say what she needed to hear. The words he'd denied them both the last time they were together.

"I need you, Maggie. More than my next breath I need you."

Her beautiful eyes filled with tears that crested and spilled over to roll down her cheeks unchecked. Her lower lip trembled, and he lifted one hand to soothe that lip with the pad of his thumb. His gaze moved over her, from her tumbled, tangled hair to the now-ruined elegant ball gown. She was magnificent and she was his. As she was always meant to be. This was a woman born to stand beside a man no matter what came at them in life. This was a woman to grow old with. To treasure.

To thank God for every night.

And damned if he'd lose her.

"Justice, I—"

He shook his head fiercely and spoke up, keeping his voice low so as not to disturb his son. "No, let me say this, so you'll never doubt it again. I love you more than should be humanly possible. The last time you left, you took my heart with you. When you came back, I came alive again. I won't let you leave, Maggie. If you go, I'll go with you."

She laughed a little, tears still spilling down her cheeks, and she'd never looked more lovely to him.

"See?" he asked. "No more pride. No more anything unless you're with me."

"Oh, God…"

"Stay with me, Maggie," he said gently, tipping her chin up so that he could look into those tear-washed eyes of hers. "Please stay. Please love me again. Please let me love you and Jonas and all the other children we'll have together."

She laughed again, a small sound filled with delight and wonder, and Justice could have kicked his own ass for taking so long, for wasting so much time, before setting things right between them.

"It's getting easier to say *please*," he told her, "and I swear, tonight won't be the last time you hear it."

"I don't know what to say," she admitted, staring up at him with a smile curving her mouth and tears glistening like diamonds on her cheeks.

"Say yes," he urged, pulling her and the baby into the circle of his arms. "Say you'll stay. Say I didn't blow it this time."

She leaned her head against his chest and sighed heavily. "I love you so much."

Justice grinned and held them a little tighter. So much relief had flooded his system in the past hour that he felt almost drunk on it. He wanted to shout. He wanted to go call his brother Jeff and thank him for sending Maggie back home where she belonged.

Then she pulled back and looked up at him again. "Am I dreaming?"

He smiled at her, bent his head and placed one quick kiss on her upturned mouth. "No dream, Maggie. Just a man telling you that you are his heart. Just your husband asking you to give him another chance to prove to you that he can be the man you need. The man you deserve."

"Oh, Justice," she said with a sigh, lifting one hand to cup his cheek, "you've always been the only man for me. You've had my heart since the moment I saw you, and that will never change."

He rested his forehead against hers and gave silent thanks for coming to his senses in time.

Then Maggie shifted their son in her arms and handed him to Justice. "Why don't we take him upstairs and tuck him in? Together."

Justice cradled the tiny boy who was the second miracle in his life and dropped his free arm around

Maggie's shoulders. Together, they climbed the stairs, and when they reached the landing, Maggie stopped and smiled up at him. "Once our son is settled in, I think I'm going to need a little attention from my husband."

Justice grinned at her. "I think that can be arranged."

Her head on his shoulder, they walked down the hallway of home, passing from the shadows into the light.

* * * * *

WEDDING AT KING'S CONVENIENCE

BY
MAUREEN CHILD

To Kate Carlisle
A great friend, a terrific writer, and the one person
I want to share a latte with before RWA meetings!
Can't wait to see your first Desire™ book in print, Kate!

One

"You think I'm charming," Jefferson King said with a smug smile. "I can tell."

"Charming, is it?" Maura Donohue straightened up to her full, if less-than-imposing height. "Do you believe I'm so easily swayed by a smooth-talking man?"

"Easily?" Jefferson laughed. "We've known each other for the better part of a week now, Maura, and I can say with certainty there's nothing 'easy' about you."

"Well now," she countered with a smile of her own. "Isn't that a lovely thing to say."

She was pleased. Jefferson read the truth on her features. No other woman he'd ever known would have been complimented by knowing that a man thought her difficult. But then, Maura Donohue was one in a million, wasn't she?

He'd known it the moment he met her.

In Ireland scouting locations for an upcoming movie from King Studios, Jefferson had stumbled across Maura's sheep farm in County Mayo and had realized instantly that it was just what he'd been searching for. Of course, convincing Maura of that fact was something else again.

"You know," he said, leaning one shoulder against the white-washed stone wall of the barn, "most people would be leaping at the chance to make some easy money."

She flipped her long black hair behind her shoulder, narrowed sea-blue eyes on him and countered, "There you are again, using the word 'easy,' when you've already admitted I'm not a woman accustomed to taking the easy way."

He sighed and shook his head. The woman had an answer for everything but damned if she wasn't intriguing enough that he was enjoying himself. As the head of King Studios, Jefferson was more accustomed to people falling all over themselves to accommodate him. When he rolled into a town looking to pay top dollar for the use of a location, those he dealt with were always eager to sign on the dotted line and collect their cash.

Not Maura, though.

For days now, he'd been coming to the Donohue farm to talk to its stubborn owner/operator. He'd plied Maura with compliments, tempted her with promises of mountains of money he knew damn well she could ill afford to turn down and in general had tried to make himself too amiable to resist.

Yet she'd managed.

"You're in my way," she said.

"Sorry." Jefferson stepped aside so she could walk past him carrying a sack of God-knew-what. His every instinct told him to snatch the heavy load out of her arms and carry it for her. But she wouldn't accept or appreciate his offer at help.

She was fiercely independent, with a quick wit, sharp tongue and a body that he'd spent far too much time thinking about. Her thick black hair fell in soft waves to the middle of her back and he itched to gather it up in his hands to feel its sleekness sliding across his skin. She had a stubborn chin that she tended to lift when making a point and a pair of dark blue eyes fringed by long, inky-black lashes.

She was dressed in worn jeans and a heavy Irish knit sweater that covered most of her curves. But winter in Ireland meant damp, cold weather so he could hardly blame her for bundling up. Still, he hoped she invited him into her house for a cup of tea, because then she'd strip that sweater off to reveal a shirt that gave him a much better peek at what she kept hidden.

But for now, he followed her out of the barn into an icy wind that slapped at his face and stung his eyes as if daring him to brave the Irish countryside. His ears were cold and his overcoat wasn't nearly warm enough. He made a mental note to do some shopping in the village. Buy a heavier coat if he could find one and a few of the hand-knit sweaters. Couldn't hurt to endear himself to the local merchants. He'd want everyone in the tiny town of Craic on his side as he tried to sway Maura into renting King Studios the use of her farm.

"Where are we going?" he shouted into the wind and could have sworn he actually *saw* the wind throw his words back at him.

"*We're* not going anywhere," she called back over her shoulder. "*I'm* going to the high pasture to lay out a bit more feed."

"I could help," he said.

She turned and looked him over, her gaze pausing on his well-shined, expensive black shoes. Smirking then, she said, "In those fine shoes? They'll be ruined in a moment, walking through the grass and mud."

"Why not let me worry about my shoes?"

Lifting that stubborn chin of hers, she said, "Spoken like a man who needn't worry about where his *next* pair of shoes might come from."

"Is it all rich people you don't like," Jefferson asked, an amused smile on his face, "or is it just me?"

She grinned back at him, completely unabashed. "Well now, that's an interesting question, isn't it?"

Jefferson laughed. The women he was used to were more coy. More willing to agree with him no matter what he said. They didn't voice opinions for fear he wouldn't share them. He hadn't enjoyed himself this much in way too long.

And it wasn't just the women, either, he mused. It was everyone he knew back in Hollywood.

Came from not only being a member of a prominent family, but from being the head of a studio where dreams could be made or shattered on the whim of an executive. Too many people were trying too hard to stay on his good side. It was refreshing as hell to find someone who didn't care if he *had* a good side.

Maura slammed the gate of her small, beat-up lorry, then leaned back against it. Folding her arms over her chest in a classic defensive posture she asked, "Why are you trying so hard, Jefferson King? Is it the challenge of winning me over that's driving you? Are you not used to hearing the word 'no'?"

"I don't hear it often, that's true."

"I imagine you don't. A man like you with his fine shoes and his full wallet. Probably you're welcome wherever you go, aren't you?"

"You have something against a full wallet?"

"Only when it's thrown in my face every few minutes."

"Not thrown," he corrected. "Offered. I'm offering you a small fortune for the lease of your land for a few weeks. How is that an insult?"

Her mouth worked as if she were fighting a smile. "Not an insult, to be sure. But your stubborn determination to win me over is a curiosity."

"As you said, I do love a challenge." Every King did. And Maura Donohue was the most interesting one he'd had in a long time.

"We've that in common, then."

"Shared ground at last. Why not let me ride with you up to the high pasture? You can show me the rest of your farm."

She studied him for a long, quiet moment as the wind buffeted them both. Finally, she asked, "Why do you want to come with me?"

He shrugged. "Honestly, I've nothing better to do right now. Why is it you don't want me along?"

"Because I don't need help," she pointed out.

"You seem pretty sure of yourself," he told her.

"And I am," she assured him.

"Then why should you care if I ride along and help out if I can? Unless you're worried that you're going to be seduced by my lethal charisma."

She laughed. Threw her head back and let loose a loud, delighted roll of laughter that touched something inside him even as it poked at his pride. "Ah, you're an amusing man, Jefferson."

"Wasn't trying to be."

"Which only makes it that much more funny, don't you see?"

Hunching deeper into his overcoat against the cold, Jefferson told himself that she was no doubt trying to reassure herself that he wasn't getting to her. Because he knew he was. She wasn't nearly as distant as she had been the first time he'd driven onto the Donohue farm. That day, he'd been half expecting her to pull out a shotgun and force him off her land.

Not exactly the picture of Irish hospitality.

Thankfully, he'd always been the patient one in the family.

Trying a different tack now, he said, "Look at it this way. While you drive me around your place, you can have the chance to elaborate as to why you don't want to take me up on my offer to rent your farm for an already mentioned *exorbitant* amount of money."

She cocked her head to study him and her black hair

danced in the cold wind like a battle flag. "Fine then. Come along if you must."

"A gracious invitation, as always," he muttered.

"If you want gracious," she told him, "you should head down to Kerry, go to Dromyland Castle. They've fine waiters, lovely food and neatly tended garden paths designed to make sure their visitors' fine shoes don't get ruined."

"I'm not interested in gracious," he told her, heading for the side of the car. "That's why I'm here."

After a moment, she laughed shortly. "You give as good as you get, I'll say that for you."

"Thanks."

She joined him at the door of the truck. "But if you don't mind, I'll drive my own lorry."

"What?" Jefferson realized he'd gone to the right side—what should be the passenger side—but in Ireland, the steering wheel was on the right. "You do realize you guys have the wheel on the wrong side of the car."

"It's a matter of perspective, now isn't it?" She shooed him off and he rounded the front of the small truck, walking to the other door. "Wrong side, right side, makes no difference, as they're both *my* side."

Jefferson leaned his forearms on the roof of the truck. "Believe it or not, Maura, I'm on your side, too."

"Ah now," she said, grinning, "that I don't believe, Jefferson King, as I'm thinking that you're always on your own side."

She hopped in, fired up the engine and Jefferson moved fast to climb in himself, since he was sure she'd have no qualms about driving off and leaving him standing where he was. She was hardheaded. And beautiful. As stubborn as the hills here were green.

Watching the big American striding across a sheep-dung-littered rainy field on a blustery day was a fine thing, Maura mused. Even here, where he was so clearly out of his element, Jefferson King walked as if he owned the land. The edges of his gray overcoat flapped in the wind like a ghost's shroud. His thick black hair ruffled as though spirits were raking their cold fingers through it and his delicious-looking mouth was twisted up into a sneer of distaste. And yet, she thought, he continued on. Carrying sacks of feed across muddy ground to tip and pour the grain into troughs for her sheep.

As the feed hit the bottom of the troughs, the black and white creatures came scampering ever closer, as though they'd been starved for weeks. Greedy beasts, she thought with a smile as they nudged and pushed at the great Jefferson King.

To give him his due, he wasn't skittish around the animals as most city people were. They tended to look on mountain sheep as they would a hungry tiger, wondering if the beasties were going to turn on them with fangs and the taste for human flesh. For a rich American, he seemed oddly at home in the open country, though for some reason, the man refused to wear stout boots instead of his shiny, no doubt hideously expensive shoes.

He laughed suddenly as a head butt from the sheep nearly sent him sprawling face-first into the muck. Maura smiled at the sound of his laughter and told herself to ignore the swift, nearly debilitating rush of heat that swamped her. An impossible order to obey, she thought as she watched the wide smile on his face lighting up his features.

Her knees went wobbly and she knew her body was not listening to her mind.

Jefferson King was a man meant to be ogled by women, she thought, eyeing his fine physique. Broad shoulders, narrow hips and large hands with more calluses on them than she would have imagined a Hollywood type to have. He had long legs, muscular thighs and a fine ass if anyone were to ask her opinion.

And he was only a temporary visitor to the lovely island she called home. She had to remember that. He'd only come to Ireland looking for a place to make a movie. He wasn't here on the Donohue Farm because he found her fascinating. He was here to rent her land, nothing more. Once she'd signed his bloody papers, he'd be off. Back to his own world that lay so very far from hers.

Well. She didn't like the thought of that.

And so, she continued to draw out the negotiations.

"They act like they haven't eaten in weeks," Jefferson said as he walked toward her.

"Aye, well, it's cold out. That'll make for heartier appetites."

"Speaking of," he hinted broadly.

They'd fallen into a routine of sorts since his arrival. Maura had hardly noticed it happening, but there it was. Jefferson spent most of the day at her farm, following her about, touting the merits of the deal he was trying to make her and then they ended the afternoon over a bowl of soup and some hot tea in her kitchen. Strange how she'd come to look forward to that time with him.

Still, she said, "You could ask the sheep to share their meal with you if you're that hungry."

"Tempting," he said, pushing one hand through his hair to sweep it back off his forehead. "But I'd prefer some of that brown bread you gave me yesterday."

"Fond of soda bread, are you?"

He looked down at her from his great height and she could have sworn she saw actual sparks glittering in his pale blue eyes. "I'm fond of a lot of things around here."

"Oh, you've a smooth tongue on you, Jefferson King." And her knees wobbled even more as she thought of the many uses that smooth tongue of his could be put to.

"Do I?"

"And well you know it," she told him, plucking two long strands of her hair out of her eyes. "But you're wasting your time trying to wheedle me into signing that contract of yours. I will or I won't and nothing you can say will sway me in either direction."

"Ah, but it's my time, isn't it?"

"It is indeed," she said and was silently glad he hadn't given up just yet.

In truth, she'd been considering his offer seriously since the moment he'd made it. Her mind had raced with possibilities. With the money he was offering her, she had tried to imagine what she could do to the centuries-old farmhouse that had been in her family for forever. Not to mention the changes she could make to the farm itself.

She already had a paid worker coming a few days a

week, but with Jefferson King's money, she would be able to hire someone full-time, to help ease the workload. And even with all that, she'd still have money left over to make a fine cushion in her bank account.

But she wasn't entirely ready to agree to his terms just yet. He'd already sweetened his offer once and she'd no doubt he would do so again. Yes, he could find another farm just as suitable for his needs, but he wouldn't find a prettier one, Maura told herself. Besides, he'd already told her he thought the Donohue land was perfect.

Which meant he wouldn't be withdrawing his offer. And Maura, coming from a long line of wily horse traders, was going to make sure she got the very best deal she could. It wasn't greed motivating her, either. Just think what a movie crew would do to her well-ordered life, not to mention her home and land. She'd need some of the money he would pay her just to put to rights the sorry mess they would no doubt leave behind.

While she stared at him, his gaze moved past her, scanning the surrounding countryside. As she'd grown up on Donohue land, and knew every inch of it as well as Tarzan knew the jungle, she didn't have to look to know what he was seeing. Green fields as far as the eye could see. Stone fences rising up from the ground like ancient sentinels. The shadow of the Partry Mountains looming behind them and the whole of Lough Mask stretching out in front of them, its silvery surface looking on this gray day like molten steel frothing in the wind. Across the way, a tumbled ruin of an ancient castle slept as if only waiting for the clang of a sword to wake it. Sheep wandered these hills freely as they had for centuries and would, no doubt, for centuries to come. The Irish wind kissed the land and the rain blessed it and those who lived here appreciated every single acre as no outsider ever could.

The village of Craic was only two kilometers down the long, twisting road and dotted along the way were B and Bs, a few more farmhouses and even one palatial mansion belonging to one Rogan Butler and his wife, Aly, who now spent most of their time in Dublin.

But here in the middle of her own fields, she and Jefferson might as well have been the only two people on the planet. A latter-day Adam and Eve, without the fig leaves, thanks very much, and surrounded by bleating sheep.

"Did I tell you," he said, shattering the quiet between them, "that my great-grandmother was Irish?"

"You mean Mary Frances Rafferty King who was born in County Sligo and met your great-grandfather when he was taking a tour of Ireland? He saw her in a pub. On a Tuesday, wasn't it?" Maura smiled. "Aye, you might have mentioned her once or twice."

He grinned at her. "Didn't mean to bore you."

"Did I say I was bored?"

"No." He stepped closer and she felt the heat of him reaching for her, charging the icy air. "But let me know if you feel yourself nodding off and I'll try harder to enchant you."

"You mean to say you've got to *try* to be appealing?" she quipped, taking a quick step or two back from him. "I'm disappointed. Here I thought you were just a born charmer."

"Did you?" he asked, closing the distance between

them again with a single, long step. "Now, isn't that interesting?"

"I didn't say your charm was *working* on me, mind you," Maura told him, enjoying their sparring far too much. It had been a long time since she'd met a man who appealed to her on so many different levels. A shame, she reminded herself, that he was only here temporarily. Better that she keep that thought in mind before her body and heart became too involved for their own good.

"You can't fool me, Maura. I'm wearing you down."

"Is that right?"

"It is," he said. "You haven't threatened to throw me off your property in almost—" he checked his watch "—six hours."

Still smiling, she said, "I could remedy that right now."

"Ah, but you don't want to."

"I don't?" That smile of his should be considered a lethal weapon, she told herself.

"No," he said, "because you actually like having me around, whether you'll admit to it or not."

Well, he was right about that now, wasn't he, she thought. But then what single woman in her right mind wouldn't enjoy having a man such as Jefferson King about the house? It wasn't every day a rich, gorgeous man showed up on her doorstep wanting to rent her farm. Could she really help it if she was enjoying the negotiations so much that she was rather dragging the process out?

"Admit it," he said, his voice low enough that it was barely more than a breath. "I dare you."

"You'll find, Jefferson," she said softly, lifting her eyes to meet his, "that if I want you…*around,* I'll have no trouble admitting it. To you or to myself."

Two

In the village of Craic, Jefferson King was big news and Maura had half the town nagging her to sign his silly papers so they could all "get famous." Not a moment went by when she didn't hear someone's opinion on the subject.

But she wasn't going to be hurried into a decision. Not by her friends, not by her sister and not by Jefferson. She'd give him her answer when she was ready and not before.

She should have thought twice about suggesting to him they go to the village pub for supper. Should have known that her friends and neighbors would pounce on the opportunity to engage Jefferson in conversation while managing to give Maura a nudge or two at the same time. But, the truth was, she had been feeling far too…itchy to trust herself alone in her house with him. He was a fine-looking man after all, and her hormones had been doing a fast step-dance since the moment she'd first laid eyes on him.

Now, Maura had to wonder if coming into the Lion's Den pub for a meal hadn't been a bad idea after all.

Of course, she was surrounded by villagers, so there was no chance at all her hormones would be able to take over her good sense. But the downside was, she was surrounded by villagers, all of whom were vying for Jefferson's attentions.

In early December, the interior of the pub was dim, with lamplight gleaming dully on paneled walls stained with centuries of smoke from the peat fires kept burning in a brazier. The floor was wood as well, scuffed from the steps of thousands of patrons. There were several small round tables with chairs gathered close and a handful of booths lining two of the walls. The bar itself was highly polished walnut that Michael O'Shay, the pub owner, kept as shiny as a church pew. And beside the wide mirror reflecting the crowd back on itself, there was a television perched high on a shelf, displaying a soccer game with the sound muted.

Michael sauntered up to their table with a perfectly stacked pint of Guinness beer for Jefferson and a glass of Harp beer for Maura. As he set them down, he gave a swift, unnecessary swipe of the gleaming table with a pristine bar rag. Then he beamed at them both like Father Christmas. "I'll have your soup and bread up for you in a moment. It's potato-leek today. My Margaret made it and you'll enjoy it I'm sure. When your movie folk arrive," he added with a grin for Jefferson, "I'll see that Margaret makes it by the boatload for you."

Maura sighed. Hadn't taken him long to get Hollywood into the conversation.

"Sounds good," Jefferson said, taking a sip of his thick black beer.

"Has your Rose had her baby yet, Michael?" Maura asked, then said in an aside to Jefferson, "Michael and Margaret are about to become grandparents."

"We are indeed," the pub owner said and gave Maura a knowing look, "so the extra money made when your film crew arrives will be most welcome."

Maura closed her eyes. Clearly, all anyone wanted to talk about was the notion of having a film made in their little village. Michael had hardly left to bustle back to his bar when three or four other locals found a reason to stop by the table and talk to Jefferson.

She watched him handle the people she'd known all her life with courtesy and she liked him for it. Surely a man like him didn't enjoy being the center of attention in a village less than a third the size of the town he called home. But rather than being abrupt, he seemed to almost encourage their chatter.

Maura listened with half an ear as Frances Boyle raved about her small traveler's inn and the good service she could promise King Studios. Then Bill Howard, owner of the local market, swore he'd be happy to order in any and all supplies Jefferson might require. Nora Bailey gave him her card and told him again that she ran a full-service bakery and would be happy to work with his caterers and finally Colleen Ryan offered her skills as a seamstress, knowing that being so far from Hollywood, his costume people might be needing an extra hand, fine with a needle.

By the time they wandered off, each of them giving Maura a nudging glare, Jefferson was grinning and Maura's head pounded like a badly played bodhran drum.

"Seems as though you're the only one who doesn't want my business," he said, then took another sip of his beer.

"Aye, it does at that, doesn't it?"

"So why are you holding out?"

"Holding out?" Maura pretended surprise. "I've not promised you a thing, have I?"

"No," he said, smiling. "You haven't. You've just sat by and let me talk and wheedle and eventually raise my offer a bit each day."

True enough and she had hopes he'd go a bit higher yet before the deed was done and the bargain struck. If her friends and neighbors could curb their enthusiasm a little.

"The whole town wants this to happen," he said.

"Aye, but the whole town won't have the disruption of a film crew camped out on their land during the height of lambing season, will they?" She considered that a point well made and rewarded herself with a sip of her beer.

"You said yourself that most of the sheep give birth out in the fields. We'll be filming mostly at the front of the house. Outdoor shots of the manor—"

She snorted. "It's a farmhouse."

"Looks like a manor to me," he countered, then continued quickly, "There may be a few scenes around the barn and the holding pens, but we won't get in the way."

"And you can promise that?" She eased back in the booth and looked at him across the table.

"I'll promise it, if that's what it takes to get you to sign."

"Desperate now?" She smiled and took another soothing drink. "Might make a woman think you'd be willing to sweeten your offer a bit."

"You drive a hard bargain," Jefferson told her with a nod of approval. "But I might be willing to go a little higher yet, if you'd make up your mind and give me your decision."

She smiled to herself, but kept it small so he wouldn't see the victorious gleam that had to be shining in her eyes. "As well I might, depending on how much higher you're talking about."

He gave her an admiring tip of his head. "Too bad your sister's not the one making this deal. I have the distinct feeling she'd be easier to convince."

"Ah, but Cara has her own priorities, doesn't she?" Smiling at the thought of her younger sister, Maura could admit to herself that she would have eventually accepted Jefferson's offer even if he hadn't paid her for the use of her land. Because he'd agreed to give Cara a small part in the movie. And since her sister dreamed of being a famous actress, Cara had been walking in the clouds for days now.

"True," he said. "If she were doing the bargaining, she might have wangled herself a bigger part."

"She'll do fine with what she's got. She's very good, you know." Maura leaned forward. "For a few weeks last year, Cara was on one of those British soap operas. She was brilliant, really, until they killed her off. She had a lovely death scene and all. Made me cry when she died."

His mouth quirked, just high enough to display a dimple in his left cheek. "I know. I sat through the tapes."

"She is good, isn't she? I mean, it's not only that I'm her sister and love her that makes me think so, is it?"

"No, it's not. She's very good," Jefferson told her.

"She has dreams, Cara has," Maura murmured.

"What about you? Do you have dreams, too?" he asked.

Her gaze met his as she shook her head. "'Course I do, though my dreams are less lofty. The barn needs a new roof and before long, my old lorry's going to keel over dead with all four tires in the air. And there's a fine breed of sheep I'd like to try on my fields, as well."

"You're too beautiful to have such small dreams, Maura."

She blinked at him, surprised by the flattery and, at the same time, almost insulted to be told that her dreams were somehow lacking in imagination. She'd once had bigger dreams, as all young girls do. But she'd grown up, hadn't she? And now her dreams were more practical. That didn't make them less important. "They're mine, aren't they, and I don't think they're small dreams at all."

"I just meant—"

She knew what he meant. No doubt he was more accustomed to women who dreamed of diamonds or, God help her, furs and shiny cars. He probably saw her as a country bumpkin with her worn jeans and fields full of shaggy sheep. That thought was as good as a cold shower, dousing the fire in her hormones until she felt almost chilled at the lack of heat.

Before he could speak again, she glanced to one side

and announced, "Oh look! The Flanagan boys are going to play."

"What?"

Maura pointed to the far corner of the pub where three young men with dark red hair sat down, cradling an assortment of instruments between them. While Michael finally made good on his promise and delivered their bowls of steaming potato-leek soup and soda bread hot from the oven, the Flanagan brothers began to play.

In moments, the small pub was filled with the kind of music most people would pay a fortune to hear in a concert hall. Fiddle, drum and flute all came together in a wild yet fluid mesh of music that soared up to the rafters and rattled the window panes. Toes started tapping, hands were clapping and a few hearty souls sang out the lyrics to traditional Irish music.

One tune slid into another, rushing from fast and furious to the slow and heartbreaking, with the three brothers never missing a beat. Jefferson watched the energized crowd with a filmmaker's eye and knew that he'd have to include at least one pub scene in the movie they would be filming here in a few months. And he was going to put in a word with his director about the Flanagan brothers. Their talent was amazing and he thought the least he could do was display it on film. Who knew, maybe he could help more dreams to come true.

Once he finally got Maura to sign his damned contract.

Jefferson's gaze slid to her and his breath caught in his chest. He'd been aware of her beauty before now, but in the dim light of the pub with a single candle burning in a glass jar on the table, she looked almost ethereal.

Insubstantial. Which was a ridiculous thought because he'd seen her wrestle a full-grown sheep down to the ground, so a fragile woman she most definitely was not. Yet he was seeing her now in a new way. A way that made his body tighten to the point of discomfort.

You'd think he'd be used to it, he thought. He'd been achy for nearly a week now, his body in a constant state of unrequited readiness that was making him crazy. Maybe what he needed to do was stop being so damn polite and just swoop in and seduce Maura before she knew what hit her.

Then a whirlwind swept into the pub and dropped down at their booth, nudging her sister over on the bench seat.

"Oh, soup!" Cara Donohue cooed the words and reached for her sister's bowl with both hands. "Lovely. I'm famished."

"Get your own, you beggar," Maura told her with a laugh, but pushed her soup toward her sister.

"Don't need to, do I?" Cara grinned, then shot a quick look at Jefferson. "Have you convinced her to sign up yet?"

"Not yet," he said, putting thoughts of seduction to one side for the moment. Cara Donohue was taller and thinner than Maura, with a short cap of dark curls and blue eyes that shone with eagerness to be doing. Seeing. Experiencing. She was four years younger than her sister and twice as outgoing, and yet Jefferson felt no deep stirring for her.

She was a nice kid with a bright future ahead of her, but Maura was a woman to make a man stop for a second and even a third look.

"You will," Cara said with a bright, musical laugh. "You Americans are all stubborn, aren't you? And besides, Maura thinks you're gorgeous."

"Cara!"

"Well, it's true and all," her sister said with another laugh as she finished Maura's soup, then reached for her sister's beer. She had a sip, then winked at Jefferson. "It does no harm to let you know she enjoys looking at you, for what breathing woman wouldn't? And I've seen you giving her a look or two yourself."

"Cara, if you don't shut your mouth this minute…"

Maura's threat died unuttered, but Jefferson couldn't help smiling at the sisters. He and his brothers were just the same, teasing each other no matter who happened to be around to listen. Besides, he liked hearing that Maura had been talking about him.

"There's no harm in it, is there?" Cara was saying, with a glance at first her sister, then Jefferson. "Why shouldn't you take a good look at each other?"

"Pay no attention to my sister," Maura told him with a shake of her head.

"Why?" he asked. "She's not wrong."

"Maybe not, but she doesn't have to be so loud about it, does she?"

"Ah Maura, you worry too much," her sister told her and patted her arm.

The music suddenly shifted, jumping into a wild, frenetic song with a beat that seemed to thrum against the walls and batter its way into a man's soul. Jefferson found himself tapping his fingers on the tabletop in time with the quickening rhythm.

"Oh, they're playing 'Whiskey in the Jar!' Come on, Maura, dance with me."

She shook her head and resisted when Cara tried to pull her to her feet. "I've worked all day and I'm in no mood for step dancing. Most especially not with my big-mouthed sister."

"But you love me and you know it. Besides, it'll do you good and you know you adore this song." Cara grinned again and gave her sister's arm a good yank.

On her feet, Maura looked at him, almost embarrassed, Jefferson thought, then with a shrug she followed her sister into the cleared-away area in front of the tables. A few people applauded as Cara and Maura took their places beside each other, then, laughing together, the Donohue sisters leaped into action. Their backs were arrow straight, their arms pinned to their sides and their feet were *flying*.

Jefferson, like most everyone else in the world, had seen the Broadway show with the Irish dancers and he'd come away impressed. But here, in this tiny pub in a small village on the coast of Ireland, he was swept into a kind of magic.

Music thundered, people applauded and the two sisters danced as if they had wings on their feet. He couldn't tear his eyes off Maura. She'd worked hard all day at a job that would have exhausted most of the men he knew. Yet there she was, dancing and laughing, as graceful as a leaf on the wind. She was tireless. And spirited. And so damned beautiful, he could hardly draw a breath for wanting her.

Without warning, Jefferson's mind turned instantly

to the stories he'd heard about his great-grandfather and how he'd fallen in love at first sight with an Irish girl in a pub just like this, on one magical night.

For the first time in his life, he completely understood how it had happened.

Cara left the pub soon after, claiming she was going to drive into Westport, a bustling harbor city not five miles from the village of Craic.

"I'll be at Mary Dooley's place if you need me," she said as she left, giving Jefferson a wink and her sister a kiss and a smile. "Otherwise, I'll see you sometime tomorrow."

When her sister was gone in a blur of motion, Maura looked at Jefferson and laughed shortly. "She's a force of nature," she said. "Always has been. The only thing that came close to slowing her down was our mother's death four years ago."

"I'm sorry," he said quickly. "I know what it's like to lose your parents. It's never easy no matter how old you are."

"No, it's not," Maura admitted, feeling the sting of remembrance and how hard it had been for her and her sister in those long silent weeks after their mother had passed away. Smiles had been hard to come by and they'd clung to each other to ease their pain.

Eventually though, life had crowded in, insisting it be lived.

"But my mother had been lonely for my father for years. Now that she's joined him, she's happy again, I know."

"You believe that."

A statement, not a question, she thought. "Aye, I do."

"Are you born with that kind of faith, I wonder, or do you have to work to earn it?"

"It just…is," Maura said simply. "Haven't you ever sensed the presence of one you lost and felt better for knowing it?"

"I have," he admitted quietly. "Though it's not something I've ever talked about before."

"Why should you?" She smiled at him again. "It's a private thing, after all."

Jefferson looked at her for a long moment and she tried to read what thoughts might be rushing through his mind. But his eyes were cool, shadowed with old pain, so she was forced to wait until he spoke.

"Ten years ago, my parents died together in a car accident that nearly killed one of my brothers, too." He finished the last of his beer in one swallow, set the glass down and said, "Later, once my three brothers and I had lived through the grief, we all realized that if they'd had a choice, our folks would have elected to go together. Neither of them would have been complete without the other."

"I know just what you mean." Maura sighed through a sad smile. Music played on in the background and dozens of voices rose and fell in waves of conversation. Yet here in the shadow-filled booth, she felt as if she and Jefferson were alone in the room. "My father died when Cara was small and my mother was never the same without him. She tried, for our sakes of course, but for her, there was always something missing. A love like that, I think, is both blessing and curse."

He lifted his beer glass in a toast. "You might be right about that."

He smiled, too, and she thought how odd it was that they would find this mutual understanding in memories of pain. But somehow, sitting in the near dark with Jefferson, sharing stories of loss made her feel closer to him than she had to anyone in a long time.

"Still," she said, her voice soft and low, "even knowing your parents were together, it must have been hard on you and your brothers."

"It was." A slight frown creased his features briefly. "I'd finally recovered from…" He stopped, caught himself and said instead, "Doesn't matter. The point is, when we needed it the most, my brothers and I had each other. And we had to help Justice recover."

She wondered what he'd been about to say. What he'd thought better of sharing with her. And wondered why, if it was so many years ago, that thought could have left a shadow of pain flashing in his eyes. His secret, whatever it was, had hit him deeply, cutting him in his heart and soul. So much so that even now, he didn't talk about it.

Maura buried her curiosity for the moment and said only, "Justice? An interesting name."

"Interesting man," Jefferson told her with a quick smile that was filled, she thought, with a bit of gratitude for her ignoring his earlier slip of the tongue. "He runs the family ranch."

Delighted by the image, she smiled. "So he's a cowboy, then?"

"Yeah, he is." He grinned suddenly, though sorrow

still glittered in his eyes. "And he's married now, with a son and another baby on the way."

"Lovely," she said, envying him his large family. "And your other brothers?"

"The youngest, Jesse, is married, too. His wife just had a baby boy a few months back." He stopped and grinned. "Jesse passed out during the delivery. We love to remind him of that."

"What a wonderful story," Maura said. "His love and worry for his wife making him faint. He must be a lovely man."

"Lovely?" Jefferson thought about it and shrugged. "I'm sure his wife Bella thinks so."

The sorrow in his eyes was fading, the longer he talked about his brothers, and Maura realized she thought even more of him now that she knew how close he was to his family. "And your other brother?"

"Jericho is in the Marines. He's serving in the Middle East right now."

"That's a worry for you." She saw the truth of that in the way his jaw clenched briefly.

"Yeah, it is. But he's doing what he loves, so…"

"I understand." Maura drew a fingertip through the ring of damp her beer glass had left behind on the table. "When Cara first left home to go to London and be an actor, I wanted to lock her in the closet." She laughed, remembering how panicked she'd been at the thought of Cara alone in the big city. "Oh, it's not the same kind of worry you must feel, I know, but at the time I thought for sure she'd be eaten alive by all manner of terrible monsters in that city."

"Worry's worry, Maura," he told her, "and it probably drove you nuts to be so far away from her."

Maura nodded and laughed to herself. "I shouldn't have bothered making myself crazy, of course. Cara sailed ahead, claiming the city as her own and making a good start to the career she wants."

"What about you?"

"What about me?" she asked.

"Your career," he said, his eyes locked on her. "Did you always want to be a sheep farmer?"

Maura gave him a half grin. "Well now, what little girl wouldn't dream of sheep dip and shearing time and lambing emergencies. It's the glamour, you see, that drew me."

Now he laughed and she thought it a wonderful sound. She was glad to see that the sadness in his eyes had all but disappeared, as well.

"So then, what made you choose to be what you are?"

"I like my life being my own. I've always worked the farm. I answer to no one. No clock to watch, no boss to kowtow to. No harried rushing about to drive into the city."

He nodded as if he understood exactly what she was saying. But that couldn't be, because the man made his living in one of the busiest cities in the world. He'd no doubt schedules to keep, people to answer to and hordes of employees clustering about him.

"I can see the appeal of that," he admitted.

"Oh, sure you can," Maura teased. "Look at yourself. Flying all around the world, looking for places to put your cameras. I'd wager you've never spent a full day away from a telephone or an Internet modem in years."

"You'd be right about that," he said with a grudging smile. "But to the travel, I do it because I enjoy it. Take Ireland for example…"

"Why don't we?"

Still smiling, he said, "The studio has location scouts, but I wanted to come here for myself. I've always enjoyed travel, seeing new places. It's the best part of the job. So I had my scout find two or three suitable properties online, then I flew over to check them out."

"Two or three?" she asked, curious now. "And which was the Donohue farm? Where did I figure on your list?"

"You were the second place I looked at—and I knew the minute I saw your farm that it was the one I wanted."

"Which brings us back to your offer."

"Isn't that handy?"

She had to give it to him. He was as stubborn as her, with a mind that continually returned to the goal no matter how many distractions got in the way. She could admire that.

Just as she could admit silently that it was time to act. To accept his offer, sign his contract and let him be off, back to his real life before she became so attached her heart would break at his leaving. Besides, she'd gotten her sister's warning glare earlier and knew that Cara would never forgive her if Maura didn't sign on the dotted line, allowing her sister to earn a small part in a big-budget American movie.

"So what's it going to be, Maura?" he asked a

moment later. "Are we going to strike a deal or am I going to have to revisit those other properties?"

In the sudden silence, Maura gave a quick look around the Lion's Den. But for Michael behind the bar and a few straggling patrons nursing a final beer, she and Jefferson were alone. The crowd had gone off and the Flanagans had packed up their instruments and left for home and she hadn't even noticed. She'd been so wrapped up in talking with Jefferson, watching his smile, listening to the rumble of his voice, the whole world could have come to an end and she'd have sat through it all without a care.

Which told her she was in very deep danger of losing her heart to a man who wouldn't be interested in keeping it. Yes, best all around to have their business be done so he could leave and her life could settle back into its familiar pattern.

She held her right hand out to him then and there. "We've a deal, Jefferson King. You'll make your movie on my farm and we'll both get what we want."

He took her hand in his, but instead of shaking it as she'd expected, he simply held on to it, stroking his thumb across her slender fingers. Her stomach jittered and her mouth went dry. Suddenly, she wished she'd ordered another beer because something cool and frothy would no doubt ease her parched throat.

"I have the papers at the inn," he said. "Why don't you come to my room now and we can get them signed."

She slipped her hand from his and chuckled. "Oh, no thank you. If I'm seen going into your hotel room at this hour, the village wags will be talking about us for weeks."

"How would anyone know?"

"In a village, there are no secrets," she told him. "Frances Boyle runs a tight ship at her inn. Believe me when I tell you she knows every person that steps across her threshold."

"Okay," he said, "then why don't we order another round, I'll go to the hotel, gather the papers and bring them back here for you to sign?"

Maura considered it, chewing at her bottom lip. She did want the deed done, but it was already late and she'd have to be up with the sun and—

"I thought you said you didn't have to run your life by the clock," he reminded her.

"Touché," she said with a nod, amused that he'd rightly guessed what she'd been thinking about. "All right then, I'll order the beer while you get your paperwork."

When he left, Maura's gaze dropped to his behind and she gave herself a stern talking-to. *You'll have a drink, sign his papers and say thanks very much and goodbye. There'll be no loitering in the moonlight, Maura Donohue. He's a man you can't have, so there's no point in wishing things were different. Don't be a fool about this, Maura, or you'll surely regret it.*

All very rational, she thought. Too bad she wasn't listening.

Three

He wasn't gone long.

The truth was, Jefferson hadn't wanted to leave her at all. He'd hoped to get her back to the hotel where he could try to slide her into his bed and seal the deal in a way that would ease the ache he'd been carrying for the last few days. But typically enough, Maura had managed to shatter his quickly thought-up plan with a simple "no." So, adjusting his plan on the fly, he thought he could maneuver her into letting him take her home and maybe he could slide himself into *her* bed instead.

When he walked into the quiet pub, Michael the barman gave him a nod of welcome, then went back to watching the news on the television. There was only one other customer left at the bar and Maura at the table where he'd left her. The single candle flickering on their table threw dancing shadows across her face and its faint light seemed to shimmer in the rich thickness of her hair.

The need he'd been carrying around inside him burst into flame. Instantly, his mind filled again with the image of her dancing. Her smile. Her regal yet somehow wild bearing. The rhythm in her body, the fast fury of her small feet, and he wanted with a desperation he'd never known before.

"That was quick," she said when he stopped at the edge of their table.

"No point in wasting time, is there?"

"None at all," she agreed, sliding out of the booth to stand beside him. "But I think we should go back to the farm so Michael can close the pub and go home. I've some wine in the fridge. We can toast the signed contract if you like."

Jefferson was silent for a moment, simply because he couldn't believe she'd suggested the very thing he'd been about to recommend. She seemed to be one step ahead of him and that was an unusual enough happening that he could enjoy the sensation. He wondered, though, if she wanted what he did. Was she simply being nice, or was she as anxious as him for them to be alone together?

He'd find out soon enough.

"Good idea." He laid one hand at the small of her back and guided her across the room. When she called out good-night to Michael, the barman merely waved a towel at them.

Then they were outside, in the stillness. The village was quiet—houses dark, streets empty. There was a hush in the air that felt as if the world had taken a breath and held it.

Or maybe, Jefferson told himself, his time in Ireland had been enough to make any man—even *him*—fanciful.

The trip to the Donohue farmhouse was a quick one, yet it felt like forever to Jefferson. With Maura beside him in the car, her scent seemed to wrap itself around him, taunting him, arousing him to the point where simply sitting still became an act of torture.

At the house he parked the car in the driveway, what Maura would call "the street," and walked beside her in silence to the front door. Neither of them had much to say, mainly he thought, because there was too *much* to say. So where was a man supposed to start?

Sign the contract?

Take off your clothes?

He knew which he'd prefer, but he had a feeling it wouldn't be that easy.

Inside the house, Maura flipped light switches on as they moved through the silent rooms to the kitchen. There, she tossed her keys onto the table and walked to the fridge. Looking at him over her shoulder, she said, "Will you take down a couple of glasses from the far cupboard?"

"Sure." Jefferson laid the envelope containing the contract on the table and went for the glasses. A moment later, she was filling them with a cold, straw-colored wine that shone almost gold in the overhead light.

He'd been in this room before, though those visits had been in broad daylight. The old kitchen was clean and tidy, its ancient appliances gleaming with the care she took with them. The counter was bare of all but a set of canisters and a teapot and the wood floor was scarred from wear but polished to a high shine.

"I suppose I should sign the papers first," she was saying and Jefferson turned his attention to her.

"Good idea. We take care of business first."

"First. And then what?" Her blue eyes glittered as she turned them up to him and Jefferson's body stirred like a hungry dog on a short leash.

"Then," he said, "we'll toast to the success of our joint venture."

A smile tugged at her lips. "Venture, is it? A fine word for it, anyway."

She took the pen he offered her and sat down to read through the short contract. He liked that about her, too. He thought a lot of people might have just taken him at his word and signed where he indicated. Not Maura though. She was careful. Not going to take his word for it that her interests were being looked after.

Was there anything sexier than a smart woman?

Her teeth pulled at her bottom lip as she read and he heard the ticking of the wall clock behind him in the strained quiet. Her head was bent over the paperwork and he had to force himself not to touch her. Not to stroke his fingers through the shining black hair that was only inches from him. *Soon,* he promised himself, reaching for the self-control that had always been a part of him.

But even as that thought rattled through his mind, he had to smile. His self-control had been mostly absent since the first moment he'd seen Maura. She tripped something inside him. Something he hadn't even been aware of in years. Something he hadn't felt since—

The scratch of a pen on paper broke the silence and

he came out of his thoughts in time to watch her put the pen down and pick up the now-signed contract.

"It's done," she said.

"It'll be good doing business with you, Maura."

"Ah, I'll wager you say that to all of the people you rent locations from."

"No," he said, sliding the contract back into the envelope then tossing them on the table. "I don't. You're…different."

"Is that so?" She picked up the wineglasses, handed one to him and took a sip of her own. "And how might that be?"

"I think you know the answer to that."

"I might at that," she mused and set her glass down again to take off the cream-colored Irish sweater she wore. Pulling it up and over her head, she shook her hair back and smiled up at him.

Jefferson sucked in a gulp of air, then chased it with a swallow of cold, crisp wine. All she'd been wearing under that sweater of hers tonight was a white silk camisole that clung to her skin and displayed her pebbled nipples with fine clarity.

"You must have been freezing tonight," he muttered.

"A bit," she admitted, "though inside the pub was warm enough and I'll admit, I thought perhaps we might end up back here tonight and I wanted to see the look on your face when I took off the sweater."

"And was it worth it?" he managed to ask.

"Aye, it was." She reached up, hooked one hand behind his head and threaded her fingers through his hair. "I've been wanting you, Jefferson."

His body jumped into overdrive, his erection painfully pushing against his slacks. "Have you?"

"I have. I think you've been wanting me, as well," she added, moving in closer to him.

"Aye," he mimicked. "I have."

Her fingers at the back of his neck felt seductive and sure and he suddenly wanted that touch all over him. He needed to feel her hands on him, to get his hands on her.

He set his glass down and reached for her. Holding her pressed tightly against him, he felt her nipples pushing into his chest and damn near groaned. Then he had to smile. "You know, I'd planned to seduce you tonight."

She grinned up at him. "Well, isn't it a fine thing indeed when two plans come together so nicely?"

"Indeed," he murmured and bent his head to take a kiss. The first of many. His mouth covered hers and she sighed into him, parting her lips eagerly, hungrily. She matched his need and as their tongues twisted and danced together, the flames they built erupted into an inferno.

He wrapped his arms around her, holding her pressed tightly to him and still it wasn't close enough. Couldn't feel enough of her. He needed her naked. Needed to feel skin to skin, rough to smooth. He needed to slide his body into hers and feel her heat surround him.

And he needed it *now*.

Quickly, he swept her up, turned around and plopped her down onto the kitchen counter. She whooped in surprise, but recovered quickly enough. Wrapping her legs around his middle, she clung to him, her tongue tangling with his, their breaths combining into a symphony of sighs that filled the quiet of the old house with the desperate sounds of passion.

Again and again, he kissed her, long, deep, short, fast. He loved the taste of her. Richer than any wine, headier than any intoxicant could be. She was all. She was everything. The world spun about her and he was pulled into her orbit with the deliberate tug of a gravity too fierce to fight.

He yanked up the hem of that silken camisole, tore it up over her head, then tossed it behind him without missing a beat. Her breasts were bared to him and he inhaled sharply as he fed the need to admire her. Full, ripe breasts with dark pink nipples, peaked now as if just awaiting his pleasure.

Jefferson cupped those milk-white globes in his hands and sighed himself with her whispered approval. His thumbs and forefingers tweaked and pulled gently at her nipples and when she writhed into him, he dipped his head, taking first one, then the other into his mouth. He licked, he sucked, he nibbled and the sounds she made urged him on, encouraged him to take all he wanted.

Her hands fisted in his hair and held his head to her breasts as if she were worried he'd stop. But stopping wasn't in the game plan. In fact, he couldn't have stopped now if his life depended on it. God help him if she were to suddenly change her mind and show him the door. He'd never live through it.

He pulled back, looked up into misty blue eyes and returned the grin she had aimed at him.

"Let's have your shirt off, Jefferson," she said. "I've a need to feel your skin beneath my hands."

He obliged her quickly, tearing off his own sweater and the shirt he wore beneath it. Then he groaned as her palms swept over his shoulders and along his back. The warmth of her touch slid into him and sent bolts of fresh need shooting through his system. Her short nails scraped at his skin. Her breath came in hard, brief pants and when she slid her hands down his arms, they were both gasping for air.

"Help me with these," she said, her voice low and tight as though she'd had to force the words from her throat.

"What?"

"My jeans, man." She had them unsnapped and was whipping the zipper down as she spoke. She'd already kicked off her shoes. "Help me out of them before I lose my mind for the wanting."

"Right, right." His head was full and spinning. All he could think about was the next touch, the next kiss. So he helped her out of her pants, lifting her off the counter so she could scoot around and free herself of both jeans and white cotton bikini underwear.

Jefferson had one shining moment of clarity when he realized that her simple, plain panties were more erotic than any scraps of black lace he'd ever seen. Then the moment was gone and he was lost in the glory of looking at her. Her milk-white skin was soft and smooth and he ached to touch her all over. Explore every curve, every line of her body until he knew her more intimately than any other man ever had.

"Now yours," she said, reaching for his belt buckle.

She grinned, tossed her hair back over her shoulder and met his eyes with her own. She was strong and sure of herself, and the sexual ache he felt went a notch higher. "I've a powerful need for you, Jefferson, and I'm not a patient woman as you might have noticed."

"Believe me, I'm grateful to hear it," he muttered, stepping out of his clothes and standing naked in front of her. His body leaped to attention, hard and thick and aching to ease itself inside her. But Jefferson had one more quick moment of reason show itself, so he said, "We should go upstairs. To your bedroom."

"Later," she countered, reaching for him, wrapping her arms around his neck even as she parted her legs and scooted forward to the counter's edge. "If I don't have you inside me this moment, Jefferson King, I'll not be responsible for what happens next."

"My kind of woman," he growled with a smile. "I knew it the moment I saw you."

Her hands cupped his cheeks again. "Then fill me, Jefferson, ease the ache."

He did.

She was hot and wet and so ready for him he almost exploded the moment he entered her. Only his immense self-control kept him from hurtling too soon over an edge he craved like a dying man wished for a few more moments of life. She threw her head back, baring her throat for him and he kissed her there, along the line of her lovely throat, lips and tongue sliding across her skin until she shivered in his arms.

He pushed himself deep as her legs locked around his hips, then pulled out and did the same again. Over and over, as he set a rhythm she raced to follow, their bodies came together, melding, meshing, sliding into a dance they had been building toward for what seemed like forever.

Her soft pants and muted sighs fueled him, fed the images in his mind, the sensations in his body. Never before had Jefferson so lost himself in a woman. He wasn't sure where he ended and she began and he knew with a blinding flash of insight that it didn't matter.

All that mattered was this moment. This one heart-stopping, mind-numbing moment in time.

Pulling his head back, he watched her as he moved one hand to the spot where their bodies joined and touched the pad of his thumb to the most sensitive flesh at her core. She gasped, trembled in his arms and shrieked out his name as her body whipped into a frenzied release.

And no more than a heartbeat later, Jefferson gave himself up, at last, to the crashing need and surrendered himself into her keeping.

Hours later, Maura stretched out on her bed and felt blissfully languid. Every cell in her body was replete. Satisfied. And even as she lay there, just an arm's reach from her lover, she felt hunger begin to stir inside again.

She turned her head on the pillow to look at Jefferson and smiled to herself. He'd been well worth the agonizing wait, she told herself even as a small voice in the back of her head warned her against feeling too much. Wanting too much.

Outside, a storm was building. She heard the first taps

of rain against her window as a cold wind rattled the panes. But here, in the cozy master bedroom of the farmhouse, a peat fire burned in the corner hearth and she lay on sweet-smelling sheets beside a man who touched her as she'd never been touched before.

Instantly, that nagging, annoying voice started up again. *Careful now, Maura,* it warned, *he's not the forever kind of man. He's not staying—neither here in your bed nor even in Ireland. He'll be off now that he has what he came for. So don't be a fool and fall in love.*

So she wouldn't take the fall. But she couldn't help feeling for the man.

He would go home remembering her and this night as something magical.

Seemed only fair, since so would she.

"I think I may be dead," Jefferson murmured.

Her thoughts crashed to a halt as he looked at her, his eyes the pale blue color of cornflowers in summer. There was the shadow of a beard on his jaws and his black hair was nearly standing on end. Not surprising considering how they'd spent the last few hours.

Maura's heart turned over in her chest. Soon, very soon, he'd be walking out her door. And as she considered it, she knew she had to have him again. One last time before he became nothing more than a sweet, tender spot in her soul.

Laying one hand on his abdomen, she slowly slid her palm lower and lower. His breath caught in his chest as she wrapped her long fingers around him and felt that hard, eager part of him leap into life again. "Not so very near death, I'm thinking," she said with a teasing smile.

He hissed in another breath, blew it out and said, "You could rouse a dead man, Maura. You've just proved it."

She grinned, feeling a delicious sense of female power rise up inside her. To know she had this effect on a strong man was a heady thing indeed. To know that he was watching her, waiting for her to make her next move, only enhanced the sensation.

Her fingers moved over him, the hard, silky feel of his skin pulsing beneath her own. Then she reached farther down and cupped him, gently rubbing, stroking until he lifted his hips off the mattress and into her touch.

"You do want me dead, is that it?" he managed to wheeze.

"Oh, no," she answered, shifting position to straddle him, "I want you alive, Jefferson King. Alive and inside me."

His hands came down on her upper thighs and she smiled at him, scooping her arms under her hair and lifting them high, displaying her breasts for his pleasure. Her hair fell down around her shoulders in a tangle, her nipples peeking through the black strands. And when his eyes narrowed, she knew she had him. Rising up onto her knees, she looked down at him as if he were her captive.

He reached for her, his hands moving over her body with a greedy touch and she nearly purred at the feel of him against her. But she wanted more. She wanted another time with him. She wanted to ride him and look down into his eyes and know that no matter where else he went in his life, he would take this mental image of the two of them together with him. Always.

She took his hard length in her hand, held him poised just at the entrance to her heat and rubbed the head of him against her until they were both at the ragged edge of control. Then finally, she lowered her body onto his, taking him, inch by glorious inch, inside her.

Maura groaned as he filled her so deeply, she felt him touch her heart and when they were firmly joined, connected as deeply as two people could possibly be, she moved on him. Riding him, her body sliding up and down atop him, setting a pace that started out slow and then became frantic. She swiveled her hips against him and leaned over so that he could cup her breasts and pull at her aching nipples.

Her gaze locked with his, she kept moving, tirelessly, ceaselessly, laying claim to his body as she couldn't his heart. And when the expectant rise of glory slammed home and shattered her, she called his name out loud. When she felt him release an instant later and heard him shout for her, she knew the echo of it would ripple through her life forever.

Dull gray light slid through the wisp of white curtains hanging at her windows and Jefferson knew the night was over. Maura was curled into him, one leg across his, one arm tossed over his chest. Her every breath dusted his skin and the scent of her hair was in every lungful of air he claimed.

He hadn't slept, yet he was more awake than he could ever remember being. For hours, he'd made love to his wild Irish woman. And when she'd finally fallen into exhausted slumber, he'd remained awake, just watching her sleep.

His time there was over and he told himself that was a very good thing. He'd become…comfortable in Ireland. In this house. With this woman. He'd begun to structure his days around seeing her. Arguing with her. Watching her laugh.

And that simply wasn't in his plan.

Jefferson didn't want to care about her. Didn't want to ever go down that road again. He would retain control at all costs to avoid the pain he'd once suffered.

Carefully, he slipped out of bed, amused more than anything else when Maura simply snuggled deeper beneath the handmade quilt they'd drawn up over themselves during the night. She muttered something unintelligible, then pulled that quilt over her head.

When they'd finally come upstairs the night before they'd carried their discarded clothes with them, so Jefferson snatched his slacks and shirt off a delicate-looking chair and drew them on. Once he was dressed, he was more in control. He felt his life slide back into place and knew that it was the best for all concerned.

One spectacular night with an intriguing woman wasn't going to change him. He was what he was and his life wasn't in Ireland, no matter how tempting the thought might be. Besides, no one had said anything about permanent. He'd deliberately avoided even thinking that word. What he had with Maura was fun. Uncomplicated. Best to leave it at that.

"You're leaving, then?" Her voice was muffled, since her head was still beneath the quilt.

"Yeah," he said. "I've got to get back to work. I've been gone longer than I planned already. And, now that the contract is signed, there's really no reason to stay any longer."

"Ah yes, the contract."

She pulled the quilt down and her sleepy, dark blue eyes pinned him. For one awful moment, he was afraid she might ask him to stay. He hoped to hell she didn't, because it wouldn't take much convincing to have him going along with that idea, and all that would do was prolong the inevitable. Make this harder—on both of them.

But she surprised him again.

Pushing her hair back out of her face, she nodded and sat up, letting the quilt pool at her waist. His mouth went dry and his body stirred, requiring all of his focus just to get it under control again. Completely at ease with her own nudity, she scooted off the bed, walked right up to him and went up on her toes. Linking her arms around his neck, she gave him a long, luscious kiss, then looked up at him. "Then I'll say goodbye, Jefferson King. Have a safe trip."

His hands rested on her bare hips and his fingers burned with the heat of her. Nothing quite like a warm, naked woman pressed up against you to make a man think of a long, lazy day spent rolling around on her bed. But he had a King jet waiting for him and a business and a life to get back to.

She smiled and he asked, "That's it? No, 'Please stay, Jefferson'?"

Shaking her head, she rubbed her fingertip across his

mouth, then stepped back from him. "What would be the point in that? We're neither of us children. We wanted each other and we had each other. It was a lovely night. Let's keep its ending just as lovely."

Apparently, he'd been worried for no reason. She wasn't going to beg him to stay. She wasn't going to cry or say how she'd miss him or ask when he was returning. None of the things he'd hoped to avoid were happening.

So why was he irritated?

"I'll see you off, shall I?" She stepped over to her closet, grabbed a dark green terry-cloth robe and slipped into it. Her body was covered now, but the imprint of her was still etched firmly in his mind. Hiding what he'd already spent hours exploring wasn't going to change anything.

"You don't have to go downstairs with me."

"Oh," she said, leading the way out to the landing and then down the stairs. "'Tisn't just for you. I'm off to brew some tea and then get to work myself."

His eyebrows rose. So much for the fond farewell. His leaving was no more than a by-product here. She was picking up the threads of her everyday life and so was he, he reminded himself. So again, why the flicker of irritation?

She opened the front door and held it wide for him. She smiled, reached up and cupped his cheek briefly. "Fly safe, Jefferson."

"Right." He stepped onto the porch and the Irish wind howled around him. "Take care of yourself, Maura."

"Oh, I always do," she told him. "And you, as well. Not to worry about your film crew, either. All will be here when they arrive."

"Fine."

"All right then." She gave him one last smile, then shut the door, leaving him no choice now but to walk to his car and leave.

With her back to the closed door, Maura wrapped her arms around her middle and held on. After a few steadying breaths, she heard his car engine fire up and she leaned toward the nearest window to catch one last glimpse of him.

He steered his car out onto the road and in a moment, he was gone, as if he'd never been. Even the echo of his car was nothing more than a hush on the wind.

"Well, now," she murmured, swiping away the tears running down her cheeks. "It's best this way and you know it, my girl. No point in laying out your heart for him to stumble over on his way out of the country."

She wasn't the first foolish woman to fall for the wrong man entirely. No doubt, she wouldn't be the last, either.

"Doesn't matter now anyway as he's gone." She headed through the quiet house toward the kitchen and a morning pot of tea. Best to get back to her life. The life she knew. The animals and the land and the world that was hers. "You'll get over him," she promised herself firmly. "Won't take long at all."

Four

She wasn't over him.

It had been two months and she still thought of Jefferson King nearly every day. Her only hope was that he was being haunted by memories, as well. That would make this whole thing more fair.

The problem was, she had too much alone time, she told herself. Too much empty time to spend in thoughts she shouldn't be indulging in anyway. But with Cara off making a film in Dublin, Maura was alone at the farmhouse with nothing more to talk to than the dog she'd recently acquired.

Unfortunately, King, named for a certain man she was still feeling fondness for when she purchased the dog, was not much of a conversationalist.

Now, along with her wild thoughts, her misery at

missing the man she never should have let into her heart, the work building up to lambing season and her new dog, she was also feeling a bit off physically. Her stomach was queasy most of the time and she'd been so dizzy only that morning in the barn, she'd had to sit down before she fell down.

"I was right, wasn't I? It's the flu, I know it," Maura told the village doctor as he walked into the examination room. "I haven't been getting enough sleep and there's so much work to be done. I'm run down is all. I thought you could give me a little something to help me sleep."

Doc Rafferty had been in the village for forty years. He'd treated everyone for miles around and he had delivered both Maura and Cara himself. So he knew them far too intimately to pull any punches, so to speak. And as he was a forthright man in any case, he met her gaze and told her the truth of the matter.

"I've got the results of your test," he said, checking the papers he held in his hand as if to be sure of what he was about to say. "If this is the flu, it's the nine-month variety, Maura. You're pregnant."

A beat of silence fell between them as those last two words of the doctor's repeated over and over again in her head. Sure she'd misheard him, Maura laughed shortly.

"No, I'm not." She shook her head. "That's impossible."

"Is it now?" The older man sat down on a rolling stool and shifted his pale green eyes up to hers. "You're telling me you've done nothing to produce such a condition?"

"Well I—" He'd examined her from head to toe too

often for her to try to persuade him she was a virgin, and why would she care to? But this? No. It couldn't be.

Maura stopped, frowned and started thinking. Odd, but she'd been paying no attention at all to her period and hadn't even noticed until now that it hadn't shown up in quite some time. Quickly, she did a little math in her head and as she reached the only conclusion she could under the circumstances, she let out a breath and whispered, "Oh my God."

"There you are, then." Doc Rafferty reached out, patted her knee. "You'll be feeling fine again soon. The first couple of months are always the hardest, after all. In the meantime though, I want you to take better care of yourself." He scribbled a few things down on a pad and then tore off the top sheet and handed it to her.

Maura couldn't read it through the fog blocking her vision.

"Eat regular meals, cut back on the caffeine and I'll have Nurse Doherty give you a sample bottle of vitamins." He stood up, looked down at her through kind eyes and said, "Maura, love. You should tell the baby's father right away."

The baby's father.

The man she'd sworn to put firmly in her past.

So much for that fine notion. He would surely be a part of her future now, wouldn't he?

"Yes, I will." Tell Jefferson that he was going to be a father. Well, wouldn't that make for a lovely long-distance conversation?

"Will you be all right with this, Maura?"

"Of course. I'll be fine." And she would. Already, the

first shock of the news was passing and a small curl of excitement was fluttering to life inside her.

She was going to have a baby.

"Do you need to talk about anything?"

"What?" Maura's gaze lifted to meet his. Kindness was stamped on his familiar features and she knew he was worried for her. And though she appreciated it, he needn't be.

"No, Doctor," she told him, scooting off the examination table. "I'm fine, really. It was a bit of a shock, but..." She stopped and smiled. "It's happy news after all, isn't it?"

"You're a good girl, Maura, as I've always said." He gave her a nod of approval and added, "I'd like to see you once a month now, just to keep a check on you and the baby. Make the appointment on your way out. And, Maura, no more heavy lifting, understand?"

When he left the room, she was alone with her news. Although...

"Not as alone as I was when I arrived, am I?" she whispered and dropped one hand to her flat belly.

Awe rose up inside her.

There was a child growing within her. A new life. A precious, innocent life that would be counting on her. But Maura was a woman used to responsibility, so that didn't worry her. The fact that her child would grow up without a father was a bit of a hitch. When she'd imagined the day she would become a mother, she'd had hazy, blurry images of a faceless man standing at her side, rejoicing with her at the birth.

Never once had she considered being a single mother.

Heaven knew she hadn't planned on this. Had, in fact been taking precautions—well, the over-the-counter precautions. It wasn't as though she had sex often enough to warrant anything permanent.

Of course, she should have insisted Jefferson wear a condom, that would have been the intelligent thing to do. But neither of them had been thinking straight that night, she admitted silently. For herself, she'd been in such a hunger to have Jefferson over, under and in her, she hadn't wanted to wait for anything.

Now, it seemed, there would be consequences.

But such wonderful consequences. All penances should be this happily paid.

A child.

She'd always wanted to be a mother.

Maura turned, looked out the window and watched as thick, pewter clouds raced across the sky. A storm was brewing, she thought, and wondered if it was a metaphor for what was about to happen to her life.

"We'll be just fine, you and I," she told her child, still keeping one hand tight to the womb where her baby slept. She would see to it that her child was safe and well and happy.

As soon as she got home, she'd call Jefferson. She'd keep the conversation brisk and as impersonal as she could, considering the situation. She'd tell him because it was right. But she'd also tell him she had no need for him to come rushing back. She wasn't over him just yet and had no wish to see him again, stirring up things that had yet to settle down.

One phone call.

Then they'd be done.

Two months later...

"Mr. King said there would be no problems."

Maura glared at the little man standing on her porch. He was short, bald and looked as though a stiff wind off the lake might blow him into Galway city. She showed him no mercy. "Aye, your Mr. King says a lot of things, doesn't he?"

He took a deep breath as if trying for patience. She understood that feeling very well as she'd been trying for weeks and still hadn't found any.

"We do have a contract," the man reminded her.

She looked past him out to the film crew setting up tents and trailers and cameras with banks of lights surrounding them. Somehow she hadn't expected the whole mess to be quite so…intimidating. As it was, she had dozens of people trampling the grass in her front yard and the complaining bleats from the sheep were as sharp as nails against a chalkboard. Swallowing her irritation as best she could, she said, "We do indeed and I'll stay to the very letter of the contract."

"Meaning?" the little man asked, his small tight mouth flattening into a grim slash across his narrow face.

"Meaning, I said you could be on my property, but nowhere near the lambing sheds."

"But Mr. King said…"

"If you've a problem with me," Maura told him, "I suggest you phone your I'm-so-busy-I-can't-bother-to-return-a-message King and deliver your complaints to him." Just before she slammed the front door, she added, "And I wish you good luck getting him on the bleeding phone as I haven't been able to manage that no-doubt miraculous feat in the last two months."

Jefferson King was juggling what felt like thirty different projects at once. It helped to stay busy. Thankfully, his position at King Studios ensured that he remained that way.

There were currently three films under production and each of them presented different headaches. Dealing with producers, directors and, worst of all to his mind, the actors, was enough to make a man wonder what he'd first enjoyed about this business. He had deals rolling with agents, a couple of smaller studios he was looking to absorb and he was in the middle of buying the rights to a bestselling romance novel to turn it into what would be, he firmly believed, a blockbuster summer hit.

So yeah. Busy. But he preferred it that way. Busy meant his thoughts were too distracted to drift toward memories of Ireland that came only a dozen times a day now. Images of deep green fields, smoky, music-filled pubs and, mostly, thoughts of Maura Donohue.

Which was just as well because every time a picture of that blue-eyed woman rose up in his mind, he was filled with a wild mixture of emotions that were so tangled and twisted into knots inside him it was impossible to figure out which had prominence.

He tossed his pen onto the desktop and scowled at the wall opposite him. Of course he remembered the passion. The chemistry between them that had built slowly and inexorably until it had finally exploded on their last night together.

Yet he also recalled clearly the calm, cool look in her eye as she walked him to the door that last morning. He gritted his teeth as he saw her face in his mind. Clear blue eyes, luscious mouth curved in a half smile. She hadn't cried. Hadn't asked him to stay. Had, in fact, acted as if he were nothing more than an annoying guest keeping her from her work.

Fresh aggravation rose inside him at the memory, so he pushed it away and grabbed his pen again. Thumb flicking madly at the pen top, he told himself it wasn't that he really *cared,* it was the principle of the thing. Women didn't walk away from Jefferson King. No matter the situation, it was *he* who did the walking. Always. But she'd thrown him off. Caught him off balance and kept him that way and a part of him wondered if that hadn't been her plan all along.

Had she been teasing him, leading him along sexually until she got the offer just the way she wanted it, and then took him to bed to seal the deal? Was she that manipulative and he simply hadn't seen it? He'd hate to think that. Went against the grain to consider it, but why else had she been so casual about a night that had damn well hit him harder than he had expected it to?

What kind of woman spent the night with a man and then turned him loose the next morning so easily?

And why the *hell* was he still thinking about her? The deal was done; it was time to move on. "Well past time," he muttered, since there was no one else in his office to overhear him.

"That's perfect," he added under his breath, "now she's got me talking to myself and the woman probably hasn't given me a single thought."

Which really fried his ass if truth be told. Damn it, Jefferson King was *not* forgettable. Women usually crowded around him, clamoring for his attention. Not just the wannabe actresses who littered Hollywood's streets every few feet, either. But women with wit and intelligence. Women who looked at him and saw a successful man, sure of himself and his own place in the world.

Women who weren't Maura.

Still grumbling, Jefferson flipped through the stack of papers on his desk, and made a few scattered notes. He was buying up an independent film company, thinking of branching King Studios out into documentaries. But it was a stretch to say his mind was focused on that particular task at the moment.

No, like it or not, he was still thinking about *her*.

But why? After all, it wasn't as if either of them had wanted or counted on a relationship. They'd had some good times together, capped by one amazing night of mind-blowing sex. So why was he so disgusted at her casual goodbye the next morning? It wasn't as if he'd been planning to stay anyway.

It had to be ego, pure and simple.

His had taken a slap and that was something he wasn't used to. How had Maura slipped under his well-honed defenses to leave such an indelible image on his mind?

"Doesn't matter," he said aloud, hearing the determination in not only the words but his tone. The memories would fade, eventually. But that wasn't much comfort in the middle of the night when he woke up with dreams of her raging through his mind.

But a man couldn't be held responsible for what his unconscious mind dredged up, could he? He pushed away from his desk and walked to the window overlooking Beverly Hills and Hollywood. The streets were jammed with cars and in the distance he could see the stalled traffic on the freeway. Smog hung low over the scene, a hazy brown blanket covering a city with millions of people all hurrying through their lives. And for just a moment, he let himself imagine the cool green fields of Ireland. The warm welcome of the pub.

The narrow road to Maura's farmhouse.

Irritated with himself and the memories that were still far too vivid, he scrubbed both hands over his face and turned away from the window. He didn't have time to waste indulging in thoughts of a woman who'd no doubt already moved on.

His phone rang and he grabbed at it with the eagerness of a drowning man reaching for a life preserver. "What is it, Joan?"

His assistant said, "Mr. King, Harry Robinson's on line three for you. He says they're having problems on location."

Harry was directing the Irish epic shooting at Maura's farmhouse. Frowning, Jefferson said, "Thanks, Joan. Put him through."

The line clicked over and he asked, "What seems to be the problem, Harry?"

The other man's voice was sharp and filled with both static and disgust. "The problem is, nothing's going right over here. It's a nightmare."

"What? What happened?"

"What hasn't?" Harry countered. "That inn you told me about? Suddenly it has no vacancies. The local caterer's prices have gone up three times in the last week and the coffee's always cold. The guy at the pub even insists he's run out of beer whenever we walk in."

Jefferson turned around and stared blankly out at the city view again. His own reflection stared back at him from the sun-drenched glass. He looked just as confused as he felt. "Run out of beer? How is it possible for a pub to run out of beer?"

"Tell me about it."

That mild swell of irritation he'd felt earlier began to bubble and churn inside him. "That doesn't sound like Craic to me."

"Yeah, well, it doesn't exactly match the description you gave me of the place, either." In an aside to someone else, Harry said, "Well, move the trough out of the shot. No? Fine. I'll be there in a minute." Then he refocused. "That's an example of what we're dealing with. There's a feed trough I want to move and Ms. Donohue refuses to cooperate."

Jefferson tugged at the tie that felt as if it was strangling him. "Go on."

"Yesterday," Harry told him, "the owner of the market

told us he wouldn't be selling to us at all and we could just go into the city for whatever we needed."

"He can't do that."

"Seems he can. I don't have to tell you that Westport's a much longer drive and it's eating up time we don't have."

"I know." What the hell was going on?

"Oh, and the market guy said that if I spoke to you I should tell you, and I quote, 'There'll be no peace for you here until someone does his duty,' end quote. Do you have any idea what he was talking about?"

"No." Duty? What someone? What duty? What the hell had happened in Ireland to turn an entire village against his film crew? The citizens of Craic had been nothing but excited about the prospect a few months ago. What could possibly have changed?

"What about Maura?" he asked suddenly. "Hasn't she been able to help with any of this?"

"Help?" Harry laughed. "That woman would as soon as shoot us as look at us."

"Maura?" Jefferson was stunned now and even more in the dark than he had been before. All right, she hadn't been as thrilled with the prospect of a film crew being on her land as her friends and neighbors had been. But she'd signed the contract in good faith and he knew she had been prepared for all of the confusion and disruption. Her own sister was *in* the movie, so if nothing else, that should have garnered her cooperation. So what had changed?

"Yes, Maura," Harry snapped. "She lets her sheep run wild through shots, her dog chews everything it can get its paws on—"

"She's got a dog?" When did she get a dog?

"She says it's a dog. I say it's part pony. The thing's huge and clumsy. Always knocking things over. Then as if that wasn't enough, one of the cameramen was chased by Ms. Donohue's damn bull."

All right, something was definitely wrong. Whatever else he could say or think about Maura, she was nothing if not meticulous about caring for her animals and the farm itself. She'd shown him the bull, and had warned him away even though the animal was an old one. "How'd the bull get out?"

"Damned if I know. One minute we're shooting the scene, the next minute, Davy Simpson's nearly flattened under the damn bull. Good thing Davy's fast on his feet."

"What is going on over there?" Frustration spiked with temper and twisted into an ugly knot inside him.

His mind raced with possibilities and none of them were flattering to the woman who'd signed his contract. Was she after more money? Was she trying to back out of the whole deal?

Too damn bad to either of those scenarios, he told himself. He had her signature on a legal document and he wasn't about to let her off any hook, nor was he going to be extorted for more money. Whatever she was up to, it seemed she'd gotten the whole village to back her play. What other reason would they have for acting as they were?

Well, it wasn't going to work.

Jefferson King didn't bow to pressure and he sure as hell didn't walk away from trouble.

"That's what I'd like to know," Harry muttered and

the words were almost lost in the static of a bad connection. "The way you talked about this place, I thought it would be an easy shoot."

"It should've been," Jefferson insisted. "Everything was agreed on and besides, we've got a signed contract allowing you access to Maura's farm."

"Yeah, the production assistant tried to remind her of that the other day. Got the door slammed in his face."

"She can't do that," Jefferson told him.

"Uh-huh. I know that. You know that. I don't think she does. Or if she does, she doesn't care."

A hard punch of irritation shot through him again and this time it was brighter, fiercer. "She damn well should. She signed the contract willingly enough. And cashed the check. Nobody forced her to."

Harry huffed out a breath. "I'm telling you, Jefferson, unless things get straightened out around here soon, this shoot is going to go way over budget. Hell, even the weather's giving us a hard time. I've never seen so much rain."

This didn't make any sense. None of it. He'd thought everything was settled. Clearly, he'd been wrong. Looked like he was going to be heading back to County Mayo whether he had planned to or not. Time to have a little talk with a certain sheep farmer. Time to remind her that he had the law on his side and he wasn't leery about using it.

"All right," he said. "The rain I can't do anything about. But I'll take care of the rest of it."

"Yeah?" the director asked. "How?"

"I'll fly over there myself and get to the bottom of

it." Something inside him stirred into life at the thought of seeing Maura again, though he wouldn't admit that, even to himself. This wasn't about his fling with Maura Donohue. This was about business. And she'd better have a damned good reason for being so uncooperative.

"Fine. Hurry."

Jefferson hung up, shouted for his assistant and grabbed his suit jacket out of the closet. He'd already scheduled a trip to Austria to meet with the owner of an ancient castle to talk about filming rights. He'd just work Ireland into the trip.

Shouldn't take long to fix whatever had gone wrong in Craic. He'd stay in the village, talk to everyone, then remind Maura that they had a damn deal. If she was playing games, they were going to stop.

Women were notoriously inconsistent, he reminded himself. God knew the actresses and agents he worked with could drive a man insane. Their moods could change with a whim and any man in the vicinity was liable to be flattened.

Besides, seeing Maura would probably be a good thing in the long run. Give him a chance to look at her without the haze of great sex as a filter. He'd see her for what she was. Just a woman he was doing business with. They could meet, talk, then part again and maybe then he'd stop being hounded by his own memories.

His assistant, Joan, an older woman with no-nonsense green eyes and a detail-oriented personality, hustled into the office.

"What's going on?" she asked.

"I'm going to need you to contact the airport. Tell the

pilot we're making a pit stop in Ireland before we head to Austria."

"Sure, Ireland, Austria. Practically neighbors."

"Funny. Something's come up." He was already headed for the door. "I'm going by my house to pack. Tell the pilot I'll be there in two hours. Have the plane prepped and ready to go."

One of the perks of being a member of the King family was having King Jets at one's disposal. His cousin Jackson ran the company, renting out luxury planes to those who willingly paid outrageous amounts of money for comfort while traveling. But the King family always had the pick of the jets whenever they needed them. Which made all the travel Jefferson did for work a lot easier to take.

Because of that, he could be in the air before dinnertime and in Ireland for breakfast.

"I'll tell him," Joan said as he walked past her. "The jet will be ready. Should I fax you those papers on the McClane buyout while you're in the air or wait until you return?"

He thought about it for a moment, then shook his head. J. T. McClane was the owner of an actual ghost town just on the outskirts of the Mohave desert. Jefferson had the idea to do a modern-day western-gothic film set in what was left of that town. But the man had been dickering over the price for weeks. Wouldn't hurt to remind the man that King Studios was going to remain in charge of the negotiations.

"Just hang on to them until I get back," he said

finally. "Won't hurt to make McClane sweat about this deal for a while."

Joan smiled. "Got it. And, boss…"

"Yeah?"

"Good luck."

Jefferson smiled and nodded as he left, and kept his thoughts to himself. No point in telling Joan that the only one who was going to need luck around here was Maura Donohue.

Five

Jefferson stopped in the village to book a room at the small inn that he'd stayed in on his last trip. He was jet-lagged, hungry and well past the breaking point. So when the innkeeper, Frances Boyle, was less than welcoming when she opened her bright red front door and gave him a grim glare, Jefferson's hackles went up.

"Well," she said, crossing her thick arms over a pro-digious chest covered by a shawl the color of mustard. "If it isn't himself, come back to the scene of the crime."

"Crime?" One black eyebrow lifted. "Excuse me?"

"Hah! A fine time to be beggin' pardon and if it's pardon you're asking I'm not the one it should be aimed at."

He closed his eyes briefly. The older woman's brogue was so thick, and she spoke so quickly, he'd thought for a moment she was speaking Gaelic. Then her words sunk in and he realized he was being *scolded* as if he were a five-year-old who'd thrown a rock through her window.

"Mrs. Boyle," Jefferson said, gathering the reins on his simmering temper and trying for a charming smile. "I've just spent too many hours on a jet, then driven here from the airport in a rental car that blew a tire on the road and now—" he paused to toss a hard stare at the lowering gray sky "—I'm getting rained on. I'm happy to listen to whatever your complaints might be after you rent me a room so I can change clothes and get settled."

"Humph."

Her snort was caught between a snide laugh and a jolt of outrage. "Used to giving orders, aren't you? No doubt your lackeys jump to attention when you snarl. Well, I'm no one's lackey, boyo, and I've no time for the likes of you, Jefferson King."

Lackey? He didn't have lackeys.

"The likes of—" What the hell had happened to this place in a few short months? Had he stepped into an alternate universe? He pushed his wet hair out of his eyes, blinked the raindrops off his lashes and asked, "What did I do? I haven't even been here in months!"

She huffed out a breath. "So you haven't, when you should've been, I say. You're a sad disappointment to me, *Mister* King."

"Disappointment?" Seriously, he felt as though he needed a translator. It was as if the older woman was speaking in code. "What the *hell* is going on around here?"

"A *decent* man would already know the answer to that question." Her features were hard as stone and her normally placid eyes were glittering. The toe of her practical black shoe tapped against the linoleum. "And I don't appreciate you swearing at me in my own home."

"I'm not in your home," he pointed out, as a cold drop of rain sneaked underneath his shirt collar and rolled icily down his spine.

"And not likely to be any time soon, either."

So, he was getting a firsthand lesson in what his film crew had been experiencing. He couldn't understand this. When he'd been here the last time, Frances Boyle had been warm, funny, *friendly*. He wasn't used to being treated with outright disrespect.

But whatever her problem was with him, he'd deal with it later. All he wanted at the moment was a room, a change of clothes and a meal. Once he was warm, dry and fed, he knew he'd be in better shape to handle not only Mrs. Boyle, but anything else that awaited him in this picturesque village.

Then he'd be ready to head off to Maura's farmhouse to settle whatever bug she had up her— He cut that thought off abruptly and tried one last time. "Mrs. Boyle. I just need a room for a couple of days," he said tightly.

"A shame for you as I'm full up."

"Full? It's not even tourist season."

She sniffed and her voice was cold enough to drop frost on her words. "Be that as it may."

Then she closed the door on him with a sharp crack of sound. So much for charm. Fine. He'd just stop at a B and B somewhere along the road. As he recalled, there was one not far from Maura's farmhouse.

Still, it stung. Hardly the welcome he'd been expecting. Jefferson turned around on her porch and looked up and down the narrow Main Street of the village. It looked like a postcard, even in this miserable weather. Sidewalks were thin strips of cement that rose up and down as the road willed it. The shops were a rainbow of colors, and smoke drifted upward from chimneys to be caught by the ever-present wind. Doors were closed against the rain currently pummeling him and early-blooming flowers in pots bent with the water and wind.

Scraping one hand across his face, he stepped off the porch and headed for the Lion's Den pub. At least there, he'd be able to get a meal and something hot to drink. Then he'd face the rest of the drive to Maura's. As he jogged across the empty street, he told himself that Mrs. Boyle's attitude was probably just a case of women sticking together. He already knew Maura was angry about something and the innkeeper was just showing solidarity. God knew every female he'd ever known would be willing to take the side of a fellow woman against a man no matter what the argument might be.

Jefferson stepped into the warmth of the pub and paused a moment to enjoy the glow of the fire in the hearth and the rich scents of beer and some kind of stew simmering in the kitchen. Then he nodded vaguely at a couple of men seated at a table, before taking a spot at the bar for himself. He'd barely settled himself when Michael came out of the kitchen, took a look at Jefferson and came to a sudden stop. His wide, genial face flushed dark red and his blue eyes flashed with trouble.

"We're closed," he said.

Jefferson muffled a groan. This he hadn't expected at all and if he were to be honest about it, he could admit to himself that he felt a bit betrayed at the moment. He and Michael had become friends the last time he was here. And now, the look on the man's face said he'd happily plant one of his meaty fists on Jefferson's jaw.

"Closed?" Jefferson jerked a thumb in the direction of the two men, each sipping a freshly stacked Guinness beer. "What about them?"

"We're not closed to them, are we?"

"So, it's only me."

"I didn't say that." Michael picked up a pristine bar rag and idly polished a bar that already shone like a dark jewel in the overhead light.

"Yeah." Jefferson swallowed his anger because it wasn't going to do him any good here anyway. Until he knew exactly what he was accused of, he couldn't fight it.

He pushed off the stool, leaned both hands on the bar and met Michael's heated stare with one of his own. "When we first met, you struck me as a fair man, Michael," he said. "I'm sorry to be proven wrong."

The man inhaled so sharply, his barrel chest swelled up to massive proportions. "Aye and you struck me as a man to do his duty."

"Duty?" He threw both arms wide. "Is everyone in the village nuts all of a sudden? What're you talking about?"

Michael slapped the bar with his palm. "What I'm talking about is you being nothing more than a rich American taking what he wants and never paying a mind to his leavings."

Jefferson straightened up like someone had shoved

a poker down the back of his shirt. He was trying to be reasonable here, but a man could only be pushed so far. "What leavings?"

"That's not for me to say but for you to know."

Great, he thought, disgusted. More code.

"Look, we obviously don't know each other as well as I thought, Michael," Jefferson told him, "so I'm going to let that insult go. But I can tell you I've never shirked my duty in my life—nor do I know anything about any 'leavings'—not that I owe you any explanations."

"Oh, on that you're spot-on," the big man muttered. "It's not *me* you're owin', Jefferson King."

"What's that supposed to mean?"

"It's time you found out, don't you think?"

"And just who should I ask?" Even as he said the words though, he knew what the answer would be.

Sure enough, a moment later, Michael said, "Talk to Maura. She'll tell you or not as she pleases. But don't come into Craic looking for friends until you do."

The men at the table behind him muttered agreement, but Jefferson paid them no attention at all. Why was the town one step short of a mob threatening to tar and feather him?

And why was he still standing there when he knew where he could go to get some answers?

"Fine. I'm here to talk to Maura anyway. I'll settle this with her and then you and I are going to have a talk."

"I look forward to it."

He left the pub at a brisk walk and headed straight for his rental car. The rain pelted at him as if Heaven were throwing icy pebbles down just to elevate his misery. He felt the stares of dozens of people watching him as he went and realized that he'd fully expected to solve this problem with ease.

He'd had friends here, damn it. What could have happened to change that so completely? And why was Maura the key?

He fired up the engine and steered the small sports car down the narrow road leading out of town and toward Maura. It was time to get some answers.

The muddy track was familiar, and despite the carefully banked anger inside him, there was something else within, too. A curl of anticipation at the thought of seeing Maura again. He didn't want it. Had fought the very memory of her for months. But being here again fed the flames he'd been trying to extinguish.

Now wasn't the time for that, though. He wasn't here to indulge in his desire for a woman who'd made no secret of the fact that she wasn't interested. He wasn't going to walk blindly back down a path he'd already traveled.

Besides, he was wet, tired and just this side of miserable when he pulled the rental car into Maura's drive. Through the heavy mist and low-hanging clouds, the manor house sat like a beacon of light. Its whitewashed walls, dark green shutters and bright blue door belied the gray day and the jewel-colored flowers bursting from pots on either side of the door valiantly stood against an icy wind.

On the far side of the yard, three RVs, a tent and the equipment that made up a film shoot were staggered. People bustled about, though Jefferson knew the actors would be tucked inside their trailers, waiting out the weather. Between the rain and the delays caused by an uncooperative Maura and friends, Jefferson could practically hear money being flushed down the drain.

Frustrated with the entire situation, Jefferson opened the car door to a fresh wall of wet, and once he was standing on the sodden gravel drive slammed the door closed again.

Heads turned. Worker bees, the PA, Harry the director, all looked at him, but when Harry made to walk toward him, Jefferson held him back with one upraised hand. He wanted to talk to Maura before he got any more information.

"And she'd better have some damn answers," he muttered, soles of his shoes sliding on the wet gravel.

With anger churning in his gut, he started for the house. He didn't notice the charm of the place now. Paid no attention to the half-dozen or so spring lambs chasing each other through the fenced front yard.

He didn't even slow down when someone shouted a warning, so he was taken by surprise when a black dog as big as a small bear charged from the corner of the house and made straight for him.

"Jesus Christ!" Jefferson's shout of surprise was raw and hoarse, scraping from his throat loud enough to carry over the deranged barking filling the air.

Instantly, the front door flew open. Maura stepped into the rain and said sharply, "King!"

The dog skidded to a stop on the gravel, its momentum carrying it into Jefferson, who swayed, but held his ground against the heavy impact. Still startled, Jefferson looked down into a smiling dog face, complete with sharp black eyes and a tongue the size of a flag lolling out the side of its mouth.

The dog's huge head was waist high on Jefferson, and the dog had to weigh at least a hundred pounds.

"It *is* a pony," he said, remembering Harry's comment.

"Irish wolfhound," Maura told him, then added, "He meant no harm. He was only greeting you, as he's a baby yet and a poor judge of character."

He ground his back teeth together and shifted a look at her. "His name's King? You named him after me?"

Her mouth twisted into a brief sneer. "Aye, I did as he's a son of a bitch, as well."

Jefferson wasn't amused. He looked into her dark blue eyes and saw a river of emotions shining out at him. They were shifting, changing even as he watched, so that he wasn't sure if she was going to throw something at him or rush into his arms, however belatedly. A moment later, he had his answer.

"Why're you here?"

The music of her accent didn't soften her words any. She faced him down as the wind lifted her long black hair into a dance about her head. She was beautiful and stubborn and the most fascinating woman he'd ever known.

Because of her, he'd hopped a plane and flown thousands of miles only to be treated like a leper by people he'd considered friends.

"You mean, why am I standing in the rain in front of a hardheaded woman who isn't honoring the contract she signed?" He snapped the words out and noticed she didn't so much as flinch. "I've been asking myself the same thing."

"Your people are littering the street in front of my house at this very moment," she challenged, "so I'm thinking I'm honoring what was between us a good deal more than you have."

"You know," he said, shoving the monstrously huge dog off his legs so that he could stalk toward the porch. And her. "I've been back in Ireland about an hour and in that short amount of time, I've been rained on, had a flat tire, got mud in my shoes and been insulted by everyone I've spoken to. So I'm not in the mood to listen to more obscure references to what a bastard I am. If you've got a problem with me," he added, stopping just short of the porch, "then tell me what it is so I can fix it."

Her eyes narrowed on him. She crossed her arms over her chest, lifted her chin and said, "I'm pregnant. Fix *that*."

Six

She slammed the door an instant later.

Eyes wide, heart pounding in her chest, Maura leaned back against the door and tried to catch her breath. She shivered slightly and couldn't be sure if it was the bitter spring weather or the ice in Jefferson's pale blue eyes that had made her feel cold down to the bone. She only knew that seeing him again had shaken her. Shaken her so badly she couldn't afford to let him see it.

Bad enough he'd shown up on her doorstep without so much as a phone call in warning. "But then," she murmured aloud, "the man obviously doesn't know how to *use* a bloody phone now, does he, since I've been calling him for more than three months now with no success."

And yet here he was.

At her front door, looking half-drowned and furious

with it and still so tempting everything in her wanted to shout for glee at seeing him again. Even though she knew better, Maura felt that familiar need for him rise up inside her. She should have been prepared for this. Somehow, she should have known.

Of course he'd come back to Ireland. If not to see her, then to check on his blasted movie people. Yet, even if she had expected to see him, she doubted she would have been prepared for the delicious licks of want and desire that swept through her with just a single look into the man's eyes.

"He had the right of it. He is a bastard." She leaned her head back against the closed door and waited for him to start pounding on it.

Jefferson wasn't the kind of man who'd hear the news she'd just delivered and then disappear as quickly as he could. Oh no, he'd be demanding entry in another moment or two. And then he'd be righteous and full of himself and expecting explanations and details.

Though she'd been trying for months to give him exactly that, right now, she was in no mind to speak with him at all.

Mostly because her stomach was still spinning from that first sight of him. And because her hands itched to slap or hold she wasn't sure which and mostly, because he was *Jefferson*.

God help her, it didn't seem to matter that she was furious with him. Her heart was still full of him and she couldn't seem to dig him out despite how hard she tried. Which only made her even *more* furious with herself than she was with him.

And who would have thought that possible?

A heartbeat later, several loud thuds came from right behind her head. She knew without looking out the window that he was using his fist to batter at her door. Her heartbeat quickened and low in her belly something stirred, buzzing awake feelings that had been lying fallow for weeks now. Like a limb waking from a deep sleep, there were pinpricks of awareness tingling across every inch of her skin.

"Damn it, Maura, open the door!"

She might have if he hadn't ordered her to. As it was, the anger she'd been carrying around for months suddenly swamped her and she pushed away from the door. "Go away, Jefferson!"

"Not gonna happen!" he shouted back. "Now, do we have this conversation loud enough for everyone to listen in or do we talk in private?"

Private.

That got her moving. She wasn't interested in having half of Hollywood listening in on her private business. Maura flung the door open and stepped back as Jefferson marched inside, followed by King, who promptly shook the rainwater off his coat and onto everything else.

"For heaven's sake," she muttered as the dog sprinted off the long hallway toward the kitchen and his bed.

Wiping water off her face, she stared up into Jefferson's eyes and almost took a step back from the glittering wrath shining there. Then she remembered just which of them had the right to be angry.

"You've nothing to be snippy about," she told him before he could speak.

"Snippy?" He pushed both hands through his wet hair, shrugged out of his suit jacket and tossed it onto the umbrella stand beside the door. His white dress shirt was soaked as well, clinging to the muscled contours of his chest and abdomen in a way that made Maura's mouth water, though she wouldn't have admitted it even with a knife to her throat.

"I'm way more than snippy," he told her. "What the hell do you mean you're pregnant?"

She forced herself to calmly close the front door before she turned to answer him. "Just how many things could I mean, do you think, Jefferson?" Oh, she'd imagined this scene too many times to count and the reactions she'd given him in her mind had been wide and varied. But in none of them had he looked as though someone had hit him over the head with a stick.

He was stunned, pure and simple, which told her flat out that no one had given him the countless messages she'd left over the last couple of months. Why did the man employ so many people if none of them could be trusted to pass on a message?

Her temper built steadily as she met his shocked gaze. "It's easy enough to understand. I'm *pregnant*. With child. Carrying. Bun in the oven." She tipped her head to one side. "Shall I draw you a picture?"

A tension-filled second or two ticked past, the only sounds in the house that of the rain battering at the windows and the wind whistling beneath the eaves. Finally, he spoke and his voice was tight with controlled emotion.

"If you think you're being funny, you're mistaken. And if you're really pregnant why the *hell* didn't you tell me?"

"Really pregnant?" She repeated the words, spitting them back at him. "Instead of only a bit pregnant, is that it?"

"That's not what I meant. Why didn't you tell me?"

"Hah! You've quite the nerve asking me that question, I'll say." She closed the space between them with two quick steps and poked her index finger against the center of his chest. "With me calling and calling that bloody studio of yours, leaving messages both long and short with that crowd of people standing between you and the public?"

"You called?"

"Repeatedly and I'll tell you now, the Pope would be easier to ring up."

"I never got any message from you," he said, pulling his tie off and opening the collar of his shirt.

Was that true? She wondered if she'd been wrong all this time. For weeks now, she'd been harboring a snarling fury toward him. She'd thought he'd been getting all of her messages and simply ignoring them. Choosing to distance himself from a woman he no longer wanted and a child he had no interest in. She'd thought him the lowest sort of man and she'd been hurt and furious with herself that she hadn't seen him originally for the snake he'd turned out to be.

Now…she had to rethink everything. She had to consider that perhaps he really hadn't known about the baby. And if that was true then what did it mean for all of them? Ah God, she needed time to think, without him standing within arm's reach of her and looking good enough to bite.

Irritated beyond measure, she snapped, "It's hardly my fault that you didn't get messages I left, now is it?"

He tossed the tie onto his suit jacket. "You're pregnant."

"As I've said."

Shaking his head, he looked as though he wanted to say something, but he bit the words back before they could escape. Instead, he swiped one hand across his face, stared at her as if he'd never seen her before, then muttered something under his breath that she didn't quite catch.

He took a few steps down the polished wood hallway, then stopped and turned around. "Does everyone in the village know about this?"

Maura sighed. It hadn't taken long at all for her secret to become public knowledge. "Nurse Doherty has ever had a flapping tongue."

"That means yes, I take it."

"It does."

"You ought to sue her," he mumbled. "Doctor-patient privilege."

She laughed shortly. "Isn't that just like an American? Lawsuits the answer to all problems? Well, what good would it do me to sue a woman who's known me since my mother was carrying me?" Maura sighed again and explained, "It wasn't Doc Rafferty who spilled the news. Trying to quiet Patty Doherty would be like holding back the tide by building a wall of sand."

She'd known the moment she left the doctor's office that fine day that within hours, word of her pregnancy would be spread across all of Craic. Not that she was ashamed of her situation. But if Maura had even guessed beforehand that she might be pregnant, she'd have visited a doctor in Westport, to keep her business her own.

"Are you well?" he asked quietly. "The baby?"

"We're both fine," she assured him.

And weren't they being civilized, Maura thought vaguely. Just two adults who'd made a child, standing in a dimly lit hall speaking to each other like strangers. The cold she'd felt earlier dropped into the freezing range.

When he'd first come to Ireland, there'd been heat. Heat that had burned bright and hot between them, ending in the inevitable. Now though, Maura thought that if he had looked at her then the way he was now, they wouldn't be in the position they were in.

It wasn't lust he was showing her now. It was…less and more at the same time. Confusing to both of them, no doubt.

All around them, a storm raged, yet here in the house where she'd lived her whole life, there was a stillness that ate at her nerves and chewed at the edges of her heart. Was he wondering what to do with her? How to keep his affair with a sheep farmer a secret from the press?

Why the devil wouldn't he *say* something?

"Must you just stand there staring at me as if I've grown two heads?"

He inhaled sharply. "It's a lot to take in."

"Oh, aye," she agreed. "What to do about Maura? Must be bloody difficult to think of the right thing to say."

He ignored that. "So, the reason the film crew's having so much trouble…the reason I couldn't get a room at the inn or a beer in the pub…" His voice trailed off, but Maura could see him thinking and knew from the expression on his face he didn't much care for what was in his mind.

"They're angry on my behalf," she told him, her voice soft, her words sharp. "Everyone in the village knows I'm pregnant and that you've done nothing about it."

"I—" He took a step toward her and stopped again. "How in the hell could I have done anything about it when you didn't bother to tell me?"

"I've already explained that I bloody well tried to tell you, didn't I?"

Maura stormed out of the hall into the main room. Through the bank of windows, she saw the gray skies, the green field where lambs played and the wide, pewter stretch of the lake. She didn't turn around to know he'd followed her into the room. She didn't have to. She would have sensed him even if she hadn't heard his footsteps.

"How hard did you try, Maura?" He grabbed her upper arm and turned her around to face him. "A man's got a right to know when he's going to be a father."

"Aye, he does. And along with that right," she countered, refusing to be cowed by the flash of indignation in his eyes, "comes a responsibility to return calls left so that he might discover what a body's trying to tell him."

"I never got any messages."

"So you say, though I left dozens. Maybe hundreds." Doubt crept in and battered at the anger she'd been carrying for weeks.

"With whom?"

"With anyone I could get on the phone, blast you!"

She yanked free of his grasp and whipped her hair back behind her shoulders. "Mostly I called your office and never got past your secretary. Oh, she was polite and all and told me how nice it was that I wanted to stay in touch, but that you're a busy man and so I was to be sure and let her know if I had any problems in the future."

"Joan. Did you tell her about the baby?"

"I did. She congratulated me as nice as you please and said she was sure Mr. King would be happy for me. *Happy* for me." She folded her arms across her chest. "I assumed you wanted nothing to do with me *or* my child."

"*Our* child."

She nodded. "As you say. So when I heard nothing from you for weeks, I put you out of my mind entirely."

Liar, her brain screamed silently. He'd never been out of her thoughts. Or her dreams. Even with the hurt and disappointment and anger, she'd thought of him, remembered that night with him and torn herself up with regrets for what had been lost.

Blast if she'd let him know that, though.

"So it seems, Jefferson, that once your contract is signed, you've no need to be polite to those you've already won over."

"I can't believe Joan knew and didn't say anything."

"Get a lot of those messages, does she?" Stung, she snapped, "Believe me or not, it's your business to be sure."

"I don't mean I didn't believe you. I meant—" His voice trailed off. Shoving both hands into his pockets, he shook his head and said, "I've had people call after the contract was signed, trying to up the amount of money they agreed to. Or to get more out of me in other ways.

Joan—my assistant—knows that and weeds out people she thinks might be causing trouble."

"Well, I might see how she could think that when, after the first few tries I made, I might have lost my temper with her...."

"Might have?" he asked, one corner of his mouth lifting.

"All right, *did,* but I had my reasons, didn't I?"

"Yeah, you did. She should have told me you called."

Jefferson blew out an unsteady breath. This was all happening so fast he could hardly think. He'd never even considered the possibility of leaving Maura pregnant. Which made him a complete ass. He hadn't worried about contraception—had just given himself over to the heat of the moment. Something he had never been careless about. But damn it, he couldn't be faulted for not acting on something he hadn't even known about.

The important thing to focus on was the fact that he was going to be a father.

Everything in him trembled. Not the kind of news a man got every day. Not hard to understand why his brain was having a tough time computing it all. He hadn't known. For four months, she'd been alone with this knowledge, thinking that he didn't care. Thinking he wanted nothing to do with her. No wonder she was spitting fire at him. Guilt roared up, took a bite of him, then Jefferson shoved it back down. Damned if he'd take the blame for something he hadn't even known about.

"I'll have a talk with Joan when I get back. Make it clear that I want to see all of my messages, not just the few she decides are worth my time." It infuriated him that Maura had been trying to get hold of him for months unsuccessfully. Still in his own defense, he said, "A lot of people call me, Maura."

"Women, I suppose," she said with a sneer.

Yes, women, he thought, though there hadn't been any since he'd last been here. Hell, he hadn't been able to look at another woman without seeing dark blue eyes and a wide, luscious mouth. His thoughts had been with Maura even when he hadn't wanted it that way.

"I saw a picture of you in one of those celebrity magazines a month or so back. You looked very handsome in your splendid tuxedo with an empty-headed blond on your arm. Yes, you were very busy."

He enjoyed the scorn in her voice. "Jealous?"

She snorted. "Indeed not. Just observant."

That might be what she was telling herself, but he was glad to know she'd been keeping tabs on him anyway. "That was the lead actress in our latest movie. I escorted her to the premiere."

"Aye, she looked the 'escort' type."

He laughed shortly. "It's my job, Maura."

"And you do it so well," she told him, dropping into a chair that looked worn and comfortable.

In fact, the whole house looked cozy, he thought, giving the room a quick going over. It had stood there for centuries and the interior of the farmhouse had the softly shabby look that spoke not of neglect, but comfort. Familiarity.

He stood over her. "You're taking shots at me. I get that. My point, though, was that a lot of people leave messages for me. It's not that surprising that yours got lost or misdirected or—" He threw his hands up in frustration.

"And how many of those messages were from women telling you they're pregnant?" She glared up at him with sparks flashing in her eyes. "Because if there's a line of us, you can tell me now, Jefferson. I won't be part of your herd. And my child won't be one of dozens of your bastards."

"Stop it." He leaned down, planting both hands on the arms of the chair, caging her neatly. The scent of her drifted to him and he inhaled it deeply. God, he'd missed her more than he'd wanted to admit, even to himself. Now, her eyes were wild with rage, but there was hurt there, too, and that bothered him.

"There's no one else. I don't have any other children. I didn't know about your pregnancy. If I had, I would have been here. Would have talked to you. Done—"

"What?" she asked, a little less battle-ready now. "What would you have done?"

"I don't know. Something."

She looked up into his eyes for a long second or two, then finally nodded. "I believe you. You didn't get the messages. You didn't know."

"Thanks for that, anyway." He pushed up and off the chair and moved away from her.

He was going to be a father. A hard thing for a man to consider. To accept. There was anticipation inside him, even excitement. But there was also uncertainty. He had to make plans. *They* had to make plans. Hell, he didn't even know where to start.

"Now I know how Justice felt," he mumbled.

"Justice?"

"My brother. The one on the ranch." He glanced at

her and gave her a wry smile. "His wife, Maggie, didn't tell him they'd had a son together until Jonas was six months old."

"Why not?"

"Because she thought Justice wouldn't believe her." To stop her from asking why again, he said, "It's a long story. The point is, at the time, I thought Justice overreacted to what Maggie had done. He was furious with her and I thought he should just get over it, deal with the new reality. But now I get it."

"Is that right? So now you're furious, are you? Well, join the club."

"No." He laughed out loud, enjoying her mercurial nature. Had there ever been another woman like her? Smiling one minute and fierce the next. She was a tangled web of emotions that a man had to be crazy to want to explore. Well, sign him up to be committed. "I'm not furious. Just…wondering where the hell we go from here, that's all."

"Well then, when you're finished doing your wondering, you know where to find me, don't you?" She stood up out of the chair and headed for the bank of windows overlooking the front yard.

"Maura, I'm not leaving until we settle this."

"I don't want you here."

"Too bad." She could push him away all she liked, he was going nowhere until he was good and ready. And that wasn't going to happen anytime soon. "I'm staying until we figure this out."

"There's nothing *to* figure out." She looked at him briefly over her shoulder before turning her face back to the window and the view beyond. "I'm pregnant. You're not. Go home."

"No."

She lifted one hand and laid her palm on the rain-streaked pane. "Tell your movie people they'll have no more trouble from me or the village. I'll see to it."

"Thanks. That takes care of one problem."

She stiffened. "I'm not a problem, and neither is my child."

"I didn't say that, either." God, she was a minefield and he was walking through it blindfolded.

"You might as well have. It's in your mind. Your heart."

"So you read minds now, too?"

"Yours is easy enough," she told him.

He caught her reflection in the glass and hated that her eyes were shining with unshed tears. He realized he'd never seen Maura cry and he damned well didn't care for the fact that he was behind those tears now.

"Go away," she said softly. "Please."

Jefferson heard the click of nails on wood, so wasn't surprised when her huge black dog entered the room and walked toward her. Automatically, she dropped one hand to the dog's head and stroked her fingers through its fur. The two of them looked like a painting together.

At the moment, Jefferson thought, there was no place for him there. Maura had drawn a line to close him out. Maybe he couldn't blame her.

That didn't mean he was going to let this go, though, and she'd better get used to that idea real fast. But for now, he'd leave, gather his forces and come back when he had things settled in his mind. He knew what needed to be done. From the moment he first heard about the baby, he'd known.

But he needed time to work out the details.

Then he'd be back and Maura Donohue would see that a King never walked away from his responsibilities.

With that thought in mind, he turned to leave, as she'd asked him to. Before he walked out of the room, though, he promised, "This isn't over, Maura."

Seven

A few hours later, Cara asked, "Then what did he do?"

"He left." Maura lifted a week-old lamb, cradled it against her chest, then held a baby bottle out for it. Instantly, the tiny, black-and-white creature latched on to the rubber nipple and began tugging at it. Maura smiled even as she tried to ignore her sister's interrogation.

Naturally, Cara wouldn't leave the thing alone even when Maura insisted she didn't want to speak about it. The only thing she could do now was hope to finish the conversation as quickly as possible.

"He just left? He didn't propose?"

Maura laughed at that notion, more to cover up her own disappointment than anything else. Until that very afternoon, she'd had dreams. Fantasies you might say, during the weeks when she was trying so futilely to get hold of the Great One himself. She'd imagined him going down on bended knee, here in this very barn. She'd pictured him proposing and, in her frustration with his ignoring her or so she'd thought, she'd pictured herself telling him no. After all, he'd been ignoring her for months, so she'd imagined the stunned surprise on his face as she told him what he could do with his belated proposal.

Then he'd shattered that lovely dream by not even bothering to give her a duty proposal. She frowned to herself and realized just how hard it was to love a man who had no idea how she felt.

"No," she said tightly. "He didn't propose and it's not likely to happen anytime soon."

"Why ever not?" Cara wanted to know. "He's given you a baby, the least he can do is make you a wife."

Maura chuckled in spite of the situation. "You know, for someone who claims to be a very modern woman of the world, you sounded remarkably like an old grandmother just then."

Cara frowned. "Being modern is one thing. Watching my sister be a single mother is another altogether. Besides, Maura, you love him."

Maura's gaze snapped to her sister, who was looking tired and near half-asleep. And why shouldn't she? Cara was balancing a waitressing job in Westport while coming back to the farm nearly every day to film her small role in Jefferson's movie. Her sister was smart, talented and far too knowing about some things.

"I'll thank you to keep that piece of news to yourself," Maura told her. "Besides, I'll not have his pity and that's all it would be if he pretended to love me now. Or worse yet, if he were appalled at the notion. So mind your tongue, Cara."

Clearly insulted, Cara drew her head back as if she'd been slapped. "As if you need tell me. I'm your sister, aren't I? Would I side with a Yank against my own blood?"

Mollified a bit, Maura nodded and put her attention back to the task at hand. She could learn to forget him, she told herself. She would content herself in the future with her farm and her child and one day, the man she loved would be no more than a fond memory she indulged in on lonely nights. For now though, Jefferson had work and so did she. And hers, she thought, was more pressing than contracts or actors or the placement of a camera.

She had a total of six lambs so far this season who needed to be hand-fed. There were two pens holding the little ones, who snuggled together to sleep in a pile beneath heat lamps that kept the spring chill away. A few had been abandoned by their mothers for whatever reason a sheep might deem reasonable. Happened every year, a ewe would give birth and simply stroll away from the lamb, ignoring its bleating calls.

The others were simply too small to be left alone with their mothers, so the ewes were penned nearby so the lambs could nurse as well as get extra nutrition from a baby bottle. The tiny, warm bodies were a constant wonder to Maura. They were so small, so helpless when new that it was difficult to remain detached, as she must. Since most of the lambs would be sold off and—

"You should be the one to tell him at any rate," Cara said and reached for one of the lambs. Grabbing up an extra bottle, she cuddled the pure white baby and smiled at the hungry sounds it made as it fed.

Her sister might have her sights set on acting, but Cara was born and bred a farm girl and knew what needed doing without being told. And for a few minutes, the two sisters enjoyed the stillness. Outside, the storm had passed, leaving only the sound of water dripping from the roof edges and the ever-present wind rattling the shingles.

"He's staying in one of the trailers, you know."

"What?" Startled, Maura looked her sister in the eye.

"I said, Jefferson is staying in one of the trailers."

Maura threw a look at the closed barn doors as if she could see through them to the yard outside. "You mean now? He's living out there? In the street?"

"In one of the trailers, yes." Cara smiled and stroked the lamb as she fed it. "Everyone else left hours ago, headed off to the B & B and some into Westport. But Jefferson is staying here. Said he wanted to be close. Why's that, do you think?"

She didn't know. And couldn't guess. Oh, she didn't like that. She'd hoped he'd be off to the city and give her some breathing room. How was she supposed to relax into her routine if she knew he was less than a hundred feet from her own front door? Her insides were fluttering and she knew it wasn't the baby moving as that hadn't happened yet. No, it was her child's father setting off swarms of butterflies in the pit of her belly.

"He can't stay there."

"Of course he can." Cara tipped her head to one side and studied her older sister. "They're his trailers, after all. And you did give him leave to park them there."

"Not to *live* in!"

Cara laughed. "Look at you. Just knowing he's close by has put color in your cheeks and a shine in your eyes."

"That's just anger is all."

"It's not, no," her sister said. "Honestly, Maura, must you be so stubborn at all times? You're flushed over him and you say you don't want him? You're having his baby, for goodness' sake. Why shouldn't you be married to the man?"

"She will be."

Both women jolted at the sound of the deep voice. They turned as one and stared at Jefferson as he stepped into the warm barn and closed the door behind him. He wore black jeans, a dark red pullover sweatshirt and heavy black boots that were as scuffed as the floor of the barn. His hair was windblown across his forehead and his mouth was a firm, grim line. The overhead lights were harsh and bright and cast unforgiving shadows over his face until he looked like some pirate with danger on his mind.

Maura's heart did a slow roll in her chest and a deep, throbbing ache set up shop low in her body. Would he always have this kind of effect on her?

"She will be what?" Cara asked.

"I said, your sister will be marrying me." Jefferson walked toward them, sidling past idle machinery and stacks of baled hay on one side of the barn. As he neared the closed-off area, one of the ewes scuttled nervously in her pen. He looked at all of the animals crowded together, then shifted his gaze back to Maura. "As soon as we can manage it."

Amazing how quickly fire could turn to ice. Here then was her "proposal." A demand from a man who clearly expected her to jump through hoops when ordered to.

"No, I'm not," Maura told him, wishing the barn were bigger. Wishing she were back in the house behind locked doors. Wishing Jefferson had never returned to Ireland. What a sorry mess.

If he thought *that* was a proposal, he was sorely lacking. Step into her barn and issue commands as though he actually *were* a king. Was he so full of himself that he expected her to fall in line with whatever he wanted? Did he really think her such an easy woman as all that?

It didn't matter, really, Maura told herself. His decisions would have no impact on her. And though her heart was galloping in her chest, she wouldn't be saying yes. She wouldn't have a man who didn't love her and she knew bloody well Jefferson King was not in love.

"Argue if it makes you feel better." Jefferson looked down at her, their eyes locked and she read pure determination in those pale blue depths. For all the good it would do him.

"And you make all the decisions you like," Maura countered briskly. "It appears you enjoy doing it no matter that nothing will come of it."

"It's all arranged." He sniffed at the mingled scents of hay and wet sheep. "Or it will be soon. My assistant's taking care of the details, but with the time difference, it'll probably take a couple of days."

"What exactly," Cara asked, when it became clear Maura had no intention of asking the question herself, "is it that your assistant is so busily arranging?"

"A marriage license, a venue." His gaze fixed on Maura. "I told Joan I thought you'd prefer to be married in the village church, but we can change that if you'd rather. Westport maybe? Dublin? Hell, we can wait and get married in Hollywood if you want."

"Hollywood?" Cara asked, saying the word a bit wistfully.

"Doesn't matter to me," Jefferson said. "As long as we get married, I don't care where we do it."

"How very thoughtful," Maura managed to choke out.

"It's not thoughtful," he countered. "It's expedient."

"And quite romantic," Maura sniped. "Why, my heart's just weeping with the joy of it all."

"This isn't about romance," he said.

"That'd be plain to a blind man."

"It's about what's right."

"Oh, and I suppose you're the one to be deciding what right is?"

"Someone has to," he said with a barely restrained snarl.

"Well then," Cara announced, effectively interrupting the argument, "I can see you two have a lot to talk about, so I'll be going, shall I?"

Maura jolted. She didn't want to be alone with Jefferson. Not now. Not yet. "Don't you dare leave this barn, Cara...."

Giving her a wink, her sister stood up, handed the lamb and its bottle to Jefferson and announced, "I wish you luck in your dealings with my sister. She can be a bit hardheaded, as I'm sure you've noticed."

"So much for family loyalty," Maura murmured.

Cara ignored her and spoke only to Jefferson. "Mind though, make her cry and I'll make your life a living misery."

"Fair warning," Jefferson said with a nod as he settled the lamb more comfortably against him.

"Good."

"Cara, blast you for a traitor, don't you leave me here with him—"

"I'll take myself off back to Westport," Cara said, lifting her voice to carry over Maura's. "I'll stay with Mary Dooley again since I've an early shift at the café tomorrow anyway. You two have a good night," she added, then looked at Jefferson. "Mind the lamb drinks the whole bottle now."

She was gone a moment later and the only sounds in the barn were those made by the restive sheep.

"I've never fed a lamb before," Jefferson said, taking a seat on an upturned crate. He looked down at the small animal in his arms and added, "I've hand-fed calves though. Shouldn't be too different, though if you tell Justice I said that, I'll deny it."

Maura swallowed hard, then realized her lamb was through feeding. She set him down in the pen, reached for the next one and began the process over again. They were too intimate here. Too crowded together in too small a space. She couldn't draw a breath without taking in the scent of him. It was fogging her mind, but not so much that she'd give way to a bully trying to force his decisions on her.

"There's no reason for you to stay," she said.

"I'm helping," he told her.

"I don't need your help just as I don't need to be told I'm getting married."

"Apparently," he said, "you do."

"I won't marry you."

"Why the hell not?" He lifted his eyes from the lamb, who was feeding as if it were the last bit of milk it might ever see. "It's the right thing to do and you know it. You're pregnant with my child. In my family, kids have parents who are married. Besides, my child is going to carry my name."

"So this is nothing to do with me," Maura argued. "It's all what you think should be done. Your rights. Your responsibility. Your child. Well go and have *your* marriage. Just don't expect me to participate."

"If you'll quit being so damn stubborn about this, you could think rationally. For the sake of the baby we made, we have to get married. Our kid deserves two parents."

"And he'll have them."

"He?" Jefferson asked.

She sighed. "No, I don't know what sex the baby is and don't want to know."

"Good," he said with a nod. "I like the surprise, too."

A part of her melted at that until she reminded herself that a man who cared for his child wouldn't necessarily care for the child's mother. This was all wrong. All of it. It broke her heart, but damned if she'd sentence either of them to a life without love.

"Do you really think I'll marry you because you think you owe me your protection?" She shook her head and scoffed at the notion. "I'm a grown woman. And this isn't the nineteenth century, Jefferson. Even in Ireland a woman alone can raise her child in peace. And the name Donohue will suit *my* child nicely."

"*Our* child," he corrected, "and there's no reason for you to be alone. I accept my responsibilities, Maura."

"Well, don't I feel warm and treasured. A responsibility. Surely that's a word every woman longs to hear from a man."

"Not five hours ago, you were pissed at me because I *wasn't* taking responsibility. Now I am."

"I don't want you to."

"That's a shame."

The ewes scuttled uneasily in their pens again as if picking up on the tension in the air.

"And," he continued, "once we're married, I'll take you back to Los Angeles. Buy you a big house in Beverly Hills."

That gave her a start. For all her idle dreams of proposals, she'd never once considered leaving the home she loved. But of course he wouldn't want to stay here. He had a life and a business in the States. She suddenly felt bereft for a dream that hadn't had a chance to come true in the first place. "I've a home right here."

"You can sell the farm," he said offhandedly. "You won't have to work so hard anymore. You can sleep in instead of running out in all weather taking care of sheep. You can have a life of luxury. Do whatever you want to do. Travel. Shop."

He seemed so pleased with himself. Didn't he hear how empty the life he described sounded? If she didn't have her farm, her work, who would she be?

"So I'm to give up my home," she said, her voice low, soft, barely making more than a hush in the quiet. "Sell the land my family's worked for generations. And then I'm to go off to Hollywood and spend your money. Is that it? Is that the life you've planned for me?"

Something in her tone warned him. Wary now, Jefferson watched her as she gently set the lamb down in the pen beside her and just as carefully picked up the last one. Her features were blank, but her eyes were glittering darkly.

Jefferson didn't see the problem. He was offering her the kind of life thousands of women would kill for. But maybe it would just take her a minute to see the beauty of it. So he gave her an easy smile and painted an even rosier—to his mind—picture than he had before. "Think about it, Maura. Lazy days sitting by a pool. Going out to lunch with your friends. Having time to play with the baby as much as you want. As my wife, you won't be expected to work every day. You can take it easy for the first time in your life."

"Take it easy. Just live to serve you, is that it?" she asked, tenderly stroking the head of the lamb suckling at the bottle she held.

In the glare of the lights, her features were in sharp relief. She looked calm, which Jefferson knew was a lie. Her eyes were bright and a flush of color filled her cheeks. No matter how tranquil she might appear, she was reining in a temper he'd seen in full force before, up close and personal.

"I don't know what you're getting all worked up over. You're not going to be serving me, for God's sake," he said, wondering why she couldn't see the simple beauty in his plan. "Maura, you're deliberately putting words in my mouth and making this harder than it has to be."

"Oh, am I? So selling my farm, my *home* should be easy? Leaving the life I love, my friends, my family, my *country*, should be a lark?" She shook her head and kept her voice low, not for his sake, he knew, but for the sake of the baby animal she held in her arms. "I'm sorry to tell you, but I've no interest at all in moving to Hollywood, with you or without you. And I can tell you now, you won't be after changing my mind about this no matter what you have your assistant 'arrange.'"

He put a lid on the frustration beginning to churn inside him. It wouldn't help a thing to just hammer back at her. Instead, he had to try to smooth her into seeing things his way. "Just think about it, all right? Before you dismiss it out of hand. You can pick out whichever house you want. It doesn't have to be in the city. We can buy something in the mountains. With some land. Whatever you want. I'll even buy you some sheep if you want and you can hire someone to do the work. I can make your life a hell of a lot easier than it's been so far. What's so wrong with that?"

Silently, he congratulated himself on being able to lay the facts out so tidily. Surely she'd see now exactly what kind of life he could offer her.

"This is how you think to convince me?" she asked, shaking her head in disappointment as she looked at him. "Am I supposed to be impressed with your station?"

"My what?" Confusion bloomed in his mind.

"You use your money so easily. Are people so eager to be purchased by you that you expect it from everyone?"

"Purchased?" he echoed. "I'm not trying to buy you, Maura, I'm trying to give you—"

"Is your life so much better than mine?" she demanded, interrupting him as she put the lamb back in the pen and stood up. "Is this the prince offering the pauper a peek at the finer things in life? Should I be awed? Grateful? Is that it?"

"Prince? Where'd you get that?" This really wasn't going at all well and damned if he could figure out how he'd blown it. But looking into dark blue eyes that were flashing with insult and anger, he knew he had.

"You're speaking to me as you would to a child you're offering a special treat. You with your money and your fine houses and your jets. Did you really think I'd be pleased to have you swoop in and throw money at me?" She lifted the lamb from his arms, returned it to the pen with the others, then snatched the empty baby bottle from him. "Well, I'm not. My life is just exactly that. *My* life. I don't care two spits about your money, just so you know. If you put a torch to it, I wouldn't so much as warm myself by the blaze."

Completely baffled, he only stared at her. "How did this get to be about money?"

"You started it, with your list of temptations, thinking to seduce me away from the home I love." Her eyes were wide and bright and her mouth was set into a furious line. "You with your fine education, pretty suits and private jets. Like all rich men, you wield power however it suits you no matter who is in the way. You've no idea at all how real people live, do you?"

"Real people?" That was enough. He stood up and looked down at her. "I don't have a damn clue what you're talking about. I'm trying to do the right thing here. The right thing for you *and* the baby."

"And I'm to fall in line, am I?"

"This is crazy," he said and grabbed her shoulders, holding her still when she would have bolted. "You're not going to make me feel guilty for offering to give you and my child a better life."

"And who's to say which life is better? You, I suppose?"

"Not better," he corrected. "Easier."

"The easy way isn't always the best way. When I marry, *if* I marry, it'll be for love, Jefferson King—and I've not heard *that* word out of you."

He let her go as if his fingers had been burned. "This isn't about love."

"And that's my point."

He pushed his hand through his hair, then scrubbed that hand across the back of his neck. Finally, when he'd eased the tension in his own chest, he looked at her and said softly, "We weren't in love when we made that child. Why do we need to be in love to raise it?"

She pulled in a slow, deep breath then let it slide from her lungs. "What we shared, neither of us thought to be a permanent thing. It was heat and passion and want. Raising a child is more than that, Jefferson, as well you know."

"There was more to that night than simple desire and you know that."

A long minute slipped past before she nodded. "I do, yes. There was caring between us, I admit that. But affection isn't love."

He couldn't give her what she wanted. He'd done love once before and when it ended, he'd sworn off. Love wasn't in his future plans. Wasn't even on his horizon. Yes, he felt something for Maura, but it wasn't love. He'd been in love before and what was now crowded in his chest, squeezing his heart, was nothing like he'd felt back then.

"There's nothing wrong with affection, Maura. Plenty of marriages have started with less."

"Mine won't," she said simply. Then she squared her shoulders and looked him dead in the eye. "You've done your duty, Jefferson King. You can go back to your life knowing you tried to do the right thing. But I tell you here and now, I won't be marrying you."

Eight

Two days later, Maura felt like a caged animal. Oh, she had the run of the farm, but she remained under the watchful eye of Jefferson King. He was everywhere she turned. She hadn't had a moment to herself since he'd arrived during the last storm. If she stepped outside the house, there he was. If she was feeding the lambs, he turned up to help. If she walked into the village, he went with her.

She'd reached the point now where she was looking for him, expecting him. Blast the man, that had most likely been his plan all along.

Though she'd set the village to rights and her friends and neighbors had once again opened their businesses to the film crew, Jefferson remained in the trailer parked outside her home. He didn't go back to the inn. Didn't move to a comfortable hotel. Oh, no. He stayed in that too-small trailer so that he could badger Maura and tell her what their future was going to be, like it or not.

"What kind of world is it when a woman has to sneak out of her own house?" she murmured to herself as she quietly closed the back door, wincing at the click of the door shutting. All she wanted was some time alone. To think. To feel sorry for herself. To do a little damn whining in private. Was that too much to ask?

Being around Jefferson was wearing on her. Love for him was caught up in her chest and strangling her with the effort to express itself. But how could she profess her love for a man who thought "affection" was enough to build a life on?

She snapped her fingers for King and the dog came running. He sprinted past her, out into the fields behind the farmhouse, chasing his own imagination and the rabbits he continually hoped to find. Maura only smiled. She'd made it. Gotten clean away and so she took a deep breath of the chill spring air. It was a fine day, and no sign of another storm yet, though she knew the good weather wouldn't last. But while it did, she wanted to be outside, with the sunshine spilling down on her and the soft wind blowing through her hair.

And as she walked, she asked herself if she could really have given up this life. Her gaze followed the sweep and roll of the green hills and fields. Stone fences and trees twisted by wind and storm stood as monuments to the only life she'd ever known. Could she have walked away?

If Jefferson had actually meant that proposal. If there had been love rather than duty prompting it. Could she have sold her farm, moved thousands of miles away and given up the cool, clear beauty of the fields for the tangled crush of people?

The answer, of course, was yes. For love, she would have tried it. She might not have sold the farm, but she could have leased the land to a nearby farmer. She could have come back to visit, though the thought of leaving tore at her heart enough to make her stagger a bit. Yes. For love she would have made the effort.

For affection, she would not.

"Are you all right?" a too-familiar deep voice called out from behind her.

She sighed. So she hadn't escaped after all.

Maura didn't turn, didn't slow down, just shouted, "I'm fine, Jefferson, just as I was the last time you asked that question an hour ago."

He caught up with her in a moment's time, her much-shorter legs no match for his long strides. Falling into step beside her, he tucked his hands into the pockets of his jeans and lifted his face to the sun. "Feels good to actually see sunlight for a change."

"Spring's a stormy season," she muttered and told her jittery stomach to calm down. Much to her own chagrin, it wasn't just his constant presence that was making her feel trapped. It was her body's, her heart's reaction to him that was eating away at her.

Even now, her heartbeat was quickening. Being near Jefferson set her blood to boiling and her nerves dancing. His scent. His voice. His nearness. All combined to make her want with an ache she knew would never really leave her.

And to have him always close by was nothing less than torture.

"Where are you off to?"

"Just a walk," she told him with a wave. "Up to the ruins and back."

"That's at least a mile," he pointed out.

"At least." She glanced up at him and smiled at the concerned frown she saw on his face. "I'm used to the exercise, Jefferson. And I don't need a bodyguard here on my own land."

He grinned suddenly. "But I enjoy guarding your body."

She flushed as he'd meant her to and the nerves already scampering through her system went on a rampage. It was probably hormones, she thought. She'd always heard that pregnant women were needier than usual. So it wasn't entirely her fault that at the moment she wanted nothing more than to feel his arms come around her. To have him roll the two of them to the sweet-smelling grass and bury himself inside her.

She took a shallow breath. No. Not her fault at all.

"Shouldn't you be working with your people?" she asked, hoping against hope to convince him to stay at the farm.

"The director knows what he's doing. I don't butt in on his job."

"But you're comfortable butting into mine," she said, smiling to take the sting out of the words.

"You're not working. You're walking."

"You're an impossible man, Jefferson King."

"So I've been told." He bent down, broke off the stem of a wild daffodil and held it out to her.

Charmed in spite of herself, Maura took it and twirled the dainty flower in her fingers. "How long are you staying in Ireland?"

"Eager to see me go?"

No. Of course she didn't say what she was thinking. "There's no real need for you to stay."

"I say there is." He stopped, turned her to face him and deliberately let his gaze slide down to her belly.

He couldn't see the small bump because she was wearing one of her thick Irish sweaters. But she felt him watching her, and felt the possession in that steady gaze and it thrilled her. In some elemental part of her heart and soul, Maura loved the way he looked at her. At the child they'd made.

But even as she admitted that, she had to also admit that it meant nothing. He was concerned for her and their baby. But he didn't love them.

Need without love was an empty thing she wanted no part of. Especially now that she had more than just her own feelings to think of.

"Don't you have work to do, Jefferson? Worlds to buy, movies to make?"

He grinned again and the sudden sweep of emotion on his face was another staggering blow to a woman already distinctly off balance.

"I've been working."

"In your trailer?" She started walking again and looked into the distance for King. She spotted him then, a black blur, racing across the open fields, and she smiled.

"With technology, I could work in a tent," Jefferson told her. "All I really need is a computer, a satellite phone with Internet and a fax machine, which I'm going to be buying today in Westport. You won't mind if I connect it in your house, will you?"

"I don't know if that's a good idea—"

"Good, thanks."

She muttered something under her breath about him being far more stubborn than she could ever hope to be. But a part of her relished what he was doing. Though she had no intention of being nothing more than a problem for Jefferson to solve, it salved her pride some to have him working so hard to persuade her.

"So, how'd the bull get out?"

His question brought a quick stop to her thoughts and it took her a second to realize what he was talking about. She cringed slightly, remembering. "Oh. You heard about that, did you?"

"Davy Simpson's still telling the story," Jefferson said, his grin spreading. "And with every telling, he runs a little faster, the bull gets bigger and meaner and the danger is more desperate."

Maura laughed at the image. "He sounds Irish. We love nothing more than a good storyteller."

"Uh-huh. The bull, Maura. Did you turn it loose on purpose?"

"Of course not!" She might have thought about it, but she never would have done it. In fact, she'd been terrified when the bull escaped, worried that it might actually hurt someone. "No, 'twas an accident entirely. I had Tim Daley in to help me that day. Tim's but sixteen and his mind is forever wandering to Noreen Muldoon."

"I know what that's like," he muttered.

"What was that?"

"Nothing," he said. "Go on."

"There's not much more to the tale. After feeding the bull, Tim, with his mind still on Noreen, forgot to latch the gate behind him and…" She shrugged. "It was an accident, and thankfully no one was hurt. Took me more than an hour to get the bull set away again."

"You put the bull away?" He goggled at her.

"And who else?" she asked. "'Tis my bull, after all."

"Your bull." He dropped his head forward, chin to chest, as he sighed.

"Aye, and his escape was a mistake, though I'll admit that the sheep running mad through your set was not."

He lifted his eyes to her. "That doesn't surprise me."

"I was angry. You were ignoring me."

King bulleted back to them through the grass, gave a happy bark, then spun around and took off again.

"You had a right to be angry," Jefferson said, "but now you're being stubborn just to spite me."

She stopped in the field, with wild daffodils blooming all around her. The sky was a soft blue, with clouds scudding its surface like sailing ships on a placid sea. The wind blew and the grass danced and in the distance, King barked, delighted with his life.

"Is that what you think?" she asked, turning her face up to his so that their eyes met and there could be no secrets between them on this. "Do you believe I'd punish you, myself, my baby all for the sake of spite?"

"Wouldn't you?"

"You don't know me as well as you think, Jefferson, if you believe me capable of that." She plucked windblown hair out of her eyes and stared at him. "I'm doing what's best. For all of us. I won't be a pity wife."

He gaped at her. "Pity wife? Where the hell did that come from?"

She smiled and shook her head. "We both know you've no interest in acquiring a wife. It's the baby worrying you and that speaks well of you. But marrying me is nothing more than feeling sorry for what you see as my 'difficult position.'"

"It's not *pity*," he told her. "It's concern. For you *and* our child."

"Doesn't really matter. I won't leave my home, Jefferson, and try to make myself into the kind of person who would belong in your world. Can't you see it would never work?"

Instinctively, she reached out, laid one hand on his chest and felt the pounding of his heart beneath her palm. "I don't belong in your world any more than you do in mine. We'd make each other miserable inside a year and that would be a punishment on a child who deserves only love."

"That's a great speech, Maura," he said and caught her hand in his. "But it's bull and you know it. This isn't about you not belonging in Hollywood. You know damn well that you'd fit in anywhere if you made your mind up to it."

She flushed and tried to pull free of his grip.

"This isn't about us, anyway. This is about our baby. I won't be an absentee father, Maura." His fingers folded around her hand, holding it fast. "I won't see my own child once a month or for summer vacations."

Clouds covered the sun and the wind sharpened.

"I'm not leaving, Maura. I'm not going to walk away so you'd better get used to the idea of having me around."

"It'll do you no good, Jefferson. I won't change my mind."

"Don't be so sure," he told her with assurance, "and don't say anything you'll have to take back later. It'll only make it that much harder on you."

Astonished at his raw nerve, she said, "You've an ego the size of the moon."

"It's called confidence, babe," he said with a smile that softened his words. Then he bent his head to hers and whispered, "And confidence comes from *always* getting what I want. Trust me when I say, I will have you, Maura. Just where I want you."

Aggravated with him and furious at the way her body was humming with a near-electrical charge, she said, "Why you miserable, softheaded—"

He cut off her diatribe with a kiss that stole her breath, fogged her mind and sent her body sliding away into a sort of dazed confusion. His tongue tangled with hers and Maura groaned at the invasion. It had been too long. Too many empty nights had passed. Too many dreams of him had haunted her.

She surrendered to what she'd missed so sorely. It didn't mean she was changing her mind. It only meant that sometimes, a bit of what you wanted was better than nothing at all.

She wrapped her arms around his neck and gave herself up to the taste of him. The feel of him pressed against her. She'd longed for this. Dreamed of this. And now that it was here, she didn't care if it was only making the situation more difficult. For this one brief moment, she would have him in her arms.

A heartbeat later, though, they jolted apart, with each of them staring down at the slight curve of her belly.

"Did you feel that?" she asked.

"I felt…something." Awed now, Jefferson came closer, laid one hand on her abdomen and Maura covered his hand with her own. She'd thought it was too soon to feel the baby move. But the doctor had told her it would be any day now and that she'd know it when it happened.

And so she had.

A flutter, then a twitch as if her child had wanted to make its presence known while both of its parents were handy. Maura was thrilled, and, looking at Jefferson, she could see he felt the same. It was magic, pure and simple. Life stirring. A life they'd created. What a gift it was to be able to share this moment with the man who'd given her the child. And how sad for each of them that they wouldn't share more.

"It's not moving anymore," Jefferson said in a worried hush. "Why did it stop? Is everything all right? We should go to the doctor—"

She shook her head and smiled. "No doctor, just wait a moment…" She was whispering, as if afraid to have the baby within hear her and stop moving deliberately.

"Maybe…*there!*" A more solid movement this time, with a sort of rippling sensation to accompany it.

Awed, humbled, Maura turned amazed, shining eyes up to his and Jefferson grinned like a fool.

"He moved."

"Aye, she did." Still caught up in the enchantment of

that moment, Maura took a second to notice the change in Jefferson's eyes. They'd gone from amused to aroused and now, they were filled with a dark determination.

"I won't lose this, Maura. Make up your mind to it." He gave her belly a possessive pat, then pulled his hand back. "Whatever it takes. That baby is a King and he'll grow up as one. Whether his mother likes it or not."

"The problem is," Cara was saying, "you're going about this in all the wrong ways."

Jefferson nodded, sat back in his chair and let his gaze scan the interior of the pub. Dark, noisy, with soft lamplight and a dark red glow of the peat fire in the hearth, the place smelled like beer and wet wool. It was raining again, so the Lion's Den was busy. Locals gathered there to have a beer with friends and listen to music. To get out of their own homes for a while. And Jefferson was surrounded by a group of them who were now, it seemed, completely on his side of the situation. All it had taken was for them to find out that he'd proposed and Maura had turned him down.

Just remembering her refusal was enough to churn his guts and have him gritting his teeth. Not once had he imagined that she would say *no*. Should have known Maura would do the unexpected.

"Maura ever was a stubborn girl," Michael said thoughtfully, waving away a customer clamoring for another beer.

"Nonsense," Frances Boyle put in, taking a sip of her tea. "She's a strong little thing is all and knows her own mind."

"She does," Cara said, "but she's also one to take a stand and then not move from it whether or not she should."

"True, true," Michael agreed, with a sad shake of his head. Then he pointed his index finger at Jefferson. "She's a fine woman though, mind, no matter what we who love her say."

"I know." Jefferson was still working on his first beer as advice swarmed around him like ants at a picnic.

It seemed everyone in the village had a theory on how he should be handling the situation with Maura. Not that he was listening to any of them. Since when did a King need help getting a woman?

Since now? a sneaky, annoying voice in the back of his mind whispered to him and Jefferson grumbled under his breath in response. He'd never had to work this hard for anything. Always, when Jefferson King set out to do a thing, it got done. He'd never before run into a solid wall like the one Maura had erected between them and damned if he could figure out how to knock it down.

An ancient-looking man on one of the bar stools offered, "Buy her a ram. That'll do it. A sheep farmer will appreciate fine stock."

Jefferson snorted. Was the way to this woman's heart through her sheep? He didn't think so. Yet as he considered it, he felt a quick stir of something remarkably like anxiety flicker through him. He wasn't trying to get to Maura's heart, was he? No. This wasn't about love. This was about the baby they'd made together, plain and simple. Telling himself that eased him a bit. "I don't see how buying her a new ram for her flock will win me any points."

"It'll win you lots of points with the ewes," someone shouted from the back of the pub.

Laughter erupted at that and Jefferson could only scowl at the whole damn room. Good to know that everyone in the village was having such an entertaining time.

"Great, that's great." What the hell was he doing here? Thousands of miles from home, from family, from sanity. He was sitting in the middle of an Irish Brigadoon trying to make sense of a woman who defied logic at every turn.

What woman in her right mind would turn down a proposal that offered her luxury? Every wish granted? He'd offered her a life of comfort and ease and she'd tossed it back in his face as if he'd insulted her.

Money and power, that's what she'd said, he reminded himself. As if having contacts and financial independence were a bad thing. He didn't understand *real people*. He *was* real people. His brothers were real. What, did she think just because a man had money, he was less than worthy?

"She's the snob," he muttered as the crowd around him continued the argument without his input, "not me."

He'd never judged anyone on the size of their bank balance. He had friends who were mechanics as well as friends who were movie stars. And though his family had money, he hadn't grown up with a silver spoon in his mouth. He'd had to work, just as his brothers had. They'd worked the ranch as kids and as they got older, their parents had told them if they wanted something, they'd have to earn it. So they'd each worked part-time jobs so they could afford secondhand cars and the gas and insurance that went with it.

Hell, he had friends who weren't nearly as well off as his family had been and their parents had paid for everything. The more Jefferson thought about Maura's accusations and generalizations, the angrier he became. He didn't need to excuse his life or make apologies for the way he lived it just because she was being self-righteous.

"You could buy her a new house," someone shouted.

"Or a new roof for the old house. It leaks something fierce in the winter," Frances said.

"Pay them no mind," Cara told him, and drew her chair closer to his. Leaning her forearms on the table, she said, "I can tell you how to win my sister."

He glanced at her and caught the brilliant smile she had aimed at him. Cara, he thought, was the reasonable Donohue sister. She knew what she wanted—to be rich and famous doing what she loved doing—and went after it. She didn't sneer at him for having money. Why would she? It's what she wanted for herself.

With an inward sigh, he asked himself why it hadn't been Cara who made his blood heat. Life would have been a hell of a lot easier.

Instead, he'd become involved with a woman whose head was as hard as the stones in her fields. Just thinking about it irritated him. Damned if he'd take it. Maura thought he was an arrogant, rich American. So he'd prove her right. If she was going to damn him for his money, he might as well make it worth her while.

His mind raced with possibilities. With ideas, notions and plans. And he liked every one of them. Time to pull off the gloves, he told himself. He'd never yet lost an acquisition he was determined to have and this wouldn't be the first time.

"Jefferson? Are you listening?" Cara gave his arm a nudge. "I said, I've a way for you to win my sister round."

"Thanks," he said and stood up. Digging into his pocket, he came up with a sheaf of bills and tossed a few of them onto the table, paying not only for his and Cara's drinks, but for most of those in the bar. "I appreciate it. But this is between me and Maura. And I've got a few ideas of my own."

He left then and never saw Cara shake her head and murmur, "Luck to you, then. I've a feeling you're going to need it."

Nine

Bright and early the next morning, Maura stepped outside, braced for the next confrontation with Jefferson. She glanced around and blew out a breath that misted in front of her face in the cold damp. Dawn was just painting the sky with the first of a palette of colors. Gray clouds rolled in from the sea and she smelled another storm on the air.

"Maybe the coming storm will keep him in the trailer," she told herself, even though she didn't believe it for a moment, and truth be told, she didn't wish for it, either. Even as annoying as the man could become, she liked having him about. Which only went to prove she really was a madwoman.

What woman in her right mind would torture herself so willingly by being around a man she couldn't have?

But what choice did she have? It wasn't as if asking him to leave her be had gotten her anywhere. Jefferson would stay until he left. Period. Nothing she could say would move him along any faster.

He'd made that clear enough.

There would be no way to escape his company and as long as that were true, she could admit, if only to herself, that she was storing this time up in her memories. Etching each moment with him on her brain so that she could draw the images out later, when he really was gone from her.

So she was prepared to have him riding as a passenger in her battered old lorry as she drove up to the high pasture. She'd even thought of a few things to tell him during the long, sleepless night. She was going to be reasonable, patient and firm. The only way to handle a man like Jefferson King. Temper wouldn't do it as the man was immune to her shouts and curses. So she'd use practicality as it was his normal weapon of choice. She could explain to him simply and deliberately that he was wasting his time staying on at the farm. She wouldn't be coerced or convinced to do something she'd no intention of doing.

She smiled to herself, called for King and stepped out of the way when the big dog raced down the hallway and out the back door.

The film crew was already busy in the front, according to the low rumbles of conversation and the sounds of engines and generators. Maura had become so accustomed to the sounds of the film crew that she had the oddest feeling she might actually miss all of the clatter and din they created each day. As she would soon be missing Jefferson, as well.

Her heart ached at the thought, but what else could she do? She couldn't marry him knowing he had no interest in loving her. She couldn't be a man's duty. His *penance*. Her blood ran cold at the thought. What kind of life would that be? For any of them?

King was barking from the far side of the barn where she'd been parking her lorry since the arrival of the film crew. Musings shattered, Maura quickened her steps, wondering what it was that had set her dog off.

She rounded the corner of the barn and stopped dead. Her battered lorry was gone. In its place sat a gloriously new and shiny truck, bright red in color, boasting a massive white bow on its roof. "What? How? When?"

"All very good questions," a deep voice rumbled from nearby.

Maura shot a look at Jefferson, leaning back against the side wall of the barn like a man well pleased with himself. The broad smile on his face told her he was responsible for this—as if she hadn't been able to guess.

"What've you done?"

"I should think that's fairly obvious."

"Where's my lorry?"

"You mean that chunk of rust with wheels?" He shrugged. "I had it towed away an hour or so ago. Surprised you didn't hear it."

She had heard more general clatter than usual this morning to be sure, but she'd become so accustomed to disregarding the hubbub caused by the film crew that she'd paid it no mind at all.

"You—" Maura looked at the new truck and felt herself being seduced by the shining paint and the large, sturdy tires—and even as her heart yearned, she closed herself off to it. "You'd no right."

"I've every right, Maura." He pushed away from the wall and walked toward her. When he was close enough, he ran the flat of his hand over the roof of the new truck and smiled, satisfied. "You weren't just trusting your own life to that accident waiting to happen, remember. You're carrying my baby. No way do I let you ride around in that old truck."

"Let me?" She gasped, pulled in air and prepared for battle. "You don't *let* me do anything, Jefferson King. I don't want your shiny new toy here—"

He smiled knowingly. "Yes, you do."

Oh, it was a hard thing to know that he could read her so easily.

"The nerve you have," she muttered darkly and stepped around him. Her gaze raked the area, hoping that he'd lied and that she'd find her old truck still here, worn and weary from too many years of work. But it wasn't. All that remained was the shiny, tempting lorry, complete with unpatched tires, uncracked windshield and—she peered in the window surreptitiously—lovely black leather seats. Wasn't it a lovely thing?

Not that it mattered, she thought as she straightened up to glare at him again. "What made you think I would be happy about this?"

"Oh, believe me," he said, opening the driver's-side door for her, "I never once thought you'd be *happy*. In fact, I knew you'd look daggers at me. You'll notice it didn't stop me."

He dangled the keys before her as he would a cookie in front of a recalcitrant toddler. "But you're too intelligent to not admit that you needed this truck, Maura."

She glared at him, then the keys and back again. Her shoulders slumped in defeat. "Clever, aren't you? Flatter me so that to turn you down makes me seem like a complete fool."

Clearly pleased with himself, he grinned. "Bottom line is, Maura," he said, "I'm going to take care of you and the baby with your approval or not. So you might as well get used to it."

Was it so wrong, she wondered, to allow him to take care of her? Was it wrong to wish for more? She'd wanted him to acknowledge their child. But she now wanted something she couldn't have. She wanted love. The fantasy.

"And if I don't?"

"You will." He cupped her cheek in his palm.

Maura shivered right down to her toes. How was it that the simple touch of his skin to hers could cause so many different sensations to course through her? And how was it that he didn't share them? That he could shut himself off from the threads of connection that bound them?

He bent his head to hers until his mouth was just a breath away. "You might be stubborn, but you're an intelligent woman and you'll eventually see that I'm right about this."

She sighed and gave him a resigned smile. "So, I'm

intelligent to agree with you and foolish to have my own opinion."

"Pretty much."

That slight curve of his mouth was a weapon, she thought. One he wielded expertly. And she was a willing victim. For heaven's sake, the man had purchased her a lorry and tied a huge bow to it. How was she to argue or stand up against a man who surprised her, not with diamonds or fancy clothes, but with the one thing he knew she not only wanted, but needed?

"You're making this difficult for me."

"Glad to hear it. Now, do you want to take her out for a spin?"

Those keys dangled in front of her face and this time, Maura snatched them. Who was she to fight the inevitable? Besides, if she was to admit the truth, at least to herself, she could say how grateful she was to have a vehicle she felt confident driving. "If you're coming," she told him with a grin, "get in and buckle up."

He did, managing to tear the white bow off the roof as he went and once they were settled, Maura fired the truck up and hooted with glee at the pantherlike snarl of a well-tuned engine. "Isn't she a beauty, then?"

"Yeah," Jefferson said, and when she glanced at him, saw that he was staring right at her as he said, "she really is a beauty."

Jefferson had the marriage license. Now all he needed was the bride. But Maura was showing no signs of weakening. He'd even moved to a hotel in Westport, to give her some space. To prove that he could be as sensitive as the next guy. But did she appreciate it? Hell no. The only thing being "sensitive" had gotten him was three days of missing the woman more than he would have thought possible.

He even missed her damn dog.

Something had to break and it had to happen soon. He couldn't stay in Ireland indefinitely. He had a life, work, waiting for him.

"Which is the only reason I was willing to try Cara's plan," he said into the phone.

"Cara," his brother Justice asked. "Who is she again?"

Jefferson gave an impatient sigh. "Maura's sister. I told you."

"You've been rattling off names of everyone in the village for the last half hour, how'm I supposed to keep them all straight? So Cara is Maura's sister and Maura's the one who turned you down."

Jefferson scowled both at the phone *and* at his younger brother on the other end. "Yes, thanks for reminding me."

Justice laughed and he sounded as if he were in the next room, not sitting at his ranch in California. "Pardon me for enjoying this, but I seem to remember you getting a charge out of watching Maggie make me miserable not so long ago."

"That was different," Jefferson said and walked to the balcony of his suite. Looking out over the river, glistening like quicksilver in the moonlight, he only half listened to the jumble of music drifting to him from a nearby pub. This harbor city, though it was nowhere near as big as L.A., was a far cry from the village of

Craic and the otherworldly quiet that he'd become so used to. Realizing that didn't put him in a better frame of mind. "That was you being miserable. This is *me*."

"Right," Justice said, still laughing, then to someone else added, "He says he *did* propose the right way." He sighed, then said to Jefferson, "Maggie doesn't believe you."

"Tell her thanks for the support." Naturally his sister-in-law would come down on Maura's side. Female solidarity at work again. He'd about had his fill of strong women lately. Especially strong women who were currently making him insane.

"So tell me again," his brother said, "what was Cara's plan?"

Jefferson frowned out at the city. Westport was awake and partying. Lovers walked along the Carrowberg River, pausing now and then for a desperate kiss beneath old-fashioned streetlamps.

It was a great view, he admitted silently. But it wasn't the one he wanted. He preferred the view of the lake out Maura's bedroom window.

Damn it.

Months, he thought, since he'd touched her. Except for that one kiss interrupted by the movement of his child. And that kiss haunted him, waking and sleeping. Need was a clawing, vicious beast crouched inside him, tearing at him constantly. The only way to assuage the beast was to be with her and the only way to be with her was to promise her something he couldn't.

He was a man caught in a web that twisted more tightly about him every time he tried to escape it.

"You still there?" Justice demanded.

"Yeah, I'm here." Jefferson turned his back on the view and said, "What were we talking about? Oh, right. Cara's plan. Well, right about now, she's telling Maura that I'm going to fire her from the movie unless Maura agrees to marry me."

"Are you nuts?"

Since he'd just thought the same thing himself, that was a statement hard to argue with. Jefferson muttered a curse and dropped onto the edge of the bed. "No. Maybe. I don't know."

"Let me get this straight," Justice said in his slow, thoughtful style, "you're planning to use extortion to get the mother of your child to marry you. That about cover it?"

Somehow, this idea sounded worse when Justice said it. "Yeah. That's the plan."

"And you think this move is going to endear you to her?"

He stood up again, feeling a swirl of something that he might have thought was panic if he'd been the kind of man to feel that particular emotion. "I never said that's what I was going for. This isn't about that at all."

"Good thing," Justice murmured.

Jefferson had thought that Justice, of all of his brothers, would understand because of his well-developed sense of honor and loyalty. "This is about marrying the mother of my baby. It's the right thing to do and you know it."

"Sure, if you love her."

Exasperated now, he demanded, "Who said anything about love?"

"I think I just did."

"Well, knock it off." Jefferson paced his bedroom and when he didn't have enough room, left to stride back and forth across the living area. "This isn't about love, Justice, and since when did you become the touchy-feely brother?"

A laugh barked into the phone. "I'm not. I'm only saying that marrying someone *just* because of a baby is a bad idea."

"That's what Maura keeps saying."

"Smart woman." Then to his own wife, Justice added, "Not smarter than you, honey." Then he was back and saying, "Jeff, don't dig yourself a hole you're not gonna be able to climb out of. You can be a part of your kid's life without being married to his mother."

Yeah, he could. Logically, Jefferson knew his brother was right. But he didn't want that. He didn't want to be a part-time father. Be one of the weekend dads that he saw all over Los Angeles. He wanted the same kind of relationship with his own kid that Jefferson himself had had with his father. He wanted a damn family for his child. That made him a bad guy? In whose book?

What was so wrong with wanting to be with his child's mother?

"That's not how it's going to be," he said firmly, feeling his resolve settle in. He'd outmaneuvered studio heads, business moguls and financial wizards. He had no doubt that he could outdo one beautiful sheep farmer.

"Your call," Justice said, "but I've gotta say, I think you're asking for trouble."

"Wouldn't be the first time," he answered ruefully.

Maura was going to be furious. But he'd had to get her here. To talk to him. And Cara's plan had been the only way.

There was a knock at the door and Jefferson's head snapped up like a wolf picking up the scent of its prey. Had to be Maura. No one else would be coming here to see him. And knowing she would show up, he'd left her name at the desk, clearing her for the elevator to his floor. "Can't talk now," he said softly. "She's here."

"I sure hope you know what you're doing, brother," Justice told him. "Let me know what happens."

With Justice's less-than-hopeful words ringing in his ear, Jefferson tossed his cell phone onto the coffee table and walked to the door. He hardly noticed the lush room. It was much like every other suite in every other hotel he'd ever stayed in. Crystal vases filled with colorful flowers standing on gleaming tables. Comfortable chairs drawn up to a gas-fed hearth where carefully monitored flames leaped and danced.

He moved quickly, but even with that, three sharp, impatient knocks sounded out again before he reached the door.

When he opened it, Maura rushed right past him, anger radiating off her in thick waves. And all he could think was, *God, she's beautiful*.

She wore dark-wash jeans and a red sweater beneath a black coat she peeled off and tossed across a chair the moment she was in the room. Her long black hair was windblown and there was hot color in her cheeks.

"You lying, sneaky, treacherous, no good…"

"Hello to you, too." He closed the door and faced her,

determined to play this out. He'd set his course with Cara, so he'd hold true to it until he got what he wanted.

Maura's complete surrender.

"Don't you hello me, Jefferson King," she shot back, lifting one hand to shake her index finger at him. "How can you stand there looking so smug and proud of yourself? What kind of man is it to do what you've done?" Briefly, she threw both hands up in disbelief. "I don't even have the words for it. How could you? How could you be so hard? So mean? So…"

"Cruel?" he helped out. "Callous? Uncaring?"

"Aye," she snapped. "All of those and more, though 'tis clear to me you've not the decency to be ashamed of it."

She was more furious than he'd ever seen her before and that gave him pause to wonder if maybe Justice hadn't been right. But it was too late now, he told himself. He'd set a course and he wasn't a man to back off just because the road got a little bumpier than expected.

"I see Cara gave you the news."

Maura bristled. Since the moment her sister had come to her at the farm, crying over an opportunity lost, Maura had been able to think of nothing else but coming here and facing Jefferson with what he'd done. She'd driven into the city like a madwoman, steering the lorry he'd given her down the familiar roads in a blind rage. The desk clerk had taken one look at her and had pointed out the elevators, obviously unwilling to take a chance on trying to stop her. A wise choice on his part.

Now that she was here, the fury riding within was bubbling to the surface. Jefferson's casual attitude wasn't soothing her any. He looked smug and sure of himself as he watched her. So much so she felt a distinct urge to kick him. Hard. And only barely resisted. Her entire body was shaking with temper and disappointment and hurt.

He'd shown a side of himself she'd never guessed at. How had she not seen what he was capable of before? How had she trusted this man? Given herself to him? Thought herself in love with him?

She looked up into pale blue eyes and saw only cold distance glittering back at her. As if he were standing right in front of her, a part of him was sealed off from this confrontation. As if his mind and heart had taken a step aside, leaving only the ruthless businessman in their place. For the first time since she'd known him, Maura saw his fierceness. The steely resolve of a powerful man who would do whatever he must to ensure he got exactly what he wanted.

Tension coiled and crackled in the air between them. She could hardly draw a breath for the iron band tightening around her chest. Her heart.

"You've gone too far," she told him, her voice hardly more than a scrape of sound.

"I don't know what you mean."

"Don't pretend ignorance. It insults us both," she said and tossed her purse atop her coat. "You've fired Cara from your movie."

He shrugged and walked past her toward one of the twin couches set in the middle of the luxurious room. "She wasn't working out."

She watched him go, vaguely noticing how at home he was in the lush surroundings. How this place, this life seemed to suit him and how it also seemed to mark the difference between them. But Maura pushed that thought aside and concentrated on her reason for being there.

"That's a lie. You told me yourself you thought Cara a fine actor. So it's not her work you've a problem with. It's *me*. You think to use my family to get my cooperation. That's the mark of a small man, Jefferson King."

"You're wrong," he said, whirling back around, returning to her, coming close enough that she could see his eyes were now shining with an inner light that blazed with banked temper and conviction. "It's the mark of a man who goes after what he wants any way he has to. I warned you I wouldn't give up. I'm Jefferson King. And a King does what he must to get what he wants."

"No matter the cost?" She searched his eyes for some sign of the man she'd fallen in love with, but he wasn't there.

"I told you going in, Maura. You're carrying my child. I'll do whatever it takes to make sure he's taken care of."

She knew, logically, that his determination to care for his child was a good thing. After all, not every man would care, would he? But Jefferson used his wealth and privilege as a club, swinging it wildly, knocking aside whoever might stand in the way of his goals and that she didn't understand. Or forgive.

"You've no right to draw Cara into this," she said, silently congratulating herself on the calm, reasonable tone of her own voice. "It's between us, Jefferson. No one else."

"You brought her into this," he said, "when you wouldn't see reason."

"And because I don't agree with you, out come the bully tactics?"

He winced, or she thought he had. The expression was gone so quickly, she couldn't be sure. "You wanted this the hard way, Maura. Not me."

"I only want—"

"What?" He grabbed her, big hands coming down on her shoulders, holding her in place. "What is it you *really* want, Maura?"

Something he had no interest in hearing, she thought sadly, staring up into his eyes and finally, *finally,* seeing the man she knew and loved looking back at her. He was as torn up by all of this as she was, Maura knew that. She felt his frustration as surely as she did her own.

And oh, what a tricky question he'd asked her. *What did she really want?* She wanted the fairy tale. What she wanted was to love him and be loved in return. To marry Jefferson King and make a family. She wanted it so badly, in fact, that she was ashamed to admit even to herself that she'd recently begun to actually reconsider his pitiful proposal. If she married for the sake of her child, it would be foolish, she knew. But oh, the temptation of saying yes. Of living with him. Being with him.

Yet even in the midst of wild dreams, she knew also that if she allowed herself to weaken on that point, she would, eventually, regret it.

So she kept those wants locked away inside her and said only, "I want you to give Cara her job back."

"And you'll do what for me in return?"

Temper drained away to be replaced by a sorrow that went soul-deep. She lifted her hands to his, linking them, as she looked into his eyes. "Not what you're hoping. I won't marry you for the sake of the child, Jefferson. I can't do that. Not to myself *or* to you. Sentence all three of us to half a life? What would be the good in that?"

He dropped his forehead to hers. "You're as thick-headed as I am," he murmured.

"We are the pair, aren't we?"

Lifting his head again, he met her gaze and said, "She has her job back."

"Thank you," she said, mildly surprised that it was taken care of so easily. Over so quickly. Her body was still buzzing from a combination of anger and desire and now…she had to leave.

But his hands on her shoulders were hard and tender and warm. Heat from his skin seeped into hers, chasing away the chill she'd been carrying for what felt like forever. She'd held strong against her own wants and needs, thinking that to be with him now would only make the parting that much harder.

Yet she was deceiving no one. Their parting would devastate her no matter the circumstances. Would one more night together really add to the pain? Or would it be an easing of sorts?

As if he could read her mind, he pulled her closer, wrapping his arms around her, burying his face in the curve of her neck. His lips on her skin sent ripples of awareness coursing through her. His hands running up and down her spine caused every cell in her body to jump up and shout for joy.

Her heart ached, her body burned and her mind knew it could never stand against heart and soul and body, so it quietly closed up shop and allowed Maura to only *feel*. For this, she didn't want to think. Didn't need to think.

This, what lay between them, was good and strong and so powerful the only thing either of them needed was their instincts, drawing them together.

"I've missed you," he said, lifting his head again, kissing her forehead, her cheeks, the tip of her nose. "I didn't want to," he admitted next, "but I did. You're in me, Maura, and now I need to be in you."

"I need that, as well." She sighed, lifting her mouth for his. He claimed a kiss, moving his mouth over hers with an aching tenderness that made her want to weep with the beauty of it.

There was a gentleness in his touch that took the hard edge off the need pulsing between them. Maura felt his quiet control and sighed for it.

Here was home, she thought, her mind sliding into a wonderfully hazy oblivion as emotion and sensation took the forefront. Here was where she wanted to be. Yearned to be. In his arms. Always.

He skimmed one hand up, into her hair to the back of her neck. He held her head steady while his mouth plundered hers and she gave herself up to the amazement flooding her system.

How had she thought she could go the rest of her life without feeling this? Experiencing this? How had she lasted months without the caress of his hands on her skin? And how would she make it through the rest of her life without him?

"Be with me," he whispered, already leading her through the seating area to the bedroom beyond.

He moved her as if they were dancing, one arm around her waist now, one hand holding hers close to his heart. She looked up into his eyes as the room slowly whirled around her and knew she'd dance anywhere with him.

"Be with me." She repeated his words to her and his swift intake of breath, coupled with a flash deep in his eyes, were all that told her how she had touched him.

Ten

In the bedroom, she saw the balcony doors were open, a soft, cold breeze sliding into the room, ruffling lacy white sheers. From the street below came the muted sounds of pub music, riding the wind. One lamp in the room was on, spilling enough golden light to chase away shadows.

Then he stopped alongside the wide bed and helped her out of the sweater she wore. Beneath was a plain white shirt that he quickly unbuttoned and tossed aside. He unhooked her bra with a surprising agility and then dispensed with her boots, jeans and underwear. In moments, she was unclothed before him and feeling just a bit hesitant about her changing body.

He hadn't seen her naked since the night they'd made their child. And since then, she'd gained a little weight and her belly was rounded with the growing baby.

She watched him as he gazed at her and she saw his eyes soften when he looked at her abdomen. Suddenly uneasy, she said, "I've changed, I know."

"Yes," he said, lifting his gaze to hers even as he laid the flat of one hand against the mound of their child. "You're even more beautiful."

"Oh," Maura told him, a smile curving her mouth, "you've the gift of the Irish for saying exactly the right thing at the right time."

He smiled, too, then said, "You're shivering. I'll close the window."

"No, don't," she told him. "The weather isn't what's making me tremble, Jefferson. It's need, is all. Need for you."

He swallowed hard and reached past her to pull back the quilt and sheets covering the bed. "Get under the covers anyway," he said and waited until she had.

Then hurriedly, he stripped out of his own clothes and joined her under the down comforter. Maura moved into him and instinctively aligned her body with his. The slide of his skin against hers felt so right. So perfect. She sighed in contentment, shifting her hands over his broad, muscled back, up to encircle his neck and then plunging her fingers into his hair, drawing his head to hers.

Lips met, tongues entangled and breath was exchanged for breath. They came together as silently, as magically as if they'd been born for this and only this.

Sensations rose up and crashed inside her and Maura could only hold on to him as he covered her body with his. He parted her thighs, she lifted her hips to welcome him and in the soft light of that luxurious room, he claimed her as he had before. He slid into her heat, her depths and in the taking, gave. In the giving, took. Hearts beat as one. Bodies moved together in perfect rhythm and sighing groans filled the air like blessings.

He kissed her as the first wave of completion caught her and she cried out his name as her soul shattered under his tender hands. Only moments later, she held him to her as his body released into hers and he collapsed atop her.

In the quiet stillness, minutes or hours could have gone by.

All Maura knew was that she didn't want this night to end. Didn't want to lose Jefferson. Yet, she couldn't think of a way to keep him. Not and keep her pride, as well. Could the man not see that he loved her? She felt it in his touch. Saw it in his eyes. Sensed the gentleness beneath the passion and knew that it didn't come only from desire. From lust. There was feeling there—and it was more than affection.

Yet, he pulled back from the mention of three small words. Held himself safely distanced from the risk of love. What was it, she wondered, that made him so determined to avoid giving his heart?

As she struggled with troubling thoughts, Jefferson rolled to one side, drawing her with him, cradling her closely against his body. Her head on his shoulder, his arms around her, he lay in the lamp-lit dark and said nothing.

How long could they go on like this? she thought desperately. How long before they tore each other's hearts to shreds and there was nothing left for either of them?

He trailed one hand idly down the length of her until

he could cover her abdomen with his palm. She sighed at the gentleness of his touch even as she remembered the fire in his passion. He rested his hand on her, fingers splayed, and she felt him take a breath and hold it— waiting for his child to move again.

As if to please its father, the baby obliged with a tiny kick that brought a smile to Maura's face despite unshed tears burning her eyes.

"He's strong already," Jefferson mused and she could hear pride ringing in his tone.

"Aye, soon he'll be trying to kick his way out," she said, surprised at the thickness of her voice.

Jefferson turned his head to look at her. "You're crying. Why are you crying?"

"'Tis foolish, never mind."

He levered himself up on one elbow and looked down at her. His eyes were the palest blue and in the darkness, they almost seemed to glow with some inner light. Maura stared up into them, then lifted her hand to smooth his hair back from his forehead.

"Are you all right?" he asked. "I didn't hurt you or the baby, did I?"

"You didn't, no," she told him, easing the fear she saw in his gaze. "I'm feeling a bit weepy these days is all."

"That's not it," he said, his mouth firming, a muscle in his jaw twitching as he gritted his teeth. "Don't lie to me, Maura."

"'Tisn't a lie," she countered, pushing at his chest to shove him away. But it was like trying to push at the walls of her barn. "I *am* weepier these days. A woman's hormones are all over the place when she's carrying."

"Fine, not a lie. But not the complete truth."

"Ah, Jefferson," she said on a sigh, "what difference does it make?"

"The difference is, we at least owe each other honesty, don't we?"

"You're right," Maura mused. "Honesty would be best. Especially now."

"So tell me why you're crying."

This time when she gave him a little nudge, he yielded and Maura pushed herself up into a sitting position on the bed. Tugging the quilt and sheets up over her breasts, she glanced out the window at the shining night beyond. When she spoke, her voice was hushed.

"I was only thinking of how much I'll miss you when you go."

"You don't have to," he said and he, too, spoke in a whisper. "You can come with me."

"We've been over this," she said, pushing her hair back from her face with both hands. "The baby is not a reason to wed."

"That's not what I'm saying this time," he told her and instantly won her full attention.

Maura stared at him and tried to read what she saw in his eyes, but the shadows in the room were too deep. "What are you saying, then?"

"I've been thinking about this, Maura," he told her as he edged off the bed, snatched up his jeans and tugged them on. He didn't bother to button them, just stalked across the room to her side of the bed and stood there, looking down at her. Arms folded across his chest, legs braced as if for battle, he said, "What just happened between us sort of solidified those thoughts. We're good together. Right. And you know it."

"I do," she agreed, wondering where he was going with this. Trying not to hope, but failing miserably, she clung to the dream in her heart and waited for him to continue.

"Good. I'm glad you can see that. It'll make what I have to say that much easier."

"What is it you're getting to?"

"In a minute," Jefferson said, wanting to get everything between them out in the open now. "We said we'd be honest—"

She only waited.

He blurted a truth he hadn't planned on telling her. "I didn't fire Cara."

"What?"

"It was her idea," he said quickly, giving her a smile he hoped would head her temper off before it got a foothold. "The idea was to make you so angry that you'd agree to marry me so that I'd take her back on the film."

She hissed in a breath. "Of all the low, despicable…"

"I know. I've heard them all." He leaned down to kiss her, quick, hard, cutting off her thread of insults before she could really get going. Then, easing back, he said, "Now, continuing with the honesty vein…marry me, Maura."

Clearly still angry over the deception, she narrowed her eyes on him. "We've been over this until the path is beaten down, Jefferson. I won't marry you for the child's sake."

"Hear me out at least. This isn't about the baby. This is about us."

"It is?"

He had her attention now, he told himself, judging by the interested gleam in her eyes. And as he relished the fact that he was back in charge, he warmed to his theme. He'd faced down hostile mergers before. This was no different. He'd convince her that he knew what was best and they'd go on with their lives.

Deliberately, Jefferson slid one hand down her warm, curvy body and settled his palm atop their child in a possessive move she couldn't miss. That simple action linked them, made the three of them a unit. As they should be.

He had to convince her. Had to make her see. He wouldn't lose this. Wouldn't lose her because of her own stubborn pride or unwillingness to listen to reason. Being with her again had brought it all home to him. He'd lay it all out for her, exactly as it had just popped into his mind and then she'd see that he was right.

The perfect solution.

"What is it you have in mind, then?" she asked.

"I'm proposing a marriage of convenience," he started and when she opened her mouth to speak, he hurried on, determined to have his say completely. "We're good together and you've already admitted it, so there's no point in denying it. The sex is great and we actually like each other."

"*Like,*" she repeated.

"Exactly." He smiled at her. "Marrying is just a good business decision. Everyone wins this way, Maura. You. Me. The baby. We know going in exactly what kind of marriage we have so there're no misconceptions. No room for hurt feelings or shattered illusions."

"Convenience," she said softly. "Marriage as a convenience."

He didn't like the hesitation in her voice, but chalked it up to the fact that she hadn't had time to fully realize all of the advantages he was offering her. Well, she was a smart woman. She'd work it out and come to the same conclusion he had, given enough time. "Just think about it for a minute."

"Oh, I am," she assured him with a small shake of her head. "And while I'm thinking, perhaps you can tell me, Jefferson, just where does love come into this arrangement between us?"

Everything in him went cold and still. He felt himself shutting down, closing off. Hadn't he couched his proposal in terms that would guarantee love wouldn't be able to rear its ugly head? He couldn't have been more clear about it. Irritation flowed through him, but he couldn't look away from her eyes, swimming with emotion.

"Why does it have to come into it at all?"

"Marriage without love would be a cold and empty sort of thing, don't you think?"

"It doesn't have to be," he argued.

Why was she making this more difficult than it had to be? Damn it. He'd laid it out for her. Explained how he felt and what they could have. But instead of being reasonable, she was going to make him confess everything. Force him to hurt her by telling her exactly why he couldn't give her what she wanted.

He blew out an impatient breath and stood up, turning his back on her to walk to the balcony and stand in the breeze still rushing in. He'd stayed too long in this place, Jefferson thought. If he'd left a couple of weeks ago, he could have avoided this. Could have spared both of them this.

But he hadn't been able to leave her. Now they'd both pay for that indulgence. He stared out at the night for a long moment before finally turning his gaze back to her.

She looked ethereal, there in his bed. Her hair a wild tangle, her mouth still swollen from his kisses. Lamplight and shadow played on her features and her eyes shone as she watched him. He steeled himself against the well of emotion threatening to choke him.

"I can't love you, Maura," he finally said softly.

"Can't? Or won't?"

"Can't." He folded his arms across his chest in a classic pose of self-defense. "I was married before."

She went absolutely still.

He didn't like thinking about it. Didn't like remembering old pain. But there was no choice but to speak of it.

"Her name was Anna and she was the love of my life," he said, needing to have this said aloud, so that Maura could understand what was keeping him from her. "We were too young to get married, but we did anyway." He smiled a bit at the memories rushing into his mind. They were soft now, hazy with time and distance, but there was still an innocence and sweetness to them that tugged at his heart.

"What happened?"

"She died."

"I'm sorry."

He nodded. "She was only twenty-one. I was a year older. It was a stupid accident. Anna was painting our bedroom. She fell off the ladder. Hit her head." He was quiet for a moment or two, recalling how she'd brushed it off, said she was fine. "She seemed all right. Wouldn't go to the doctor. Said it was silly to make a big deal over a little bump. She died in her sleep that night. The autopsy found a hemorrhage in her brain."

"That's terrible, Jefferson," Maura said softly. "I'm so sorry for you and for her."

Mentally, he pulled away from the past and said briskly, "When she died, I swore that I'd never love another woman the way I loved her."

She drew in a long, deep breath but still remained silent. He hoped she understood. Hoped she could now see that what he was offering her was the best he had inside him. This was it. Take him as he was, or they would have nothing.

Walking back to her, he stood beside the bed and said, "I want to marry you, Maura. Not just because of the baby, either. I like being with you. I like having you beside me at night. I think we could make a good life together."

Still she was quiet and the shadows had deepened so that he couldn't even read her eyes now.

"I'm offering you my name," he told her. "I'm offering to build a life with you and raise our child. But don't expect love from me, Maura, because I won't love you. Ever."

The distant music from the pub on the street below sounded overly loud in the strained silence. Time ticked past in long, drawn-out seconds.

"Without love, we have nothing," she finally said and Jefferson's hopes crashed and burned at his feet.

Instinctively, he reached for her, but she scooted off the opposite side of the bed, avoiding his touch. Moving quickly, she gathered up her clothes and started pulling them on.

"Maura," he said, giving himself points for the calm restraint he heard in his own voice, "if you'll just be reasonable about this…"

"Reason," she muttered, buttoning up the front of her shirt with shaking fingers. "The man wants reason when what he's speaking is nonsense."

"Nonsense?" He came around the edge of the bed and took her upper arm in a hard grip. "I'm trying to be honest with you. To tell you exactly who and what I am so that there'll be no more misunderstandings. I don't want to hurt you anymore, Maura. Can't you see that?"

She yanked herself free of him, stepped into her boots and shook her hair back from her face. "You're not being honest, Jefferson. Not with me or yourself, come to that. You're hiding from the future by staying in your past. And that's cheating not just me, but yourself of what you might find if you'd open your eyes."

"I'm not hiding," he said in a snarl, insulted that she would take what he'd offered and throw it back at him. "I don't hide from anything."

"And the truly sad part?" she asked quietly. "It's that you actually believe that."

She pulled her sweater over her head, scooped up her hair and drew it free to lie on her shoulders. Jefferson's hands itched to touch it. His whole body yearned to have her back in that bed. Back to where they'd been together just a few short minutes ago.

She stalked from the bedroom into the living area and Jefferson was just a step or two behind her. "Where are you going?"

She sighed. "I'm going home, Jefferson. As you should."

"What?"

Maura turned to look at him and she knew her aching heart had to be shining in her eyes, for the pain was staggering. She'd had hope, until tonight, that he might wake up and see that love was staring him in the face. She'd hoped he might let himself take the tumble. See what they could have together if only he'd allow himself to love.

Now, that hope was ground into dust. The man was just thickheaded enough to cling to a promise made by a heartsick boy so long ago. And if she couldn't have all of him, she'll not have him at all.

"Do you think this is what your Anna would have wanted for you?"

"We'll never know that, will we? Because she's *dead*." His voice was tight and hard.

"And so are you, inside, dead as your lost love," Maura told him. "The difference is, I believe if she were given the choice, your Anna would choose *life*. You've chosen to stay in the shadows and there's nothing anyone but you can do about it."

His features were as remote as if his face had been carved from granite. "You wanted honesty. I gave it to you."

"So you did. I thank you for your offer, Jefferson King, but I won't marry without love. Or at least the hope of it."

"Maura, you're being ridiculous."

"I don't think so," she told him, keeping her voice even and steady despite her urge to shout the roof down and howl out her misery. "I'm sorry for you, Jefferson. I truly am."

"I don't want your pity," he snapped.

"That's a shame, for you have it." She picked up her coat, slung her purse over one shoulder and said, "If you won't let go of your past, what chance do we have of making a future? No, Jefferson, 'tis better this way, you'll see."

"How is this better?"

She walked to the front door, put her hand on the knob and paused for one last look at him. Instead of answering his question, she said, "You can come and see our child anytime you're able. You'll always be welcome, though you won't have me."

"Maura, think about what you're doing."

"I have. And I also think you should go home now, Jefferson. Back to Los Angeles and the empty life you're clinging to with such steadfastness."

"My life's not empty," he countered as she opened the door and stepped through. "But you're right about one thing, Maura. It's time for me to go home."

She watched him walk toward her, his features a study in blank isolation. Maura curled her fingers into fists to keep from holding out a hand to him. It would change nothing, only prolong this wretched ending to all of their possibilities.

Maura wanted to brace herself for the pain that was building within but all she could do was wait for it.

Impossible to prepare for a crippling misery that she knew would be with her for the rest of her life. But damned if she'd let him see that he had so much power over her heart, her mind, her very soul.

He wouldn't learn from her that she loved him and always would. No, she'd send him back to his life, his world, as cleanly as she had before. And as before, she would take comfort in knowing that he would think of her—and their child—often.

His eyes were cool as glass as he looked down at her. "I'll be by in the morning to see you before I leave."

How businesslike he sounded. As if they were no more than acquaintances who'd happened upon each other. Already he was stepping away from her, closing the door on all they'd found, all they might have shared. And she wondered how it was she could love a man so bone-deep foolish.

"That'll be fine," she told him smoothly. "I'll expect you then."

"Good night, Maura," he said and shut the door as she stood there.

"Goodbye, Jefferson," she murmured as the first tears fell.

The pain lasted a week.

Maura had cried until she'd no more tears left in her body. She'd wallowed in her despair until even her sister, Cara, had lost all patience with her. She'd watched the last of the film crew pack up and leave when their work was done, severing that final thread connecting her to Jefferson.

Every night she dreamed of him and every day she missed him. Finally though, anger jostled her out of her self-pitying stupor. She hadn't actually believed he would *leave*. Maura had left the hotel convinced that when he came to say goodbye, they would instead have a good clearing-the-air fight, followed by spectacular sex and pledges of eternal love.

Instead, the tricky man had come to her home cool, detached, handed her a bloody sheaf of papers, then walked away, as calm as you please. He hadn't even looked back at her, the low skunk of a man, she thought with a hearty stomp in the mud.

The fury that had been growing inside her for the last couple of days seemed to explode all at once. Blast Jefferson King, she saw him everywhere she went. His voice haunted her home. His smile chased her across fields and even driving into town was no escape, as she was sitting in the bright red lorry he'd purchased for her.

He'd invaded her life, upset the balance and then disappeared. "What kind of man does that?" she asked aloud of no one.

Automatically, she checked the latch on the barn door where the ewes and their lambs were safe from wind and rain. Then continuing on toward the house, she asked King, "Am I that forgettable, then? Is it so easy to make love with me, then say 'thanks very much, bye now'?"

The dog whined in response and she appreciated the support. "No, you're right. I bloody well am not forgettable. The man's crazy for me and doesn't even know it."

She remembered everything about that last night with Jefferson and hoped to Heaven he was remembering, too. And hoped it was tearing him apart. But even if she were sure that he was being tortured by the memories of what he'd tossed away, it wouldn't be enough to ease the emptiness inside.

"How does he dare turn his back on me? On *us?*" She muttered dark and vile curses, all aimed at his handsome head, as she stomped through the farmyard, King dancing at her heels. "What gives him the right to say 'tis over? Am I to listen to him and go away quietly, like some schoolgirl afraid of punishment?"

The dog barked and Maura nodded as if the beast had agreed with her. She crossed the yard, ran up the short flight of steps to the back porch and kicked off her Wellington boots. As if in sympathy with her dark emotions, it had been raining steadily for the last few days and the farm was hardly more than a river of mud. King loved it, of course, which was why she also kept an old towel and a tub of water by the back door.

"In you go," she ordered and the big dog daintily stepped through the water and out the other side. Maura dried his paws, tossed the towel over the porch railing, then opened the door, letting them both into the warmth of the kitchen.

"Thinks I'll just sit with my mouth shut, does he? Accept what he says as a declaration from the mount and go on with my life?"

She took the teakettle to the sink, filled it with water and set it on to boil. As the flames licked at the base of the copper pot, she tapped her fingers impatiently against the stove top. "And why shouldn't he think that, Maura, you great idiot? Didn't you walk away, as well?

Didn't you let him slip through your fingers without ever once telling him that you love him?"

Lowering to admit as it was, Maura had to concede that she'd allowed her own pain and disappointment to color her responses to Jefferson on that last night. If she hadn't been so stunned by his announcing that as he'd loved once he couldn't love again, she might have stood her ground. She might have told him exactly what she thought of a man too afraid to love. She might have—

"And this is doing no good at all. Not for either of us. What good is it to shout the ceiling down when he's not here to listen?"

He had to listen, she thought. She had to *make* him listen. Her thoughts slammed to a stop and she whirled around, staring at the yellow phone on the counter.

Before she could think better of it, she walked directly to the drawer by the telephone and pulled out the four sheets of paper Jefferson had left with her.

Phone numbers and addresses of everyone he could think of, all neatly typed and printed out. He was nothing if not efficient, her Jefferson—and he *was* her Jefferson—the stubborn mule of a man.

She looked at the list. His cell-phone number, numbers for his brothers, his cousins, his office, his home, his vacation home in the mountains and even for the places he kept in London and Paris. He'd said that last morning that he didn't want her to have trouble contacting him again.

The man was a font of information when he wanted to be, she mused, running the tip of one finger down the list.

She wouldn't be calling Jefferson directly though,

she told herself. No. What she had to say to him could only be said in person so that she could knock some sense into his head if need be. So that left her with at least three choices. She picked the one whose name seemed the most familiar and dialed his number.

When a gruff voice answered, she said, "Hello. Is this Justice King, brother to Jefferson?"

A long pause, then, "It is. I'm guessing from your accent that you must be Maura."

"I am," she said, grateful to know that at least the dunderheaded man she loved had spoken of her to his brothers. "I've something to say to that great lout of a man, personally. I was wondering if you could help me."

There was a low, deep chuckle that rumbled through the phone line and then Justice answered, "You planning a trip to L.A.?"

"I am, yes," she said, plans forming in her mind even as she spoke. "As soon as I can get a plane ticket."

"No need for that," Justice told her. "When can you be ready to leave?"

Steam shot from the spout of the teakettle and Maura walked to turn off the stove. While she did, she decided on whom she would ask to take care of the farm for a few days and when she had it set in her mind, she said, "I can have things arranged by tomorrow night."

"Then pack a bag, Maura," Justice said. "I'll have a King jet waiting at the airport for you. All you'll need is a passport."

She gasped, surprised at the generosity of the offer. "'Tisn't necessary," she told him, "I was only calling you to see if you could arrange to have Jefferson somewhere we can talk."

Justice laughed and she enjoyed the sound, feeling as though she had an ally in this oh-so-personal battle.

"Maura, trust me. Sending the jet is a selfish move. My brother's been in a black mood since he got back from Ireland. My wife tells me there's a reason for it and she thinks it's you."

She grinned now, knowing that Jefferson was as miserable as her. "Isn't that a lovely thing to say," she murmured.

Justice laughed again. "Oh yeah, you and my Maggie are going to be great friends. I can see it already." There was a pause and then he said, "So, once we get you here, what's your plan?"

Maura leaned back against the counter and told Jefferson's brother exactly what she had in mind. Between the two of them, they refined their strategies. By the time she hung up, Maura felt her self-assurance slide back into place, for the first time in days.

"Jefferson King, you've no idea what's in store for you."

Eleven

"What was so damned important I had to come all the way out to the ranch?" Jefferson slammed his car door and faced down his brother.

"Just a few things we need to discuss," Justice told him. "But first, I've got to get that yearling back in his stall."

He followed Justice out to the paddock and watched as his brother hopped the rail fence and loped across the dirt enclosure without so much as a limp. Months after the accident that had brought Justice and Maggie back together again, his brother's leg was as good as new.

"Hey, you're here!"

Jefferson turned around to spot his youngest brother, Jesse, headed toward him. A former professional surfer, Jesse was a successful businessman now, running King

Beach, surf and sportswear. And by rights, he should have been in Morgan Beach. So what was he doing at the ranch? Suspicion flitted through Jefferson's mind, but he couldn't quite put his finger on what the trouble might be, so he let it go. For now.

"What are you doing here?" Jefferson asked, shifting a glance to Justice, who was taking a young horse by the bridle and leading him off to the barn.

"Bella wanted to visit with Maggie, so I tagged along. What are you doing here?" Jesse grinned as he said it. "Who's making movies if you're out wandering the ranch?"

"I'm not wandering. Justice said he needed to talk to me about something. And where are Maggie and Bella?"

Jesse shrugged. "Shopping?"

Wariness had him turning for the barn. Something was definitely up. The wives were gone. Both of his brothers here. Grinding his back teeth together, Jefferson headed for the barn. Stepping into the shadowy interior, with Jesse right on his heels, Jefferson called out, "Justice, are you going to tell me what you wanted to see me about?"

Justice ignored him as he led the horse into a stall. Once the task was finished, though, he faced him and smiled. "Jesse and I thought it was time we got you out here to talk about what the hell is wrong with you."

"I knew you were up to something the minute I saw Jesse here." He looked from one brother to the other in disgust. "This I wasn't expecting. You're trying to tell me this is an intervention?"

"Call it whatever you want," Jesse told him, slapping

his back. "The time has come, big brother, to stop acting like a bastard and tell us what's going on."

"Screw this," Jefferson said, turning on his heel to walk to his car. "I'm going back to the office. You two can sit around and psychoanalyze each other."

"No one at the office wants you there," Justice told him in his slow, patient voice.

That stopped him. Jefferson glared at each of his brothers in turn. "You're telling me they were in on this setup?"

"Joan thanked me," Jesse said on a laugh. "Seems you've been miserable to deal with since you got home."

He couldn't argue with that, Jefferson thought, pushing one hand through his hair in a gesture fraught with frustration.

Back a week now and nothing was the same. He'd expected to come home, slide into work as if he'd never been gone and pick up the threads of his life. But that hadn't happened. He was restless. Dissatisfied. He felt it and couldn't find a way to combat it.

His mind continued to drift toward Ireland. The green hills, the farmhouse.

Maura.

Compared to what he'd left there what he'd returned to was lacking. That he hadn't expected. He'd always liked his life, damn it. So why then did Los Angeles and the job he loved seem suddenly to be nothing more than plastic and illusion? Why did he feel alone surrounded by hundreds of people? Why was he waking in the middle of the night, reaching for Maura?

He knew why, of course. The simple truth was he

wasn't the same man anymore. The bright sunlight and hot Santa Ana winds felt alien to him and his heart yearned for what he'd lost.

"So." Justice stopped for a private word with his foreman before steering Jefferson to the ranch house. "You going to talk to us about this or what?"

"Yeah," he said. "Yeah, I'm coming."

Justice's study was a man's room. Leather chairs, shelves lined with books and a massive desk against one wall. Of course, the toys strewn across the floor marked the fact that his son, Jonas, spent plenty of time in the room, too. The three brothers settled into chairs, each of them holding a cold beer from the bar refrigerator.

After a couple of long moments passed, Justice finally asked, "So what is it? What's crawled into you and died?"

Jefferson smirked. "Very nice."

"Not interested in being nice. We want to know what's going on."

Jefferson stood up, took a swallow of icy beer and then began to pace. Nervous energy pumped through him, feeding his steps, stoking a temper that seemed to be continually on the boil lately. "Damned if I know. I feel wrong, somehow. As if I made a bad turn on a highway and now I'm lost."

"Easy enough to turn around again," Jesse commented.

"Is it?" Jefferson stared at him. "When turning around changes everything, is it really so easy to do it?"

"Depends on what you gain and what you lose with the effort," Justice mused, giving their youngest brother a hard look demanding patience. "So, where'd you make the wrong turn, Jeff? Was it Maura?"

"I'm starting to think that leaving her was the mistake I made. But what the hell else could I have done? She wouldn't give an inch. A more stubborn woman I've never known."

"She sounds perfect for you," Jesse offered and received a glare for his trouble.

Jefferson looked at Justice. "I told you she's pregnant."

"Yeah, you did."

"I asked her to marry me." He took a swig of the beer.

"So you screwed up the proposal?" Jesse asked. "That's easily fixed."

"That's not it." He took a breath, then studied the label on the beer bottle as if the printing there held the answers to every question he had. "She wants a real marriage."

"Imagine that," Jesse mused.

Jefferson's gaze shot to their youngest brother and seared him to his chair. "If you can't help, then be quiet."

"You don't need help," Jesse countered. "You need therapy. Why the hell can't you give her a real marriage?"

"Because I've already been in love. Anna."

Instantly, both of his brothers went quiet. Not so full of answers now, were they?

"Don't you get it? If I admit to loving Maura now," he said, "I'm essentially saying that Anna didn't count. That what we shared was replaceable."

Justice shook his head, stretched out his legs in front of him and balanced his beer bottle on his flat abdomen. "That is the *dumbest* thing I've ever heard." He shifted a look at Jesse. "How about you?"

"Oh yeah," he agreed. "It's right there with the top

three." Then to Jefferson, he said, "What, you're only allowed to love one person in your life?"

"No," Jefferson muttered, realizing just how foolish that statement sounded when said aloud. "That's not what I meant."

"What did you mean, then?" Justice asked. "Are you saying Anna would want you alone and lonely for the rest of your life to prove that you loved her?"

Jefferson thought about the young woman he'd loved and lost so long ago. "No," he admitted, "she wouldn't have."

Odd, but for the first time, he realized that the mental images he had of Anna and their time together had grown hazy. To be expected, he guessed, since time had a way of dulling the edges of pain or grief. Leaving behind only the vaguest feeling of guilt for having to live on. To keep breathing while the one you loved was gone.

"Jefferson," Jesse said softly, "if you had a child already, would you be able to love the one Maura's carrying?"

"That's a stupid question," he shot back.

"Is it?" Jesse laughed at him. "You're standing there telling us that you can't love Maura because you already loved Anna. How does that make sense?"

It wasn't just loving Maura that made him feel as though he were somehow betraying Anna, Jefferson thought with a glaring flash of insight. It was the fact that what he felt for Maura was so much more than what he'd once known. But he couldn't tell his brothers that. They already thought he was crazy.

While it was hard, he realized that the love he'd had for Anna had been a young man's love. Innocent in its way and it had ended before it could be tested. But he could love more now, deeper now, because he'd lived longer, knew more, had experienced more. His life had made him more than he had been at the time, so he was capable of feeling more than he'd been able to at twenty. Was it really that simple? Had he missed this revelation somehow because he'd been so determined to give Anna the loyalty he'd thought she deserved?

Justice was right. Anna wouldn't have wanted him to be alone and empty for the rest of his life in some bizarre tribute to her. A heavy load slid off his heart as he drew a deep, easy breath for the first time in weeks.

"God knows I'm no expert," Justice was saying. "Took long enough for me to realize what an ass I'd been in letting Maggie go. But I wised up in time. Are you gonna be able to say the same?"

Jefferson's hand tightened around the beer bottle. He knew what he wanted now, but would he be able to make Maura believe him?

"Yeah, I am," he said aloud, imagining the look on Maura's face when he showed up on her front porch at the farmhouse. "I'm going back to Ireland."

"For how long?"

He looked at Jesse. "Permanently."

"What about the studio?" Justice asked.

"I can handle it by phone and fax," Jefferson said, setting his beer down onto the closest table. "And I can be back here easily enough if I have to handle something in person."

"You? On a farm?" Jesse asked with a broad smile.

"Me on a farm," he repeated, already mentally arranging his move to the country, the woman he loved. "Why's that so hard to believe? Hell, we grew up on a ranch! Maura would never be happy anywhere else and I can work from anywhere. Besides," he added with a wide smile, "I have to get back. Find out if Michael's grandchild has been born. See if Cara's moving back to London. And it's lambing season, so Maura will be shorthanded…"

"Lambs?"

Jefferson laughed at Justice's horrified expression. "I know. You're a cattleman to the bone, but you're going to have to come visit our sheep."

God, he felt like he could climb mountains, run all the way to Ireland with his feet never even touching the water. He knew what he wanted. And he wouldn't settle for less than all. If Maura didn't agree right away, he'd just kidnap her, haul her in front of the village priest and marry her whether she liked it or not.

"I've gotta go," he said, checking his watch and mentally calculating the time he would need to tie up some loose ends and then get to the airport.

Jesse and Justice exchanged a glance and ordinarily, Jefferson would have been curious. But at the moment, he was too busy planning his reunion with Maura. He left the house, his brothers right behind him. But when he got to his car, he stopped.

"What the hell happened?"

All four tires were flat. The small, sapphire-blue sports car was practically resting on its rims in the dirt of the drive. Jefferson looked at his brothers. "Do you know something about this?"

"Hey," Jesse said, lifting both hands, "don't look at me."

Justice scrubbed one hand across his jaw and muttered, "I told the man *one* tire."

Before Jefferson could say anything to that, the throaty purr of an expensive engine rolled toward them. He looked up to watch a King family limo, all shining black paint and chrome, glide up the drive. "What the…"

Justice clapped one hand to Jefferson's shoulder. "This is why the flat tires. We had to keep you here. Although, Mike was a bit more thorough than I'd planned."

"What are you talking about?" His gaze was still fixed on the limo as the driver hopped out, opened the rear door and Maura stepped from the car, looking straight at him.

"Don't screw it up," Jesse muttered.

Justice shoved him and said, "We'll be in the barn. You two take your time."

Jefferson never even saw them leave. His gaze was fixed on the woman he loved and he couldn't have looked away if his life had depended on it. He wasn't betraying Anna by moving on. He knew that now. The living had to live. And he had no interest in doing that without Maura.

From the moment she'd stepped foot onto the King family jet, Maura had felt as though she were walking into a fairy tale. Surrounded by luxury, she'd flown halfway across the world for this moment. She'd slept in a bed thirty thousand feet in the air. At her arrival in Los Angeles, she'd been swept into the private opulence of the limousine and driven off down freeways choking with more traffic than she'd seen in her lifetime. And through it all, she'd had one thought in her mind. Getting to Jefferson. Making him see all that he was giving up when he turned his back on what they'd found.

When the limo turned into the long, winding drive of the King ranch, she had felt a slight stirring of nerves. Anxious, she had worried that going with her instincts might not have been the best idea. But she was committed to her plan and she wouldn't back out now that the moment had arrived.

Yet when she stepped out of the car, all she could do was look at Jefferson. He looked wildly handsome in his white shirt and black slacks with the wind ruffling his hair across his forehead. Even the baby inside her jumped and kicked, feeling the excitement of being with its father again.

Maura felt the hot, dry wind tug at her hair and burn her eyes. Surely that was the reason her vision was blurring with unshed tears. The King family ranch was a lovely place, what she noticed of it, but her gaze locked unerringly on Jefferson.

"Maura," he said, taking a step toward her.

"No. Stay there, if you please." Instantly, she held up one hand to keep him at bay. If he came too close, she might give in to her urge to run into his arms, when what she needed to do was stand her ground and speak her heart. "I've come all this way to have my say, Jefferson King, and you'll do me the courtesy of standing there to listen."

"You don't have to say anything," he said.

"That's for me to decide," she told him and paid no

attention as the driver of her limo discreetly slipped off in the direction of the barn. "I've spent the last several hours thinking of exactly what I want to tell you and now I will."

"Fine," he said, stuffing his hands into the pockets of his slacks. "Have at it."

"Good then. Where to begin?" She took a deep breath, met his eyes and said the first thing that came to her mind. "You're a bloody fool to walk away from me, Jefferson King."

"That's what you wanted to tell me?" he asked, smiling. "You came all this way to insult me?"

"That and more. I'll say this to your face as it's not something a woman wants to tell a man over the telephone." She walked toward him then, steel in her spine and fury in her steps, despite her earlier hesitation to be too close. "The reason I refused to marry you when you offered me a cold, empty marriage for the sake of our child or for convenience's sake was because I *love* you, you great ape of a man."

He gave her a slow smile. "You love me."

"I did. I do. But don't hold that lapse against me." Sputtering now, as thoughts crashed through her mind in a kaleidoscope of images and words, she wondered where her carefully rehearsed speech had disappeared to. Then she gave it up and spoke from the heart. "Though I love you, I won't marry a man who won't love me back."

She glowered at him, seeing him now through her tears and anger and wanting nothing more than to throw herself into his arms and taste his kiss on her lips again.

"So I've come to tell you that refusing to love another out of loyalty to your first wife is a foolish waste—though I'll say it speaks well of you to remember her and care for the memory."

"Thanks," he said, then added, "God, I love you."

She rolled right over his words, intent on telling him everything that was inside her. "Still, the living must live, Jefferson. Denying your heart is just another kind of death. I won't do that. And I hate that you're willing to. I'll tell you now, I will love you till I die, but I won't stop living. I'll be there, in Ireland, when you come to your senses."

"Maura," he said, "I love you."

"I've not finished," she told him sternly. Why couldn't the man be silent and let her get this said? "You'll miss me, Jefferson, and the life we could have had. You'll pine for me and I swear you'll regret ever walking away. And when, in your misery, you finally realize that loving me is what you were meant to do, remember it was I who told you. 'Twas me who came here to look you in the eye and give you one last chance. And blast it all, remember it was *love* that brought me here."

"I said I love you."

"What?" She whipped her head back to shake her hair out of her eyes and blinked up at him as if he were suddenly speaking Gaelic. "What was that? What did you just say?"

"I said, *I love you.*"

She looked up into his eyes and read the truth of his words shining back at her. A bright burst of light exploded in the center of her chest and Maura thought with those words ringing in her ears, she wouldn't have need of a plane to get back home. She'd simply float across the Atlantic.

"You love me."

"I do," he said, grinning now as he reached for her.

She went willingly, throwing herself at him as she'd longed to do from the first moment she stepped out of that long, elegant car. Her arms came around his neck and she clung to him as she muttered thickly, "Well, why the devil didn't you say so?"

He laughed out loud and, arms wrapped around her waist, he lifted her off her feet and swung her in circles around the drive. "Who could get a word in when you're on a rant?"

"True, it's true. I've a terrible temper, I know, but it's just that I hurt so badly and I wanted you to be as miserable as I was feeling," she whispered into the curve of his neck, inhaling his scent, feeling the hard, solid strength of him pressed against her.

"I was," he confessed, his strong arms crushing her to him. "Without you, there's nothing. I know that now."

"Oh, Jefferson, I've missed you so."

"I was coming to you," he told her, his voice husky and filled with emotion. "I'd just decided to go back to Ireland and convince you to marry me, even if I had to abduct you."

She laughed a little, relief and wonder tangling up inside her. "I'm almost sorry to have missed that."

"I'll make it up to you," he promised. "I want to live in Ireland, with you and our baby, at the farm."

She pulled her head back to stare up at him in

wonder as the last of the dream slid into place. "You'd live in Ireland?"

"It's not a hardship," he told her. "I think I love the place almost as much as you do."

"You're a lovely man," she said on a sigh. "Have I mentioned that lately?"

He grinned. "Not lately, no."

She'd come so far, hoped and dreamed so much and now that she had everything she had ever wanted in the circle of her arms, she could only hold on to him, reeling at the happiness coursing through her. Finally though, he set her on her feet, but left his hands at her waist as if he couldn't bear to let her go.

"I'll still have to do some traveling at times," he was telling her, "but you and the baby can come with me. We'll have so many adventures, love. Our life will be full and happy, I promise you."

"I believe you," she said, lifting one hand to cup his cheek.

"Maura," he said softly, staring into her eyes like a man who'd just awakened from a long sleep to find his heart's desire landing at his feet. "I'm going to ask you again. The right way this time. I want you to marry me. For real. Forever."

"Ah, Jefferson, now I'm going to cry," she said, and felt the tears sliding along her cheeks.

"Don't," he whispered, bending to kiss her briefly, hungrily. "Don't cry." He smoothed her tears away with his thumbs and smiled into her eyes. "I'm really not worthy of you at all, am I?"

She laughed and leaned into him, relishing the sound

of his heartbeat beneath her ear. Wrapping both arms around his middle, she said, "Oh, you darlin' man…if every woman waited for a man who was worthy of her, there'd be no marriages, would there?"

He laughed aloud and pulled her tightly against him. "You're the one for me, Maura. The only one."

"And you for me, Jefferson. I will love you always."

"I'm counting on it," he told her, and gave her a soul-searing kiss that promised a lifetime of love more powerful than either of them had ever imagined.

And when that kiss ended, they parted to the sound of hearty applause and sharp whistles. Looking toward the barn, Jefferson grinned, took Maura's hand in his and said, "Come with me. I want you to meet my family."

"*Our* family," she corrected and laid her head against his shoulder.

Then together, they walked away from the past and into the future.

* * * * *

14_ST_1

MILLS & BOON®

Why shop at millsandboon.co.uk?

Each year, thousands of romance readers find their perfect read at millsandboon.co.uk. That's because we're passionate about bringing you the very best romantic fiction. Here are some of the advantages of shopping at www.millsandboon.co.uk:

* **Get new books first**—you'll be able to buy your favourite books one month before they hit the shops

* **Get exclusive discounts**—you'll also be able to buy our specially created monthly collections, with up to 50% off the RRP

* **Find your favourite authors**—latest news, interviews and new releases for all your favourite authors and series on our website, plus ideas for what to try next

* **Join in**—once you've bought your favourite books, don't forget to register with us to rate, review and join in the discussions

Visit **www.millsandboon.co.uk**
for all this and more today!